MW01234971

Other Books by the Author

ANY GIVEN DAY
ANY GIVEN NIGHT
SPLINTER
NORA OAKLEY

Coming Soon...

ANY GIVEN CHOICE
STRUGGLE
LETTER CARRIER
119TH ELEMENT

the
Devil's Pods

by Annegret Werner Shaw

"The Devil's Pods"
an original novel by author Annegret Werner Shaw

Copyright © 2015 Annegret Werner Shaw
Author Photo by: Stephanie Quates

For information regarding copyright issues please contact:

Celsius Publishing
Attn: Publisher
PO Box 194
Tomball, TX 77377-0194

ISBN: 978-0-9912373-1-9

Printed in the USA

CELSIUS
PUBLISHING

Dedicated
to:

Fritz Werner

"The great dragon was hurled down – that ancient serpent called the devil, or Satan, who leads the whole world astray. He was hurled to the earth, and his angels with him."

Revelations 12:9

And the angels fell from the heavens above and the feral wind blew them over the earth and one of Satan's angels blew into a protective, hidden cave inside a cliff, which pointed straight to the heavenly sky, where it took root and flourished, content to do Satan's work from such an isolated place. And the mountain on which the cave was located lay next to a slumbering green valley, where animals still grazed the luscious green grass and drank the clear cold mountain water, the basin still undisturbed by men. But Satan's angel had time, all the time in the world. He knew that in time men would come and inhabit this valley and fall prey to his temptations.

Prologue

September 2007

Young Russell twisted and turned in his sleep. The rapid eye movements beneath his closed lids fluttered as his lips formed unheard whispered words of regret.

"Sorry, I didn't mean to. I'll never do it again. Don't hurt me. Please don't hurt me."

His unconscious mind comprehended what his conscious mind couldn't. Deeper and deeper he flew through the dream, following the treacherous path up to the plateau of the mountain and passed the three large cliffs pointing to the sky. Effortlessly he flew over the edge high above the canyon and floated down the steep rock face on the other side until he found the hidden opening of the cave. He came to rest on the hard rock surface and followed the narrow, cold and damp tunnel inside, until he found the famous alcove he had heard about for years. The moonlight fell softly through the large slits in the cave wall and illuminated the grotto. He knew that he would at last put his eyes on the illusive flower he had yearned to see above everything else in the world; the famous Trumpet Angel. To know its hiding place would be invaluable to him. He was obsessed with finding it, ever since he saw the oil painting of the flower four years ago. He remembered that day so well when he accidently walked into Adam and Robin's guest bedroom looking for the restroom. The painting had hung over the bed and literally pulled him closer. He couldn't release his stare. The picture looked so mystical…ripped straight out of a fantasy world he didn't know existed. Stepping closer he read the words underneath the painting.

"The Trumpet Angel"
Adam Fletcher, September 2004

Oh, what he would have given to own that painting; to be able to look at it every day. He had asked Adam about it, but back then he had been just a teenager and believed Adam when he told him that he painted the flower from his imagination. It was only when he turned eighteen that he found out that the flower really existed.

And now he saw it in the cave growing in front of the back wall, like it had been waiting for him all along, for all this time. His first sight of the beautiful plant took his breath away with its overwhelming beauty. The moonlight illuminated it just right and he lingered as he stood taking in its magnificence. No words could do it justice. The descriptions he heard told for so long were inadequate. He saw the plant the way only a few people had seen it before. The way Adam had seen it and painted it; full with large, brilliant black flowers, as big as his fist, looking like trumpets. The branches and flowers were dancing to the small breeze coming through the rock openings, creating goose bumps on his exposed skin. He never felt more alive and savored the feeling, not realizing it was just a dream, his last dream. The multitude and perfection of the dark angel trumpets hanging from the branches didn't release his stare until he counted at least fifty blossoms. He heard faint trilling sounds coming from the plant luring him to come closer, teasingly and…irresistibly.

Never before in his twenty years had he been captivated by anything more intense and faultless. Then he saw the brown peapods lying around the trunk and his heart started to beat harder in his chest. He carefully bent down and collected all of them, tucking them inside a brown paper bag he had brought along for just this purpose. They were his now, all his…and no one else's. He finally knew the secret, found the hidden cave and located the flower.

The pods were in his possession and he knew his plan would work. He would bring the pods to the awareness of his professors and he would be remembered as the man who made the most important discovery of modern history.

But Russell didn't comprehend that the plant was just teasing him with this new found knowledge, already planting the irreversible outcome deep inside his brain. The plant had been aware of Russell's intentions for weeks, had warned him over and over again, but Russell had ignored the bad headaches he suffered from and didn't listen to the whispering of unspoken words in his unconscious mind.

"Don't do it… don't do it. You will die! As sure as I have survived for millions of years, you will die a horrible death. I will play with you and control your mind and think of a death worthy of your attempt to destroy me, because nobody will ever take me outside this valley. Many men have tried, but none have succeeded and neither will you. I have done it this way for centuries and I will do it again and nobody can stop me. Nobody! You are just another pawn in my game of collecting souls."

The dream faded away and the words were forgotten. The moon crossed the night's sky and the young man slept in his bed unaware of the deathly danger he was in. The wind softly blew the curtains into his room as the crickets finished their nightly concert.

The next morning Russell woke up to the shrill sound of his alarm clock, unaware that he had received a warning, unaware that his fate had been decided. He jumped out of bed in a good mood ready to start his day. He used the restroom, brushed his teeth and then walked downstairs where his mother had his cup of coffee waiting for him, like she did every morning. One day he would make her proud of him, he thought.

He was the only child of two devoted parents. No child could have asked for a better childhood. His father, Alfred Bradley, was a hard working carpenter, who worked long hours to put him through college. His mother, Maria, was from Puerto Rico and even though she spoke fairly good English she raised him speaking Spanish. She was a stay-at-home mom and he loved her for it. She was always there for him, helping him with school work, taking him to sports events and challenging him to become the best he could be. She was devoted to him and he knew that he was the center of her universe. His dream to make them proud of him and pay them back for all their sacrifices became an obsession with him. It had become his mission, his ultimate goal. And today was the start of this goal. Today was going to be the day which would change his life and the lives of people suffering from incurable diseases. He was excited. He knew that he had done his research well; knew that his chances were good, better than good, that something miraculous and ground breaking would come out of the discovery he had made. It could mean a medical breakthrough for so many horrible diseases still incurable; Alzheimer's disease, Pick's disease, cancer… the possibilities were endless.

Russell was in his third year of Med school, but only this year did it occur to him that the valley's secret pods were special, more than tripping balls, more than a quick fix for leaving everyday problems behind for a couple of hours. The realization that the pods had never been recorded in any biology or medical book had astounded him, but more than that, it had really shocked him that all the oaths muttered at the valley's Festival of the Pods were not just superficial, trying to make the valley a more interesting place to live in or create a tight-knit community by a shared secret. No, the oaths had been for real and protected the flower from outsiders from the time it had been discovered hundreds of years ago.

Centuries of secrecy had protected the plant's existence. But all this was going to change now and it was he who was going to change it. Instead of one plant they would grow hundreds, and instead of sixty to seventy pods they harvested each year, they would harvest thousands of them, all with the intent to cure diseases.

"Morning mom," Russell told his mother, bent down to the five-foot-two woman and placed a kiss on her chubby, soft cheek, like he had done so many mornings before, except for one thing, this morning was going to be the last time he would do so.

"Morning," his mother replied, sitting at the table, eating a bowl of cereal. "How many classes do you have today?"

"Just one," he answered and took a sip of his coffee then walked back upstairs with his cup in hand, showered and got ready for the best day he was sure he was going to have. He couldn't wait to show Doctor Harrison the pod, couldn't wait to stand next to him while he looked at the blood-red peas inside and then examined a small sample under his microscope. He would see the same thing he had seen yesterday when he opened the pod and dissected one of the peas under his microscope at home. It would blow his mind. He just couldn't be wrong about it. He was the best in his class, would become the best in his field, and this discovery would catapult him to the top. Russell could envision the headlines in the medical magazines now, no, not just the medical magazines. He could envision himself on the cover of Time Magazine and all the other major magazines. He could see himself pose for pictures and in his mind he already could see the headlines.

"Newest Discovery in Medical Science"
Russell Bradley brings hope to millions of people ailing from incurable diseases.
"Miracle Plant discovered in Hunter's Valley"

"Medical Discovery of the Century!"

And of course there would be a picture of him to go along with the article. A good looking young man with short, dark brown hair and two dimples in his cheeks the girls couldn't get enough of. He would finish Med school and then get his doctorate, all the while knowing that billion dollar pharmaceutical companies would offer him the job of a lifetime. He could see his parents in his mind, how proud they would be of him, their only son. Of course he would move away from Hunter's Valley and take them with him. No, this tiny valley wouldn't mean much to him anymore once this discovery would become public. Of course he would always be grateful that he had the chance to grow up in this valley and was handed the opportunity to discover the potential of the peas the valley had kept a secret for so long. He would move to the big city where he could enjoy all the things a large town had to offer. Yes, he definitely could envision a future for himself, a good future. And Hunter's Valley would profit from this discovery also. Tourists would come and bring money to the small community and the valley would prosper and grow larger. He would buy his parents a larger house in the city and his father could retire. He had it all planned out in his head.

Russell came back downstairs fifteen minutes later dressed in his new jeans and the new shirt his mother had bought him for his last birthday. She looked up surprised.

"What do you have going on today?" she asked him, looking him up and down. "You look nice, really nice."

"You could say I'm going to have an interesting meeting with one of my professors," he replied. "Don't ask me more. I will tell you all about it when I come home tonight. I promise." He grabbed a bowl out of the cabinet and filled it with his favorite cereal then ate it standing up, too nervous and anxious to be on his way.

"I have to run, Mom," was the last thing she heard him say. A kiss on her cheek and he was out of the kitchen door which he slammed shut. She shook her head with a smile. How many times had she told him not to slam that door? Probably, since the day they moved to the valley when he was five years old. But he was a good son. Never gave them any trouble and now he was in Med school. She was so proud of him. There would be a doctor in their family. She smiled.

"That boy is always up to something, but he'll tell us about it tonight at the dinner table," she mumbled to herself, as she watched him back his old Ford Mustang out of the garage. "Maybe I should fix something special for supper," she thought as she started to wash the morning dishes.

Russell turned the car around in the driveway and drove down the incline disappearing behind the trees. He was in a good mood. He took the bag with the opened pod and the two peas out of his pocket and placed it inside the glove compartment, then pushed the play button on his CD player and turned the music louder as he drove over the dam. His car windows were down and he enjoyed the fresh morning air coming inside his car, tousling his dark brown hair. He didn't care. He could comb it when he reached the city later. It was just too beautiful of a day not to take advantage of it. Russell turned left after he crossed the dam and drove along the isolated gravel road, not wondering why he hadn't turned right to get to the highway, his usual every-day route to reach the campus of the university forty-five minutes away.

He drove two miles on the gravel road, leaving the lake behind him singing to his favorite song by the Black Eyed Peas. He followed the curved road through the north side of the valley until he reached the small narrow turn-off path which would lead him up to Manitou Hill. Not thinking about it, he turned right and slowly drove up the narrow mountain road. The grass had grown tall in the middle of the path with the occasional wild flower placed in harm's way to become the victim of the Mustang's tires.

Never before had he taken the Mustang up the mountain. It was wiser to use an all-terrain vehicle, but today it didn't seem to occur to him that the Mustang was ill equipped to handle this drive. It took him over ten minutes of careful driving to reach the top of the mountain, taking each hole and bump in the road slowly, though as not to damage anything on the Mustang's undercarriage. He loved his car. Two more years of payments and it would be paid off and belong to him. His dad had bought the Mustang for a bargain price from his old friend Chuck and surprised him with it over a year ago. He was going to pay his dad back every penny and the way it looked to him right now, it would probably happen sooner than later, if everything went the way he figured.

The last time he had been up to the top of Manitou Hill was over a year ago with eight of his college buddies, including three girls. They had brought their sleeping bags, a lot of beer, and everything to grill hot-dogs and hamburgers. They made a small fire in the fire pit they had created by collecting rocks for just that purpose. Wood was everywhere and within ten minutes they had collected enough to last them through the night. They drank beer and spent the first part of the night celebrating the end of their second semester. Since then Russell thought often of that night and remembered with fondness how Jennifer had snuggled up to him. That night had been their first time together and he dated her ever since. They were good memories and he enjoyed thinking of them.

Strangely enough though, Russell didn't wonder why he was driving up to the top of Manitou Hill this morning. After all, his meeting with Doctor Harrison was in less than an hour; a meeting so important that he wouldn't forgive himself if he was late for it. He reached the top and parked the Mustang in the grassy area before the large boulders, next to the remains of the fire pit. Man, did he love this car. It had made it up this incline without any problems. He reached inside the driver's door pocket and took out a paper napkin he had saved from a Sonic Drive-in last week for just this kind of purpose. He spit on the napkin and polished a smashed bug off the Mustang's front windshield. Ever since he owned this Mustang, red had become his favorite color. He heard that police were more likely to stop red vehicles for speeding than any other car, but he didn't care. He always drove cautiously so why should he worry about statistics? Coincidentally, it was the same color as the peas he had chewed for the second time last year. He had been on such a high each year; the experience didn't come close to anything he had tried before, and he had tried a lot of things.

Only last year did the thought occur to him that he had something special in his hands. He had asked around, but nobody in his class or professors had heard about the pods. He went on line and researched them; described the plant, the pods, the juicy blood-red peas, their taste, and the hallucinations and erotic effects they had on him after he chewed them.

He found nothing…nothing at all. No matches, and that's when he figured out that he had become a part of something bigger, something undiscovered, and he put two and two together. The promises the users uttered before they were given a pea pod moved from just a ridiculous valley tradition to something serious. The valley and its two harvesters were protecting a one of a kind plant; one that never made it into any biology or science book, but he wasn't scared about the consequences of breaking his promises to protect the plant's secret and not to take the pods out of the valley. After all, what could the harvesters do to him? They wouldn't even know what he had done until it was too late and by then he would be famous.

He knew his parents were users, had known it for years. Even as a small kid he had picked up on the importance of the valley's special celebration; the Festival of the Pods.

As a young boy he had enjoyed the celebrations; a day of picnics and games, and the fun he had swimming in the lake or paddling the paddleboats with the other valley children to see who was the fastest, were still some of his favorite childhood memories. He loved the festival and looked forward to it as much as his parents did. At night he was tucked into bed and his parents told him they would go to the dance for an hour or so and if he was a good boy they would buy him a new toy. He had been good and received a new toy every year.

Only much later did he find out that his parents returned to the lake, not for the dancing, but for the handing out of the pods. And he also remembered how happy his parents were for days after the festival, letting him do whatever he wanted to do. He was allowed to watch television until late at night when his parents had already gone to bed. He was allowed to eat as much candy and chocolate as he could find, and the best thing was, that he couldn't do any wrong. Once, when he was about twelve- years-old, his father found him smoking one of his cigarettes in the basement, but all he said was, that he shouldn't make a habit out of it and that it was bad for his health. Usually his parents were extremely strict, but the festival had a strange effect on them; they eased up on him and he loved it. Only years later did he put it all together.

It was the year that he turned eighteen, about two weeks before the next Festival of the Pods. That year he was approached by Doug Manchester, the Senior Harvester, and was told that he was now old enough to participate in the Festival's evening celebration and thus receive a pod if he chose to participate. He had always addressed the older gentleman as Mr. Manchester, but that night, he insisted that Russell call him Doug. It was like graduation night for him; graduating from an innocent child into an adult who could be trusted with a secret that was centuries old. Hunter's Valley's secret. A secret he didn't even know existed until then.

Doug explained to him about the rare plant which grew in a cave somewhere up in the mountains and he talked about responsibility, honor, and about the importance of keeping the secret safe from outsiders. He instilled values in him, simply by trusting him to do the right thing and he felt privileged to participate and enjoyed the pod's fruits tremendously.

He learned that Doug was the Senior Harvester, an important job, which he carried out with pride, and Adam Fletcher was the Junior

Harvester, the only two people alive who knew where the plant grew. Russell felt important that night…man did he feel important. Doug had warned him to take his time and to seriously think about becoming a user, that it was a life-changing commitment and not to be taken lightly. He never found out if his parents knew that the Senior Harvester had approached him. If they did know, they avoided talking to him about it.

It was like sex education. They hoped that the school system would do the job explaining the facts about the birds and the bees to him; a job they were supposed to do, but didn't. It was the unwritten law of the valley, circumventing parental interference. He didn't discuss it with them and two weeks later received his first pod filled with three blood-red peas. He chewed his first pea and it had been an incredible experience he repeated two more times that weekend and for days afterward felt on cloud nine. His ability to concentrate in class improved and so did his capability to retain information, especially the Latin names of plants and medications. It was like he had a power boost which lasted for months. He had been mesmerized, totally enthralled with the pea's potency and the effect it had on him and couldn't wait for the next year's festival to arrive.

Russell stood on the plateau of Manitou Hill next to the big pine tree and looked into the small valley below. It was a breathtaking view with the lake and a few houses visible between patches of trees. How he loved this valley. Pretty soon he would be rich and would leave it. He would marry Jennifer and have a wonderful life. Life would be so good. Strange, that nobody else figured out how valuable the peas were. Was he the only one in the valley with a high IQ? To hell with secrets and promises - a chance like this wouldn't come along again and he was smart enough to realize that and grab it.

Why was he on Manitou Hill, he suddenly asked himself. He looked at his watch and panicked. What was happening? Why had he come up here when he had such an important meeting with Doctor Harrison? He stared with disbelief at his Mustang. Had he really driven it up here? His forehead wrinkled with worry and he looked again at his watch. Damn, he was late now. This fucking day dreaming wasn't getting him anywhere. He ran toward the Mustang, but stopped abruptly. He looked confused down at his legs, wondering what was happening to him, then his thoughts vanished into nothingness; an evil, strong force entering his mind, taking over his body, controlling every movement. He was a puppet.

His movements became awkward as he walked toward the trunk of the car, his legs stiff and cumbersome. He opened the trunk. The hose he was looking for lay curled up on the bottom of the black carpet where he had placed it earlier, before he backed the Mustang out of the garage. He pulled the hose out and bent down on one knee, not caring if his new jeans were getting stained by the dirt. Without any trouble he slipped the hose over the exhaust pipe and checked that it was on tight. He guided the other end to the driver's door, opened it, rolled down the window just enough to put the hose inside and then rolled the window back up so it wouldn't fall out. He walked like a robot, performing tasks he didn't tell his limbs to do. It was like his reasoning was shut off, all he could feel was his heavy frantic heartbeat. He was watching himself carrying out unheard orders, unable to stop. He was scared, scared to death of what was happening to him.

He started screaming, but nothing came out of his mouth. Russell sat down in the driver's seat and closed the door. The small grey blanket he always had in his car was on the back seat. A blanket once used to keep lovers warm was now used to fill the gap in the window around the hose. He wanted to stop, but didn't know how; something inside of him didn't let him. The strength inside of him faded away and he became a helpless pawn in a death game. He stopped screaming, all he was able to do now was to observe his self-destruction.

His body rested back against the seat and his face turned into a mask without emotions. His right arm reached forward and turned the key to start the motor which sputtered into motion. Couldn't the motor just once not start, was his last logical thought. He pumped the gas pedal a couple of times, the loud noise of the motor shaping his facial muscles into a smile he didn't feel. Russell looked into the rear view mirror; a strange face, faintly familiar, stared back at him with large blood-red pupils. He knew then something horrible evil was inside of him - that he was going to die. He lowered the seat into a reclining position and waited, sucking the carbon monoxide deep into his lungs. Death came within the hour.

A huge search was started after his parents reported him missing. They found him dead inside his car after the Mustang was spotted by a search helicopter. His parents were inconsolable and the whole valley was in shock. It was a clear case of suicide. Not one person could understand why a nice boy like Russell, uncomplicated, full of life, with such a promising future, would commit suicide. Nobody knew, except Doug Manchester, the Senior Harvester; he knew damn well why.

He went, as most valley residents did, full of grief and gave Russell's parents his condolences. Before he left their property he walked over to the Mustang, which was now parked behind the garage of his parent's house. It was strange how he knew where to look, but he found the bag with the pod in the glove compartment and put it in his pocket.

Doug asked himself a thousand times; could he have prevented this horrible suicide from happening? But how could he have known that Russell was going to kill himself on Manitou Hill? The words of Chester, the Senior Harvester before him, came to his mind; "And all that stands between the suicides…and the plant…is you. Prevent them… when you can…let them happen when you can't."

In this case he couldn't save the boy. Somehow he sensed that the plant meant it to be this way, but it wasn't that damn easy. He hated his fucking job.

The funeral was held three days later and Russell was laid to rest in Hunter's Valley's graveyard. His mother suffered a breakdown and had to be hospitalized. His father didn't talk much anymore after that and one year later they moved away from the valley, never knowing what had killed their only son.

Chapter One

August 3, 1755

T he rock face was visible from miles around; three tall cliffs next to each other, high on a mountain top, pointing straight to the sky, looming more than a hundred feet above the rest of the rocks and boulders. The mountain itself was impressive enough, being the highest one around, but the tall cliffs with their distinct shapes were the reason Bulk named the mountain Pitch Fork Mountain. The rock columns were located at the west end of the half-mile long mountain and the vertical cliffs dropped steep into the canyon below. To the north-east side of the mountain lay the valley. A valley so beautiful and rich in sustenance that it still took Bulk's breath away each time he came up the mountain to look at it from high above. The small lake glittered in the late afternoon sun. He took such pleasure in his little log cabin that was tucked to the side; smoke coming from the chimney he had built out of the stones so abundant around the vicinity.

He knew that his evening meal was simmering over the hot fire and he knew that she was waiting for him, but he couldn't resist coming up here on his way home, and today the urge to do so had been especially strong.

He stood on the plateau tall and wide shouldered, his feet spread apart, the narrow, leather strings of his deerskin leggings fluttering in the wind. Bulk was a handsome man in the prime of his life, and he was proud that he could call the valley below his home. It was a good place to call home, a real good place. He and Loretta had done all right by themselves. Their first winter had been hard; more snow than he ever thought possible coming down on their little one room log cabin.

The lake had frozen over and the pass out of the valley had been impassable. But they had cut enough firewood and stayed warm. The five chickens and one rooster they had brought with them had survived. He was glad he had followed his instinct and built a solid two stall barn with a chicken coop inside before he concentrated on the cabin last summer. The three horses had made it through the winter and so had the cow they depended on for milk. The hay ration was tough on the animals, but they had put any lost weight back on this spring, eating the rich luscious grass which was so plentiful. The animals looked better and healthier than they did before he started his trek west. The valuable wagon had been the only thing left outside, unprotected against the rough elements of winter and after the first snowstorm only the half-circle wooden hoops stood out of the snow. The wagon had survived, but Bulk doubted that it would withstand the elements a second winter. He knew he had a lot of work to do before it turned cold again.

He and Loretta were the only ones living in the valley. When he had first seen the three large rock columns from a distance, he had felt an intense impulse to climb up the mountain to investigate and take a look around the area to see if there was a way through the mountain or if they had to drive the long way around it.

That's when he put his eyes on the valley nestled on the opposite side totally surrounded by mountains. He was amazed at its beauty; a large lake with plenty of pasture land ready to use. The ground was fertile, dark and rich, perfect for a garden or planting crops. The valley was perfect, better than what he ever expected to find. It was August a year ago that he had stood right here and realized that they had reached the end of their journey. He had left Loretta in the wagon at the foot of the mountain waiting for him to return and he joyfully climbed down to tell Loretta that he had found the place where they would live and build their future.

Bulk had spotted the pass from above and guided the horses and wagon through the half mile long corridor before it became impassable due to a severe thunderstorm visible on the horizon. Loretta was just as excited when she saw the valley for the first time coming through the pass. Together they chose the site for their cabin and barn and together they worked hard to finish it before the harsh winter set in.

Reminiscing, Bulk sat down on the outer edge of the boulder overlooking the picturesque valley below to his right, but he also kept his eyes on the strikingly beautiful sunset. Leisurely he pulled his pipe out of his knapsack. It was almost dusk and he wanted to enjoy the sundown from this spot before heading home to Loretta. He indulged in his one luxury; smoking the pipe he had received from his father before they left town to head west. Smoking his pipe right here in this isolated spot had become one of his favorite things to do. It was like he was thinking clearer up here. He laid the pipe next to him and searched his knapsack for the flint he knew was inside. He didn't know how it happened, barely saw it out of the corner of his eye, but his pipe slipped down the boulder and disappeared from his sight into the canyon below. He reached for it, but it was already too late. How in the bloody hell did that happen? Cock and Pie! That was my good pipe, he thought. He could have sworn that the boulder angled up and not down. Was it a visual trick? Cursing, he leaned over the edge to see if he could spot it below. Heavy in his heart, he knew deep down that it was lost to him forever. To his surprise he saw it resting on a little overhang he had never noticed before, sixty to seventy feet below.

Hope surged through him. Damn, if he wasn't the luckiest man on earth. Maybe the pipe wasn't lost to him after all. It looked like it was still in one piece. Looking around for a way to climb down, he realized that it was impossible. The cliff had no crevices, no cracks or holes to put his feet or hands in. It was as smooth a surface as he'd ever seen one; no footholds, nothing.

Bulk looked around and noticed a good size boulder close to the plateau's edge where he was sitting. If he tied the rope he always had with him around the boulder he might be able to lower himself down and retrieve his pipe. With any luck it would work. He wasn't an experienced climber, but he wasn't afraid of heights and he was physically fit, so it shouldn't be too difficult. He walked to his horse which was tied to a pine tree sixty feet away. The rope hung from one of the saddle bags. He patted his mare then grabbed the rope and hoped that it would be long enough. First he knotted the rope every five feet then secured it around the boulder. Taking a deep breath he lowered himself down the cliff. The sunset painted the steep cliff into a warm yellowish-orange color, tingling his eyes with its glittering brightness. The cliff felt warm to his touch and he felt the warmth of the last sunrays through his shirt. Slowly he worked his way to the small overhang below, cautious not to look down into the canyon's depth. Step by step he carefully repelled himself one foot at a time. He almost reached his precious pipe when he noticed the cliff opening up below him.

Surprised at this unexpected discovery, he lowered himself past the opening he guessed to be seven foot by four foot and placed his feet next to his pipe. Strange, he thought, how you can't see this opening from above and even stranger that his pipe had landed on this small overlap. It didn't make any sense to him that it hadn't broken to pieces or bounced off and fallen to the bottom of the canyon. To him, the odds that it had fallen and stayed on this small overlap seemed too great to be possible, but he didn't analyze it any further. He was just too damn happy to have it back and satisfied, stuffed it deep into the pockets of his pants.

Having done that he looked around more curious, wondering how deep the opening went inside the cliff. He let go of the rope and climbed over several small rocks inside. A narrow tunnel opened up in front of him and he stepped carefully inside and followed it. The walls felt wet to his touch as he moved deeper inside. The thought of it being a cave for bats entered his mind and he stepped cautiously not to arouse any sleeping occupants since it was almost time for the bats to go hunting. It started to get dimmer; the light from the opening was unable to reach this deep inside the tunnel. He wished he had a torch, but how could he have anticipated this turn of events. He considered turning around to come back another day with a torch when he noticed a brightness coming from ahead. He turned around a bend and saw a large cave closed from all sides with four slits of vertical openings, six feet high by one foot wide, in the west side of the cliff, allowing airflow and light to enter the cave. What a curious cave, he thought. I must be under the columns of the pitch fork by now. Bulk marveled how serene and peaceful this place felt and looked out the narrow openings at the gorgeous sunset. The sun was now an orange globe in the sky.

Even though he hated to leave this place, he recognized the danger of lingering much longer in this cave and decided to climb back up before the sun disappeared and it would turn dark on him. Climbing up the steep cliff could become dangerous, especially with a new moon tonight. Bulk turned away from the openings and started to walk back to the tunnel when he was stopped short by the sight of the plant. His mouth fell open, totally taken aback by its beauty. It was like he saw the plant exactly at the moment it was meant to be seen, when it was the most radiant, when the last sunrays entered the cave openings, creating a brilliant yellow-orange glow around the plant.

Bulk never got goose bumps, but he did in that moment…right then…standing in front of the plant, marveling at its existence. The feeling that he had just discovered something rare and special overwhelmed him. He stood there frozen in place, minutes ticking by, as he watched mesmerized how one trumpet-like-flower after the other slowly opened up its black shinny pedals as the last sunrays vanished outside the cave. How did something this strikingly beautiful thrive in a hidden cave like this, Bulk wondered?

The plant was about four feet tall with multiple branches reaching in all directions from its thorn covered thick green trunk to the heavy green spade like leaves. But all of it was overshadowed by the beautiful black flowers opening up. It was like they were swinging to the soft evening breeze, now coming warm and tingling through the openings. Hanging upside down they swayed and he felt he could hear a sweet high pitched sound but, of course, it must have been in his mind.

He felt an incredible pull toward the plant, like the flowers were gesturing him to come closer. Captivated by the unexpected display, he moved nearer to inspect this unusual plant. He carefully touched one of the pedals and marveled at its softness. Delicate narrow blood-red veins ran the length of the pedals to its outer edge, giving it the most fragile look. He bent down and smelled the intoxicating perfume, which started to fill the cave. The scent filled him with sensual desire so strong that it took him by surprise.

His thoughts flashed to his young, beautiful wife…how striking she was and how much he wanted to make love to her when he reached the cabin. A picture of her slim, naked body, washing herself in the river entered his mind. Bulk shook his head to clear his thoughts. How strange it is that I'm craving Loretta like this, he thought. Wiping his eyes as if to divest himself from this vision he noticed how dark it was getting. In another minute or two it would turn pitch-black inside this cave and it would be too dangerous for him to climb back up. He hated to leave this peaceful place and felt strong regrets in doing so, but he knew he had no choice. He tediously felt his way back to the rope, part of the tunnel already too dark to see. Slowly he climbed back up the steep cliff, twilight turning to solid darkness. His horse was still tethered to the tree and whinnied softly as he reappeared, like she had been waiting for him and wanted to get back to the barn and her nightly portion of grain. Bulk left the rope tied to the rock knowing that he would return the following day. Satisfied, he climbed onto his horse and rode the steep path carefully back down, glad about a few twinkling stars in the dark sky and the surefootedness of his mare. He reached the valley and his small cabin one hour later.

Reaching the barn he unsaddled his horse, fed it some grain and then opened the gate of the corral he had built this spring to let the mare graze through the night. He slapped her hind quarter and heard the mare snorting satisfied trotting off to the rich grass waiting for her. Bulk could smell the venison stew before he opened the wooden door to the cabin.

Loretta looked up from stirring the stew in the kettle, which was suspended over the wood fire in the hearth. They had brought the heavy twenty pound iron kettle with them on the trek and even though the one inch thick walls gave her a challenge to heat the food evenly, Loretta had mastered the technique and had become an excellent cook.

"Tis late, Bulk. Suffer me the cause to worry," she simply stated. He wouldn't have blamed her if she had yelled at him, but she didn't. She never did. She was all alone in this valley with him being her protector, and he came home this late. He shouldn't have made her worry. He walked over to her and put his large arms around her slim waist. She was so tiny, her head only reaching to his chest. Every time he looked at her he wondered how a big oaf like him had ended up with a beautiful woman like her. He turned her around and kissed her on the forehead, lovingly and gentle.

"I'm sorry Loretta."

"Tis all right, Bulk. You're safe and sound, standing right here in front of me and that's all that matters."

He didn't deserve her. She was too good for him. Once in a while she would get angry, and once she even threw a cooking pot at him when he had gotten drunk, but those occasions only happened rarely and he knew he had them coming.

"The most peculiar thing happened to me today. I dropped my pipe down the cliff sitting up on Pitch Fork Mountain. When I went to retrieve it, I found a cave in the side of the cliff. I checked it out and you know what I found?" he asked Loretta, but before she had a chance to answer him he continued. "I found the most beautiful flower I've ever seen in my life. It was quite unusual; the pedals were in full bloom as I stepped inside the cave. They were black with red veins going through them, looking like small trumpets. Have you ever heard of a flower looking like that?" he asked her, still excited by his discovery.

"No, I never heard of a plant having black flowers. Tis quite unusual. Are you hungry? The stew is ready. Wash up and come 'n eat," she told him. And then as an afterthought, not being able to resist she added, "You're really late husband. You had me vexed."

Bulk walked to the hand basin, soaped his hands with the homemade soap and cold creek water, then splashed his face and ran his wet hands through his dark shoulder length hair. He knew she was right. If the shoe were on the other foot he would be mad as hell.

"Husband," she continued, "I love this valley as much as you do, but what am I to do if you don't come home one day? I would be all alone with nobody to help me and I have no way of getting in touch with someone."

"I'm sorry, wife. You're right of course," he told her again, then tried to explain his inconsiderate action. "I don't understand it myself. I was going to ride straight home, but then the urge to ride up the mountain came over me and I couldn't resist it, like some unknown force was pulling me toward it."

She started laughing. "Bulk Horswell, if I didn't know you better I would think you're trying to pull wool over my eyes. Nothing and nobody can force you to do anything against your will, you big oaf. I know it's your favorite spot up there, to look down on our valley and smoke your pipe and I have no problem with that, but next time let me know so I don't have to worry about you, tis all I'm saying."

His deep chuckle made her smile and she forgave him for making her worry so much.

"The good news is, we won't be in this valley by ourselves much longer. I mailed a parcel to Hank and Emma. You'll see, they're going to come. One more winter and then they'll be here."

"It can't come soon enough for me," she replied. "I miss the company of another woman." She looked up into his soft brown eyes, a smile covering her face. "I'll forgive you for scaring me, if you tell me what you're building in the barn for me."

"Woman, you be the death of me with your nosiness. I'll not be blackmailed into telling you and that's it." They both started laughing, having played this game many times before.

"Come now and eat, you big bully," she told him, turned to the hearth and filled two bowls with the hot venison stew then carried them to the table he built for her just three months ago. Two chairs made out of heavy oak matched the table. If she could just figure out what he was building her next. They sat across from each other holding hands, thanking God for their blessings and then started eating the delicious stew, every so often looking into each other's eyes.

"The flower's fragrance made me think of you," he told her flirtatiously.

"Oh, really? What did you think about?"

"Well, I would tell you, but I think your ears are too delicate to hear such thoughts spoken out loud," he answered her with that sensual smile of his.

"You are a rascal, Bulk Horswell. Finish eating your stew and keep your mind on what you're building me in the barn," she told him and both laughed.

"I'm going back to the cave tomorrow and bring you back some seeds. I think you're going to like this plant, seeing how much effort you're putting into the garden and flower beds. I would take you with me, but it's too treacherous of a path and you would have to climb down a rope," he told her, finishing his bowl. "Tis really good, wife. You can cook handily," he told her and winked at her. "May I have more?"

"You know you can," she answered him; laughing that mesmerizing laugh of hers he loved so much. She stood up and moved to the cooking pot, swinging her long skirt provocatively, reminding him of the thoughts he had in the cave. Slowly she ladled the rest of the stew into his bowl. She loved it when he asked her for more.

After supper Bulk went to the barn to work on the night table he was building for Loretta to put next to her side of the bed. For now she used a round stump, which he had cut several months ago. Appreciating the useful trade of carpentry he had pursued before he left the city, he devoted at least an hour each night to build her more furniture, enjoying her happiness when he presented her with a new piece.

He had been so lucky to find and marry her. Not only was she incredibly beautiful and smart, but she possessed the same kind of adventurous spirit that he did and was able to cope with the severe weather conditions and their lonely existence in this forlorn wilderness. When he had suggested the long trek across undiscovered territory she didn't flinch about the dangers ahead of them.

He taught her how to load and fire his Kentucky Long Rifle and she was surprisingly good at it. She had practiced over and over until she perfected it. He had been so proud of her; watching her pour the right amount of black powder down the long barrel then place a piece of greased linen over the muzzle and use the ramrod to gently push the lead bullet on top of the gunpowder encased by the linen. It took patience and repetition to go through all the steps, but she learned quickly, even anticipated the lag of the pull of the trigger and the actual ignition of the gunpowder. In the end he had purchased a second Kentucky Long Rifle for her and she always kept it close. Loretta had shot her fair share of rabbits and turkeys out here and he had taught her how to skin a deer and clean and dress fowl. The one thing he hadn't taught her was to cook.

There was no need since she proved herself to be a damn fine cook. Whatever he brought home she could turn it into a savory meal.

But he had to agree with her. If something happened to him out here she would have hell to deal with to make it out of this valley alive. No, he would praise the Lord the day his brother and wife would arrive in this valley. Until then, he would just have to tread carefully not to get hurt or killed.

Smiling to himself he remembered last winter when he had gone hunting on snowshoes, leaving Loretta behind in the warm cabin. He was at least forty minutes away when he heard a faint shot coming from the direction of the cabin. Scared to death of what could have happened he rushed back through the knee deep snow, waiting for a second shot. He had always told her that if she needed him in an emergency to shoot twice into the air, but this had been only one shot.

Horrible pictures flashed through his mind of Loretta being attacked or killed by natives, even though he had never encountered any in this remote area. Five minutes later a second shot echoed through the valley, and in a way the second shot worried him more than the first one. He knew she could load the rifle faster than that. He ran back to the cabin as fast as he could, the snow shoes making it almost impossible to hurry. His heart was beating out of his chest with fright. When the cabin came into view he could see from a distance that a dark mound was lying in front of it. In his mind he tried to figure out if it could be Loretta. Had she worn such dark clothing that morning? He ran and was sweating even though it was horribly cold. When he finally reached their dwelling he came to an abrupt halt as he recognized a dead bear lying in the snow thirty yards from the cabin door. Rushing inside to look for her he noticed the deep scratches the bear had inflicted on the wooden door and his angst only disappeared after he opened the door and saw Loretta standing by the fireplace giving him a victorious smile, stirring a stew, totally at ease and calm.

"Husband, have you ever eaten bear stew?" she asked him, laughing her special laugh. He was totally dumbfounded, his heart beating hard underneath his ribs.

"Are you all right?" he yelled at her and rushed toward her. "What happened?"

"I think the bear was hungry. I was making bread when I heard something crashing against the door. He scratched it pretty bad, snarling the whole time, but the door held up. Then I watched him through the small windows searching all around the cabin and then he walked toward the barn. I was so afraid he would kill the cow or get the chickens, so I got my rifle and opened the door. He heard me and turned around and I shot him as he charged me," she told him as calm as could be.

"Bloody, you could have been killed, Loretta!" he shouted at her angrily, the thought of her being charged by a bear made him see red. "Wife, the rifle could have misfired or you could have missed the bear," he shouted at her angrily.

"But it didn't and I wasn't," she snapped back at him.

He turned around, realizing he had to calm down. He stomped back outside and slammed the door shut then walked over to the bear and looked at him closer. He couldn't figure out why the bear wasn't hibernating in a cave somewhere. It was way too late in the season for him to be foraging for food. Loretta stayed where she was, stirring the stew, giving him the time he needed to realize that she was all right. He came back inside ten minutes later and sat at the table not saying a word, still upset.

"You know," she finally told him. "I have felt the way you do many times before, every time you go out hunting, every time you make the long journey to the next settlement and leave me behind. I never know if you will come back to me. Life out here is terribly hard, and to survive we both have to be strong and do what we have to do to stay alive. Do you want a wife who shrivels up with fear when it comes to protecting the few things we have out here? I have to do my part."

Bulk looked at her with amazement. "You're right, but did you have to start out by killing a bear? You scared me so badly, Loretta. I was so worried when I heard the shot. I thought I had lost you…but I'm proud of you and I'm glad you're all right," he added.

"To tell you the truth, I trembled when the bear charged me. He went down immediately after I shot him, but I held my breath for a long time afterward to see if he would get back up. Only after I started breathing again did I decide to be on the safe side and shoot him again. Only then did I calm down and thought to surprise you with a bear stew. I cut the meat out of his hind quarter from underneath so as not to destroy his fur coat. Will you skin him and make me a nice rug? I want something warm to step on when I get out of bed in the mornings."

"Count on me, good wife" he told her and kissed her with a passion equal to his earlier fear. Only several minutes later did he let go of her and walked outside to take care of the bear. The bear rug was lying in front of her side of the bed now and the meat kept them fed through the whole winter with the occasional mule deer, turkey, raccoon, and rabbit stew. And the added benefit of killing the bear was that Loretta loved his fat for frying.

Luckily nothing else happened that first winter and they had eaten all the meat, Loretta using her skills as a good cook to make it taste delicious. The night table he was working on started to look good. A couple more evenings and it would be finished. Carefully he carved the words "Anno 1755" into the front drawer of the night table. He knew she would love it. She deserved to have nice things and furniture was something he could build thanks to the three years of being a carpenter's apprentice in his home town. The next thing he was going to build was a rocking chair. He could picture her sitting in it and rocking their baby to sleep, if they finally would be blessed with one. They had been married for three years now and every month Loretta was disappointed to find out that she was not with child, but Bulk was convinced that one day he would be building a cradle; a cradle for his son.

Later that night he went through his pocket almanac. He didn't remember how many times he had read it from front to back. It looked used, earmarked and worn out, but he still lived by it. The front page looked faded; the words barely readable.

An Almanac for the Year of Our Lord 1752

The little book automatically opened to the page he looked at the most; the picture of a human body and the words: 1751 - The Anatomy of Man's Body as governed by the Twelve Constellations. He knew beforehand that he wouldn't find anything about the mysterious plant, but still felt compelled to flip through the pages. As predicted, he couldn't find it.

Chapter Two

August 4, 1755

T he following morning, Bulk woke up earlier than normal and started his chores right after breakfast so that he would have enough time to ride up the mountain and look at the beautiful plant again. He couldn't really understand his own need and motivation in doing so; after all, he never really was interested in flowers before. He received his pleasure from the livestock and dreamed of raising cows and horses, but plants? He still mourned his dog, Hans, who had died on the long trek to this valley. He had owned him since he was a young boy and when he died he left a void. As an afterthought, Bulk wondered why he hadn't written his brother to bring him a pup.

Bulk returned to the mountain ridge shortly after lunch and climbed down the rope, just as he had done the day before, except now it was daylight. He entered the opening and followed the tunnel to the cave with the four openings, where the sunlight entered the cave and brightened every crevice and corner of the large alcove. The flowers were closed up and hanging limp from the branches. It was hard to believe that it was the same plant he had seen the evening before, when it looked breathtakingly radiant. The flowers now looked lifeless and drooping. The sweet perfume of the blossoms had long since dissipated and he didn't feel the previous overwhelming awe. The plant is sleeping, waiting for the night to come to bloom once more, he thought.

He looked around the cave, seeing some of the niches and alcoves clearly for the first time. What had been dark and ominous the night before was now visible to him. And then he saw one single bone sticking out from behind a rock wall in the farthest corner of the cave. Taken aback he moved closer to the small alcove to get a better look. Was it an animal bone? It couldn't be human, could it? Not up here in this cave.

Astounded he recognized the skeletal remains of a human being. There was no doubt in his mind when he saw the complete skeleton and the detached skull, lying with empty eye sockets, staring into nothingness behind the rock wall. It appeared to Bulk that the man had been trying to hide during the last moments of his life, why else would he be behind this rock wall? But what was he hiding from? Why wasn't he at the entrance of the cave where he could shout and be heard? Did he live all alone in this valley? Who was he and why did he die in this cave and what had he been doing up here in the first place, Bulk wondered? Could it be that the cave had another entrance to it? He searched the cave but could only find one way out and that was the way he had come in.

He wiped his hand over his lower jaw thinking; a habit he had since he was a small boy when he was pondering what to do next. He looked at the skeleton closer and noticed a strange looking axe lying next to the hand bones. The blade was made out of an arrow shaped, sharp stone and was held together by a worn out leather string. He picked the cutting tool up to inspect it closer, but the stone fell off and Bulk thought it a sign not to disturb the dead and placed the worn-out wooden handle back where it had been before. One thing was for sure; the axe was old, really old. The thought crossed his mind that it had been in this cave for centuries. But he didn't know for sure, he wasn't an expert. Whatever happened to the man, it happened a long time ago and had nothing to do with him. Maybe back then the whole valley belonged to cave dwellers and it wasn't up to him to figure it out.

A high pitched tinkling noise made him turn around. Where did that come from? Maybe the wind coming through the openings of the cave, he first figured, but that couldn't be. It wasn't windy at all. Maybe a rodent in the back of the cave or a bat, he figured next. Those animals were known to make high pitched sounds. That's it, a bat, Bulk mused. The tinkling sound stopped and he looked one more time at the bones. Let him rest in peace, Bulk thought and made a cross over his chest then walked back to the plant.

He had brought the journal along his brother Hank had given him as a goodbye present before he left. Bulk sat down across from the plant and pulled the book out of his knapsack. He had wanted to take daily records about the trek through this unknown country over a year ago, but he never had. Not one word had made it inside the journal. It was time that he used his brother's present for something. The idea to draw the plant and describe its beauty occurred to him last night lying in bed next to Loretta, who had already fallen asleep. Bulk got up and started searching for the ledger by the dim light of the hearth. He finally found it tucked away inside Loretta's large wooden trunk.

Yes, he would use it for this unusual plant. After all, wasn't it the duty of a pioneer to keep records of undiscovered plants and animals the world had hidden away in isolated places? He hadn't drawn anything since he was a small boy and now he tried hard to sketch the plant. When he finished, he labeled each segment of the plant. He drew the pea pods he overlooked the day before lying around the plant's trunk. Now in the daylight they were clearly visible; three inches long and dark brown and they felt dry to his touch when he picked one of them up and inspected it closer. It was strange how tranquil and peaceful he felt as he sat close to the plant, like they were meant to be together; like the outside world didn't exist.

What a ridiculous thought, he chided himself. Such nonsense! What's wrong with me to have such sappy thoughts? He had no idea why this plant had such a strong effect on him and marveled at his response. How he wished he could smell the flower's fragrance again. He almost craved the scent. Bulk knew that he had to wait to return another day at sunset so he could see the flowers open up and smell the intoxicating scent once more. Yes, he would definitely come back.

He sat there for at least an hour perfecting the sketch of the plant and writing a report of how he had found it the day before. He described the cave and how in his opinion the plant had managed to survive the harsh elements of winter, with its taproot descending deep into the crevice of the rocky cave floor. He dated and signed his drawing then stood up and picked up some of the pods from underneath the plant's trunk. He placed them carefully into his knapsack. Somehow he knew he was going to see the plant again, he felt drawn to it. The plant had become an essential part of his being. Why he felt such a deep connection with the plant remained a mystery to him. His only plausible explanation was that he felt a certain responsibility toward it, since he discovered it.

Not analyzing his motives too much, Bulk climbed back up the cliff and removed the rope from around the rock. Sure, he and Loretta were the only people in this valley, but anyone else could come along just the way he had and discover this rope. No, it was better to leave no trace of the plant's location. He was the only person who knew where this plant grew and he was going to keep it that way.

Several minutes later he rode his mare carefully down the path into the valley, knowing that it had been a good decision to keep a record of his discovery. A sense of accomplishment and success flowed through him. When he reached the cabin he pulled out the ledger and showed the sketch he had made to Loretta.

"Gracious me. I knew not you were so gifted, husband!" she told him. Bulk just grumbled then continued to tell her about the skeletal remains he found inside the cave.

"It causes one to ponder who he was?" she responded. "I always believed it unanswerable that we were indeed the first people to live in this valley."

"I know. So did I, but whoever he was, he died hundreds of years ago. We'll most likely never find out," Bulk told her then changed the subject. "You have the green thumb in this family. See if you can make them grow."

He placed the pods he had picked up on the table. Loretta sat down and looked at the dark-brown shells then picked one of them up and turned it around, inspecting it from all sides.

"They don't look so special to me," she remarked and counted them. Bulk had brought her eight pods. "They remind me of the flat reddish-brown seeded pods I've seen hanging from a small tree a couple years ago, but I know not their name. I know it bloomed in the springtime and had gorgeous pink to reddish-purple flowers. I was told that you could boil the flowers and pods of this plant and eat them, sometimes even raw. I never tried it. Do you think these are good for eating?"

"I don't know. But I don't want to find out. They could be poisonous. Eight pods are not enough to get a malady over. We'll figure it out in good time. I'll make inquiries on my next trip to the settlement. Someone might know something about a plant which looks like the one I found, but that won't be for another couple of months."

"Did you open one of them up yet?"

"No, didn't occur to me, but go ahead. We have enough left to plant." Curious Loretta opened one of the shells and found three shriveled up peas inside, as red as blood, but when she pressed one of them flat between her fingers she was surprised to see red juice running out." The instinct to lick her fingers overcame her so strongly that she lifted her fingers to her mouth, but Bulk grabbed her hand and firmly told her no.

"Careful, wife," he raised his voice.

"But they look like currents, just juicier, like they are both young and old at the same time. Oh, how I miss currents. Remember the parcel we brought along on the trek? You have to write Hank to bring us some more. Then I'll be able to make you a bread pudding with currents," she told him and wiped her fingers on the cloth. Bulk grinned at her.

"Yeah, I'd like that. Now go and plant the pods. I feel better knowing they're in the ground."

Thinking how to best go about it, Loretta placed some pods in the soil of her garden, next to her root vegetables, and some in a rock bed close to the cabin, simulating the conditions of the cave Bulk had told her about.

"I'm going to put the two peas left from the opened pod into this dirt pot and place it in the window facing west, the same direction of the openings in the cave wall."

"When I saw the plant today the flowers were closed, all of them," Bulk told her. "It was disheartening to see the plant so lifeless, like it was sleeping."

He watched her. For some reason he was afraid that she would eat the left-over peas. Only after she had planted them in the pot did he leave her presence, feeling reassured that she was safe. He never found a good enough reason to explain his feelings, writing them off as irrational.

"I find it queer, husband, that you take such an interest in this plant. You never take any interest in my garden," Loretta complained to him. "What is so special about this plant beyond their peculiar black flowers?"

"I really don't know. I feel like I have a connection with it. What if it is the only one of its kind? What if I'm the first person to discover it? I feel like I was meant to find it. Like my pipe was meant to fall

40

down there. I can't really explain it," he answered and walked over to where she stood. "You will see, once it takes root and grows how special it is. Maybe I will name it after you. What do you think about that?" he teased her and smiled. "The Black Loretta." She laughed out loud at his suggestion.

"That's a ridiculous name for a plant," she teased him. "And it sounds somehow sinister and frightening, not a very good name at all for a one of a kind, fine-looking flower."

Neither one of them knew at the time how close Loretta came to the truth. Bulk still had to unsaddle the mare and put her in the corral, so he went to the barn and did his chores while Loretta stirred the stew. When he came back inside, he opened the journal and drew the insides of the pea pod and the way the peas looked and described them to the last detail. Loretta finished making corn cakes and carried them to the table.

"Let us eat. The rabbit stew is delicious," she told him, handing him his bowl. They ate together contented with their circumstances and happy to be in each other's company. Life was good.

Chapter Three

August, 1756

Even though Loretta watered the seeds and put them into different soils - from dirt to small rocks - nothing happened. Not one single pea grew. Bulk went to the cave and checked on the plant many times since he discovered it. The flowers and leaves started to wilt and dropped to the ground during the last two weeks of September until the plant looked bare, dreary and dismal. Looking at it then, absolutely nothing reminded him of the incredible spectacle he had witnessed the first time he laid eyes on it. If it would have looked like this the day he entered the cave he wouldn't have spent another second thinking about it. But he did see it and experienced its incredible allure and he couldn't wait until he could experience it again.

He had climbed down to the cave in the dead of winter and found the plant covered with snow, which had drifted in through the open crevices of the cliff. He had worried about it through the cold days and ice-cold nights, but especially during the worst snowstorm they experienced that winter. It had been so severe that he had to tie a rope to a hook next to the barn door and his cabin, the only way to safely guide his way through the raging strong blizzard. He left the cabin twice a day to feed the animals and check on their well-being, otherwise he stayed put in the cabin. The blizzard created such a blinding whiteness that he easily could have lost his way if he stepped just a couple of feet into the wrong direction.

The storm lasted three days - three days of being cooped up together – three days where Bulk had no other obligations besides cleaning hides and whittling with wood. They had been good, warm days, with enough food to last them through the storm, enough firewood to keep them warm, and enough love between them to cherish every minute of being snowed in. It was a short respite from daily chores and obligations. Life in this wilderness was lonely, but during these three days they didn't mind being isolated from the rest of the world. The wind howled around the corners and the snow piled up high against the north side of the cabin, but they didn't care. They were safe in their little haven and they had each other.

Bulk went to check on the plant the first day of April and found that it had grown new green twigs and little vines which were budding out of the old, dead bottom branches. He devotedly removed the dead branches and discarded them through the cave openings into the canyon below; happy he could perform this task for the plant. He entered his findings into his ledger and returned three weeks later to check on the plant again. He was totally astonished by how much the plant had grown in just three weeks' time. It had almost returned to its former size and this time he noticed small little buds which had formed all over. The plant had gone through an incredible growing spurt. Bulk couldn't wait to once again watch the blossoms open up and smell the intoxicating perfume in the warm evening air. He wanted the heady feeling back, which overwhelmed him so much the year before and had created the elevated sensual response in him. Yes, he wanted to feel it all again. It was like his insides were tingling with anticipation at the mere thought of it. He wasn't going to admit it to anyone, but he had become a slave to the plant.

The pass out of the valley finally cleared in mid-April and Bulk was able to make the long trip to the next settlement for much needed supplies. When he came back three days later, he excitedly showed his wife the parcel which had been waiting for him for the last three months. His brother Hank and his wife Emma had agreed to make the long trip to the valley and would arrive late September. The thought that they were already on their way at the same time he showed Loretta the letter filled them both with happiness and excitement.

Soon a second family would call this valley their home and for them to be their own kin was incredible. It was a dream come true for both of them. The letter also notified them that Hank and Emma had become parents since Bulk and Loretta left New York. They had a little boy now and it made their arrival that much more special. To have a little child in the valley would bring joy to them all. It brought tears to Loretta's eyes and she was beaming with happiness at the thought of it. In the evenings she sat down in front of the hearth and worked on sewing little buckskin leggings and a shirt for the little boy. Bulk had taken all of the animal hides except the softest and lightest one into town and traded them for supplies. She had planned on making Bulk a shirt out of the soft skin, but now it would have to wait until he killed more game and restocked his hides. There was time enough for her to make him a shirt and Bulk understood her need. He knew he would get his new shirt in due time. It was more important to him that she was happy; realizing how disappointed she was each month to find out that she was not with child.

He recorded the plant's blooming and seeding cycle. He found out that the plant started growing the pods in the beginning of May and the flowers started blooming in mid-June. He went several times during this time not to miss the opening of the blossoms, and when it actually happened he was on an incredible high. The same strong perfume engulfed him and he gave his fantasies free range, not holding back this time, breathing in the potent vapors, enjoying every second of it.

The strong urge to check on the plant again overcame him in August with such intensity that he saddled his horse and rode the hard treacherous trail up to Pitch Fork Mountain. He couldn't really afford to lose another half-day of work, especially since he was not only getting his place ready for another harsh winter, but also planning ahead for the arrival of his brother and his family. Each day he cut down several trees for his brother's cabin, so that when he arrived they could start building without any delays. But on this day Bulk just couldn't fight the urge to see the plant. It didn't make any sense to him why he felt so strongly about the plant that particular day and when Loretta asked him why he wanted to venture up the mountain again, he couldn't explain it to her. All he knew was that he had to see the plant. He had dreamed about the plant the previous night; how the flowers opened up and started swaying in the evening breeze, how he felt teased and taunted by the smell of its perfume, the headiness making him ache with desire. He woke up in a sweat, feeling like he had cheated on Loretta. Bulk looked at his beautiful wife lying next to him in the bed, with the light of the moon outlining her sleeping form. He snuggled close to her and prayed that his obsession with the plant would come to an end. But it didn't.

The next day, late in the afternoon, Bulk rode back up the mountain path to the plateau and climbed down to the cave below. He had timed it perfectly, it was almost dusk. He sat in front of the plant and waited anxiously for it to stir. A minute seemed like an hour, but finally the flower started to move and sway as he sat there and watched it happen.

The blossoms slowly opened up to the disappearing sunlight and it was like the first time. Time stood still for him as he absorbed it all; the beauty, the sensuality, the incredible allure of forbidden fruits. He had come prepared and brought a small lantern and in the dim light of the flame he admired the overwhelming exquisiteness of the plant. It seemed like it had surpassed its size of the year before and had more flowers. He was mesmerized by the handsome plant and the irresistible perfume which now filled the cave. He just sat there staring at it and inhaled the fragrance deeply into his lungs. He was heady with the intoxicating smell and started to get light headed; fantasies assaulting his thoughts, fantasies like he never had before. Loretta dancing naked in front of him, teasing him with her sensuality, indicating for him to come closer and... irritated at himself for his lustful wanderings, Bulk shook his head to clear all the intimate thoughts out of his head.

And then he put his eyes on the pods underneath the branches and he realized why he had come. It was his job now to collect them. Not analyzing his motives he stood up and carefully picked the pods off the ground and placed them in his knapsack, then extinguished the lantern. He would leave it behind for the next time he came, so he once again could stay past dark and enjoy the miracle of the plant. Even though he hated to leave the cave he knew that he had to. Loretta was waiting for him with supper and he didn't want to worry her. Still lightheaded he reached the opening of the cave and took several deep breaths of the crisp, clean night mountain air to clear his head before climbing up to the plateau above.

Once he safely reached the top, Bulk undid the rope by the soft moonlight and walked back to the mare who snorted with anticipation, eager to get back to the barn. Bulk climbed into the saddle and started his way back down the mountain. His head had cleared up and he started to think clearly again. It wasn't the first time that he ascended in the darkness with only the moonlight to guide him. It was a full moon and the night was beautiful, the light from above throwing shadows around him.

He was disappointed that his wife's efforts at growing a seedling had failed. Not one of the peas had taken root. Maybe Loretta was right and the peas weren't meant to be planted in the dirt, but a fruit or vegetable to be harvested. Maybe it was time for him to test this theory. The way he figured he was twice as heavy as Loretta so any negative effect the peas would have on his body would be half as bad as they would have on Loretta's body. No, he should definitely be the one to try them, and he would try them right now before she could give him any grief about it. Yes, he would try one right now.

Oh, he was in a weird mood, the desire to taste the little red peas becoming stronger, impossible to resist. What was wrong with him lately? He acted like a spoiled member of the female gender. Of course, they could be poisonous, so he decided to only try one. If the pea tasted bitter he would spit it out immediately, before any harm could be done. One way or another he would find out tonight.

Bulk halted the mare while he opened the saddlebag and retrieved the little pouch. He took a single pod out and excitedly opened the brown shell. Three blood-red peas were inside. He turned the shell upside down and dropped them into his large hand. Carefully he picked one of them up and put it in his mouth. To his surprise it was deliciously sweet and even though a minute before he cautioned himself to only taste one, he ate the other two peas without hesitation. It was definitely a fruit, a delicious small little fruit. He almost felt euphoric realizing the discovery he had just made. It was so strong in flavor that he felt pretty sure that Loretta could make a jelly or even a fruit wine out of it. He urged the mare on to continue down the path.

The desire to eat and chew more of the peas on his way down entered his mind, but he refrained from doing so, thinking that he wouldn't have enough left for Loretta to use. No, he was going to wait and taste one or two more with Loretta, excited to see what she thought about this incredible sweet flavor. He rode down the path thinking of all the uses, the moonlight giving him the needed light to find his way back down to the valley. He looked up to the moon and the stars and was mesmerized by the sheer number of them. It felt like he looked at them for the first time, noticing their clarity, their numbers. An incredible feeling of happiness floated through his body.

The thought crossed his mind that if he didn't know better he felt kind of giddy, like he had too much ale to drink. Laughing out loud at this thought he shook his head to clear his senses, which seemed to be in overdrive. He could smell the strong scent of the pine trees, as strong as if he had just cut one down. And what about the mare he was riding? How come he could suddenly smell the strong horse flesh underneath him, which he never smelled before? What was happening to him? He inhaled deeply through his nostrils, differentiating the smells from the vines climbing up on the trees to the pollen of the weed bushes growing between the rocks on his path down the mountain.

He felt euphoric, yet he also felt serenity the likes he had never experienced and he relaxed back in his saddle and gave himself up to the feeling of bliss and ecstasy. The details of the stars in the sky, the needles on the pine trees and the rabbit scurrying into a hole close by overwhelmed him with their clarity, even though it was almost dark. It was like nothing existed in the whole universe other than what he was experiencing right now; what he saw, heard, smelled, tasted and felt. Nothing else mattered, nothing except this moment where every cell in his body seemed alive and exploding with pleasure. He closed his eyes, the darkness behind them igniting into colorful bursts.

He didn't pay any attention to the path, didn't worry about the deep, dangerous drop next to him into the canyon below. He heard the birds chirping and felt like it was the nicest sounds he ever heard. He saw the moon twinkling through a cloud and thought he never experienced a nicer night, the perfect breeze tingling the skin on his arms and face and he smelled the incredible aroma of God's green earth in his nostrils, every little hair tingling with enjoyment. He felt more alive than he ever had in his whole life.

Only by the grace of God and the sure-footedness of his mare did he reach the bottom of the valley in one piece. The mare knew her way home and thirty minutes later stopped in front of the barn unaware that her rider was in a fantasy world of his own. Bulk sat on the horse not realizing he was home, totally unaware of his surroundings. He sat there and followed the imaginations in his head, half asleep, half awake, and the mare waited patiently for him to get off. And that's how Loretta found him five minutes later, looking through the small window of the cabin, wondering where he could be. Bulk was sitting on his mare not getting off.

"Husband! What is wrong with you? Why aren't you getting off the mare?" she shouted at him from the cabin entrance. "Bulk!" she shouted again when he didn't answer.

Then she noticed how his head was hanging down on his chest and a fear the likes of which she never experienced before went through her. Maybe he was shot. Maybe an Indian put an arrow through him. She ran toward him screaming his name now. "Bulk… Bulk… what's wrong?" In her haste she tripped and fell down hard on the ground, bruising her right knee. Any other time Bulk would have rushed toward her and helped her up, but he didn't move a muscle. Scared to death she pushed herself off the ground, grabbed hold of her long skirt and ran toward him.

She reached the mare out of breath and looked up at him. His eyes were halfway open and he wore a strange smile on his face, mumbling words she couldn't understand.

"Bulk, are you hurt?" Loretta shouted at him, her breathing labored, looking him up and down for an injury, but didn't find one.

Her head barely reached the mare's back and it was hard for her to tell if he was hurt with only the moonlight above. The only other chance for her to look him over was for her to get him off the mare, but how was she going to do that? She looked at his face again. He didn't look like he was in pain and she couldn't detect any blood on the mare either. The smirk on his face started to irritate her, and then she remembered; didn't he wear the same irritating smirk the day his brother got married and he had too much ale to drink? Yes, it was the same smirk, his eyes slightly blood shot and half open. Suddenly it dawned on her. Her husband was drunk; stinking drunk.

"Get down from the bloody mare right now, Bulk Horswell, or I shoot you off myself," she shouted at him, getting madder by the second, her former anxiety now replaced by anger about his drunken stupor.

"By all that is holy, how could you, Bulk Horswell? Get off the horse."

Bulk didn't move, didn't register what happened around him. He was oblivious to all, in a fantasy world of his own making and nothing could penetrate it. Loretta loosened Bulk's fingers from around the reins and then pulled hard on Bulk's arm. She used all the strength she possessed to make him lose his balance and fall off the horse. She succeeded the third time and her husband fell off the mare hitting the ground hard, creating a dust cloud around him. The mare danced away, unaccustomed to such a dramatic exit off her back. Loretta left her husband lying in the dirt and walked over to the mare, petting her soft, warm muzzle to calm her down.

"Thank you, Betsy. I can always count on you girl to bring the rascal home to me. You're a good girl and deserve a second ration tonight." She took the reins and led the mare to the barn where she took the saddle bags off and hung them up, then loosened the wide belt around her girth, pulled and tugged on the heavy saddle until it slid off the mares back into her waiting hands. She grabbed the heavy saddle and swung it over the wooden saddle horse, all the while wondering where Bulk had gotten drunk.

Loretta filled a bucket with two helpings of grain and hung it from the hook inside the corral then led the mare inside the fenced area.

"You deserve it girl," she told her and patted her hindquarters then locked the gate behind her and walked back to where her husband was still lying in the dirt. He had rolled onto his back, and now, hearing her approach, opened his eyes and grinned at her conniving. Loretta looked at him and started laughing; she just couldn't help it; he looked too funny lying on the ground all dusty, his long hair loose around his handsome face and looking more pleased then a cat who just ate a bowl full of cream. Damn that man of hers. She reached down and grabbed his hand.

"You can either try and get up or I let you sleep out here tonight for the wolves and bears to find."

"I love you so much, Loretta," he mumbled and this time she understood him.

"Sweet talking me won't get you anywhere," she told him. "Now get off the dirt and inside the cabin before I lock you out."

He chuckled at her feistiness, his befuddled mind slowly clearing up. He lifted his hand, got to his feet and wobbled next to her, his arm around her shoulders, to the cabin, all the while telling her what a fine fetch of a woman she was. She smiled and remembered how amorous he had been after his brother's wedding. They reached the inside of the cabin and she maneuvered his oversized body onto the kitchen chair where she tried to take his boots off. Drunk or not drunk, he wasn't going to sleep with his boots on. She wouldn't have it.

"I love you so much, Loretta," he mumbled again and pulled her slender body onto his lap.

He kissed her and to her surprise she didn't taste the bitter flavor of ale nor did he smell like he imbibed in the brew. What happened to him? If it wasn't ale, what had gotten him into this kind of state? She freed herself from his amorous attention and tried to take his boots off, straddling one of his long muscular legs, her skirts hanging down over each side, exposing part of her bare legs. Loretta pulled as hard as she could. Bulk just sat there and watched her efforts, rambling on about how happy he was and that she was the prettiest thing he ever put his eyes on. And then he told her that she shouldn't present her backside to him and tempt him so sorely without expecting any ramifications.

The first boot came off and fell onto the wooden floor. He appreciated her backside with her small hips and ample behind and his imagination fueled as he admired her shapely, soft, pale legs exposed to him once more as she worked on the second boot. Every movement of her trying to get his boots off put him in a more amorous mood until he grabbed her from behind and pulled her on his lap again. She screamed and protested his advances, but Bulk kissed her until she gave up fighting him. He stood up, suddenly strong and sober and carried her to the bed still wearing one dirty boot; the only thought on his mind now was the woman in his arms.

The next morning Bulk woke up not able to remember how he ended up in bed the night before. He felt refreshed and happy and eager to start the new day. Loretta was already up and he could smell the bacon she was frying for breakfast. He stretched leisurely and then got up putting his pants on. Looking for his boots he found only one discarded next to the bed. Wondering where the other boot was he looked around and saw it lying under the kitchen table. Strange, he thought, then walked over to the kitchen chair and put both of them on. Loretta didn't turn around from the hearth as she did every morning to greet him.

"Good morning," he finally told her.

"What happened to you last night?" she asked him curiously, still not looking at him.

"What happened to me last night?" he repeated, not quite sure what she was getting at, as he placed a kiss on her neck, then walked outside to the pump thinking about her question. What was she talking about? He washed his naked chest, armpits, neck and face with the clear ice-cold mountain water, musing about what she meant with her question. Refreshed he shaved the stubble off his face reflecting back to what he remembered about last night. He suddenly paused dumbfounded, halfway shaved, a memory flickering into his consciousness, just a tiny one, and then it hit him full force.

He remembered the night before and it took his breath away with its clarity. What a rogue he had been. The things they had done together and how incredible it had been. And then he remembered the peas he had eaten and the way they had made him feel and he put two and two together and realized the enormity of it. He had eaten the peas, all three of them, and was totally out of it coming down the path. How had he even made it without falling off his horse into the steep canyon below? The peas were stronger than any ale or wine he had ever tasted, even stronger than whiskey. And the effect they had on him was so exhilarating, so… He turned his face to look at the cabin and saw Loretta standing in the door frame, watching him the whole time while he performed his morning grooming ritual. He grinned at her from a distance, an – 'I remember now' - grin, and even from where he stood he could see her blush.

Angry at being caught ogling him, Loretta turned around, slammed the door and disappeared inside the cabin. She heard his deep laughter from where she leaned against the door, her heart beating hard in her chest.

When he finally finished he returned to the cabin. Loretta faced him, her eyes direct, tolerating no more from him.

"Where did you get alcohol, Bulk Horswell?" she asked him resolutely. "I shall not tolerate alcohol in this house, and you know this well."

"I had no drink, Loretta," he answered.

"You, Bulk Horswell are a fraud. You were drunk. And the way you behaved. It was appalling."

"I seem to remember that you enjoyed last night as much as I did," he answered her with a wink and a smile.

"I did no such thing. You remember it wrong."

"Loretta, I'm telling you the truth. I didn't have any ale or whiskey. I chewed three of the plant's peas on my way down from the mountain, wondering if they were edible. Well, they were. They made me drunk; drunk with happiness and well-being and love. They made me feel like I was the most content person in the world. It was incredible," he told her excitedly. "Everything I heard, smelled, tasted and saw last night was so intense, so strong. Your kisses were incredible;

your skin felt so indescribably soft. It was fantastic, everything we did together."

Blushing again by the memories Loretta turned around. "Stop it. I won't hear more of it. How do you know the peas weren't poisonous? What if they damaged something inside of you?" she asked him.

"I have never felt better," he answered, picked her up and swung her around the room. "I still feel so happy. It's like total, complete happiness entered my body."

"Throw them away. We don't need something like that in our cabin," she told him vehemently. "Go get rid of them right now." She pointed to the door after he put her back down, unwavering in her demand. "This is a God-fearing house and I won't tolerate such elixir."

"Hold it woman! You want me to throw the pods out? What if there's healing inside of them?" he argued back with her.

"Bulk, take them away. Just knowing how ungodly we two behaved last night is enough for me to throw them out. Please do as I say. Where are they?"

"I figure they're still in the saddle bag where I put them."

"Go and get rid of them now."

He gave her a stern look, but knew there was no reasoning with her. He knew her well enough to know she wouldn't change her mind. He walked angrily outside. Why did she have to be so strict in her ways of thinking? What should he do, just open the bag and discard the pods to the four winds? To hell with the woman inside, this was one time where he wouldn't listen to her. Sometimes a man had to stand his ground and follow his own gut feeling. And his feeling told him to keep them. Yes, he was going to keep them.

He walked toward the barn and found his saddle bag hanging from the hook on the wall. His saddle was placed neatly on the wooden saddle horse and just thinking of how his small wife of one hundred pounds had to wrestled with this saddle half her weight to place it on this tall wooden rack, brought a smile to his face. Boy, she was something else. He remembered her body from the night before and the way she had responded to him and felt a shiver of delight going through him. There was no way he could get rid of the pods. He opened the leather strings of his saddle bag and took the pouch with the pods out. Looking around for a good place to keep them, he spotted the hayloft. Smiling to himself he climbed up the ladder and hung the pouch from a nail on the far side. They would be safe there. Loretta never ventured up the loft.

"Is it done?" his wife asked him when he came back inside to eat his breakfast which was waiting for him on the table.

"It's done," was all he said as he sat down. They sat in silence for a while.

"When do you think Hank is arriving?" she asked him to change the subject, thinking that she had won the fight.

"I hope in another month or so if the weather stays fair."

"I can't wait to have another woman to talk to and a little one to play with will be so nice. I miss another woman's company so much."

"I'm going to cut more trees today for their cabin. I'll be on the east side of the lake if you need me." Bulk stood up, walked to the oak coat-rack and put his shirt and jacket on, glad to get to work without having to lie again. Ten minutes later she watched him ride down the path. She remembered the night before and her face turned flush with remembrance. What a wild guy she had married.

Unbeknown to her, Bulk chewed one of the peas every Saturday night for the next eight weeks, making sure he chewed only one of the peas, so as not to be overwhelmed by the strong powerful juices like he had been the first time. He knew that if he took more, Loretta was sure to find out and he didn't want that to happen. To his greatest disappointment, he noticed that the strength of the peas wore off with time and after four weeks he had to chew two peas at once to get the same strong effect. By the end of September the peas were dried up and became ineffective. Disappointed, he wrote all of this into the brown leather journal and discarded the leftover pods.

Chapter Four

September 26, 1756

It was one of the last warm days of the year. The summer had been long and pleasant and the fall transformed the valley into a color palette from deep red-orange to yellowish-brown of all shades. Loretta loved the fall with its refreshing winds and invigorating frisky mornings and she loved lying in bed at night listening to the howling of the wind around the cabin.

The midday sun was shining down on the valley, its sunrays reflecting off the blue lake creating an incredible display of splendor and brilliance. Pretty soon the lake would be covered with ice. Loretta could hear the faint sounds of Bulk's ax on the east side of the valley where he was cutting trees for Hank's and Emma's cabin. She saw the cow and the two draft horses, impervious to the valley's beauty, grazing down by the lake, enjoying the rich grass before the harshness of winter would set in.

Not a cloud was in the sky as Loretta wrung out the last piece of clothing she had just finished scrubbing hard against the tin washboard. Her knuckles hurt, but she was glad that the weekly washing day was nearing its end and she was almost finished. It was hard work cleaning all the clothes, but she took pride in it and the pleasure of fresh smelling clothes was always rewarding to her when she picked them off the clothesline after they fluttered and dried in the fresh air for a couple of hours. Loretta put the wet buckskin shirt into the vine clothes basket Bulk had fashioned for her and carried it toward the back of the cabin where the clothesline was located. She knew that the soft warm afternoon breeze would dry the clothes before the sun had a chance to set. It was hanging up the clothes which she enjoyed the most.

It was a satisfying feeling to know everything was clean and the hard task of scrubbing was behind her. The clothes fluttered in the wind and she just stood there taking a breather, then walked toward the front of the cabin. She heard the barking of a dog. Surprised she lifted her head toward the sound and was overjoyed to see a wagon coming up the steep path. Tied to the back of the wagon was a horse, a bull, and a dog was running alongside it. Loretta dropped the empty clothes basket and started running down the path, waving and shouting excitedly at the two people sitting on the buck board.

"You're here, you're here!" she yelled over and over again, running toward the wagon, the dog running toward her, barking at her. Her untied bonnet fell off her head into the dirt, but she didn't care. They were finally here. When she reached the wagon she smiled up at the travel weary occupants, her hand shielding her eyes from the bright sun.

Her brother-in-law, Hank, and his wife, Emma, who was holding a sleeping little infant in her arms, were smiling back at her. Loretta walked next to the wagon up the path until the wagon came to a halt in front of the cabin.

"I can't believe you're finally here," she told Hank as he climbed off the wagon and gave her a bear hug, lifting her off the ground.

"Tis good to be here. Where is my brother?" Hank asked Loretta as he looked around for him, but then noticed that Loretta had her eyes on his little son Emma was holding; her face full with unfulfilled longing. Hank turned around to his wife, took the sleeping boy out of her arms and handed him to Loretta.

"Meet your nephew," he told her proudly then put both his hands around his wife's waist and lifted her easily off the buckboard. Loretta looked at the little sleeping baby with such longing and tenderness that Hank and Emma exchanged some knowing glances, realizing that Loretta was aching for a child of her own. Loretta finally noticed both of them staring at her how she admired the little boy and was ripped out of her daydreaming of becoming a mother. Emma and Loretta greeted each other like long lost sisters and immediately started talking about the little one. Loretta just couldn't keep her eyes off of the baby. "He's so handsome. What a fine boy he is," Loretta stated over and over again.

"So, where is Bulk?" Hank asked her again.

"Oh, I'm supposed to shoot the rifle to let him know you have arrived," she explained and was about to hand the baby back to his mother to fetch the rifle from inside the cabin.

"Hold it, sister," Hank stopped her and grabbed his own rifle off the buckboard, then stepped to the side and fired a shot into the air. The little boy woke up with a start and started screaming. When he saw who was holding him, he stopped and stared at her. All three of them laughed. Three minutes later they heard a horse galloping in the distance. Expectantly, they turned toward the path and Bulk appeared around the bend riding like the devil was after him. Coming to a stop in front of the three he jumped off his mare and grabbed his brother hard, slapping him on the shoulders. After that he picked up his sister-in-law and swung her around, making her beg him to stop.

"It's about time you all got here. What took you so long?" he asked them, then saw the little boy who was staring at him with big round eyes.

"And who do we have here?" he asked, taking the small child out of his wife's arms. "My, he is a fine lad and heavy, has to be at least twenty-five pounds. What did you name him?"

"Ben, after father," Hank answered.

"Father is proud, no doubt. How is the old man doing?"

"Ornery as ever. He's never going to change. I tried to talk him and mother into coming with us, but mother wouldn't hear of it. She wants to stay put in Boston."

"I expected as much. I'm glad you finally made it. Did you have a hard time finding the valley?"

"For a while I thought we were not on the right trail, but then I saw the three cliffs you mentioned from the distance. They were our beacon."

Bulk laughed. "That's what brought us here too. I named the mountain after the cliffs. Pitch Fork Mountain." Bulk turned toward the talking women and handed the child back to his wife. "You women folk go inside and get the food ready. Hank and I will take care of the animals. I have to check out that fine bull he brought along."

Followed by his brother, Bulk walked toward the huge beast tied behind the wagon.

"That's what took us so long in getting here. I let him graze wherever there was good grass along the way. Isn't he a fine specimen?" Hank asked Bulk proudly.

"Surely he is," Bulk answered, inspecting the bull from all sides, patting his enormous dark brown hindquarters. "Brother, he is a great beast! He's just what we need to start that herd we talked about." Grinning from ear to ear, satisfied with Hank's selection of the bull, Bulk turned to the horse tied on the opposite side of the wagon and slapped his brother teasingly on the shoulder. "I see you brought Old Faithful along." He walked over to the brown gelding tethered to the wagon.

"I just couldn't leave him behind. I've had him for too long and I figure he has a couple good years left before I put him out to pasture." They both laughed. "Got him when I turned twelve and here I am twenty years later and he is still with me."

"Let's get him and the draft horses into the corral. They've done their work for today and the bull will go into the stall inside the barn," Bulk told his brother. He noticed the large dog by Hank's side.

"Glad to have a dog in the valley again. I lost Hans on the trek," Bulk told his brother.

"Sorry to hear that. He was a good dog."

"That he was."

They worked in unison until the animals were taken care of, just like they had done so many years ago when they were growing up on the farm. Good memories of his little brother following him around came back to Bulk's mind. This is good, he thought. This is really good. Together we'll make this valley work; get good crops and start a cow herd. We will make a name for ourselves.

"Now can we go inside and eat some meat? I'm starving," Hank teased his older brother.

"Let's go eat. Loretta put a venison stew on the fire several hours ago. The meat should be nice and tender by now. I still can't believe you're finally here."

"I have to say, when you described this valley, you didn't exaggerate. It's as beautiful and rich as you said."

Bulk was about to say something when he heard soft whining noises coming from the wagon. He turned and looked and was surprised the see a small puppy peering out over the planks at him.

"I figured I would let him decide when to introduce himself to you. He's yours," Hank explained. "Figured you could use a good dog by now. He was only six weeks old when we got him from another wagon trail going south. Look at him now, he is six months old and built as solid as you are." Bulk walked over to the wagon and untied the dog from underneath the seat where he had been sleeping.

"Looks like a wolf breed." Bulk smiled as he picked him up and placed him on the ground. "Brother, you must have read my mind. I missed having a dog around...You couldn't have gotten me...thanks," Bulk stumbled over the words. "Hell, I like him. Come on pup. You're home now."

They washed up outside in the big metal bucket, getting the water out of the rain barrel which was filled to the brim with rain water.

"One day I will build a contraption for Loretta which will bring the water directly into the cabin. I just need more time." It was Bulk's responsibility to always keep the barrel filled with clean water from the creek running next to the cabin if it didn't rain for a while.

The puppy followed him inside the cabin and laid down next to the hearth and when Loretta spotted him she nodded her approval, a happy smile on her face. She had cried when Hans died and they had buried him together.

They all sat down at the table and thanked the Lord for a safe trip, then ate and talked for hours catching up on what happened since Bulk and his wife left almost three years ago, what happened to Hank and his family on the trail and their plans for the future. They also caught them up on the latest news concerning Boston.

The women and the baby slept in the small cabin and the brothers took their pallet in the barn, going to sleep listening to the movements of the animals and the soft snorting of the huge bull. The puppy slept in the crook of Bulk's arm and Hank's dog slept close to the barn door having accepted his job as the protector of the pack a long time ago.

The next day Bulk showed Hank where he figured his cabin should be built. He showed him the trees he had cut and stripped, ready to be used. He pointed out the small creek running close by and the ideal spot to build the barn and the horse corral. Hank told Bulk that he couldn't have picked a better spot. They rode around the lake and inspected the pastures where Hank marveled at the rich ground. Bulk pointed to the place where he reckoned a dam should be built to limit the flooding down below and thus gain more pasture land and Hank readily agreed. He became familiar with the valley and the more he saw of it, the more he liked it. It would be a good place to call home, raise a family and be prosperous.

They started to work side by side the following day, building a one room cabin and a barn. The months flew by and by the time the first snowflakes fell on the valley, the cabin was dried in and the animals had a place to call their own. At one point during the long days of hard work, Bulk told Hank about the beautiful plant he discovered and its strange powers. They laughed together when he told him about the part where Loretta had pulled him off the horse fuming mad at him for getting drunk and he fell onto the dusty ground. But Bulk only hinted at the incredible sexual desires he experienced. He promised Hank to take him along the next time he went to the cave.

Annegret Werner Shaw

Chapter Five

August 1757

Another harsh winter followed a beautiful fall with so much snow that Bulk had to work hard to clear a pass to the barn. Two severe snowstorms hit, but the two families stayed warm inside their small cabins. Hank and Bulk went hunting together and came back with a mule deer and an elk, which kept all of them busy cutting the meat and using the hides.

The valley looked beautiful covered with snow, but belied the hardships the two families endured. Bulk worked a lot in the barn building Loretta a cabinet for her pots and pans, which still hung from hooks on the log wall. By the time spring arrived everybody breathed a sigh of relief and threw themselves into the hard work of getting the ground ready for planting new crops, including new seeds Hank had brought with him, which had laid dormant through the winter months.

Spring turned into summer and August arrived. Bulk had eagerly awaited his trip up to Pitch Fork Mountain and now that it was upon him, he was edgy with anticipation. He couldn't wait to see Hank's reaction when he saw the plant. Would he feel the same things he did? Would he become as mesmerized as he had been the first time he saw it? Late one afternoon, after a hard day of work, the two men saddled their horses and rode up to Pitch Fork Mountain.

Loretta told Bulk to leave the plant alone with its wickedness, but he just laughed at her and didn't listen. Hank saw firsthand how beautiful the valley looked from the plateau. Bulk knotted and tied the rope around the boulder the same way he had done the year before and repelled down, encouraging Hank to do the same. Hank followed him down the cliff to the opening. Curious now he followed his brother inside the dark tunnel until it opened up and he was inside the big cave. Just like Bulk, he first noticed the four vertical openings and was impressed by the view they offered. The cave was bright, filled with light and the air was fresh, not musty, wet and dark like the tunnel was. Bulk just stood back and watched his brother take in the view.

"You can see for miles up here. I can even see part of the valley to my right." Hank turned around to look at his brother and that's when he noticed the plant. "Bloody hell, it sure is something!" "Sit here next to me and wait just a little longer. You haven't seen anything yet. Get ready for a spectacle the likes you've never seen," Bulk replied and indicated the spot next to him.

Hank did as he was told and together they waited. The cave turned darker as the sun set lower on the horizon, painting the cave with radiant colors. The two brothers didn't talk. They just sat there enjoying the peacefulness of the cave, keeping their eyes on the plant. Not a single leaf moved; nothing stirred. It was a calm windless evening and the only thing they heard were the drops of water trickling down a crevice somewhere inside the tunnel.

Hank was surprised at Bulk's eagerness to show him the plant. Sure, it was totally out of place here in a cave high up on the mountain top, and the closed black flower petals hanging upside down were unusual, but he couldn't quite join in his brother's enthusiasm. The cave itself was incredible. So he sat next to Bulk and stared at the plant and waited, not really expecting anything grandiose to happen.

"I named the plant the Black Trumpet Angel," was all Bulk said.

The grey wall behind the plant turned orange-yellow as the last sunrays entered. It was as if the plant had waited to be in the spotlight.

Then without warning a soft breeze entered the cave and stirred the flowers and Hank watched, fascinated at how the limp blooms moved in harmony, slowly opening up to become big, beautiful, gleaming, black flowers. They came alive and the evening breeze touched them and carried the sweet seductive smell to the brothers who sat transfixed, barely breathing. The blood-red thin veins inside the blossoms danced and glittered as if they acted on their own accord, teasing and taunting, pulling the two men deeper into its spell.

Each brother watched captivated, each in their own fantasy world now, their eyes shiny with want, unable to look away. It was like the plant was singing to them, lulling them to hallucinate. But neither one of them could have sworn to it that it was indeed the flowers and not their imaginations which made them hear the beautiful high pitched sounds. Yes, it was all in their heads and they only imagined the fine trilling sounds coming from the blossoms.

Bulk was the first one to regain his senses. He stood up and collected the pods lying around the trunk of the plant and placed them carefully into his little leather bag. Hank was still caught up in the plant's spell. Bulk looked at him and saw the same amazement written on Hank's face as he took it in.

Finally he put his hand on his brother's shoulder and squeezed hard enough to get his attention and told him that it was time to go. Reluctantly, without talking about what had happened, Hank followed Bulk to the opening of the cave and climbed up the cliff, where Old Faithful and Betsy were tethered to a tree. On the ride home neither one of them spoke, both of them thinking about what they witnessed and how it had made them feel. Only when they reached Hank's cabin did Hank turn toward his brother and asked him the question which was on his mind.

"Tell me," he started out. "Did you fantasize a lot about Loretta when you smelled the flower's fragrance?"

"I sure did," Bulk answered him back.

"I mean, did you think of her in an impure way, if you know what I mean."

"I know exactly what you mean. It happens to me each time the flowers open up and release that scent. It takes your breath away, doesn't it? Wait until you chew your first pea tomorrow night, and pray, don't tell Emma about it. Loretta told me never to chew the peas again, and if I know my wife, she probably told Emma not to let you use them either," Bulk warned him. "Brother, you're in for a treat."

Both laughed and parted ways and only after Bulk rode on did he remember that he didn't show Hank the skeleton he had found inside the cave. The plant had taken up all his thoughts.

The next evening, after working side by side all day, Hank and Bulk sat by the lake and each savored the sweet juicy flavor of a single pea. They both smoked their pipes afterward while they waited for the effects of the peas to kick in. They didn't have to wait long.

Never did smoking tobacco taste better, never did the lake look more beautiful. They both lay back in the grass and stared up at the darkening night sky, the moon and stars looked glorious, sparkly and glittery. Peace and tranquility filled their beings and they were totally content with their lives.

They walked home two hours later, the feeling of happiness anchored deep inside of them. But Loretta noticed the shiny eyes of her husband and recognized his playful banter and guessed the reason why. She figured out the year before that Bulk hadn't thrown the pods out like she told him to, but didn't question him about it; instead she enjoyed his amorous behavior. Now it was different, he had involved h0is brother. The next morning, after a passionate lover's night, she asked him if he had chewed the peas with his brother and he didn't deny it.

"Loretta, I only chew one pea at a time and they do me no harm. I'm a God-fearing man, but what harm does it do us if I chew the peas? They are only good for such a short time. God created them for a purpose, didn't he, and one day the peas will heal the sick and comfort the suffering. Think about it. How can something so good be bad? If you would just try one of them, just one time, you would understand," Bulk told her.

"I will do no such thing, husband!" she shouted at him and they argued about it, but in the end there was nothing she could do. She confided in Emma who had noticed herself that her husband had come home with shiny eyes and in a happy mood and had wondered why. She agreed with Loretta that she wouldn't partake in chewing the peas, even though they admitted to each other that they both had enjoyed their husband's attention toward them. In the end they decided that it was better to pretend to be glad that the peas had such a short lifespan, then to admit the truth to Bulk and Hank. The brothers chewed the peas until the end of September and it was bittersweet. They knew they had to wait another ten months for another harvest and it seemed like an eternity to them.

It was during a bad snow storm that following winter that the lives of the two families were interrupted by a wagon train making camp next to the lake. There were four wagons along with several riders and a small herd of cows. Bulk and Hank rode down to them and found out that they were on their way west. The four women and three children were invited inside the cabins while the men stayed in the barns. It became a long hard winter, but thanks to the ever running spring and the abundant wildlife they all had enough food and water to keep them nourished and enough firewood to keep them warm.

When the wagon train moved on in early spring, two families stayed behind. Newlyweds Augustus and Agnes Mueller, German immigrants who came to the continent just three years ago, who were looking for a chance to own land and farm it, fell in love with the valley and the families living in it. The second family consisted of Leroy and Martha Theiss and their two sons, eight-year-old John and six-year-old Frank.

Chapter Six

September 17, 1758

T he green valley lay below him bathed in the early morning sunrays. Small dew drops were even now holding on tightly to the leaves of bushes and trees, refusing to get absorbed into the hot day which was sure to follow. Bulk had left the cabin way before dawn to go hunting and was lucky to shoot a big rabbit for supper within the first ten minutes. He enjoyed these early morning hunts, watching squirrels jumping around in the trees and listening to the birds announcing the new day with their chirping. It gave him time to ponder the day to come and what he wanted to accomplish. Hank would arrive at his cabin in an hour so they could together work on the new addition to his barn. The cow had her first calf this spring and he needed more room to get the livestock through the winter. Life was good and he thanked the Lord every day for his blessings.

He stood on the mountain ridge looking at the valley below when he heard the first faint scream echoing up the mountain. He instantly became tense. Someone was in trouble down there. At first the screams sounded faint and far away, but then they became louder and he knew that they came from Loretta. What had happened to her in such a short time? When he left her an hour ago she was still asleep in bed. He had kissed her softly on her cheek and marveled once again at the size of her swollen belly. His child was growing inside of her and he had placed his hand protectively over her stomach feeling a small little kick. He could feel the unborn baby move underneath her skin and he carefully pulled the blanket over her sleeping body, making sure both of them were warm and comfortable. Just two more months and he would become a father. Thank God Emma knew something about birthing babies.

But all that was forgotten now as the terrible screams echoed once more up the mountain. Panic engulfed him. He dropped the rabbit unceremoniously onto the ground and started running down the path, his heart hammering hard in his chest. Terrible fear tightened the muscles inside of him and his mind envisioned horrible things happening to his wife. He would reach the cabin faster if he veered from the small path which twisted and turned down to the valley. He jumped over rocks and thistle bushes, full with purple bloom this time of year. His rifle kept hitting him solidly between his large shoulder blades each time he jumped, but he didn't care. He had to get to her. Another agonizing scream tore through the valley, now louder and he could hear her scream his name. He stumbled and fell down hard on the rocky ground, ripping his deerskin leggings, drawing blood from a deep gash on his right knee. It hurt badly, but he didn't take the time to bind the wound. He had to get to her. Bulk jumped up and ran again, vines and bushes tearing at his clothing. Three little foxes scared by the sudden intrusion ran inside a fox hole. Any other time, he would have stopped and admired the little guys, but not today, not now. He barely registered their existence. He ran as fast as his long, bulky legs allowed him to and reached the valley below completely out of breath.

He ran over the dirt dam and the wooden bridge, where the spill of the lake water descended to the green pastures below, his heavy boots thundering across the wooden boards, creating their own rumbling echo. Thank God, Augustus, Leroy and Hank had all helped build the dam less than a month ago, constructing a wall out of logs, stones and rocks. It would save him at least ten minutes in getting to his cabin. Just a couple more minutes and he would reach it. Out of the corner of his eyes he saw his brother Hank running toward the cabin, coming from the north side of the valley where their cabin stood. He saw short little Emma following him at a distance, carrying Ben in her arms.

Bulk reached the cabin first and ripped the door open. To his horror he saw Loretta lying on the wooden planked floor, writhing in pain, holding her extended abdomen with both hands, her beautiful black hair matted with sweat to her contorted face. A shattered clay container lay in pieces around her feet and spilled milk glittered in contrast to the dark wooden floor.

"Bulk!" she screamed. "Bulk! The baby is coming. It's too early. Something is terribly wrong."

He rushed over and kneeled on the hard floor next to her, taking her small hand into his and squeezing it comfortingly.

"It will be all right," he told her in a soothing voice. "I saw Emma heading over here. She will know what to do."

"I'm scared," Loretta cried, before another pain ripped through her small body, making her scream with agony.

He felt so helpless. His wife was thrashing about in pain in front of him and he couldn't help her. What was taking Emma so long?

His brother Hank reached the cabin and rushed inside through the wide open door, out of breath, taking the situation in without asking questions. The brothers exchanged looks; no words were needed. Bulk picked his wife up and carried her to the bed which was located next to the log wall underneath the small window, just a couple steps away. Loretta barely weighed one hundred and ten pounds carrying a baby inside of her and he had marveled at her stamina each day she did her chores during her pregnancy. He shouldn't have let her do the wash and standing in front of the hearth for hours, cooking a meal for them. He shouldn't have let her do a lot of things, but she always insisted that she was fine and could do it. What had gone wrong?

His brother walked over to the fireplace at the opposite side of the room and placed several chopped pieces of wood out of the fire box onto the small fire still burning from when Bulk had added them before going hunting. They would need water to heat, so Hank grabbed the bucket and walked outside the cabin toward the creek, passing his wife who was out of breath reaching them.

"Loretta is in labor. She needs you," he told her, grabbing his small son from her arms, carrying him with him to the creek. The child wasn't frightened, and he was proud of the fact. He filled the bucket with ice-cold water and carried both back to the cabin where he poured the water into the black iron kettle hanging over the now blazing hot fire. Emma came walking over to him, leaving Bulk, who was tending to his wife, speaking encouraging words to her.

"It's not going to be good," she told him. "It's too early. Go get Bulk out of here."

Hank walked over to his brother, still carrying his son and put his hand on Bulk's wide shoulder.

"Let the women do their task, brother, and we will do ours. Get your pipe and let's wait outside…What will be, will be. It's in God's hands now."

He saw the worried eyes of his brother and felt deeply for him. Bulk looked at Loretta. She nodded her head in agreement with Hank. She didn't want Bulk to see what was coming. He squeezed her hand and bent over to kiss her one more time on the mouth, then slowly stood up and walked toward the fireplace where he grabbed his pipe sack, dreading the wait to come. Hank closed the door behind them and walked toward the small barn sixty yards away. Four large wooden stumps surrounded the stone fire pit on the right side of the barn where the four valley families had spent many happy hours singing, dancing and eating good food, watching the fire until it was time to retire to their cabins. Good memories now overshadowed by the torturing hours they knew were in front of them.

The Devil's Pods

They sat down and Hank put the child on the ground and both men quietly watched the boy playing innocently with sticks and stones, totally unaware of the disheartening deeds occurring inside the cabin. If he could just do something, Bulk thought, anything at all, he would gladly do it, instead of sitting here waiting helplessly for the outcome of the birth. But there was nothing he could do and the feeling of helplessness flowed fiercely through him. How could he take the pain away from Loretta, how could he make time go by faster? He tore himself up with blame. Why hadn't he helped her more? Why? Why? Why? He stood up, too tense to sit one more minute. He started pacing in front of the barn, back and forth, and back and forth again, keeping his eyes on the front door of the cabin. He didn't see the logs stacked to the side of the barn in preparation for the new stall he had been so excited about just a short hour ago, now forgotten in the drama which was unfolding.

It pained Hank's heart to see his brother this way. They had waited so long for a child and now it was taken from them because God willed it so. How could he make his brother understand that there was a time and reason for everything? Even if he couldn't understand and see it right now, there was a reason for it.

Hank stood up and walked to his brother.

"You think that you have no control right now, but the control will come later, brother. Come and sit down again." Bulk followed him back and once again sat down on the wooden stump. He stuffed his pipe and lit it, then took strength from watching his nephew play in the dirt.

Both men were thinking their own troubled thoughts. Bulk was smoking his pipe, keeping his ears tuned toward the cabin, waiting for the first cry of his baby. Hank was worried how his brother would take the bad news, only he and Emma knew was coming. He knew Bulk and Loretta had looked forward to their baby's arrival. They had waited a long time for God to bless them with a child, and now that he sent one their way something went horribly wrong. He knew God had His reasons

75

and they had to trust Him to know that He always made the right decisions. But why was it so darn hard to do? Why?

Hank had always looked up to his older brother. All his life he had admired him for his strength and determination. Hell, if it wasn't for Bulk and his adventurous spirit he wouldn't have ended up in this small valley and would still live in Boston fighting to carve out a decent living for his family. No, coming here was the best thing he ever did and it was all because of Bulk.

Hank looked worriedly at his brother. The stress in Bulk's face was clearly visible, changing his otherwise handsome features into a now dangerous looking individual. He knew Bulk would do anything to save Loretta and his baby; no matter who or what stood in his way, he would get it done. But in this situation, Bulk was totally helpless and that made it all the worse. Heck, he had watched his brother lift a tree trunk single handedly off a man who was caught by one which had fallen during a bad storm when he was a teenager. By the time Hank had reached his side to help him, the man was able to get out from under it. Later he had tried to lift the trunk by himself, but couldn't move it an inch. That's how his brother had earned the name, Bulk, for the sheer mass of him, standing six foot four, his shoulders wide as an ox, his upper arms thick as tree trunks. Even as a small child he had amazed his parents by carrying as much fire wood inside as a grown-up. He, on the other hand, was the tall skinny one. No matter how much he ate, he never put on more weight. Thank God he had inherited the same good looks as Bulk; dark wavy black hair, brown eyes and high cheekbones, and they both had inherited their fathers cleft chin, which Emma always teasingly told him made him irresistible to her.

An hour passed and the men didn't talk. Then the horrible screams started again and this time both stood up, unable to sit still any longer, unable to do anything but wait for the outcome. Hank put a comforting hand on Bulk's upper arm, reassuring him to stay put, to let Emma handle the situation. Then the screams stopped and five minutes later Emma appeared in the door motioning for them to come back to the cabin. Bulk ran toward her, searching her eyes for clues and when he reached her, he read them and his world collapsed.

"Is she alive?" was all he asked, fear in his heart.

"For now," Emma answered, totally at a loss for words, tears running down her face. She had done everything in her power, but the baby had been way too early and came out the wrong way on top of it. Loretta had endured so much pain and lost too much blood to be able to make it. Sure, she was a fighter, but how could she survive this? Emma just didn't see any hope.

Bulk pushed past her, ducked his head so as not to hit the door frame, and stormed inside the small cabin, which had been their home for such a few years. His brother tried to follow behind, but Emma held him back by the arm.

"No, it's their time together, Hank," she told him. "There is nothing you can do but to let them be together until it's over." Hank realized the truth of her words and stayed outside with her, hugging her hard in his need to comfort and be comforted. The little boy came running after the men and reaching his mother pulled at her long skirt trying to get her attention. Emma picked him up and Hank hugged them both, realizing how lucky of a man he was.

Bulk stood next to the bed and looked at his wife who lay with her eyes closed on their bed. He stood on the bear rug she was so proud of, he saw the night table she had been so excited to get, and saw the small baby cradle he had built for his child, all the things she had enjoyed and been so happy about, and now...? What would he do without her? What would his purpose in life be? He didn't want to live without her.

He noticed the small bundle of clothes in her right arm; saw the pile of bloody towels and sheets in the basket next to the door, to be washed by Emma. How much would he give for just one scream from the child? He stood still, just took it all in. It hit him hard - so hard in his guts that he froze from the misery inside of him. He took several shaky breaths to get back in control, then slowly walked toward the bed and sat down next to her. She felt the weight of the bed shifting and opened her feverish, blue eyes.

"Bulk," she whispered barely audible. "We have a son. A beautiful little boy just like you wanted."

The smallest hint of a smile appeared on her exhausted face. He smiled back at her, the hardest thing he ever had to do, realizing that she didn't know that the child was dead. He reached for the little bundle and took it out of her arm. Slowly he opened the cloth to get a look at his stillborn son. The baby was so tiny, so deathly pale, his eyes closed, his body motionless, ten tiny little fingers, ten tiny little toes, the umbilical cord hanging bloody from his little belly button. He was perfect, the most perfect little boy he had ever seen, the son he always wanted... but he was dead. Their son was dead. Bulk's eyes hurt with the weight behind them; unshed tears waiting for release, but he couldn't cry in front of his wife. He had to be strong and pretend to be happy. He had to stay in control. Was that the control Hank had told him about earlier? If it was the last thing he was going to do, he would make sure she would be happy during the last couple hours of her life, not knowing that their little boy was dead. It was so hard, so incredibly hard to do. He didn't know what to say to her. Deep sorrow engulfed him. His firstborn son lay dead in his arm and soon he would lose his wife. He saw her expectant face and forced himself to look at her with a smile.

"He is beautiful, really beautiful," was all he could utter. How would he be able to go on without her? She was only twenty-five-years-old.

"He is, isn't he?" she whispered, interrupting his tormenting thoughts. Her words tore his insides out with their innocence.

"Yes, he is," he answered again. The barely audible words of his made her eyes shine with happiness. A shear film of perspiration covered her skin from the high fever raging uncontrollably through her small body.

"Can I hold him again?" she asked and he closed the cloth and placed the dead baby back into the arch of her arm. He bent down to kiss his wife gently on her fevered lips and then watched her fall asleep. Bulk stood up and walked outside totally numb with pain. Hank and Emma were waiting outside and little Ben was chasing a squawking chicken around the yard.

"Loretta thinks the baby is alive," was all he could utter before tears ran down his face. "What should I do? I can't tell her the truth. I just can't."

Hank put his arms around his brother and held him tight, his own eyes full of unshed tears. He had to be strong for Bulk and not lose it. This was one time where his brother could lean on him and not the other way around.

"Pray, and let her have her time with the baby, before she goes. She needn't know. Let her die happy," was all he answered. Bulk slowly got a hold of his emotions, then nodded his head in agreement, wiped his face and walked back inside to sit with his dying wife. Emma came back inside and placed a container with cold water and a cloth on the night stand.

"Keep her cool and comfortable with the wet cloth," she told Bulk. "It won't be much longer. Shoot the rifle when you need us." She picked up the basket with the dirty linen and left the cabin, closing the door quietly behind her.

Loretta slept a lot and when she woke it was always with a smile, still holding the dead baby. Bulk wiped her face and forehead and the length of her arms with cool water. Time passed and the morning turned into afternoon and Emma and Hank returned to bring him food, but Bulk refused to eat. Just the thought of food nauseated him. He couldn't possibly eat with his wife dying a few feet away from him. Emma changed the sheets and made Loretta comfortable. She woke up shortly and whispered unheard words to her then fell back into a deep sleep.

After two hours they went home, expecting death to arrive during the night, while Bulk sat next to her and waited. Darkness invaded the small cabin and he stood up to add more firewood to the hearth. He sat for hours watching her sleep, watching her chest rise and fall with each breath she took, wondering if it was going to be her last. He nodded off sometime around midnight just to wake up startled half an hour later to keep an eye on her once more.

Her face looked peaceful even if it was covered with perspiration. It was relaxed and once in a while a soft smile formed, as if she was having a beautiful dream. If it wasn't for the high fever he could almost imagine that she was just resting from a difficult birth. He wiped her forehead again and rinsed the cloth in the cool water then folded it and placed it around her neck to keep her cool. She didn't wake up for hours holding the dead baby in her arms the whole time, holding it tight. The moon shone through the small window, making its path slowly across the dark sky. It was a peaceful picture for him to look at; a picture of love and innocence; a mother sleeping with her newborn baby in her arm. The reality was too harsh for him to think about right then. He just sat there and waited and thought about the past.

He envisioned Loretta and how she had looked when they rode through the valley last summer; she on Betsy and he on the big draft horse. They had such a great time. Her laughter had always been so infectious and he saw her how she looked the day she told him that they were going to have a baby. She was filled with happiness that day and every day since then, and now this happened.

He stood up frustrated. There was nothing he could do now but wait and be there with her when she died. He paced the small cabin several times, added more wood to the fire and then sat down next to her to hold her warm hand as she slept. He cooled and wiped her hot face with the wet cloth when she became restless and was burning up with fever and talked to her in soothing words. He must have fallen asleep in the pre-dawn hours. When he woke up to the lightened room he was surprised to see Loretta looking at him, her eyes wide and clear. The fever had left her. Hope surged through him, but her words brought him instantly back to reality.

"We need to feed him and change his cloth," she said and handed the dead baby carefully into his waiting hands. "And we need to give him a name, Bulk."

"We will give him a fine name, Loretta," he told her as he took the dead baby from her. She smiled at him and her eyes were full of happiness, then she fell back asleep. It's the silence before the storm, Bulk thought. She is delirious.

He placed the dead baby into the crib then sat down at the table, lowered his face into his hands and started to sob uncontrollably. His shoulders shook with his grief and it was some time later that he got a hold on his emotions. Emma returned half an hour later, surprised that Loretta had survived the night. She fixed him coffee and something to eat which Bulk refused. They were sitting at the rough table talking in low voices when they heard murmuring from the bed. They walked over to the bed and watched Loretta wake up. She slowly opened her eyes, looked at both of them and said in a much stronger voice; "I'm so hungry and thirsty. Can you make me something to eat, Emma?"

Bulk and Emma looked at each other with utter amazement, hope returning to them with the simple request from the deathbed.

"Where's the baby?" Loretta asked next with concern in her voice.

"The baby is resting comfortably in the crib," Emma answered. She stood up and walked to the fireplace where the breakfast oats she had fixed earlier were simmering over the fire. She ladled some up into a bowel and carried it to the bed where Bulk was holding his wife's hand, telling her how much he loved her. He took the bowl from Emma and started to feed her. And Loretta ate, ate beyond their expectations and even drank half a cup of water. Bulk saw determination in his wife's

81

eyes and he began to believe that she would survive, survive for the son she couldn't leave behind, the son she didn't know was dead.

"We will call him Charlie, after my father," she said.

"That's what we will call him. It's a good name," he answered. A happy smile crossed her face and then she rested again.

Bulk turned around to Emma. "What will I say when she wakes again?"

"We will have to tell her the truth," she answered, "but for now we need to bury the baby. We need to do it right. Your brother and Augustus are digging the grave right now. We'll do it at noon. Bring the baby at noon to the high spot where the three large oaks grow, halfway between our cabins. Hank thought it would make a good graveyard for the valley; where all of us will come to rest one day. It's so beautiful there and the big oaks will shade his little grave. Hank hoped that the spot will meet your approval."

"It's a good spot for a graveyard," Bulk answered her. Emma helped Bulk to dress his son in his christening gown and wrapped his small little body in the hand-crochet blanket Loretta had finished only a week ago. She left the cabin when they finished and walked home, passing the spot they had selected for the grave on her way. Hank and Augustus had just finished digging the grave; the hole made for two, now too big.

"Loretta is going to live. It's a miracle." Hank looked up surprised at her words and then grinned from ear to ear.

"Praise the Lord. Loretta is going to live. Bulk isn't going to lose her. Hallelujah!"

"Bulk will bring the baby at noon. Let's go home and prepare for the service," she told the men. Hank shook Augustus' hand and thanked him, then grabbed his gritty son, who was playing contently on the dirt pile, and together they walked home. A father carrying his son, holding his wife's hand, grieving for his brother's loss, at the same time being happy that his brother's wife was going to survive. He was a man counting his own blessings.

Two hours later all the valley people stood by the grave. Augustus, his wife Agnes, Leroy, Mary and their two sons, and so were Hank, Emma and little Ben, resting on his mother's hips, everybody dressed in their Sunday best.

Bulk walked up the trail carrying his son in his arms. When he reached the other mourners he placed his son into the small wooden box his brother had built. Hank closed the lid over the little body and hammered the nails into the boards. He stood up and spoke words he had memorized from the Bible;

"None of us lives to himself, and none of us dies to himself. If we live, we live to the Lord, and if we die, we die to the Lord; so then, whether we live or whether we die, we are the Lord's. For to this end Christ died and lived again, that he might be Lord both of the dead and of the living."

Romans 14:7-9

A tear ran down his cheek as he stopped speaking. Hank got onto his knees and lowered the little wooden box carefully into the large hole. What should have been a day of rejoicing and celebrating was a day of sorrow and weeping. Bulk grabbed the shovel leaning against the large oak tree and started scooping dirt onto the casket; the hollow sounds of the dirt falling onto the wooden box reverberated the eternal suffering of mankind and imprinted itself into his mind, painful and forever, never to be forgotten. His brother saw the hurt on his face and took the shovel away from him.

"Be with Loretta," he told him and started to shovel the dirt over the small casket. Bulk gave him an appreciating nod. Augustus and his wife came up to him and shook his hand and offered their condolences and so did Leroy and his family. He appreciated them all, but was numb to their consoling words, the only thing on his mind now how he was going to tell Loretta that their son was dead.

He walked back to the cabin, the task in front of him weighing heavy on his shoulders. He didn't want to do it, but he knew there was no way around it. He couldn't avoid it any longer. She needed to hear the truth. Loretta was awake when he entered the cabin, looking almost like her former self. She had brushed her beautiful long hair which was now softly framing her even now pale face, coming to rest on the front of her white cotton night shirt. She looked like an angel sitting there, resting her back against the headboard. Her blue eyes searched his eyes expectantly and when they met she read all his sorrow and pain in them.

"The baby is dead, isn't he?" she whispered, knowing that it was so.

"Yes, he is dead," he answered, not able to say it any other way to ease her pain.

"I was so afraid to think it. I was hoping that Emma had taken him to her house to take care of him so that I could rest, but somehow I knew deep inside of me that I had lost him." Her body slumped and her face turned paler than it already was.

"Loretta, we still have each other. Look at me," Bulk told her with a strong pleading voice, but she already turned her back toward him and lay back down. He could hear her softly crying and then she started to wail. All the anguish she felt came out in her wailing. The loss of her child was too much for her to handle, and it was too hard for him to listen to, the agonizing sounds slowly ripping his heart out of his body. He couldn't take it, couldn't stand her sorrow one more minute and couldn't stand the fact that he couldn't do a damn thing about it. He turned around and walked outside to look for something, anything to take his pain out on. He saw the woodpile and stumbled toward it a broken man. He grabbed the ax and split the logs until he couldn't split any more then he crumbled to his knees and wept.

Two days later Loretta was still in bed refusing to eat. She looked like a forlorn child who had lost her way in the wilderness. She looked like she'd given up on life and was just waiting for death to take her home. Her eyes were without life, her willpower gone, and nothing Bulk told her penetrated her grief-stricken mind.

"I want to die too," she told him over and over again when he tried to encourage her to eat and get better.

"But you would leave me behind with hurt that would never heal," he answered her, at his wits end of what to say to make her realize he still needed her.

"You're strong, Bulk. I'm not," was all she replied.

"But you're strong too. Don't you remember all the hardships you endured during the long trek out here? Don't you remember how hard we worked together to get everything ready for our first winter in this valley? Don't you remember the day you shot the bear and scared me out of my wits? Please, Loretta, don't give up on me. I need you so badly."

But Loretta just turned away from him; nothing was important to her any more. Another day passed and she was getting visibly weaker. Hank and Emma were in the cabin around dusk, unable to rouse life back into her. They even let little Ben climb on her bed, thinking a little guy like him could snap her out of her depression, but all she did was give him a smile, turned away and started crying softly.

"What about the peas?" Hank whispered, as they sat around the table, all out of ideas. "They always gave me a feeling of wellbeing. Why can't we give them to her? What can they hurt?" All three looked at each other, hope entering their eyes. Emma nodded her head.

"She won't last much longer without taking food," Emma commented and looked at Bulk expectantly to make a decision.

"But she always refused them before," Bulk answered.

"I refused them also, but this is different. I could grind them into a powder and fix a tea for her. She will drink the tea. She doesn't have to know that we added the powder of the peas."

"How many do you have left, Hank?"

"Only two pods. But they'll have to do."

"I have one left. All right then. Go home and get the pods. It's a chance I'm willing to take. I will gladly take the blame if she should find out later what I did. I would love for her to yell at me. Oh, God, how I would love for her to get mad at me. I want her back so badly. I'm willing to try anything."

One hour later Bulk helped Loretta sip the lukewarm tea which contained two ground-up peas. Loretta sipped the tea and told Bulk with a smile that the tea tasted delicious. Ten minutes later she fell asleep. Hank and Emma took their son home to put him to bed, knowing the effects of the peas too well. When they opened the front door to leave, a heavy wind whipped around their clothes, flattening Emma's long skirt around her slim legs. Dark ominous clouds were coming over the mountains from the north.

"Bulk, get the cow and calf inside, a storm is coming," Hank yelled at his brother, then picked up his son and grabbed his wife's hand, and was off hurrying down the dirt path, trying to reach their cabin before the clouds would burst.

Twenty minutes later Bulk came back inside the cabin soaked to the bone. The cow and her calf were safe in the stall now, but he had left the horses in the pasture. They could take care of themselves. It wasn't the first bad storm to hit this valley.

It was dark outside now and the storm pushed through, the loud thunder rumbling off the valley's mountains, making it seem worse than it was. The lightning flashes entered the windows of the small cabin, illuminating the inside with incredible clarity and detail. How strong nature can be, Bulk thought. Any other time he would have enjoyed a storm like this, making him feel safe inside his small cabin, making him feel like a good provider to his wife, who certainly would have felt the same, but not tonight. Tonight the outside storm resembled the turmoil he was feeling inside his body. He wanted Loretta to stay on this earth with him and not go to the Lord's paradise. He was selfish, unbending in his request. He wanted to keep Loretta.

The thunderstorm went on for hours but Bulk never relinquished his demands. He paced the floor of the small cabin to the rumbling of the thunder outside. The soft glowing embers in the fireplace illuminated only the front part of the room, leaving the bed in shadows, barely outlining his wife's sleeping form. He looked at her never the less and each time the lightning flashes illuminated the room, he could see her small body lying in the bed, clear as day. The lightning brought such brightness to the cabin that he felt like being teased; teased by its clarity, teased by its simplicity. She looked so small in those seconds, so vulnerable. She wasn't aware of the weather, wasn't aware of his anguish and just drifted away to a land unknown. She was still sleeping peacefully and hadn't moved a muscle since he left her to take care of the animals, but now, as he sat down in the chair by the bed she slowly moved her arms and reached for something only she could see. Was it a reaction from the peas, Bulk wondered?

She looked comfortable with the blanket covering her body and nothing else happened. He added a couple more logs to the fire and sat back down, watching her expectantly. The storm continued its path and half an hour later he could only hear the occasional thunder rumbling in the far distance and the crackling of the wood in the hearth. The fire was blazing and it started to get warm inside the cabin. Loretta kicked the sheets off in her sleep. She looked so beautiful and innocent when she was sleeping. He was wondering if he should cover her back up when she started to move and moan pleasant sounds; her hips started to move in an erotic manner and the yellowish-orange glow from the fire threw the dancing shadows of her arms, legs and hips against the log walls. She reached for things only her mind let her see with a smile on her beautiful lips. Any other time he would have found it erotic to see his wife move in this fashion, but not this night. This night was different. This night would decide their future. He watched fascinated how her body reacted to the peas and prayed to God to give Loretta back to him.

After a while Bulk started to get worried. Maybe he should have given her only one pea instead of two. He remembered how totally out of it he was when he had taken three peas the first time he chewed them, after all, he was a two hundred and thirty pound man and she weighed less than a hundred pounds right now in her famished condition. But then again, the peas were not as strong anymore since it was nearing the end of September. Praying that he had done the right thing he sat with her as she continued her feverish behavior for another four hours until she was completely worn out and spent and stopped her erratic movements.

Loretta woke up in the early morning hours and asked him for food. She didn't mention the baby, just smiled at him. He fixed her the same tea two more times in the following days, hoping that it was enough, since the peas were now all gone. Her appetite returned with an astonishing speed. On the third day Loretta felt strong and well enough to get out of bed and returned to doing her daily chores.

Emma was so excited she baked Loretta her favorite pie. A week later Loretta and Bulk walked up the hill to the cemetery to visit the small grave of their son. It was the first time that she visited the place of her son's eternal rest. Bulk was worried that she would fall back into a depression, but she didn't. They reached the grave and Bulk held her hand, giving her strength and comfort with his presence. They stood there not talking, just looking at the small little dirt mound and the wooden cross, feeling the heat of their hands, knowing they still had each other. Bulk looked at her and saw one single tear running down her cheek.

"You did a fine job making the cross," she told Bulk, as she caressed the carved letters inside the wooden cross.

In Memory of
Charlie Horswell
September 17, 1758

"You know we haven't really talked about what happened," she said, looking at him, knowing that sooner or later it had to be said. "You saved my life by giving me those peas." He looked at her surprised that she knew what he had done.

"You know then?" he answered.

"How could I not? I wanted to die, but when you gave me the tea it put the will to live back inside of me. The sorrow which held my heart and mind captive disappeared after I drank the first cup and suddenly I wanted to live. I remembered the taste of the peas from your lips and the tea you gave me had the same taste, but I drank the second and third cup fully aware that the powder of the peas were mixed in it. I never felt like that before. A feeling of incredible well-being flooded through me, just like you described. It was like peace came over me and I was able to let go of our son. I still can't explain it, not even to myself. I'm happy right now, even though we lost him. I know he's in a better place. Thank you Bulk, for not giving up on me." She turned toward him and looked into his brown eyes.

"One day we will have another son or daughter," he told her softly and kissed her tenderly on the mouth.

"I know we will. You were right. We are both strong...strong enough to survive the loss we have suffered. But because I got well and received a second chance at life, I want to celebrate the peas. You were right all along; there must be healing powers inside of them. What would you say if we celebrate the next harvest of the peas with a festival? Everybody in the valley could participate and we declare the day a holiday from work and have a picnic by the lake. In matter of fact, we should have a big celebration each year," Loretta told him excitedly.

"If that's what you want, that's what we're going to do. We will make it a valley tradition," Bulk answered her, so thankful that she had survived the terrible ordeal. When they came back to the cabin, he wrote her suggestion down in the journal. The valley was going to celebrate the plant's mystical healing powers by having an annual festival every second Saturday in the month of August and he named it the Festival of the Pods. They would start the day off by having an outside church service to rejoice and pray for the miracle plant God had bestowed on them.

Bulk couldn't help but praise the day he discovered the plant. Without the plant's healing powers Loretta surely would have died. God works in mysterious ways, he thought, and from that day on he became even more protective of the plant. It was clear to him that he had a special connection to it, but was still amazed that he was the one God had chosen to be the link between the valley people and this miracle plant.

He had this extra ordinary aptitude to sense what the plant wanted from him, the knowledge that the plant didn't want to reproduce, that it was one of a kind, and most importantly, that it never wanted to leave the valley and only be used by its' residents. Bulk read the Bible daily and was aware that God had chosen many men before him to become His tool of spreading the message of Christianity. To become His instrument to do good was the highest honor bestowed on him. To Bulk, it also answered the question about the skeleton he had discovered inside the cave. The poor soul was probably a man just like him, chosen to protect the plant. That's why he found a hatchet next to his body.

He thought about the plant at least once or twice a day, fleetingly, with fondness, looking forward to the next harvest. As God's instrument, he sat down and wrote the rules in his ledger. A set of rules he hoped would be handed down from one generation of valley people to the next through the coming centuries.

Had Bulk known at this time how wrong he was, that it was Satan getting inside his thoughts and not God, he would have turned away in horror. But he was clueless; the thought of evil never once entering his mind.

Annegret Werner Shaw

Chapter Seven

August 1766

More than a decade had passed since Bulk discovered the plant and its pods. The valley had grown to eight families; the newest members a family from New Orleans who had settled in the valley three years ago; Edward Thompson, his wife Mary and their two little daughters who were now six and eight years old.

After all these years, Bulk still considered finding this valley one of the luckiest days of his life. The valley people flourished, the soil was perfect for their crops and produced large quantities, the animals thrived from the rich grass, and the surrounding wooded mountains were full of game and fowl and the valley's lake full of fish. Trading furs from beavers, deer, and bears with the next settlement was still one of the brother's favorite pastimes.

Bulk's little cabin had increased in size to three rooms and Loretta and he had finally been blessed with a little baby boy five years ago. They called him Ludwig and he was the apple of their eyes. He had become Bulk's shadow, not wanting to leave his father's side and it was all right with him. Hank and Emma had increased their family by three additional children and the total of children in the valley outnumbered the adults by twenty-one children to sixteen adults. On summer days the children could be heard playing together and having fun by the lake, their laughter and screaming echoing up the hills to the cabins and barns where the women hung up the laundry or cooked and the men worked in the barns or in the fields. During the winter, the lake would freeze over and the children would glide across the thick ice and slide down the small hill next to the lake on the sleighs their father's had built them.

The dream Bulk and Hank had of raising cows became a reality as well. The bull was producing several new calves a year.

The location of the plant was only known to Bulk and Hank and each August they rode the dangerous path up to Pitch Fork Mountain and climbed down the cliff to harvest the pods. It seemed that the plant thrived in the same way as the valley and its people did and grew larger and more beautiful each year. The amount of pods also increased in number so that there were always enough peas for anybody who wanted to participate in the annual Festival of the Pods.

It had become the most anticipated day in the valley and each year the residents looked forward to giving themselves a pass to celebrate and be merry and most of all, to be totally carefree with no obligations for the day. Each year the festival started off with church service where the valley people gave thanks to another successful harvest of the pods.

Several years ago Bulk and Hank had finally given the skeleton inside the cave a respectable burial, carrying small rocks in their backpacks down to the cave and covering the bones up, until the rocks formed a nice looking mount. The unknown stranger finally had a decent grave. They laid his broken hatchet on top of the stones and painted a cross on the cave wall above the grave with dark charcoal from a fire and wrote the letters R.I.P on it.

Another festival was just around the corner and it was time for the brothers to plan a trip up the mountain. The women folk in the valley were already preparing all kinds of dishes for the picnic and the young children looked forward to the jolly time they would have by the lake.

But in contrast to all the other trips the brothers had made up the mountain, it was the first time that Bulk felt deep worries inside of him. He had the sense that something was wrong, very wrong, that the plant's well-being was at risk. And the weird thing was that this fear he felt came with a mental image; the mental image of his friend's face. Edward Thompson's face.

He couldn't explain it. He always thought of Edward as a kind man, a God-fearing man and a man of his word. He was easy to get along with, a hard worker and a good family man, and always willing to help and pitch in. Edward and his family had participated two years now in the festival and twice he and his wife had received pods. Sure, he had noticed Edward's interest in the peas after he used them for the first time, but it was nothing out of the ordinary. Most valley residents had asked him, one time or another about the plant; where did it grow, could they get more pods, or, could they go with him to see it in person? Questions like that were normal for him. Usually, when he explained the situation, the person would be satisfied with his answers, but not Edward. His fascination with the plant was different. He constantly talked to Bulk about it and when he didn't get anywhere with him he tried to pester Hank. Edward also wanted more pods and wasn't satisfied with his ration. He asked the brothers over and over again to show him were the plant grew and begged them to let him go along on the harvesting trip, but Bulk always told him no.

The sense of uncertainty and fear persisted inside of Bulk; the bad feeling moving to his gut, making him physically sick. He felt pressure inside his chest and felt helpless, not knowing what to do about it. The worst part was the increasing headaches he suffered the closer the day of the harvest approached. The mental picture of Edward was stuck inside his head and was accompanied by an incredible throbbing in his temples. What was he supposed to do? He prayed for an answer, but didn't receive one.

Bulk planned the trip for a late afternoon. He was extremely nervous when they rode out; the feeling of being watched came over him. Hank noticed his uneasiness and wondered what was wrong with him. Bulk was usually so certain and confident, but today he was nervous and constantly looked over his shoulder. Hank finally asked him what was wrong and Bulk told him that he had a bad feeling that Edward was watching them; that he was trying to find out where the plant grew. Hank knew that Bulk had a special connection with the plant and didn't question him any further. He looked around, but didn't see anything out of the ordinary. His brother was merely more concerned than usual, that was all.

They rode the treacherous path up to the mountain plateau. Bulk's headache increased and he was in a foul mood. He had looked forward to this trip for so long and enjoyed it every year and this year wasn't supposed to be any different. Darn these horrible headaches and darn this uneasy feeling inside of him, Bulk thought.

But he didn't feel better. The uneasy feeling clung to him like sweat on a humid day. A voice inside of him warned him to be careful, but no matter how often he looked over his shoulder to see if they were being followed, he never saw anybody. At one point Bulk told Hank to wait behind a large boulder to see if someone was following, but it proved unsuccessful. After fifteen minutes of quietly waiting and watching the path below, he called himself paranoid and they rode on, his horse following Hank's horse up the trail. Damn these premonitions. He never suffered from them before.

The two brothers reached the plateau and tied their horses to the big pine tree, as they did every year, and knotted the rope around the boulder. The weather was extremely nice and they could see for miles. Even after all these years it still took Bulk's breath away to see the beautiful valley with its blue lake sparkling up at them. He tore himself away from the gorgeous view and lowered himself down the rope, followed by Hank. His headache had finally receded some and he felt better. They entered the opening and followed the tunnel to the cave. It still amazed Bulk, as it did every year, how much he was still drawn to the plant, like it was his first time to put his eyes on it. Watching the plant's flowers open up was irresistible to him and his brother and they always planned it so that they arrived shortly before sundown. It had become an unspoken, annual ritual for them.

Together they sat in front of the plant and waited, and after a short while the blossoms opened their shiny black petals and the intoxicating fragrance, they remembered so well, drifted out and filled the cave. The brothers inhaled the heady scent, getting lightheaded from its potency. Their imagination began to play tricks on them and they heard beautiful music coming from the flowers. Fine trilling sounds filled the cave. They sat in silence mesmerized by the plant's beauty and the lure of the melody. Sensual visions filled their minds and the feeling of supreme happiness engulfed them.

Suddenly Bulk was startled out of his visions of ecstasy and bliss by an unfamiliar loud noise behind him. He sensed a presence and turned around. Utterly shocked he saw Edward standing in the opening of the tunnel, staring at the plant, smiling from ear to ear.

"I told you I would find out where the plant had its hiding place," he told them with satisfaction. Bulk and Hank jumped up aghast to see him standing there. Edward walked closer toward the plant, fascinated just like they had been. He stopped three feet away from it to admire the flowers closer up. Bulk watched him totally taken off guard by his sudden appearance in the cave.

"It's as beautiful as you described it, Bulk," Edward turned around and told him, then stepped closer and tried to reach down to touch one of the flowers. To Bulk's amazement the branches and flowers receded from his touch. Did the plant do that or was it the wind, he thought, but he couldn't feel any breeze inside the cave on this wind-still evening. He couldn't hear the trilling melody any longer and the

97

fragrance had disappeared. It was like the magical moment from just a minute earlier had vanished…never existed, except in his mind.

"You shouldn't have followed us, Edward. I told you before that it's the valley's rule. Only the two harvesters can know of this place," Bulk told him, trying to stay calm. What was he supposed to do now? Change the rules? He sensed anxiousness inside of him and something else. He suddenly had a strong feeling that something horrible was going to happen, but he had no inkling what. Hank on the other hand didn't have any such premonition.

"You should go, Edward, before something happens to you," Bulk told him in a stern voice following his intuition. "Go now before it is too late and don't tell anyone of this place."

Edward started laughing, his mirth echoing back from the cave's walls; repeating the loud sounds over and over until it sounded like sinister cackling, raising the hair on Bulk's neck.

"You're joking, right? The valley's rules? You mean your rules; don't you mean that, Bulk? You made up these ridiculous rules to keep the pods to yourself and your family. I didn't come all this way just to turn around, my friend. Don't you see what kind of treasure this plant is? Can you imagine how much money we could make if we grow this plant in large quantities and sell the pods? The pods are stronger than alcohol, stronger than tobacco or any medication I've ever taken. We can sell them in the surrounding settlements and become rich. Can't you see that, Bulk? What about you, Hank? Think about all the money, all the nice stuff you could buy for your wife and children."

"I think you better listen to Bulk and leave," Hank answered, showing Edward that he was on his brother's side and would stand by him.

"I'm going to leave after I get what I came for," Edward told them, pulled a small sack out of his jacket pocket and kneeled down by the plant, his hands reaching for the pods. It was like the plant came alive, or was it the wind again? The thorns scratching Edward's hands and arms as he reached underneath the branches, the vines entangling his limbs. He didn't let the vines get in his way and ripped several of them off his arms before he was able to collect the pods. Satisfied he stood up and grinned at the two brothers.

"I knew you two wouldn't get in my way. You're good God-fearing people. I won't forget you two when the pods become famous. I promise you both." He turned around and walked away, leaving Hank and Bulk staring after him, realizing that he was right. Neither Bulk nor Hank would have raised a hand against him.

They watched him walk away toward the opening of the tunnel, stunned and defeated. Abruptly Edward stopped in mid-step and turned around to face them once more.

"I'm getting a bad headache from the scent of the flowers," he said and rubbed his temple with his free hand. His face, which two seconds ago had looked triumphant, now turned ashen and uncomprehending. The hand which held the full sack of pods tightly, suddenly opened up and the sack fell to the ground spilling the pods. The brothers looked at each other, not understanding what was happening in front of them. It had become deathly still in the cave. The brothers looked at Edward's face and watched horrified how it transformed itself; his pupils turned large and then a blood-red glimmer appeared in them; not one of his facial muscles moved or twitched, not a sound escaped his lips. It was like he was frozen in place all of a sudden. All they focused on was his horrible hollow stare and his eyes glimmering back at them. What could cause such a transformation in a man, Bulk thought? Helpless they watched as Edward slowly turned away from them, his movements now awkward and sluggish.

"Edward, stop!" Bulk yelled at him, suddenly his terror turning into action; his need to help Edward greater than the worry about the plant. He rushed after him, a terrible fear gripping his heart. All he knew was that he had to stop him, but Edward's awkward movements now sped up and he ran through the tunnel toward the cave's opening, Bulk and Hank right on his heels hoping to stop and talk to him before he climbed back up. And then...they watched...stunned and appalled...how Edward didn't stop at the edge of the cliff, but jumped to the depth below, his body disappearing out of sight. They didn't hear him scream, not a single sound escaped Edward's mouth. And in the end, all they heard was a single loud thump when his body hit the rocky ground below, broken beyond repair.

Bulk and Hank looked at each other totally horror-struck with what they had just witnessed. What possessed Edward to do such a thing? They hadn't been a threat to him. There was no need. Why did he do it? He had killed himself in front of their eyes. They were quiet for a while, just stood there at the cave's entrance at a loss of what to do next.

"There was nothing we could have done to stop him," Bulk finally said into the silence, hoping the simple statement would bring some normality back to their lives, but it didn't. "Let's go, it's getting dark." He turned around and went back to the spot where Edward had dropped the pods and collected them, placing them in his pouch, then followed his brother up the cliff. They rode the path down in silence, Hank pulling Edward's horse behind him. Halfway down the mountain, Bulk realized that the tightness in his chest had vanished, that his headache had totally disappeared and his premonitions and bad feelings about the safety of the plant were gone and then he remembered the last sentence Edward had spoken: I'm getting a bad headache from the scent of the flowers.

It was the exact moment that Bulk realized that both their headaches had come from the flower and that single thought made him halt the mare, physically and mentally weak, totally nauseated. He slipped off his horse and dragged himself to the edge of the path where the ground disappeared deep below him into a gorge. His stomach twisted and knotted itself as he bent over into the bushes and threw up until he couldn't throw up any longer. He dry heaved until he was spent; the bile in his throat tasting horrible, but he didn't care.

Nothing mattered to him. Images flooded through his mind; the way the plant looked the first time he saw it, the feeling the peas created inside his body and mind, Loretta drinking the tea and getting better, the plant's intoxicating smell, the plant inside his head, and the plant... the plant... the plant... the pictures didn't stop and they were all connected to the plant and he finally understood. The plant was evil, pure evil. It wasn't God's instrument, but the devil's, ensnaring mankind into his web of addiction and greed, tempting them until they fell into his trap. How could he have been this wrong? A Bible scripture entered Bulk's mind as he collapsed exhausted onto the dirt path. He had read it many times and knew it by heart. It was Matthew 7:15-23

"Beware of false teachers who come disguised as harmless sheep, but are wolves and will tear you apart. You can detect them by the way they act, just as you can identify a tree by its fruit."

A tree by its fruit, he thought, and he knew with a certainty that the plant was put in the cave by Satan himself, to lure people into his trap, as sure as Adam and Eve ate the forbidden fruit at the beginning of creation. And it was his fault. He had tasted the peas first and brought the fruit to the valley. Bulk knew with a certainty that he had become Satan's pawn and the realization was killing him.

"Be sober, be vigilant; because your adversary the devil, as a roaring lion, walks about, seeking whom he may devour..."

The Bible verse, Peter 5:8, went through his head over and over again and Bulk realized that the devil had walked about and chosen him and he was being devoured slowly and painfully until he took his last breath.

Hank stopped behind Bulk wondering why he was getting off his horse. It was a clear night with a full moon overhead, but it was still too dangerous to get off the horse on this narrow path. When he heard his brother's retching he understood and waited in silence, holding the reins of Edward's horse, until Bulk regained his strength.

Hank himself had a hard time dealing with what happened to Edward. Nothing of what occurred made sense to him. They hadn't been a threat to him…why did he jump? Why did he look so… so evil… so satanic? Why did his eyes glow red? He didn't have the answers and it wasn't a good time to ask Bulk.

After a while they continued the trip down the path to the valley. Edward's cabin came into view from a distance. His wife came out of the barn carrying an oil lamp and a basket, followed by her two young daughters laughing at something the mother had said. The brothers stopped and looked at the idyllic picture knowing it would be shattered within minutes. The girls were chasing each other now, while the mother stood back and watched them. It would be a long time before they would be happy again.

"Let them have five more minutes of happiness," Bulk told his brother as they sat and watched Edward's family being unaware of his demise. "Five more minutes," he repeated to himself as he watched them in the moonlight.

If I could just turn back time, Bulk thought. If I had only listened to Loretta all those years ago and thrown away the pods this would never have happened. If I had never tasted the peas… if I never… never… but I did… I did… and I did fall prey to the temptations, just like Adam had when he tasted the forbidden fruit in the Garden of Eden. Bulk's thoughts were tormenting him to the core of his being.

"Let's go," he told Hank, unable to sit still another second and kicked his horse unnecessarily hard in the flanks. It was as much his fault that Edward was dead as it was Satan's. If he hadn't been so weak, so damn weak. Sure, Satan had lured and tempted him with the plant

102

from the beginning, but he had given in to the temptations of desire and cravings and had become Satan's tool. Without him it would still grow unnoticed in the cave. And in his mind Bulk saw it clearly now, how his pipe had slipped down the boulder…in slow motion…all those years ago, as he was sitting on the rocks. Satan had lured him to his hiding spot and had groomed him to do his bidding, getting more and more people under his influence. He now knew that Satan had planned it all; it had been inevitable.

Mary saw them coming and waved, but then stopped when she noticed Edward's horse being led by Hank. She just stood there and waited for them to get closer, her face already sad with the news she knew would come. The girls stopped next to their mother, but she told them to go in the house and fetch her shawl, not wanting them to hear the details. Bulk and Hank climbed off the horses and respectfully took off their hats.

"Is… Edward… dead then?" she asked Bulk, the question more a statement than a question, like her mind had already accepted the worst.

Bulk nodded his head. "Yes, Mary, he is dead." He saw the last glimmer of hope die in her eyes with his answer.

"How did it happen?"

He told Mary the truth, except for the end, where he told her that Edward tripped and fell down the cliff, not jumped. That was a lie he gladly told. There was no reason for her to know that her husband jumped to his death. That fact would just cause her unnecessary pain and would leave her to constantly wonder why her husband committed suicide. And what damage would it do to his two girls, knowing that their father left them behind in this wilderness? He couldn't blame Mary if she decided to move back to the city. It would be hard for her to survive out here without a husband. He knew that all the men in this valley would help her with the hard chores like chopping firewood, shooting game, and also with the farming of the fields. Everybody liked

Mary. She was one of them, but who would blame her if she decided to leave.

"We're going to retrieve his body tomorrow. It was too dark to find him tonight," Bulk told her. He paused, then added, "I'm really sorry, Mary. Edward was a good, fine man and a good friend to everybody in the valley."

Hank guided the mare away, unsaddled her and put her in the corral. Bulk wished it could have been him putting the mare up, instead of telling Edward's widow that he tripped and fell down the canyon.

"I'll send Loretta to your cabin to stay with you and the girls tonight. You know we will help you, no matter what you need or decide to do. We're really sorry. There was nothing we could do." What else could he tell the woman in front of him who now looked pale and unsteady on her feet? No words could erase her pain or could make her feel better. Her whole world had just collapsed.

The girls came running toward their mother laughing and shouting a friendly hello to the two men, then handed Mary her shawl. When they saw their mother all quiet and deathly pale, they asked her what was wrong. Mary put her arms around each girl's shoulder to steady her, then turned away from the men and walked with her two daughters to the cabin, where they disappeared inside. Bulk wondered how much Edward had told his wife about following them up the mountain.

The brothers climbed back on their horses and left, feeling utterly miserable, but before they parted ways Hank asked Bulk the question which had been on his mind ever since he saw Edward jump to his death. Bulk knew it was coming, had dreaded this question and had hoped that his remark had gone unnoticed, but he also knew that he had to tell Hank the truth; the awful truth of what he now knew was true. He had avoided acknowledging it out loud, a response so gruesome and unbelievable that it blew his reasoning.

"Bulk, how did you know that something awful was going to happen to Edward?"

"I just knew. The knowledge was deep inside of me. I felt the plant's anger at what was happening. I knew it wouldn't let him take the pods out of the valley...I really hoped that I was wrong, that it didn't make any sense to feel such a thing, but I wasn't. The plant killed Edward as sure as I'm your brother and it will kill anyone else who tries to take it out of the valley. It put its thoughts inside of me. I've become the plant's conspirator. It needs me to protect it; that's why it sends me the horrible premonitions and feelings of upcoming doom. It made me its henchman and there is nothing I can do about it. The plant is Satan himself."

"What do you mean when you say that the plant is Satan himself? You can't be serious. How could that be? You sure it's not just the compulsion to get to the peas which made Edward act crazy like that, to the point of committing suicide. You saw him; he acted totally out of character."

"Then how do you explain his eyes? Did you see them? His eyes were glowing for heaven's sake. He was possessed by the devil!" Bulk shouted at him.

"If that's true, what are we going to do about it?" Hank asked.

"No, no, Hank. Don't you ever say or even think about doing anything to the plant. The plant will kill you as sure as it will kill me if I try to interfere with its plan. I'm sure of it. Leave it be and never share this knowledge with anyone, not Emma, not Augustus or anyone else in this valley. It's too powerful. I will deal with it the best I can. Promise me you won't harbor any bad thoughts about the plant or take any action. Promise me, Hank!" Bulk shouted. "Promise me, damn it!"

"All right, I promise," Hank finally replied.

"Good then, there is nothing we can do. Remember that."

The truth hung between them as they rode on. Hank didn't argue with him and accepted Bulk's answer, realizing his brother was right.

He had seen the plant's power with his own eyes. It was the devil at work.

Two days later, a second grave was dug in the small graveyard and Edward Thompson was laid to rest next to the little boy Bulk and Loretta had lost so long ago. Bulk attended the funeral and he was aware of the irony. Two graves, two deaths. One, a baby, whose mother was saved by the plant and the second, a man who was killed by the plant. The plant had played him. Made him believe that it saved Loretta; that it did a good thing, a miracle. But what it had done was set a trap for him and he had blindly believed it.

"Beware of false teachers who come disguised as harmless sheep, but are wolves and will tear you apart."

The Bible scripture came back to his mind. Where would it all end? Even Loretta, the woman who wanted him to throw out the pods so many years ago, was now a user and a believer in the powers of the plant. She even gave the plant's healing powers credit for getting pregnant and carrying the baby full term, telling him several times how glad she was that the plant existed. He knew that this suicide was only the beginning, but the beginning…of what? What was he supposed to do? Everybody he loved and cared for were users, except the children of course. But then again, were the children the exception or were they also tainted through their mother's milk? Did the plant have control over them as well? The thought made him nauseous and he turned away from the mourners who were listening to Augustus praying for Edward's soul. His soul, Bulk thought, that's what Satan wanted. He wanted his soul. The devil was collecting souls.

He walked up the small hill behind the graveyard to get his nausea and emotions under control. Loretta looked after him with confusion on her face. Only Hank understood him, was aware of what was ailing him. To hell with you Satan and your plant, Bulk thought.

I'll never go to the cave again. An intense pain shot through his temple reminding him that he really didn't have a choice.

"I'll make you commit suicide just like I made Edward jump off that cliff and then I'll turn to Loretta, and Hank, and Emma, and of course little Ludwig. I'll erase your family from this valley, but don't worry. You will see them all again in hell."

The thoughts came out of nowhere. They weren't his. He would have never thought that. He was possessed and there was nothing he could do about it, not without risking his own and his family's lives.

Bulk wrestled with the decision to tell Loretta about the plant and what he had witnessed and now knew for sure, but in the end he refrained from doing so, sensing that the plant didn't want him to. Only Hank and Bulk knew that Edward committed suicide and it had to stay that way.

Bulk would have given his right arm to cancel the Festival of the Pods, but the power the plant had over him was too strong and he couldn't do it. He felt torn between the two obligations in his life. He felt it was his job to protect his wife, family and friends from the evil which loomed over this valley. On the other hand he had to protect the plant or pay the ultimate price with his death or the death of a loved one. Without his consent, he had become the plant's champion. The plant made its wishes and worries known to him and he spoke for the plant, wrote down the rules it wanted him to write and oversaw that they were followed. He wrestled with his responsibilities, making sure each person who received a pod knew of the peas potency and swore an oath of secrecy to protect it.

It was like a double edged sword. He was absolutely powerless. However, there was one thing he did change and it happened without the plant's objection. He cancelled the church service which had always preceded the Festival of the Pods. He kept on writing his thoughts down in the ledger and explained the horrible situation he was in. He also warned any future Harvester to heed his warnings and adhere to the plant's rules. He wrote down the date Edward Thompson committed suicide and by what means, insisting that any future Senior Harvester keep careful records of any suicides in the valley.

Convinced that he had seen the devil himself in Edward's eyes, Bulk renamed the plant from Black Trumpet Angel to Satan's Angel. And as he sat there writing the new name into the ledger, it occurred to him for the first time that it was indeed Satan's Angel come to earth, working for his master. He opened his Bible to Revelations 12:9 and read:

"The great dragon was hurled down – that ancient serpent called the devil, or Satan, who leads the whole world astray. He was hurled to the earth, and his angels with him."

The plant was Satan's angel put on earth to do his Master's evil deeds. Bulk now knew for sure what he was dealing with and heavy heartedly performed his duties as the plant's guardian to the best of his capabilities, knowing full well there would be hell to pay if he didn't.

Chapter Eight

March 1770

F our more years went by without further incidents. Bulk carried
the burden of his knowledge with a heavy heart. He felt like he
betrayed the valley people by not warning them not to chew the
peas, not to become a user, but he couldn't do anything about it. Just the
mere thought of doing so created throbbing pains in his temples. Every
way he looked at it, the plant would win by either killing him or someone
he loved dearly. The day of the festival and the following two months
became the most dreaded days of the year for him, and every year he
breathed a sigh of relief when the festival passed without any incidents
and the peas lost their potency two months later. Only then could he
look forward to the next ten months.

Every year Bulk tried unsuccessfully not to chew the peas, but
realized he had become addicted to them, the urge too strong to suppress.
It was the wicked lure of the flesh, the feeling of being happy and
carefree for a couple of hours, which attracted and enticed him each year
until he gave in. The obsession and infatuation with the peas
overshadowed his common sense. Bulk felt weak in character afterward
and despised himself. He cursed his lack of determination and
willpower. Begging Loretta not to use them any longer gave him the
severest headache, so severe he had to throw up for hours. But Loretta

didn't understand why she should quit the peas if they made her feel so good, being just as addicted to them now as he was. He didn't know anyone in the valley who ever quit the peas once they tasted them.

In late March of 1770, eight-year-old Henrietta Mueller developed a severe cough and even though her parents, Augustus and Agnes, took good care of her she didn't get better. She suffered through the whole spring months, not joining the other children when they were playing outside. She started to cough up blood at the end of August of that year and her parents were beside themselves with worry. They had heard of a disease where the afflicted person spit up blood, but certainly their only daughter couldn't suffer from that disease since it was known to be very contagious and no one else in the valley suffered from it.

Lying in bed at night, Augustus worried about her and tried to figure out what to do. Should he take Henrietta and make the long arduous trip to the closest settlement to find a doctor? He discussed it with Agnes who was totally against it, fearing that in the frail state her daughter was in she wouldn't survive the trip in a wagon and instead suggested that it was wiser for Augustus to ride out by himself and bring a doctor back to the valley.

He lay in bed debating his options, when suddenly the peas entered his mind. Out of nowhere the thought occurred to him that maybe the peas could help Henrietta get better. The peas always gave him the feeling of well-being for weeks after using them. Why couldn't they help his daughter get better? Strange that he had not thought about this possibility earlier. He chided himself for being so selfish. He had chewed his ration of three peas two weeks ago, not once thinking that they could benefit Henrietta. Of course, the rules said that they couldn't be given to children, but what if they could? What if they could heal her?

It was the first time in the valley's history that they desperately needed a doctor. No one ever had been seriously sick during the last decade and the need for a doctor didn't exist, but all this changed now.

Augustus decided the only thing to do was to seek Bulk out and talk him into giving him more peas. A serenity he hadn't felt for weeks came over him and he fell asleep without worrying about his daughter, sleeping all through the night without waking up. He felt sure that he was making the right decision and felt at peace with it.

The next morning he woke up and rode out to Bulk's cabin after eating breakfast. He discussed his idea with Agnes and she agreed that it was a chance worth taking. Loretta was hanging up clothes in the back yard when Augustus approached her and told her that he was looking for Bulk and she directed him toward the north pasture where the brothers were working together. He found them cutting hay for the winter twenty minutes later.

"Good morning Bulk, Hank." He nodded his head toward the younger brother. "I need to talk to you," he told Bulk as he shook his hand, then waved him to the side, indicating to him that it was a private talk. Bulk followed him to the large oak tree where they could stand in the shade while they talked. He leaned his wooden scythe against the trunk of the tree, then turned his attention toward Augustus.

"What's on your mind?" Bulk asked him.

"It's Henrietta. I'm really worried. She is spitting up blood now and fading fast. I don't want to lose my child, Bulk," Augustus told him.

"How can I help?" Bulk asked him.

"Well, I have an idea and I want to run it by you, seeing as you are the Senior Harvester. Every time I chew the peas they make me feel so good for weeks to come. It occurred to me last night that maybe the peas could help Henrietta get better. You told me a long time ago how they helped Loretta. Will you give me another pod so I can give the peas to Henrietta? I don't know what else to do. She is too frail to make the long trip to the next settlement to see a doctor."

Bulk was silent and didn't answer Augustus right away. He hadn't had a headache for so long that he sometimes forgot for days on end about the evilness of the plant. Why didn't he sense this problem

111

coming on at all? Was the plant's power fading? He couldn't be happier if this was true.

"You do understand, don't you, Bulk? I want you to give me your blessings and give me more pods."

"You know it's against the rules," Bulk told him. "One pod per adult user, that's the rule." He sounded harsh, but he couldn't help himself. The last thing he wanted was for the plant to feel threatened by Augustus' request. He wanted to help Henrietta and he felt anguish and sorrow for Augustus and Agnes, but could he dare give them another pod? Could he break the rules and allow a child to chew a pea? He expected the throbbing in his temples to start, but nothing happened. Deliberately he thought the same thought over and over again, forcing a reaction inside his head. I will give a pea to Henrietta…I will give a pea to a child…I will give a pea to a young child…but nothing happened, no pounding headache, no sense of wrong doing, no mental picture of his friend. He felt calm and at peace, as if the plant was in agreement with his thoughts.

"Bulk, you're a father. You know what it's like to lose a child. Give me another pod. I have to try and do this."

"Believe me, I do." He paused, giving Satan's Angel one more chance to interfere, but again there was no reaction inside of him. "I tell you what we can do instead, Augustus. I will break the rules and make an exception with Henrietta. You're right, we have to try and see if the peas can help her, but we are going to do it my way."

"What is your way?" Augustus asked him.

"I will give them to her in a tea. We will start with half a pea tonight," he answered.

"I'm willing to try it. I'm willing to try anything to help her get better," Augustus answered him.

"There is one more thing however. You can't tell anyone about this. Do you hear me? Only you and Agnes can know. Do you promise me not to tell anyone?" Bulk asked him.

The Devil's Pods

"I do. I promise and Agnes will also," he replied immediately.

"I'll come over tonight then and give her the tea. If she reacts well, I will come by and give her the tea every morning and every night for three days. If that doesn't help, I will ride with you and bring a doctor back to the valley. Is that a deal?"

"It's a deal. Thank you, Bulk."

Augustus turned around and walked back to his horse and thought that Bulk was a good, reasonable friend. Satisfied he climbed on his horse and rode home to tell Agnes the good news.

That night Bulk came to their cabin and asked Agnes to swear not to reveal that they were breaking the rules by giving the peas to a child. Agnes swore right away, her eyes bright and filled with hope. Bulk added the mashed up part of half a pea to the tea Agnes had fixed and stirred it until all of it dissolved into the fluid then walked over to the bed where a feverish Henrietta was tossing and turning. Moaning sounds escaped her mouth which tugged at his heartstrings.

Carefully, he lifted her small head off the pillow and slowly fed the hot liquid to the feverish girl. She took little sips until half the cup was empty then refused to drink any more. Bulk desperately hoped that it was enough. Henrietta looked up at him with blue, shiny eyes, her face pale, her long blond hair braided into two pig tails and the top of her small little head was covered by a white night cap. After a couple of seconds she started to cough and her mother rushed over to wipe her mouth. Traces of blood stained the clean cloth and the three adults looked at each other horrified. After the coughing spasm stopped, the weak girl nodded her head toward the cup. Once more Bulk held the cup to her mouth and watched her drink the rest of the tea. When she was finished she rested her head back on the pillow, closed her eyes and fell immediately asleep. She looked so helpless, so weak, just like Loretta had looked when she was sick.

Bulk hoped and prayed that he had done the right thing, that the peas would help this child get better. He left the cabin shortly afterward,

113

promising to return in the morning with the second dose. When Loretta asked him where he had been, he didn't answer her. He didn't want her to know and he didn't want Hank to know either. There was no reason to involve them. That way if the plant sought retribution it would have to turn toward him.

He paced the cabin half the night, not being able to go to sleep, plagued by doubts and worries. His conscience was riding him hard, but the worst thing was that he couldn't share his worries with Loretta who asked him ten times that night to tell her what was wrong. But how could he? How could he tell his wife that he was mixed up with evil and that there was no way to get out of it without suffering the severest of consequences? He finally fell asleep in the rocking chair and jumped up when Loretta brought him a cup of coffee in the early morning hours. He drank it gratefully and kissed her good morning, then told her that he had to leave, but would be back for breakfast. He couldn't wait any longer to find out how Henrietta fared through the night. Nine-year-old Ludwig opened the door of his small bedroom and ran toward him as he was halfway out the front door.

"Dad, where are you going this early? You didn't have breakfast yet," he asked him surprised to see him leave. Bulk smiled at him, his heart filling with pride when he looked at the fine lad.

"Son, I have to do something very important," he told him. "I'll be back in half an hour and after we eat breakfast we will go to the field together and you can help me with the hay, all right?"

"Yes! Can I handle the team the way you taught me last time?" he asked Bulk, his eyes large with expectation. Bulk chuckled.

"You sure can." He closed the door behind him and walked to the barn where he found the utensils he needed to grind up the second half of the pea. Hopefully Loretta wouldn't miss them for a couple of days. He had snuck them out of her kitchen yesterday to use them for this purpose. There was no way he would involve her.

He rode his horse to the other side of the lake with the mushy pulp inside the tiny tin container. Augustus' cabin was located on a small hill with beautiful pasture land surrounding him. From a distance he saw the smoke coming out of the chimney and as he came closer he saw Augustus coming out of the cabin walking toward him. Bulk looked anxiously into his face trying to figure out if he was going to tell him good or bad news about his daughter, but he couldn't read his friend's expression. He climbed off his horse and tied the mare up to the hitching post then turned around to face Augustus.

"Well, how did she fare last night?" he asked him.

"She had a peaceful night, except for talking and laughing in her sleep. She woke up half an hour ago. It didn't get any worse and she seems to have an appetite this morning. Agnes is feeding her scrambled eggs right now."

They entered the cabin and Bulk walked toward the girl's bed. Henrietta gave him a weak smile then started coughing, but not as hard as the day before and without any blood coming out. The two men agreed to give her another dose and Bulk added the pulp of the pea to the cup of tea Agnes already had waiting by the fire. He was so relieved that Henrietta hadn't turned sicker. Her fever had dropped slightly and her pretty eyes were not quite as shiny as the day before. Could there be hope? Bulk lifted the cup to her mouth and she took little sips until it was empty. She smiled up at him and somehow he knew then that she was going to make it.

"It sure tastes sweet," she whispered with a hoarse throat, the first words she had uttered in a week. All three adults smiled at her comment. Yes, there was definitely hope.

Bulk came for three days every morning and every evening and repeated the procedure. Henrietta looked better each day, her appetite improved and her coughing became less and less. By the end of the third day she begged her parents to let her get up and play outside. The color had returned to her pale face and her voice was stronger and filled with life, like it had been so many months ago before she fell sick.

Agnes and Augustus couldn't believe the change in her. Bulk worried the whole time that he would get premonitions and start getting headaches as he did when Edward wanted to know where the plant grew, but it never happened. The plant let him get away with breaking one of its rules not to let children taste the peas. Bulk could only wonder at its ulterior motives, but couldn't come up with one. Why didn't the plant punish him? Why didn't the plant put suicidal thoughts into his mind? Why did it help the little girl get better? What was Satan's Angel up to? For the life of him, Bulk couldn't figure out how it all fit together.

Only a short year later would it become crystal clear to him how Satan's Angel had once again manipulated and toyed with him and used his goodness toward satisfying its own agenda of collecting another soul.

Chapter Nine

Henrietta's health returned to normal and the valley once again enjoyed the laughter and cheerful playing of all the children. Life was good and even Bulk relaxed knowing that a tragedy had been averted and a child's life had been saved. The harvest that year was exceptionally good and people in the valley were happy and content. Late summer turned into a mild fall. The days turned shorter and one late November morning winter announced itself with its first snow storm and covered the valley with thirty inches of snow. Columns of gray smoke climbed out of the eight chimneys into the sky and the smell of burned wood lay heavy in the air.

Bulk, Hank and the six other men went hunting regularly in the surrounding woods and came back with plenty of mule deer, rabbits and the occasional fowl, which were skinned and quartered by the men, processed by the women and divided up equally among the families. The days were short and filled with hard work, but the evenings were long and warm sitting in front of the fireplace and spending time as a family. Bulk liked the winter months. He liked the cold weather and appreciated being warm. He felt content, not thinking too much about the plant, instead enjoying his daily blessings. Life was good and the people in the valley were satisfied with their lot in life.

Mary Thompson had married again two years ago. A trapper named Gustaf Olson came through the valley and took a liking to the widow and her two daughters and when he asked her to marry him, she agreed. It was the first wedding in the valley with Augustus performing the ceremony.

She now was Mary Olson and they were awaiting the birth of their second child together. The horrible suicide of her husband had faded into the past and Bulk sometimes caught himself doubting his assessment of the plant from four years ago. Maybe he had been wrong. Maybe everything had just been a horrible coincidence. Maybe he had been mentally sick with obsessive thoughts about the plant back then. For that reason alone, he refused to give many thoughts to the plant and instead concentrated on building Loretta a kitchen cupboard for Christmas.

The winter months passed slowly and spring was around the corner. Henrietta didn't turn sick during the winter months, not a cough or an ache in her body. Even when her older two brothers caught a cold, she stayed healthy to the amazement of her parents.

The way Augustus saw it, it was the peas which healed his daughter and he thought of them as a cure for any ailment. Agnes and he kept their promise and didn't tell any other person in the valley what had cured their daughter, but the knowledge that the peas saved his daughter's life festered inside of Augustus' head and he couldn't let go of it, thinking about the peas as an incredible healing source.

Many times a day, Augustus looked at Henrietta and marveled how lucky he and his wife were to have had the peas available to them. Without the peas his sweet little Henrietta would have died. They were certainly a miracle cure.

It all came to a head in early 1771 when the first courier rider came through the valley, carrying the latest newspaper from Boston. The families finally received news of what was happening outside their little valley. The paper contained articles from Boston, seaboard colonies, foreign news from England and the West Indies, obituaries, and commercial shipping news. The families were thrilled and read the paper from front to end several times. The stories of the latest encounters with Indians and fights with pirates and French privateers, who plagued the oceans, were read to the younger children who seemed to want to hear those stories over and over again.

One of the articles written in the Boston Gazette was about a Scottish surgeon in the British Royal Navy named James Lind, who discovered that citrus fruit prevented scurvy. Scurvy had killed Augustus' father who had been a sailor all of his life. To him, it was the discovery of the century; too late for his father who had died over twenty years ago, but not too late for many other sailors. James Lind had even written a book about it. It was strange how this news affected Augustus. How many lives would be saved by this man's discovery? How many children wouldn't lose their father like he had back then? And then he thought about the peas and how they had saved his daughter's life and he drew comparisons and suddenly he knew what he had to do. He had to bring the healing powers of the peas to the awareness of the rest of the world just like James Lind did.

He lay awake at night thinking about the rules concerning the peas. He had made an oath not to take the peas out of the valley, just like he promised not to tell any person that his child had received peas in her tea. He was a man of his word, but how important was it to keep a promise when you compared it to all the suffering in the world? He thought of all the people who died every single day because there were no cures for so many diseases. How could he live with himself knowing what he knew; that there was a plant growing high up in these mountains which could cure illnesses by chewing its fruits.

No, if the pea would save just one life it would be worth breaking his promise over. It was his duty as a Christian to share this knowledge.

What right did Bulk have to make him promise not to talk to anyone about it? It wasn't Bulk's plant, even if he and his brother were the only two people who knew where it grew. Did that make it his plant? Not in Augustus' mind. The way he figured the plant belonged to everyone, not just this valley. The more he thought about it, the more he became resolute to follow through with his idea. He shared his concerns with Agnes, and seeing how plagued her husband was with this heavy burden, she encouraged him to go and talk to Bulk.

"Bulk was so reasonable last time you talked to him. He will see the wisdom of your words. Go talk to him Augustus."

So on a beautiful early spring morning he approached Bulk who was shoeing one of his horses inside the barn. The beautiful stallion was tied up to a stall and Bulk was busy turning a pair of iron pliers, holding a horse shoe in the hot fire, forcing air into the coals by pumping the billows with his foot.

"Morning, Bulk," he greeted him as he walked through the open barn door.

"Morning, Augustus," Bulk looked up, then turned back to inspect the shape of the horseshoe. He used a hammer and formed it into the desired shape over the anvil, creating loud clanging sounds which echoed through the valley, up the mountain ranges. Augustus waited for him to finish. He understood that Bulk couldn't quit in the middle of his work. He walked outside and leaned against the corral fence. The morning air was fresh and he could see little breath puffs coming out of his mouth as he anticipated the meeting. After a short while Bulk joined him outside.

"What brings you to my company this beautiful morning?" Bulk asked him smiling and in a good mood. "Beautiful weather we're having for an early spring, isn't it?"

"Sure is," Augustus replied. "As to my reason for being here… well… it's the business with the pods. I have given them a lot of thought lately. I want to talk to you about the promise I made to you when Henrietta was sick."

"What about the promise?" Bulk asked him, his heart starting to beat a little bit faster, his good mood suddenly overshadowed by anxiety.

"Well, I can't honor my promise to you any longer, but I want you to know why."

Bulk's eyebrows crunched and Augustus thought that he looked weary and tired all of a sudden.

"Well, it's just not right to keep that kind of knowledge to ourselves. We're just a few people here in the valley. Our use of the plant's healing power is so minimal compared to the rest of the world. We have no right to keep the pods to ourselves. We owe it to the rest of the world to bring healing to all the sick people, to put an end to so much suffering because of incurable diseases," Augustus started his explanation off.

Bulk frowned at him. He had been in such a good mood and now here he was listening to Augustus rambling on about the healing power of the plant and sharing it with the rest of the world.

"Listen, I'm sure you read about James Lind, when the courier rider came through the valley a week ago and brought us the Boston Gazette. When I read the article it really hit home with me. He was the man who discovered that citrus fruit prevents scurvy and that got me thinking. You know my dad died of it. Well, the way I see it, we have an undiscovered fruit on our hands. It is our obligation to make the rest of the world aware of its healing powers. We have to take the pods to the next settlement to send them to New York to have them studied, don't you see that. Just think about how many lives could be saved. Let me out of my promise, Bulk."

"I will do no such thing and I advise you to hold fast to your promise for reasons I can't discuss with you," Bulk answered him, his voice raised, his tone almost threatening now. "Don't you dare take them out of this valley! They saved your daughter. Let it be good with that."

"Why, Bulk? Why? Give me one good reason why not?" Augustus tried to reason with him.

"Because you will die if you try to take them out of the valley, that's why!" Bulk shouted at him.

Augustus looked at him dumbfounded. Of all the arguments he had expected, he didn't expect this one.

"You're going to kill me?" he asked him astonished. "Why would you do that? You're a God-fearing man."

"I'm not going to kill you," Bulk shouted at him, shocked by Augustus' thoughts. "No, I won't kill you - the plant will. I tell you - it doesn't want to be found and taken out of the valley. The plant has this…" Bulk started to say more, but an abrupt painful headache seized him. His hands went to his temples and rubbed them, furious to feel this unmistakable pounding inside his skull again. It was the same throbbing as he experienced four years ago, when Edward jumped to his death. It was a warning. The plant was trying to tell him to back off…not to reveal too much. He stopped talking. After a short moment of just staring at each other he yelled one more final warning.

"Don't you dare go against me on this one, Augustus! Don't you dare!" Bulk turned around and walked back inside the barn ignoring his good friend and neighbor, leaving him speechless, staring at his back.

It was the first time he had ever yelled at him and lost his composure. But he didn't care. It had to be. It couldn't be any other way. He was sure about it and hoped that his warning hadn't fallen on deaf ears.

Slowly Bulk's headache receded and a great calmness came over him, reassuring him. Everything is going to be all right now, he thought. I must have made my point with him.

Mad as hell, Augustus stomped off in the opposite direction to where his horse was tethered and rode away. He hadn't expected this kind of reaction from the man he had come to know as a friend for so long. Bulk had been totally unreasonable and overreacted to his simple request. Augustus was extremely bewildered by Bulk's reply and behavior. He had known him for a long time now, but never did he hear him raise his voice against him. And what about what he had said; the plant was going to kill him. What had gotten into him? He knew him as a reasonable friend who he could discuss anything with and receive good advice, who he could count on for help. He knew him to be strong in his faith, a good friend and family man. Why couldn't he have discussed this matter without threatening him? Why did he believe that the plant would kill him? Such stupid nonsense. He never heard anything more ridiculous. I will wait a while and give him time to think about it, Augustus thought. I planted the seed in his mind and when Bulk has time to think about it he will come to see that I'm right in wanting to share nature's gift with the world. Let him ponder on it, Augustus thought, as he reached his cabin and climbed off his horse.

Spring arrived to the valley and blessed the countryside with an unusual amount of wildflowers. They were growing everywhere; on the grazing lands, on the hills and along the trails they traveled; flowers of all colors and shapes, from small ones to big ones, to thistle bushes. Flowers were everywhere. The whole basin became one colorful painter's palette. Mild winds and temperatures turned the usually hard work into pleasant chores. Finally summer arrived and drove the temperatures to such a high that it wasn't uncommon to see several families cooling off by the lake, going swimming at night after the chores were finished.

The men in the valley stayed busy with work. Augustus and Bulk never discussed the peas again and returned to their former friendship, both hoping that the other man had changed his mind. The closer the Festival of the Pods came, the calmer Augustus turned about his decision and looked at his calmness as a sign from his savior. Hadn't the plant been fashioned by the Creator of Heaven and Earth for just this purpose? It was like Augustus' destiny had been decided. He would take the pods to the next settlement and send them to a medical institution for tests. It didn't matter to him how Bulk felt about it, not any more. Bulk's empty threat had just been a weak attempt to keep the pods in the valley for their personal use. He was just being plum selfish and ridiculous and one day he would see that he had been wrong and appreciate what Augustus had done.

The day of the festival arrived. The harvest had been extremely good and every user received two pods. Bulk gave Augustus a stern look as if he was trying to look inside of him to see if he still felt the same way as before, but Augustus gave him an encouraging smile, like he wasn't pursuing his dream any longer. Since Bulk didn't suffer from a headache, he thought it would be all right to give him his pods. Augustus uttered the usual oath but knew he wouldn't keep it. To hell with trying to keep the plant a secret and to hell with Bulk's warning that the plant would kill him. How could anyone hold him to an oath if it could bring cures to the world's diseases? No, the plant was special, very special, but to attach all this hocus pocus to it was ridiculous. Did Bulk really think he would sacrifice this greater cause just so the people in this valley could chew these peas once a year and celebrate its existence?

The urge to use the pod was strong that night but, with the help of his wife, Augustus managed to get through the difficult hours and fought the cravings inside of him. They both went down on their knees and prayed to God for strength. He never expected it to be this hard, the desire so powerful that it overwhelmed him with its intensity. After all, he had been so sure of what he was going to do, so why was it so hard to stay away from them? Agnes was his strength during those hours. She didn't suffer any urges, since she had never tasted the plants' fruit. She was the only person in the valley who didn't participate and for once he was glad about it. Every year he had encouraged her to try them, but she had vehemently argued against it. On this night he asked her to hide the pods and under no circumstances break down and reveal the location to him until he left for his trip in the morning. Eventually, after being on his knees for what seemed like hours, Augustus crawled exhausted onto his bed and fell into a deep sleep unaware of the warning he received. He experienced the last joyful moments of his life; falling prey to Satan's

Angel, teasing and taunting him in his unconscious state, letting him experience it all; the hidden cave, the beautiful black trumpet flowers opening up, the soft harmonic trilling sounds of the blossoms and the heavy tantalizing fragrance of the flower's nectar. His eyebrows lifted and his lips opened up with astonishment. Everything was so beautiful and Augustus never wanted to leave, wanted to stay in this state forever, tortured by all his senses to unbearable heights.

But none of this remained in his awareness when he woke up the next morning, rested and resolute to pursue his goal. The exquisite experience vanished into nothingness, like it never happened.

Augustus rose early and Agnes fixed him a huge slab of bacon, homemade biscuits and scrambled eggs for breakfast, which she hoped would sustain him during the long ride ahead. She also prepared a knapsack of food just in case the unforeseen should happen and night would catch him on the trail. It was a long way to the next settlement and they had learned long time ago to always prepare for the unexpected. They lived in a vast expanse of undiscovered, isolated territory and danger waited everywhere for a lonely rider. Anything could happen; Indians, wild animals, bad weather, or heaven forbid his horse would break a leg in the rough terrain. No, it was better to be safe than sorry, one of Augustus' favorite sayings.

The first sunrays crossed the mountain caps and caught Augustus' attention as he walked to the barn to saddle his mare. He had no idea that it was going to be the last sunrise he would ever witness. All he thought was that it was going to be a gorgeous day. Nature was on his side. He didn't need any bad weather to slow him down. The way he saw it, the faster he took the pods to the next settlement the sooner he would be free of the urges to use them and Agnes agreed. He felt he could handle his urges while it was daylight, but what if he was delayed somewhere out there in the middle of nowhere? Could he withstand another night without Agnes by his side? Even now the pods were in the back of his mind, haunting and tempting him. Just knowing that they were going to be in his possession; two pods, six juicy peas inside - and he could chew them anytime he wanted to on the trail, away from the cabin. No, damn it... he had to think about other things. Think about Agnes and Henrietta...think about anything but the peas. He had to get going or he would go insane. He had never hurt his wife in his life, and he never wanted to hurt his wife, but the thought of forcefully getting the pods back from her last night had occurred to him and it scared him. He felt ashamed for even thinking it, felt weak and not in control. No, he wanted nothing more than to leave this valley behind him, get to the settlement and get rid of the pods.

The saddlebags and leather water pouch were already fastened to the saddle when Agnes walked inside the barn and handed him the pouch with the pods. He took the pouch and smiled at her. It was supposed to be an encouraging smile, but he failed miserably. It was almost as if his hands tingled when he took the pouch from her and tucked it inside the saddlebag. His imagination was getting the better of him. One thing was for sure; it was going to be a long miserable day. He finished tying the last knot around the sleeping blanket behind the saddle. In his heart he knew he was doing the right thing. Henrietta and her two older brothers stood next to Agnes and all hugged him tightly before he waved one last goodbye to them and then road off into the glorious sunrise.

It would take him at least nine hours of hard riding to reach the settlement and he wanted to get going. Getting caught by darkness in this wilderness wasn't an option for him, especially not tonight, not with the peas in his saddlebag. He had plenty of time to reach the town before sundown.

To redirect his mind from the pods he started to think about the valley. It was thirteen years ago when they found it. He remembered the incredible snow storm and how his party had found the pass into the valley hoping for shelter and camped next to the lake, surprised that two families already called this remote spot their home. Agnes fell in love with this peaceful little valley and became fast friends with the other two women who were carving out a living next to their husbands in this forlorn wilderness. He didn't need much convincing to stay behind even though he didn't let on, enjoying Agnes beguiling efforts of changing his mind. They had only been married for nine months at the time. The trek moved on north without them and three months later they finished building their own small cabin with the help from Bulk and Hank. He never regretted his decision to do so and still didn't to this day. They had been very happy here until Henrietta turned sick with the fever.

Augustus was nearing the pass and his thoughts turned toward the night. He would get a room in a cheap boarding house, but not before he located the settlement's doctor and handed the pods to him to send to the medical institution. He would show him what he thought to be the rarest fruits of a plant not yet discovered. There was no way that he would spend another night knowing he could use them, feel those incredible sensations and mind-blowing hallucinations. Stop it, he scolded himself. Stop it and watch the rocky pass before the mare breaks a leg.

Bulk, yes, he would be upset with him once he found out that he went against him, but he would cross that bridge when the time came. Even Bulk had to acknowledge sooner or later that he was justified in revealing the secret of the valley. He would see the logic in bringing help to so many people suffering from incurable diseases. No, Bulk was a religious man and wouldn't stand in his way. After all, they had been friends for thirteen years and he knew that Bulk cared for his family.

How stupid and irrational this whole tradition was anyway. The first time he chewed one of the peas was thirteen years ago, his first year in the valley, and he was overcome with beautiful sensations. He had listened to Bulk when he told him about the pea pods and was captured by the story of how he had found the plant. Back then he could tell how proud Bulk was; how the plant had saved his wife's life and that he would be forever grateful. The last couple years however were different. Bulk's speech had changed from being proud to being cautious and now he warned the residents not to betray the trust he had in them. And then Bulk had told them that they were cancelling the church service before the festival and it had really upset Augustus. To not praise the Lord and give blessings to His incredible creation just seemed improper, downright blasphemous. But no matter how hard he tried to change Bulk's mind, he stuck to his decision. He never gave him one good reason why he cancelled the church service, and when he approached Hank, his brother had simply told him, "Bulk knows what he is doing. Leave him be," and walked away from him. To hell with trying to guess Bulk's motives, and to hell with Hank for always being on his brother's side, Augustus thought.

He slowly rode into the long pass. Steep cliffs went up on both sides of the rocky trail. There was only one way in and one way out of this valley and he always felt vulnerable riding through this pass. It would be the perfect trap for Indians to capture him. He shook that possibility out of his mind. He had never seen a Red Skin within hundred miles of this place.

He felt raindrops hitting him. Surprised and knocked out of his reverie by the hard hitting drops, he looked up and saw a dangerous cloud overhead, heavy with rain, low in the sky above him. The whole pass suddenly looked dark and foreboding. How in the hell did that creep up on him? Even though the rain was a welcoming sight to Augustus, he wasn't thrilled about the thunder and lightning accompanying the downpour.

The crops could unquestionably use the water. It hadn't rained for three weeks and now here he was riding out of the valley and the raindrops started pelting him hard riding through the pass. It was just his bad luck. He gave his horse the spurs and tried to outrun the cloud above him. It was a good thing that he, as well as his mare, knew every hole on this rocky path, otherwise he wouldn't have dared to try such a maneuver. At a neck-breaking speed, he raced halfway through the pass. Finally he slowed down, looking behind him, the rain had subsided and the cloud had disappeared. Strange phenomenon, he thought, as he turned back around. He could see the large opening signaling the end of the pass with one final curve around the cliff and then the trail led down and out of the mountains. Soon he would leave the mountain behind and be on the flat open range.

Augustus had ridden this way many times before and knew that he had to go slow around the cliff and down the last rocky decline before he reached the better traveled road below. It was the most dangerous part of this trip and he was well aware of it. Of course it was more dangerous coming around it with a wagon, but the ground was still wet from the rain and the rocks were slippery, so he was particularly cautious.

All of a sudden, without any reason, without any thoughts, he pushed the spurs of his boots deep into the horse's flanks. The mare whinnied and instinctively shot forward, its ears back, upset by the rough treatment it received from its rider. Being of sound mind, the mare slowed down again and started to calm down, when Augustus repeatedly kicked it hard in the flanks, leaned forward and screamed into its ears.

"Run, you miserable piece of horseflesh! R…u…n! Run like the devil is behind you!"

Panicked, the mare flew down the pass and tried to run around the cliff, tried, because its life depended on it, but Augustus yanked the reigns to the opposite side. The horse screamed in protest, stumbled and attempted to stop in time to avoid the depth below, but it was too late. It didn't stand a chance in hell. The momentum of the equine's speed forced the heavy creature and its rider over the pass' overhang. With the most horrible scream of animal and rider, they disappeared down the canyon below.

Annegret Werner Shaw

Chapter Ten

The first time Agnes felt ill-omened vibes going through her body was when she was hanging up fresh scrubbed laundry in the back of her yard, the same morning Augustus left. The terrible sensation touched her spirit deep inside of her and made her want to double over and vomit into the dirt. She didn't have any idea why she suddenly felt so miserable and dismissed it from her mind after the feeling passed. But as time went by and Augustus didn't return home the next night, she knew in her heart that something awful had happened to him. She always was a worry wart so she gave him one more day, just in case he had to spend the night on the road.

But the next day came and went and he didn't return home. She was beside herself with worry and after spending another sleepless night she walked over to Bulk's place the following morning. He was the only person she could think of to turn to for help. It was early in the morning, but he was already up and working on the roof of the barn before it turned too hot in the valley. He waved at her from a distance and shouted a good morning, thinking that she had come to visit Loretta. But Agnes stopped at the barn and yelled up at him that she needed to talk to him, that Augustus was long overdue to return from his trip to the settlement. A strong foreboding overcame Bulk as he climbed down the handmade wooden ladder. He looked at Agnes and saw how red her eyes were from crying and how deathly pale she looked.

"Why did he leave the valley without letting me know?" Bulk asked her, suddenly sure what her answer would be.

"He felt so strong about the pods. He took them to the next settlement to send them to a medical institution. He was sure that they had strong healing powers. He didn't want to anger you, that's why he left alone three days ago."

"Three days ago? I warned him not to go. Why didn't he listen?" Bulk shouted at her, angry at Augustus for tricking him and angry at himself for trusting his feelings that everything was all right. Why didn't the plant warn him and why didn't he suffer from any headaches the last four days? Why? And then he knew the answer. The plant didn't warn him because Satan's Angel was ready to collect another soul. He had been tricked again. It all made sense now. The way he and Augustus had been played from the beginning. That's why the peas healed Henrietta, to put the thoughts into Augustus' head that he should share the peas with the world, all the while knowing that he was a God-fearing man and would do it for that reason alone. And it was the God-fearing people of this valley who he was after. Good against evil - and evil had won again. Augustus and he had both played their part, the outcome determined before the game began. The only reason Satan's Angel made Bulk suffer from the headaches was to show him that he controlled him and that he was powerless to change anything he decided to do.

Bulk was furious with himself. He should have talked to Augustus again before he gave him the peas, but these thoughts didn't help his wife right now who was standing in front of him a broken woman. Hank came walking up from behind the barn carrying two boards they had needed. When he saw Agnes he nodded a greeting, but then stopped short realizing something was wrong.

"What's going on?" he asked curiously.

"Augustus left the valley three days ago and hasn't returned," Bulk filled him in. Bulk's worried look at him spoke volumes. Hank lived in this wilderness long enough to realize how serious it was if someone went missing.

"Hank and I will go and find him, Agnes. Go home and be with your kids," he told Agnes and put his hands comfortingly on her shoulder. "The women will come and stay with you until we return."

"Oh, Bulk. I'm so afraid something bad has happened to him. I'm so afraid," Agnes sobbed and started to cry hysterically. Loretta came out of the cabin. She realized right away that something bad had happened when she saw Agnes standing there crying and her husband comforting her. She picked up her long skirt and ran across the dusty yard toward the barn.

"What happened? What's wrong, Agnes? Is Henrietta sick again?" she asked her friend who now turned to her and hugged her. Bulk explained what happened and Loretta agreed with him that she would stay with Agnes. The women disappeared inside the cabin so Loretta could grab a couple of things she needed before they headed to Agnes cabin. Emma and Mary joined them later; the hours ticking by way too slow, waiting for the news.

Bulk turned to face Hank as soon as the women left.

"We will need the clapboard wagon," he told him. Hank looked at him dumbfounded.

"Why do we need the wagon?" he asked. "We'll be much faster on horseback."

"We need the wagon to bring Augustus' body back," Bulk answered him in a monotone voice then turned and walked inside the barn.

One hour later they neared the entrance of the pass. They slowed down and entered it, keeping a lookout for danger, Hank riding with his rifle in his hands ready to shoot if he needed to. Halfway through the pass, they caught sight of the tall cliff which indicated that they almost made it out. One more dangerous curve and they would be heading down to the wider path below and it would become easier to travel with the wagon. Simultaneously, the brothers noticed vultures floating and gliding high in the air on the shifting winds close to the last cliff. They knew from experience that it could only mean one thing; something was dead in the canyon below.

With foreboding and apprehension, they rode the clapboard wagon around the treacherous cliff and down the decline. Bulk stopped the wagon as soon as he reached the bottom twenty minutes later and put the brakes on, then pulled his rifle out of the leather shaft attached to the wagon seat. Together they walked through the heavy underbrush to where the birds where flying overhead. They heard the angry squawking before they saw three vultures fighting over the carcass of the mare, lying all mangled and twisted up in a clearing close to the canyon's edge; her long neck bent into an awkward angle, one leg torn off, her stomach ripped open by a bear who was resting close by, protecting nature's free hand-out from other carnivores. The bear stood up and growled at them, getting ready to charge, but Bulk fired a shot into the air, scurrying the vultures and the bear into the nearby woods. Silently they walked past the carcass of the mare. Augustus had to be close by and Bulk prayed silently that they would find his body in one piece to bring home to his wife; a whole body, not just left over bones, so that she could look at him one last time before they buried him.

They carefully searched the rocky area but couldn't find him. Bulk's heart turned a little lighter, hoping against all hope that Augustus had been able to walk away from this accident. Maybe he jumped off before the mare fell down the canyon, or, if he went over the edge as well, he was not dead but badly injured and crawled into a safe crevice or hole to avoid the bear? Was it possible that he had survived? They shouted his name and looked for another fifteen minutes, but didn't find anything; no blood, no pieces of clothing, nothing at all. What in the hell happened to him?

Frustrated, Bulk looked up the cliff, wondering how anyone could survive such a fall. And that's when he saw Augustus fifty feet above, twisted and mangled into a grotesque looking corpse, hanging between the branches of a pine tree which had found a foothold in the outcropping of the cliff. With horror he caught sight of two black vultures picking away at him. Outraged, he screamed, raised his rifle at the monstrous sight and killed one of them with a single shot; the other flew away squawking angrily, throwing up part of its meal. Bulk looked back at Hank who had caught up with him and witnessed the horror on his face. He watched his brother swallow hard and his face turned pale. Both men needed a few seconds to catch their bearings, to exercise their strength and get their feelings under control. There was no use for weakness in this forlorn wilderness. There was nothing either one of them could do for Augustus now, besides getting him down. Bulk told Hank to return to the wagon and retrieve the rope and the hatchet he always carried with him, while he looked for a way to climb up the cliff.

After checking out the massive rock wall, he found a possible way to climb up to the left of where Augustus was hanging from the tree. It wouldn't be easy, but it was physically possible. He hung the rope around his shoulder and climbed up the cliff slowly, making his way sideways to the pine tree. Augustus' corpse was lodged between two branches and the only way to loosen him was to cut one of the branches off. The closer he climbed to the tree, the harder it was for him to avoid looking at his friend's torn body; but he had to, and just one glance at his friend's corpse made him heave so hard that he tasted strong bile in his mouth. Half of Augustus' face looked like a hardened horror mask; the other half was ripped and picked away by the vultures; his empty eye socket in stark contrast to the second eye which was wide open, clouded over by death. Augustus' guts were hanging down the branches, his torn shirt fluttering in the light breeze. He tried to get the image of Augustus' broken body out of his mind, tried to get his emotions under control; his friend didn't deserve to die this way. Augustus was a good man trying to do a good thing for mankind, but he didn't have an inkling that he was dealing with Satan.

Bulk threw part of the rope down to Hank who tied the hatchet to it, then pulled it back up. He untied it and then took several deep breaths to steady himself before he was able to tie the rope around Augustus' body and anchored the rope around a thicker upper branch. He grabbed the hatchet and started hacking away at the lower tree branch until it gave way to the dead weight. With tears in his eyes he lowered the corpse slowly down the cliff and then climbed down after him. The brothers carried Augustus to the clapboard where they wrapped him in a blanket Bulk had brought along for this purpose. He wished to hell that he had been wrong, but he wasn't.

They walked back to the horse cadaver and retrieved Augustus' saddle and blanket smeared with blood and guts. Hank carried both back to the wagon as Bulk took the leather halter off of the mare's head. Then he looked for the saddlebags he knew Augustus had with him. The bear must have dragged them off into the bushes. Bulk found them thirty-five feet away, scratched up, but the contents safe. He untied the knot of the leather strings and searched for what he knew was inside. The brown leather pouch was tucked underneath some clothing inside the left bag. Bulk poured the contents of the pouch into his palm. Two pods fell into his hand. Carefully he placed them back into the pouch and put it into his pocket. Why didn't Augustus listen to him?

The ride home was made in silence. Bulk hadn't told Hank about the discussion he had with Augustus so many months ago. He saw no point in worrying him. It was his job to deal with the plant and the less Hank knew, the safer he was. He looked at him from the side. He could see the stress on his younger brother's face; his forehead crunched and his lips tight. He knew he would eventually ask him questions he didn't want to answer. At this point he probably had no idea that Augustus' death was connected to the plant.

Hank noticed Bulk looking at him and turned to face him.

"What happened, Bulk? Augustus knew this trail, rode it many times before. What in the hell happened?" The dreaded question was finally out there, but how was he supposed to answer him? That the plant collected another soul; killed their friend for wanting to bring the pods existence to the attention of the rest of the world?

"I don't know," Bulk answered him, knowing full well that he was avoiding telling him the truth, still trying to absorb it all himself. To him, it was so much more than the death of a friend. Augustus had died a horrible death...but everybody died someday, somehow, but not this way, not by suicide. It was the second suicide in the valley and he was the only one aware of it and he was going to keep it that way if he could help it.

"Maybe he was caught in the storm we had a couple of days ago which seemed to loom over the pass, remember? Maybe the mare slipped on the wet rocks. Hell, I don't know and we will probably never know," he answered Hank.

He felt bad for lying to his brother, but it was for his own good. Only he knew that it was the plant who planted suicidal thoughts into Augustus' mind, just like it had done to Edward. Bulk could have stopped him. He knew what would happen if Augustus took the pods out of the valley. Sure, he had warned him, but it hadn't been enough.

It became unbearable for him to know the truth and he was ridden with guilt and self-reproach. He was the one to blame. He could have tried harder to convince Augustus of the danger, but he didn't, and he would never forgive himself. It was the second time that the plant had tricked him and deep down inside he knew that it was the last time.

They drove the wagon to Bulk's cabin and locked it inside the barn. There was no way he was going to let Agnes see her husband the way he looked. And even though she begged and pleaded with him to let her see him one more time, he didn't veer from his decision. He told Agnes that Augustus had had an accident and that a bear got to him before they found him. It was a horrible lie, but it was better than telling her the truth, that he killed himself.

Bulk built him a wooden coffin, working all through the night, the last thing he could do for his friend. Augustus was buried the next day in the small valley's graveyard.

Life changed for Bulk after that. He wrestled with his conscience day after day, night after night, the guilt never leaving him. It started to affect his daily life. He rarely smiled and Loretta worried about him and asked him constantly what was ailing him, but he couldn't share his heavy burden with her. In the depths of his despair he turned toward the Bible and read the book for hours to find comfort and reassurance in the scriptures. At the same time his headaches increased in frequency and strength and he realized that Satan's Angel and he were on a collision course where only one would survive. He kept on reading the Bible despite the pain in his throbbing temples, hoping that the book held the answer to defeat Satan's Angel. One night he came upon the scripture of Ephesians 6:13-18:

"Therefore put on the full armor of God, so that when the day of evil comes, you may be able to stand your ground, and after you have done everything, to stand. Stand firm then, with the belt of truth buckled around your waist, with the breastplate of righteousness in place, and with your feet fitted with readiness that comes from the gospel of peace. In addition to all this, take up the shield of faith, with which you can extinguish all the flaming arrows of the evil one. Take the helmet of salvation and the sword of the Spirit, which is the word of God. And pray in the Spirit on all occasions with all kinds of prayers and requests. With this in mind, be alert and always keep on praying for all the saints. "

When he read this particular scripture he knew he found what he'd been looking for. His heart filled with understanding. He could defeat Satan by praying.

Be alert and always keep on praying...always keep on praying.

The words kept going through his mind over and over again. As long as he prayed, Satan's Angel couldn't control his thoughts. He finally found the answer. God and his faith were his weapons. Bulk spent hours memorizing his favorite scriptures. He would do battle and he would win as long as he didn't let his guard down. A plan formed in his mind, but he wasn't sure if he should act now or wait for the dead of winter when the plant was sleeping. In a way he knew that it wouldn't make any difference; no matter how deep asleep the plant was, it would wake up and fight him. He pushed the day of his plan further off and prayed to God to help him prepare.

And then the decision to push the inevitable further off was taken out of his hands the day Loretta told him she was with child. A day which should have been filled with rejoicing and happiness was overshadowed by the knowledge that he had to act soon. There was no doubt in his mind that the day had arrived to stand firm against evil. He couldn't bring another child into this world, into this valley, while he was still a slave to Satan's Angel. He just couldn't stand the thought. The day had come to destroy the plant, but he had to stand firm. The risk was high and he knew that his actions could be fatal, a risk he was now willing to take. There wouldn't be a day of happiness left in his life if he proved to be a coward. He was prepared and prayed constantly. The more he prayed, the more his headaches increased and he felt the constant presence of the plant inside his head. Reading the Bible for hours gave him strength and he found that his faith was stronger than ever. Psalm 23:4 gave him the greatest solace of all and he read it over and over again.

"He makes me lie down in green pastures, He leads me beside quiet waters, He restores my soul. He guides me in paths of righteousness for His name's sake. Even though I walk through the

valley of the shadow of death, I will fear no evil, for thou are with me, Thy rod and Thy staff, they comfort me."

Chapter Eleven

September 23, 1771

B ulk picked a Sunday, the day of the Lord, to defeat evil. He rode up the mountain path determined to put an end to Satan's Angel's reign over the valley. The headache reappeared when he tied the rope around the boulder and he knew that the battle between good and evil had started. He began to pray hard and loud and concentrated on each word he was saying. The headache increased in severity, pounding his temples, making it hard for him to concentrate. Bulk lowered himself down the rope, now shouting the words of Psalm 23, the Psalm of David, loud and clear; his words echoing down the canyon. It was hard for him to think. He couldn't form his own prayers any longer.

"The Lord is my shepherd, I shall not be in want. He makes me lie down in green pastures, He leads me beside quiet waters, He restores my soul. He guides me in paths of righteousness for His name sake. Even though I walk through the valley of the shadow of death, I will fear no evil, for You are with me; Your rod and Your staff, they comfort me. As I walk through the valley of the shadow of evil...I walk through the valley of the shadow of evil...I will fear no evil...I will fear no evil...you hear me...I will fear no evil!"

As soon as his feet touched the hard rock surface of the opening he grabbed his hatchet, which he had sharpened for just this purpose, from his belt and stormed through the tunnel.

"I will fear no evil!"

He reached the cave and rushed toward the plant, not wavering for a second. The branches and vines twisted away from his hatchet as his deathly assault started.

"I will fear no... evil!"

He hacked off one large limb, the hatchet going through the texture easily, all the while hearing the plants ear-piercing, high pitched screams. His head felt like it was going to split in half, but yet, he kept on shouting and hacking away at the plant.

"I will fear... no evil... I walk through... through the shadow of death, but I will fear... no evil!"

He chopped and hacked and when no branches were left, he attacked the trunk. His feet were surrounded by the cut branches and vines which still twisted and turned in the aftermath, trying to twist around his boots. He stomped on them, adrenaline rushing through his body, giving him the extra strength to destroy the plant until nothing was left. The more limbs fell to the ground, the clearer his thoughts turned, the less intense the headache became. But he was prepared for Satan's trap and kept on praying;

"And we know that in all things God works for the good of those who love him, who have been called toward his purpose."

No way was he going to stop praying until the last part of the plant was destroyed. Sweat was running down his neck and back as he chopped the last part of the trunk apart. He hacked and kept on hacking at the twisting limps and vines until the high pitched screaming stopped and nothing moved. Only then did he sit down a couple of feet away and looked at his massacre. The headache had vanished and he felt good. Calmness he hadn't experienced for weeks came over him and he knew he had won. He had defeated Satan's Angel. Bulk stopped praying and started laughing out loud; the laughter echoing up and down the walls of the cave. He laughed until he could laugh no more, tears of mirth running down his cheeks.

"I did it! I destroyed you!" he yelled. "I destroyed you!"

All the fears he had bottled up inside of him came now bubbling to the surface and changed to unbelievable feelings of happiness. His life would become normal again. He would see his new child, be a good father to his children and a good husband to Loretta, and he would praise the Lord until the end of his days. The plant was dead, couldn't control him any longer. He had destroyed Satan's tool of collecting souls and he would never come back to this cave again. He would go home to Loretta, Ludwig and be there when the new baby was born. Bulk never felt better, never felt more alive than during these short few minutes of rejoicing.

But the few minutes passed all too soon. All of a sudden Bulk's headache returned with a vengeance and he heard a high pitched teasing sound reverberating through the cave, first quietly than getting stronger and louder. Totally taken off guard, Bulk looked at the empty spot where the plant had stood tall and regal such a short time ago and realized that the sound came out of the crevice in the rock. Be alert and always keep on praying, he remembered the scripture he had read so often, and in that moment Bulk realized that he had made two fatal mistakes; he hadn't destroyed the taproot growing deep inside the rock and he had stopped praying the second he thought he destroyed the plant. He had let his guard down.

His face turned ashen with the devastating knowledge that he was defeated. His smile disappeared and complete shock took over his body. Nonetheless, he jumped up ready to fight again; the hatchet firm in his hand. Through the intense pain of the headache he tried to form coherent thoughts. How can I destroy the taproot? How can I get to it with my hatchet? He started to pray again.

143

"I fear no evil. I fear no..."

It was too late. The plant had seized the opportunity the moment Bulk let down his guard. Now it laughed with victory; eerie, evil laughter, high-pitched, inhuman sounds piercing his ears. Bulk's headache became unbearable and the last lucid thought he had was of the skeletal he had found in the cave so many years ago. He now knew why the man had died with the hatchet by his side. The man had tried to destroy the plant the same way he had tried to and lost. And Bulk knew he was going to die. The hatchet dropped out of his hand, hitting the rock floor with a loud clanking thud. He knew it was all over.

Chapter Twelve

B ut Satan's Angel was vengeful. He knew he would get Bulk's soul in the end, but a simple death like jumping off the cliff wouldn't do for the one who had dared to butcher him. No, he was not through playing with him yet. He had the man's actions totally under control; every muscle, every bone, every nerve would do what he asked of it and he would ask a lot, a whole lot.

Bulk had become a pawn; a pawn in a death game. His movements didn't belong to him any longer, but yet, he managed to climb up the rope. He reached the plateau and pulled the rope up so he could take it with him. His body walked toward the mare, who snorted with fear, not recognizing the person approaching her. His movements were stiff, his face a frozen mask and his glowing blood-red eyes were staring out of his rigid head. The horse danced and sidestepped nervously as the stranger tied the rope to the saddle and climbed on. Bulk rode down the path, then turned and headed toward the furthest corner of the lake. It was an isolated deep part of the lake where once in a while he would come and fish in solitude, smoking his pipe. He had even brought Ludwig here to teach him how to fish, but had been careful to keep an eye on him so he wouldn't fall off the large boulder into the deep water below. But today he had no thoughts, just watched what was happening to him from the inside out; his heart beating fast and hard in his chest, the only thing in his body not controlled by the evil force inside of him. He climbed off the horse, but didn't tie the mare to his usual tree, just grabbed the rope off the saddle. He watched without thoughts how the horse galloped off into the distance. Satan's Angel had to hurry now. People would search for the man. He guided the man toward the lake, walking stiff and cumbersome, keeping his eyes on the rocky ground.

Bulk didn't even know what he was looking for until his body bent down and picked up a huge odd looking rock and carried it to the edge of the large boulder. He tied the rope around the odd rock, took out his knife and cut the rope shorter and then tied the other end around his own ankle. He looked around one more time; a man with a mask on his face, a man trapped inside his own body, a man with no way out. Bulk picked up the rock and jumped into the deep, shadowy water; his blood-red eyes slowly being extinguished by the cold clutch of death.

The mare galloped home and arrived at the barn the same time Hank came outside Bulk's cabin. He had needed his brother's help, but hadn't found him home. Loretta told him that he had left early that morning, not telling her where he was going. They both were shocked when they saw the rider less mare coming to a stop in front of the barn and ran over to where the mare was dancing, foaming at the mouth, snorting with fear.

"Something happened to Bulk!" Loretta shouted, dread filling her being.

"You really don't know where he went this morning?" Hank shouted at her. Loretta couldn't answer; her body too numb with shock. She shook her head, tears running down her face.

"Something awful has happened to him. I feel it," she moaned. "Find him Hank. Please find him and bring him home."

Hank organized a small search party. The riders split up, each man looking in a different place in the valley. Hank himself rode up the path to Pitch Fork Mountain having an inkling that his brother might be there. Maybe the mare had torn herself loose from the tree Bulk always tight her to? He arrived at the plateau, but didn't see Bulk's rope around the boulder. Where was his rope? Maybe it came loose and he now waited for help down below? He tied his horse to the tree and walked to the edge of the cliff.

"Bulk, are you down there? Bulk, can you hear me?" Hank yelled down over the edge and listened, but didn't receive a reply. "Bulk... Bulk!"

Something inside of him told him to climb down and investigate to make sure his brother wasn't there. He used his own rope and tied it to the boulder. What he found inside the cave made him stagger with disbelief. The plant lay destroyed at his feet; branches and leaves looking wilted and dead, scattered around the ground. But where was Bulk? Hank called his name several times, but only heard the answer of his own echo. Then his foot hit something. Hank looked down and saw the metal head of a hatchet lying on the ground. He picked it up and instantly recognized it as his brother's. His initials B.J.H. were carved lengthwise into the wood and the handle was covered with worn-out rawhide. It was Bulk's favorite hatchet, more lightweight and shorter than the other one he owned. He would never have left it behind. Never. Frustrated he looked around, not sure what to do when he heard the fine trilling sounds. Even though the sounds were beautifully composed, an eerie feeling went through him as a cold breeze swept through the cave touching his skin. He sensed that his inner essence was stroked by evil and he wanted to shake it off, but couldn't. He moved closer to the sound and realized that it came out of the rock where the plant had grown. Hank bent down on one knee and moved several dead branches out of the way and then he saw the crevice. Horrified he watched how little roots wiggled and grew in length, multiplying rapidly from a dark brown taproot. It survived and is healing, he thought. What is going on?

The large taproot disappeared deep inside the crevice, with no end in sight and the roots squirmed and danced to the dramatic trilling sounds of violins and trumpets, the music resembling a celebration march. It was a dramatic tune, catching his ears, and then he heard the laughter, like the plant noticed his interest in the melody and teased him with it. How can a plant make this kind of music, he thought? Is it possible?

You like this melody? You do? I will whisper it into a man's ear one day and make him very famous.

How come he could hear the plant? Was he going crazy or just imagining these thoughts? Shocked he straightened back up. He heard the laughter again, dark and sinister.

I'm inside of you now and there is nothing you can do about it, and I will stay inside of you until the day you die.

"Nooo!" Hank screamed and jumped up and looked all around him to fight whoever was present, but, there was nobody, only this nauseating gut feeling that evil was inside of him. And then, all of a sudden, he understood and he knew that his brother was dead…dead because he had dared to fight the plant.

Yes, I killed him. He tried to destroy me, but he failed. Come back next year and I will be as I've always been; potent, powerful, majestic and invincible. Don't dare to cross me. I own you now. I am your new Master.

Hank turned away, nausea ripping through his body. He was immobilized by the weakness of his body and realized the magnitude of the power the plant held over him now. He was defenseless to do anything about it and moreover didn't understand how it was possible. How could a plant control a human being's mind? But then he remembered what Bulk had told him long time ago; that he could feel the plant's anger and that he knew what the plant was thinking. Bulk was dead now… and he was alive. He had been selected to carry on the job of protector of the plant, against his will. And he remembered that

Bulk had told him that the plant was Satan himself. He stood up and screamed into the cave from the bottom of his lungs.

"No… No… No!" he screamed over and over again until his strength was spent. His frustration and anger slowly turning into determination to defeat the evilness inside this cave, but first he had to find his brother. He had to find his body and bring him home to Loretta, and only then would he deal with the plant. He would resist the evil presence inside of him for now and later finish what his brother had started. First, he would give Bulk a Christian burial. It was the last thing he could do for him.

Laughter followed him through the dark tunnel into the bright opening. As Hank closed his eyes to the intense sunlight, he whispered to himself, "How can the sun still shine this brilliant when my world has collapsed?" He knew he would come back.

They searched the canyon below, but couldn't find Bulk's body. Two days later one of the searchers found part of Bulk's rope on the boulder next to the lake. Hank recognized the knots in the rope at once and knew that he would find Bulk at the bottom of the lake. He took his buckskin clothes off and dove into the cold mountain water and found his brother weighted down by the heavy rock; little fish nibbling on his face. Hank took out his knife and cut the rope, then grabbed his brother around the torso and brought him up to the surface.

The funeral was held two days later. Loretta was devastated by the knowledge that she was alone now and miscarried her unborn child the same day Bulk was laid to rest. She couldn't understand why Bulk had killed himself. There were no answers for her and Hank was tight lipped about the whole situation, mourning his brother harder than he had ever mourned anybody. The valley residents were stunned. They had lost two good men in such a short time. Bulk was laid to rest next to his still-born son. The small valley graveyard now consisted of three suicide victims, but only Hank was aware of it.

Hank had found the ledger he had given to Bulk so many years ago, in his own wooden trunk the day of the funeral. The book was tucked inside Hank's good jacket. He must have known that I would wear this to his funeral, Hank thought as he picked the book up and opened it. A piece of paper with Bulk's handwriting lay inside.

It read:

Hank, the plant is Satan's Angel come to earth to collect souls. I have been his helper for too long. I can't do it any longer. It needs to end today, before another person commits suicide. I have decided to destroy the plant and if I succeed you will never find this ledger. God willing, I will survive. If I don't, please take care of Loretta and the children. Be reassured that I would never commit suicide on my own accord. God help me. God help us all! My faith will carry me through.

Don't follow in my footsteps. The responsibility lies with you now. Read this ledger and you will understand everything.

Bulk Horswell, September 23, in the year of our Lord 1771

Hank read every single entry Bulk made into the ledger and finally began to understand. Everything started to make sense to him. He realized that he was the only one who knew where the plant grew now. It was he who would be used by Satan's Angel to do his bidding.

He returned to the cave one week later. Bulk's hatchet was lying in the same spot he left it in. He picked it up and threw it into the canyon below then fell to his knees sobbing. He sobbed for several minutes, crumbled into a heap, his face close to the hard ground. He grieved terribly for his brother, felt the pain of his loss deep inside. If Bulk could have just told him what he had planned to do. Maybe together they could have accomplished what he alone wasn't able to do. But then again, perhaps both of them would have died. It was probably the reason Bulk kept it a secret from him.

Suddenly Hank became aware of the fine trilling sounds coming from the roots of the plant, like it was trying to soothe him, trying to make him feel better. He lifted his head and stared at it. He was now the Senior Harvester, the new protector of the plant and people in the valley. He knew his choice of killing the plant had been taken away from him. Reading the ledger he understood now that he would die if he tried to. There would always be something left of the taproot. No, he would keep the plant safe; the alternative too horrible to imagine. His brother had asked him to take care of his family and he would honor his last wish. Bulk had made a fatal mistake. Hank couldn't afford to do the same. In his heart he knew Bulk had done the right thing by trying to save the souls of all the people in the valley, but Hank wasn't that brave.

When he reached his cabin he opened the ledger and made his first entry, tears smudging the ink.

Bulk Horswell – September 1771 – He was my brother and died a hero. He tied a rock to his leg and drowned himself in the valley's lake after trying to destroy the plant with his hatchet.

Hank also noted that he was now the new Senior Harvester and was going to offer Leroy Theiss the position as the new Junior Harvester. And then he made one final entry for the day.

If anybody is brave enough in the future to follow in my brother's footsteps... destroy the tap....

A severe headache assaulted him. His temples throbbed to the point of explosion. He stopped writing…and closed the ledger and the headache disappeared and he knew why.

Chapter Thirteen

June 18, 2009

"Look, over there. What a beautiful lake!" Erica exclaimed excitedly, pointing to the little blue lake down below. "Look, there are several paddleboats, a picnic table and even a wooden platform in the middle of the lake."

Cotton looked to his left and saw the beautiful little valley coming into view.

"I hope the house is within walking distance of the lake," he answered. "It would be nice to throw a hook in and catch supper."

"Mom, can we go swimming?" five-year-old Lucas piped up from the back seat. "Please mom. I was good the whole trip, wasn't I?" he continued pleadingly.

"You know we have to unpack our stuff and wait for the movers to show up. Your swimsuit is in one of the boxes in the moving truck. Don't worry, the movers promised to be here soon," Erica answered him. "I have a feeling the lake will become our favorite hangout."

Cotton drove down the gravel road and turned left at the row of mailboxes. The road angled down toward the lake.

"Look dad, we're going to go over a bridge," Lucas shouted excitedly. "And there is a waterfall where the water comes out from underneath it."

"We're driving over a small dam," Cotton replied. "That waterfall over there is where they regulate the water coming out of the lake, depending on how much water is in it."

He rolled the windows down and drove slowly over the dam, giving each person time to take in the idyllic look. Cotton looked down to his left side where a steep drop of forty feet opened up to a luscious green pasture with a gurgling stream running through the middle, splashing over rocks and curving around large boulders. Three horses grazed in the distance, their long tales swatting invisible insects.

"Man, this valley looks peaceful, almost too good to be true," Cotton mumbled to himself. They reached the end of the dam and a fork in the road made him stop the car. "What was the name of the street we have to turn on?"

"Aspen Lane, it's right there, turn right here and then left on Pineknot Drive," Erica pointed to the small green road sign. They followed the road alongside the lake until they found Pineknot Drive. Cotton turned left and counted three houses.

"Oh, my goodness, it's beautiful. And you can see the lake from here. Brad was right when he told us we wouldn't be disappointed," Erica told him excitedly.

"I told you we could count on him. This house will be perfect for us, you'll see, and Lucas will love it here. This is exactly where I want my son to grow up. This place is ideal. He can run and play outside, learn how to drive a four-wheeler, learn to ski and we will go on long hikes and be out in nature every day. I love it, and the weather is so pleasant, not as hot and humid as in Texas and no crime to worry about either. This is such a small community. I bet we'll know every person in this valley within the first month of being here."

She gave him a big smile. "You're right about everything. I never expected it to be this pretty."

Cotton turned onto the gravel drive and parked in front of the detached garage to the left side of the house.

"Come on, get out of the car, I can't wait to see what the inside of the house looks like."

All three of them got out. Dino, Lucas's Golden Retriever, ran down the drive then turned around to bark at them, totally excited to finally be out of the vehicle.

"Come over here, Dino!" Lucas shouted and ran toward the house, the dog racing after him. Cotton and Erica laughed then walked hand in hand up the small incline toward the wooden stairs leading up to the front door.

"I have to get used to this. I never lived in the mountains before, never lived in a log house where you have to climb stairs to get to the front door," she told him overwhelmed. Together they climbed the stairs to the porch which continued around three sides of the house.

"Oh, wow. You can see the lake from up here even better," Erica exclaimed, leaning against the wood railing, taking in the spectacular view. Cotton searched his pocket for the house key the real estate lady had given him. He put it into the lock and opened the door.

"Come on in," he told her, then entered a small foyer which opened to two sides. A large kitchen was to the right and the living room with a nice stone fireplace to the left. Erica followed him inside, hearing Lucas's footsteps on the stairs. The kitchen was modern with oak cabinets and a large kitchen island.

"It even has granite counter tops," she exclaimed.

"It was remodeled before the previous owners moved away," Cotton told her.

"Why did they remodel the house and then move away?" Erica asked, curious how anybody could leave such a wonderful home behind. "It doesn't make any sense to me. Do you know why they moved, Cotton?" she asked him.

"I do know, but do we have to talk about it right now?"

"Why? Did a murder or something like that happen in this house?" she teased her husband.

"No, but I didn't want to spoil this moment by someone else's loss," he answered her.

"What happened, Cotton? I want to know. Tell me."

"The family moved away because their twenty-year-old son killed himself on one of the mountains around here. He put a hose on his car's exhaust pipe and fed it into the inside of his car."

"Jeez, that's horrible." Erica was quiet for a while, unable to imagine what that would do to a family. "Why did he do it?" she asked.

"Nobody knows. That was the worst for the family, not knowing why he did it. Brad told me that the parents couldn't stand living in this valley any longer."

Cotton looked at Erica who looked shocked at the sad news. It was a somber moment and he regretted telling her, but he promised years ago that he wouldn't lie to her again and he wasn't going to start today. They had the biggest fight of their marriage back in 2004 when he came home from Iraq. He was stationed eleven months in Baghdad and was waiting for his leave at Camp Stryker, which was part of Baghdad International Airport. Several days later he was sent to South Forward Operating Base, but continued to lie to Erica that he was still at Camp Stryker, that the worst thing which could happen to him there was that he could cut himself shaving. He continued to lie to her for three more months not wanting to worry her, while he was on patrols for route clearance, where IED's were a daily occurrence. She was livid when she found out.

Lucas came running into the room followed by Dino, interrupting the sad moment.

"Where is my room?" he asked them excitedly and the awkward moment was broken by his enthusiasm.

"Well, let's see if we can find it," Erica told him and took his hand. Together they climbed to the second floor and peeked into the three bedrooms, one of them clearly was the master bedroom.

"Well, you get to pick one of these two. Which one do you like better?" Cotton asked him. Lucas walked importantly into both rooms and looked out the windows.

"I like the view out of this room better. I can see the lake. I want this one," he told them.

"All right, this one is yours. All we have to do now is wait for the moving truck to get here. Why don't you go and get your luggage out of the car and take it to your room. I want to check out our bedroom with mom, all right?" Cotton told him as he took Erica's hand and led her into the large master bedroom. A double door led outside to a beautiful patio. They stepped outside and looked at the panoramic view. It was breathtaking with several mountain tops visible in the far distance, some covered with trees, others with solid rock faces and tall cliffs.

"Look at that mountain over there," Erica told him excitedly pointing west. "Doesn't that look like a pitchfork sticking up into the sky the way those cliffs look?"

"Brad told me that the tallest mountain in this area is called Pitchfork Mountain, so that must be the one. It sure looks beautiful…majestic."

"I might never want to move from here," Erica told him, facing him.

"It will be a while before I get transferred again. Let's not worry about it for now," Cotton told her and kissed her passionately.

"I just appreciate that we don't have to live on base. And I also appreciate that you're willing to make the one hour trip to work every day."

"I never liked living on base, you know that. One military base looks like the next. You've seen one, you've seen them all. Just two more years and I have twenty years in. Maybe, I'll retire and we'll settle down right here in this valley," Cotton told her.

"You never mentioned that before. Would you really do that? You love what you do so much."

"Why not? I could always find something else to do, especially if we like it here and want to stay. Let's play it by ear." He nibbled on her ear creating the most tantalizing sensations. "Talking about ears, I really like yours," he whispered, producing goosebumps all over her neck.

"Talking about ears," she retorted back, pulling herself away. "I think I hear the moving truck." She turned around and looked from the patio toward the loud rumbling of a diesel motor. Sure enough, a large moving truck was just crossing the dam and would be at their house in less than five minutes.

"Let's go downstairs. I think it's going to be a very busy afternoon."

And it was. Erica had her hands full, delegating the three movers to the correct rooms and telling them where to place each piece of furniture and the boxes with all their belongings. Lucas proudly showed them where he wanted them to put his bed and started to follow them around until the bookshelves were put against the wall in his room, then he unloaded the box filled with his tractors, his prize possessions, and placed them on the bookshelves. When that was done his interest in unpacking faded and he ran outside to play with Dino. Erica tried to keep an eye on her son and the movers at the same time and looked over the patio to yell at Lucas not to leave the yard. Cotton was helping one of the movers put the king size bed frame back together and shouting to her about what box he had packed all his tools in.

Four hours later the three of them sat exhausted around the kitchen table eating peanut butter and jelly sandwiches. They all agreed that they were too tired to go swimming.

Chapter Fourteen

It was going to be a warm day; the sun was lingering softly on Erica's sleeping face. Lucas came running into the master bedroom and jumped on the bed, his small body already dressed in blue shorts and his favorite Indiana Jones tee-shirt.

"Get up you guys. Remember that you promised to go down to the lake swimming with me today. Wake up, Dad."

Erica opened her eyes sleepily.

"Is it morning already?" she asked, pulling the pillow over her head, blocking the sunshine which irritated her eyes.

"Yes, Mom. Come on, get up. You promised, remember? Last night at the table," Lucas pleaded and tried to pull the pillow away from her face. "Dad, help me. Mom won't let go of the pillow."

"She won't let go of the pillow?" Cotton repeated still drunk with sleep. The next thing he felt was Lucas jumping on his back, making him groan from the impact.

"Get up, Dad. I mean it," Lucas insisted with a surprisingly strong and tough voice.

Cotton laughed out loud, hearing his son sound that demanding was unusual.

"All right, I'll get up," he said knowing full well that he wouldn't get another minute of sleep, not with his son being this excited about going swimming in the lake for the first time.

"Let's pull Mom's blanket off together," he told Lucas and together they pulled and tugged at her blanket until she relinquished it laughing and squealing, kicking her legs in protest.

"Let's go swimming right now," Lucas demanded.

"Honey, nobody in this family is going swimming until they have a good breakfast in their belly, all right," Erica answered as she walked toward the bathroom. "Go downstairs and watch Saturday cartoons until we're showered."

"Why do you have to take a stupid shower when you go swimming later on anyway? All you have to do is put a swimsuit on, Mom," he answered her back as he slowly climbed down the steps, not comprehending his mom's way of thinking.

"He is right, you know," Cotton told her as he grabbed her from behind and placed a soft kiss on her neck.

"Right or not," she mumbled leaning into him, "I need a hot shower in the mornings to wake up."

"Strange, so do I," Cotton answered, then closed the bathroom door behind them.

An hour and a half later they were walking down the path toward the lake. It wasn't even eleven in the morning yet, but several people were already there enjoying themselves. Three children were splashing and squealing in the water while adults sat around the picnic table visiting with each other.

Cotton held Erica's hand as they walked across the dam toward the grassy beach area on the other side. She was wearing her black bikini under her summer dress, but wished that she had put her one-piece swimsuit on, not expecting for anyone to be swimming this early. When they reached the picnic area they greeted the people sitting at the table.

Cotton introduced his wife, Lucas and himself to the group as the newest members of the valley.

"We just moved here yesterday. Lucas was dying to go swimming as soon as he saw the lake," he said to the group. A tall man around forty stood up and shook his hand.

"My name is Adam Fletcher and this is my wife Robin, and the red haired boy over there splashing around in the water is our five-year-old son Logan." Cotton shook his hand and liked him instantly. He had a firm handshake, almost painful. They were about the same age and he could tell that Adam was athletic, maybe an inch or two shorter than himself. The man sitting next to Adam also stood up and reached for Cotton's hand.

"Jack Rutter. If you ever need dirt work done, I'm your man. I live over there. He pointed to a nice log house, the closest one to the lake with a beautiful patio. I saw the moving truck yesterday when I drove by. I'm glad somebody finally bought the house. It's been sitting empty for too long, you know," he told him, ready to explain the circumstances if Cotton showed any interest and was willing to listen.

"Yes, I know," Cotton answered to stem any further discussion of the former owner's tragedy and then added with a smile. "Nice to meet you, Jack."

He was in his fifties and looked somewhat rough, his face extremely weathered, a small scar across the left side of his mouth. "My wife and I have been living in this valley for over twenty years now. You couldn't find a better place to live," Jack replied before sitting down.

The fourth person at the table was a young woman of no more than thirty years. She was wearing a red bikini and a smile on her face. She waved at the newcomers.

"Nice to have you in the valley," she said. "My name is Rachel Young and I live on the north side of the lake right over there," she pointed to a Cedar house halfway up the mountain. "You will find out everything about every person living in this valley within a week, so I might as well tell you. I'm divorced and live with my dog Tiger and on rare occasions my boyfriend Mark sleeps over." She laughed an infectious laugh and the whole group joined in. The ice was broken and Cotton and Erica sat down at the long table. Erica ended up sitting next to Robin and Rachel. They seemed very nice to her.

"Can I go in the water now, Mom?" Lucas asked her impatiently, standing next to her, pulling at her dress to get her attention.

"Yes, you can. Do you want to wear your floaties?" she asked.

"Mom, floaties are for babies. I'm not a baby anymore," he told her.

"Of course you're not," she replied. "But don't go into the deep part. Don't swim out too far."

"Okay," he answered and ran toward the water. Dino followed him and stood at the edge of the water watching Lucas. Erica noticed a second dog, a good looking Golden Retriever, sleeping next to the paddleboat, now stretching and walking toward Dino. She jumped up anxiously, not knowing if the dogs would like each other and get into a fight.

"Cotton, there is another dog. Do you think they're going to get along?"

"That's my dog," Rachel told them. "Yeah, that's Tiger. I've had him for six years. He's pretty mellow and won't hurt a fly. What's your dog's name?"

"Dino," Erica replied as she watched the dogs get acquainted with each other, at the same time keeping an eye on Lucas splashing in the water.

"It's so cold," he yelled, but kept on going deeper. Erica looked at Cotton and he understood her look.

"Wait for me, Lucas!" he called after his son. He took his shirt off and ran after him plunging deep into the cold water. Lucas squealed with delight and soon both were splashing and laughing in the cold water together. A deep feeling of being in a good place came over her. Yeah, I think we're going to like it here she thought as she sat back down.

"This is really nice. I feel like I'm on vacation. The lake is so beautiful with all the mountains in the back ground. How many people live in this valley?" she asked the two women.

"Just one hundred twenty-four, not counting you three…yet. In one more month it's going to be one hundred twenty-five. Sarah David is scheduled for her C-section," Robin answered.

"Do you have a home owner's association here?"

"No, once a year each homeowner pays eighty dollars and we get the lake stocked with fish or buy new gravel for the upkeep of the roads. Only home owners are allowed to fish in the lake. When something needs fixing we just divide the cost among the owners, like when we built the floating wooden platform over there in the lake. It was a community project and a lot of fun. Now we all enjoy it. We built this picnic table the same way. And the paddleboats, kayaks and canoes can all be used by everyone. Everybody helps when they can, that is what makes living here so nice. We all look out for each other," Robin explained to her.

"Who do the two girls in the water belong to?" Erica asked.

"They belong to Sarah and Lee David. They live on the south side of the lake. Identical twins as you can tell. They are eight and a hand-full. They also have another younger daughter who is five. Sarah is going to be here shortly. I'm giving her a break and keeping an eye on them for her. She looks ready to burst! She wanted a boy this time but is carrying another girl. She's a brave woman, if you ask me…four girls. Poor Lee…he has to live with five women in the house," Rachel explained and laughed.

"Well, I'm going in. Are you two coming?" Robin asked them both as she slipped out of her short pants and sleeveless top.

"Let's do it," Rachel answered her, then both women looked at Erica for an answer. Erica laughed out loud. She had the feeling she just made two good friends.

"All right, let's do it," she answered and took off her summer dress. All three walked to the edge of the lake and stepped into the refreshing cold water. The ground was soft and squishy with the occasional rocks. They waded out together then took the plunge and swam to the middle of the lake where the wooden platform was anchored. A little white plastic ladder, attached to one side of the wood, made it easy for them to climb up. All three lay down on their stomachs. Delicious goosebumps covered Erica's skin. She thought it felt heavenly; better than getting an expensive spa treatment. It felt wonderful to lie on the hot wood as her back slowly dried from the intensity of the sun. She heard Cotton and Lucas splashing and having fun in the distance as she closed her eyes for a short retreat. Yes, she definitely could get used to this. She loved to swim and this lake would give her the opportunity again to swim on a daily basis during the hot summer months. She was extremely happy that once again she had water in her life. Life was good; she loved this valley and the people living in it, at least the ones she had met so far.

Chapter Fifteen

T he weekend had been wonderful. They had met neighbors and residents of the valley and every one made them feel welcome. The people were down to earth and friendly and offered their help willingly. All the advice they received was overwhelming. They now knew where to find the best parks and playgrounds, where the best restaurants in the city were located, where the best fishing spots could be found, the nicest nature walks, the longest hiking trails, and that for a $10.00 fee you could get a permit to cut firewood in the national forest surrounding them. They had received two invitations for parties, but the best thing of all was that Lucas found a friend his own age. He had really bonded with Logan, Robin's and Adam's son, and they lived just around the corner, not even a five minute walk away.

Cotton's first day of work arrived the following Monday. He dressed in his uniform and kissed his sleeping wife goodbye at five in the morning, hoping that the traffic would be good once he hit the highway fifteen miles north of the valley' s pass. He gave himself an extra fifteen minutes, but hoped that it would take under an hour to get to work. Being late for his first day wasn't an option.

Erica woke up three hours later, the sun shining in her face. She made a mental note that getting curtains or mini blinds for the master bedroom window was a top priority.

"I have to buy a window cover today," she mumbled to herself, as if saying it out loud would make it happen right then and there. She turned her head into the pillow and hid her face underneath the covers. But then she thought of the coffee waiting in the kitchen and stretched and got up. She wanted to drink her coffee on the patio and enjoy the view. School was out and Lucas was still sleeping. She walked quietly passed his room and tip-toed downstairs. Cotton was such an angel. He had refilled the coffee pot for four cups and all she had to do, was to push the on button. She contemplated what she and Lucas would eat for breakfast, as she walked barefoot to the refrigerator; waffles with syrup or a bagel with cream cheese and strawberry jelly? She pulled out the frozen waffles and put two of them into the toaster.

Armed with coffee and waffles drenched with syrup she walked outside. Dino followed her, excitedly waving his tail. Erica sat down in the comfortable wooden chair, propped her feet up on the railing and started to eat her waffle, all the while keeping a close eye on Dino who ran downstairs and was inspecting the surrounding area, finding just the perfect spot to do his business.

She sipped her coffee thinking about how lucky they were to have found this house. They had definitely hit the jack pot with this one. She was used to moving from one state to another every couple of years, being first an Army brat and then an Army wife. She had married Cotton twelve years ago and had lived in Texas, Georgia, North Carolina, Germany, South Carolina, and Colorado and now she was here in the mountains. Of all the places she had ever lived, this was certainly the nicest place. She was used to being by herself when Cotton was on his tour of duty in Afghanistan or Iraq and knew she could handle the stress it brought to her, watching the news every day as soon as she woke up in the morning to see if any troops had been killed.

To actually think of a future where Cotton didn't have to risk his life every day would be a dream come true. The thing was, he had really surprised her when he mentioned that he might quit after reaching twenty years in the military. She thought she would never hear him say those words; that he liked to settle down and pursue another line of work. Could he really give it all up? He loved the adrenaline rushes he received from doing his job. It was just too much to hope for and she realized, from her own experience, how hard it was to give up a job where the adrenaline rush was a daily occurrence.

Before they had Lucas, she worked at SeaWorld in San Antonio training Killer Whales, but now she was happy to be a stay at home mom and enjoyed every minute of it.

She remembered the adrenaline rush she got every time she entered the water with the huge three ton mammal, using the orca as a surfboard, surfing through the water in front of a huge crowd. The incredible strength the whale had, pushing her in a long underwater dive and then propelling her thirty feet into the air; the feeling was indescribable. The killer whale would beach himself in front of a crowd, just to be rewarded with a couple of fish.

Her one-on-one relationships with the mammals had been wonderful. They were so smart and communicated with her in a way which made her never want to quit her job. But when she found out that she was pregnant, everything changed. She wasn't going to take any chances getting hurt. Even the smallest miss-step with such an enormous mammal could have caused her to miscarry. Sure, she missed the adrenaline rushes she received from training and performing with the orcas, but living with Cotton was an adrenaline rush all by itself and she didn't regret making the decision of quitting her job. But all this happened a long time ago. No, being the mom of Lucas was much more important and rewarding to her.

This move had been particular hard on her, not because of all the friends she had left behind, but because of the friends Lucas had left behind, his first friends. He had cried when he had to say goodbye to them and it had tugged at her heartstrings and brought back memories of her own youth. She didn't want him to suffer like she had every time her father had relocated to another base. For that reason alone did she dread moving to such an isolated place, but now Lucas had made a new friend and she felt better. She was happy. She was like a lioness protecting her cub, and no matter what happened, her son's happiness came first, and he was happy, and that's was all that mattered to her. This valley was making her happy. Maybe her dream of settling down would become true after all.

Erica took a sip of the hot black coffee and another bite of her waffle. Her imagination was running wild with her; a future in this valley, a permanent place to call home, Cotton's retirement from the military, maybe even another child, wouldn't all that be wonderful? It sounded too good to be true. She yearned for a normal home life with a husband who came home from work every day and didn't have to leave for months on end. For heaven's sake, Cotton even missed the birth of his son when Lucas was born two months premature. Cotton had arrived after the birth, after all the drama was settled, but she had been so happy to see him that she really didn't care. She loved him and would follow him to the end of the world if she had to. And this valley was far better than the end of the world.

Erica sat on the porch sipping her hot coffee reminiscing about the past. They had fallen in love during the first hour that they met. It was instant attraction the minute they sized each other up. And they did that without words, just looks and glances for the first forty minutes, the time it took to walk from an airport gate to the luggage area to pick-up the bags and then to the parking garage.

She had met him through Sandy, her best girlfriend since fifth grade, who had begged her to drive with her to the airport to pick up her boyfriend Andy who was on a two week leave from the military. Well, as it happened Andy had invited Cotton along and it was to both girls surprise when the two handsome soldiers walked out of the gate together. Erica had noticed the tall, dark handsome man instantly and hoped against all odds that it wasn't Andy. And it wasn't and she felt like she had been handed a present.

Sandy and Andy ran toward each other and hugged and kissed for an embarrassing long time while Cotton and she stood across from each other staring into each other's eyes, sizing each other up. He was tall, at least six foot two with dark short hair barely half an inch long. His broad shoulders and strong chest were in stark contrast to his narrow waist, and his butt…even in his uniform was something to look at. And then there were his hazel eyes; the softest eyes she had ever looked into. When Sandy and Andy joined them, Sandy introduced them.

"Erica, this is Andy and Cotton. Andy and Cotton, this is Erica, my best friend." They all said hello to each other and that was that. Sandy and Andy were too much involved with each other to worry about the two of them, so they walked next to each other and followed the couple in front of them to the luggage pickup area, not talking; just incredibly aware of the person next to them. She thought he was good looking, but she didn't want to be the one to make the first move so she acted aloof.

They stood next to the conveyer belt until the bell rang, staring straight ahead at the luggage being sent down the opening and falling onto the conveyer belt below, like it was just another boring evening at the airport. They waited patiently next to each other for the luggage to arrive and then she watched him lift the two heavy military duffel bags off the belt and carried them toward where Sandy and Andy were waiting, still carrying on like two long lost love birds, kissing and talking and not paying attention to anything happening around them.

He handed Andy his bag and they again walked behind the couple to the VW in the parking garage. The constant talking and laughing from the couple in front of them was in stark disparity to their own silence. And then they were in the parking garage and got into the car. Erica sat in the back seat behind the driver's seat expecting the two guys to sit in the front due to their long legs and the car being so small, but Cotton walked next to her and simply said: "move over," and she did. She never was more aware of a person in her life than she was during that ride, sitting next to Cotton in the small back seat of the VW.

Her heart was racing and her palms in her lap were sweating and she hoped to God that he didn't notice. Andy and Sandy were talking ninety miles an hour in the front seat of the car. And then they looked at each other and Cotton gave her that crooked smile of his, which took her breath away and sent shivers down her spine, and that was that. It was the beginning of their life together. That special smile of his, which he gave her many times since then, and it still had the same effect on her now, as it did back then. She had looked at him and gave him a smile of her own and he reached over and took her hand off her lap and held it in his warm, soft hands for the rest of the ride. They had gotten into the car strangers, but stepped out of the car as a couple in love without ever having said one word to each other. They held hands the rest of the night and spent every day of the next two weeks together. Just three short months later they were married by the Justice of the Peace in the same little town.

Erica remembered the wonderful times they had dating, drinking the rest of her coffee. Mornings like this brought out the happiness inside of her and gratitude of how fortunate she was to be married to him. Every day with Cotton and Lucas was a gift from God, she thought, as she savored the fresh morning breeze and the singing of the birds in the nearby trees.

The patio door opened up behind her and a sleepy-eyed Lucas came barefoot outside, still wearing his Captain America pajamas. Oh, how she loved this little munchkin; a little replica of Cotton. Yes, she thought, a little baby girl would be all right with her.

"I'm hungry, Mom," was the first thing Lucas said and jumped onto her lap. "Can I eat that waffle?" he asked her, pointing to the untouched second waffle, sitting on the plate on the railing.

"Of course you can," she answered him, "but first I need my good morning Mom kiss."

He reached his little face up to her and placed a kiss on her lips. "Good morning, Mom," he whispered, his soft, sweet smelling night breath engulfing her. How she loved these mornings when he kissed her. Pretty soon he would be too old to climb on her lap and she would miss being that close to him. Yes, she and Cotton should have another baby, she thought, and this time he would be home for the birth. She decided to talk to him when he came home that evening. She was thirty-two now, still young enough to have a baby and he was thirty-nine. She reached for the waffle and handed it to Lucas as he leaned back against her chest and started to eat, both of them quiet, following Dino's movements down below. When he finished his waffle he sat up straight and looked at her.

"Did you know I made a new friend?" he asked her. "His name is Logan and he lives one street over."

"Yes, I saw you two having a lot of fun. I talked to his mom for quite a while," Erica answered him. "Did you know that he is only one month older than you are and you're going to the same grade when school starts up in September?"

"Can I play with him today?" Lucas asked her, looking expectantly into her face. "Please, Mom. I really like him. Maybe he can come over and play with me in my room for a while?"

"That's fine with me, but it's still too early to call him. Let's get our chores done first and then I will call his mom, all right?"

"Yeah, first I'm going to get dressed and then I'll…"

"Remember, first you have to feed Dino. It's your job to take care of him."

"Yes, Mom." He jumped off her lap. "Dino!" he yelled too close to her ear. Dino heard him and came running up the steps, excited to see him. "Good boy," he told the dog affectionately. "It's time for breakfast, Dino." He petted him behind his ears and opened the screen door to let the dog inside the house.

Cotton called Erica half an hour later checking in with her and asking her about her plans for the day. They chatted for a while and he told her to expect him home by six that evening. Shortly after she hung up the phone rang again and she assumed that he had forgotten to tell her something. She was surprised to hear Robin's voice on the phone.

"What are you two up to?" she asked Erica. "Logan and I are planning a picnic by Trout Creek. Do you two want to come along? Logan is dying to play with Lucas."

"Oh, that sounds like a wonderful idea," Erica replied enthusiastically. "Lucas asked me just a minute ago if he could play with Logan today. What can I bring?"

"Well, I have some left over drum sticks in the refrigerator. What do you have?"

"Let's see." She opened the refrigerator and looked inside. "I have potato salad left over from last night's meal and a third of an apple pie."

"Great, sounds like a meal to me. I'll bring some juice for the kids and a couple of Diet Cokes for us."

"All right, I think I have a bag of chips to go with that. What time?" Erica asked her.

"I'll pick you guys up at eleven-thirty. Will that work?"

"Sure does. See you then, Robin," Erica answered and hung up the phone.

Lucas was excited when she told him about the picnic at Trout Creek.

"Mom, do you think Dino can come too?" he asked her concerned.

"Well, you will just have to ask Ms. Robin when she comes to pick us up," Erica told him as she looked at her watch. She still had enough time to start a load of laundry, get the dishwasher unloaded, and maybe unpack a couple more boxes, which were still sitting in the hallway.

She really liked Robin. Robin was four years older than she was, but they both had the same interests and best of all their children were the same age; strange how simple life could be sometimes. They had been in the valley for only three short days and both Lucas and she had made friends.

Punctually at eleven-thirty Robin drove up the drive to their house in her off-road, army-green jeep. She honked the horn and yelled up at them. "Let's go! Time is wasting." Erica and Lucas ran down the steps, Erica carrying the picnic basket, both giddy and excited for their new adventure to come.

"Ms. Robin, can Dino come along?" Lucas asked Robin when they reached the car. "He is my dog."

"Sure," she laughed. "He goes where you go, isn't that the way it's supposed to be?" she asked him.

"Yes, Ma'am," Lucas answered her, grinning from ear to ear.

"I didn't know you owned an off-road jeep. This is so cool. Lucas, climb in and put your seat belt on, Honey. This is going to be fun."

Lucas climbed into the back seat next to Logan, beaming with excitement. Dino sat between the two boys, first licking Logan then licking Lucas.

"Behave yourself, Dino. You're in Ms. Robin's jeep now," Lucas told him with a stern voice. The women looked at each other and smiled. It was going to be a fun day.

They all laughed and screamed, being shaken up by the uneven terrain as Robin headed up the hill and took a small rocky path to the left, which led over the mountain and down on the other side to a beautiful creek.

"This jeep is so much fun," Lucas shouted over the laughing and squealing of the passengers when they were jolted around by the bad road. Twice they drove through a stream of water coming down the mountain and the water splashed up high on the sides of the jeep, making the boys scream with delight when they were splashed.

"Way to go, Mom," Logan shouted at her, proud of his mother's driving skills. It took them thirty minutes to reach the creek, stopping once on the mountain top to view the spectacular sight, before heading back down on the other side to reach the beautiful creek.

Robin parked the jeep alongside the small, narrow dirt road when they reached their destination and all four of them walked down to the creek, blankets and picnic basket in hand. The water was gurgling and splashing and making such inviting sounds that the boys immediately stripped out of their clothes and put on their swim trunks. It was a wonderful warm day. They squealed when their toes touched the icy-cold mountain water, but soon were too involved designing and building a small dam out of all the rocks lying close by to notice the cold water. Erica and Robin sat on the picnic blanket drinking an ice-cold Diet Coke.

"This is just heaven," Erica told her. "How long have you and Adam lived in this valley?"

"It's going to be ten years next month. We were camping at Pike's Campground about twenty miles south of here. We took a small detour home and found this valley by accident and fell in love with it. We sold our house in the city and bought one here after waiting a whole year for someone to sell their house. But it was definitely worth the wait," Robin stated. "I couldn't think of a better place to raise our son. I feel so safe in this community. Everybody is looking out for each other."

"Yeah, I guess everybody wants to stay here. I don't blame them. I would love to stay here forever myself," Erica answered. "There are only...what... about thirty-five or so houses in this valley, right?"

"Thirty-seven to be exact. We bought our house from a woman named Muriel Mass. She wouldn't have sold the house, except that her husband committed suicide and she didn't want to live there after his death. They were both in their fifties, so she was alone after he died."

Isn't that a strange coincidence, Erica thought. It was exactly the same reason why their house had come up for sale. That was just too weird to be true.

"You're kidding me, right?" Erica asked her, stunned by what she just heard.

"Kidding you... about what?" Robin asked her confused.

"About the owner of the house committing suicide? You're kidding me, right?"

"No, I wouldn't kid about something like that. I felt bad about it, but it had nothing to do with the house so why shouldn't we buy it?" she replied, not understanding Erica's question.

"I can't believe it. It's such a weird coincidence."

"What is? You are talking in riddles, Erica."

"Don't you see how strange this is? You bought a house which was sold because the owner committed suicide, right? We did too. Cotton told me that a med student killed himself in his car and that his parents moved away from the valley because of it. We bought their house. It just blows my mind. We both bought a house because of a suicide."

"Oh, my gosh. You're right. That is weird. I had forgotten about Russell Bradley and I don't think much about the former owners of our house any more, but now that you mention it. You're absolutely right. That is a strange coincidence."

They both were quiet thinking about what they had just found out, the laughing of the boys the only sounds in the background. What a somber coincidence.

"How did he kill himself?" Erica asked her after a while.

"Probably the most horrible way I can think of. He cut his leg off with a chainsaw and bled to death in his tool shed. Can you imagine that? How can somebody cut their whole leg off? There was an investigation of course to rule out foul play, but they couldn't find any. They checked out the chainsaw to see if it maybe had gotten stuck, you know malfunctioned because he couldn't turn it off, but it ran fine when they tried it."

"His wife was in shock and had to be hospitalized. She never came back to the house and moved out of state where her sister lived, when she was released. Movers packed up all her belongings and took them to her. She asked a reasonable amount of money for the house and we bought it. That's pretty much the whole story."

"Was he going to cut a tree down?"

"No, that was another strange thing. He told his wife that he wanted to go to town to do business with a man she didn't remember the name of, but instead he walked outside to the shed and started the chainsaw. There was nothing to cut. She checked on him ten minutes later when she saw his car still parked in the driveway and found him inside the shed lying dead in a large pool of blood." Robin stopped talking. She remembered how horrible she felt at the time, then she finished her explanation. "The first thing we did was tear down the small shed and build a beautiful flower bed there instead, kind of in honor of him. It made me feel better about the whole situation that we did that."

"How horrible that must have been for his wife."

"Hey, enough of the sad talk. Let's get the food out. I'm starving," Robin declared. The last thing she wanted to do was to think about that horrible suicide again. It had haunted her for a long time before she could let go of it.

"Sounds great to me, but first I want to put my legs in the creek." Erica jumped up and took her shoes off and then walked carefully over the rocks and sat down on a boulder hanging her feet into the cold water.

"This feels so good!" she shouted to Robin and soon both women were sitting on the boulder with their feet dangling in the water, splashing the boys who squealed with delight.

Later they all sat down on the picnic blanket and ate the drumsticks and potato salad and afterward the boys stuffed themselves with potato chips and a tiny slice of apple pie. It was a wonderful afternoon, but when clouds came up the boys started to shiver from the cold water and they made them get out of the creek and get dressed. Robin drove a different way home and pointed out different hiking trails. She knew these back roads by heart. When they reached her house Robin invited them inside for an ice cream pop and Erica readily agreed. It had been such a beautiful day and the picnic had been so wonderful. She entered Robin's house for the first time and was amazed at her style of decorating.

"Wow, you really did a good job decorating this house. I can tell you like southwestern art. It is all so tastefully done," she told her friend.

"I'll give you a tour of the whole house after the boys get their ice cream pops."

That accomplished, Robin indicated to Erica to follow her.

"You know, most of these oil paintings you see were done by Adam. He loves to paint with oil, mostly during the winter months. She showed Erica the living room, kitchen, master bedroom, Logan's bedroom, where the boys were already engrossed in playing with Legos and then she showed Erica the spare bedroom.

Erica was instantly drawn to an unusual painting hanging over the bed. It was of a beautiful flower in full bloom; black blossoms hanging in abundance from its branches, some tiny green tendrils twisting around the limbs, a full moon and stars shining in the background. The painting was done mostly with subtle dark colors with the exception of the moon and stars, but radiated beauty and serenity. Erica felt like she looked at an intimate scene.

"Wow, that's an awesome painting," Erica remarked. "It's so unusual. I've never seen a plant with black flowers and look at the fine red arteries veining themselves through the black pedals. It gives you the illusion that it's alive. Did Adam paint this one?"

"He sure did. Read the little commemorative inscription on the bottom of the frame," she told Erica. Erica stepped closer and read the small, black lettered words.

The Trumpet Angel
Adam Fletcher, September 2004

"Wow, the picture is mesmerizing, like it doesn't want to release your stare," Erica remarked.

"Adam told me it's his favorite painting of all the paintings he ever did. I remember when he painted it. He was like possessed until he was finished with the painting, spending every spare minute working on it. The picture was all he could talk about during that time. It took him three months to paint."

"I'm certainly impressed by his talent and visualization. The way he combined colors and light is absolutely remarkable."

"You know, he didn't imagine this plant. He saw it with his own eyes. That's how come he had to paint it. He told me he never saw a more beautiful flower than this one."

"You're kidding me? This plant really exists?" Erica exclaimed. "It looks like a fairytale flower."

"Man, you don't want to believe anything I say today, do you?" Robin teased her. "He told me he saw the plant up in the mountains. Let's go back to the kitchen and I'll tell you about the valley's secret," Robin replied. "You're going to find out about it soon enough."

Erica couldn't tell if Robin was joking or serious. The kids were still playing in Logan's room with the Legos Logan had received for his birthday so they had uninterrupted time together. They sat down at the kitchen island and Robin filled both their glasses with ice tea.

"All right, tell me about the valley's secret," Erica teased her, not expecting too much of a mystery.

"Well," Robin started off after drinking half her glass empty. "Adam and I moved to this valley almost ten years ago, right?" Erica nodded her head in agreement. "Well, it was my neighbor, Mrs. Wagner, who first told me about the mysterious flower shortly after we moved here. I first thought she was teasing me, then I thought maybe she was going senile, but in the end she was right. Have you ever heard of an Edelweiss, a flower which grows on the most remote and dangerous mountain cliffs in Europe? I think in the Alps?" Robin asked her.

"Sure, I have heard of the Edelweiss. Many climbers lost their lives picking them from hard to access ledges," Erica replied.

"Well, we kind of have our own version of the Edelweiss right here in this valley. Only two people in the valley know where it grows and the secret is guarded fiercer than the Queen of England."

"You're kidding me, right?" Erica replied, and started laughing at Robin, realizing she had said the same sentence for the third time today.

"No, I'm not. Listen, it gets even better. Once a year the two people who know where the flower grows, climb up to the place in the mountain and harvest the pods of the plant. We call them the pea pods or pods. Inside the pods are three blood-red peas. The legend has it that when they first discovered this plant hundreds of years ago they tried to grow it, but nobody and nothing was able to make the seeds take root. It just couldn't be done. Well, finally someone tried to find out if the little peas were edible and ate them. And guess what happened?" Robin paused.

"What?" Erica asked. "Tell me."

"Well, the peas tasted incredibly sweet, but more important… the peas created the most intense feelings of wellbeing and happiness. People hallucinate when they take them, some of them say that they experience extreme sexual desires so strong… well you get the point. Now comes the good part; once a year the valley celebrates this plant's existence by having a huge party. It's called the Festival of the Pods and is held every August, to be exact every second Saturday in August. The Harvesters, that's what the two people who know where the plant grows are called, go up the mountain and collect the pods and then they divide them out among the people of the valley on the day of the festival, only

179

to users of course. Nobody is forced to participate in the celebrations or become a user. It is a strict affair, only the residents of the valley are invited, nobody else. Every user gets one pod. If you decide to become a user you have to swear never to reveal the secret of the plant and its powerful effects to anyone outside the valley and the most important rule is to never take the pod outside the valley."

Robin stopped talking and Erica looked at her the way Robin had looked when she first found out about the valley's secret. She started laughing.

"I'm a user for eight years now and I can't wait for the Festival of the Pods to get here. It's our favorite day of the year, our favorite weekend. Adam takes off work the following Monday so it turns into a three day celebration for us. I guess you can figure out how the peas affect us. You have to use them within two months, after that they lose their potency."

"And that is the plant Adam painted?" Erica asked her. "He has seen the plant in person then?"

"He was chosen to be the Junior Harvester in 2004 after one of the two Harvesters died. That's when he saw the plant for the first time. He was absolutely taken by its breathtaking beauty and he painted it from memory the following winter."

"Why does he call the painting the Trumpet Angel?"

"I asked him the same thing. He told me that the flower looked like an angel trumpet his mother grew in her yard many years ago. Of course that one was white, but the form and the size of the flower were the same. That's where the name came from I guess."

"Do I know the Senior Harvester?" Erica asked full of curiosity now.

"Maybe, Doug Manchester is the Senior Harvester. I don't know if you met him yet. He lives on the other side of the lake on Antler Drive. He's been a Harvester for almost twenty years now. One day Adam will become the Senior Harvester."

"Is it dangerous to chew the peas?"

"Not at all, and you can't detect them in a pee test either. We have two nurses living in the valley who participate in the festival each year."

"Is it like pot?" Erica asked her.

"It's better, much better. You will feel so good, so carefree with a totally new outlook on life and the sense of wellbeing is overwhelming. Your senses are in overdrive and a flower or cloud becomes the most beautiful thing in the world to you. It lasts only for a couple of hours, but the happiness I get from it lasts for months. It's like an anti-depressant... well...it's hard to describe... It's a total happy pill."

"You sure make it sound good, but the last time I took a hit was in college, way before Lucas was born and I promised Cotton that I wouldn't do it again."

"Well, it is totally up to you. Just remember, you can't tell anyone about this, except Cotton of course. No one outside the valley knows about the plant and it must stay that way. If we have company I always tell them that the painting is a fantasy picture. I had to make the promise to Adam, before he let me hang it up in the spare bedroom, but you live in the valley, so it's all right to tell you."

"What happens if the secret gets out?" Erica asked.

"All I know is that it doesn't. A while back, a non-user, Old Man Cobb, that's what everyone in this valley called him, rattled it to a doctor in town and he called the FDA. They came down asking questions, but nobody talked. Of course Old Man Cobb didn't have any proof that the plant existed so they snooped around for a while, but couldn't find anything. Cobb died in a car crash one month later."

"Wow, that is certainly weird," Erica commented. "Can I look at the painting again?" she asked.

"Of course." They stood up and walked to the spare bedroom. This time Erica studied the oil painting closer. It was beautiful. At least fifteen black flowers were fully open and hanging upside down from the plant's branches. The dark shapes were slightly standing out from the night's darkness, pencil-thin blood-red fine lines running the length of the flowers to the edge of the pedals.

"And Adam has never told you where the flower grows?" Erica asked her again.

"No, he takes his job as Junior Harvester very serious and gets mad at me when I ask him," Robin replied.

"You said the festival is in August?"

"Yes, this year it falls on August 8th. You'll have to come no matter if you chew a pea or not. It's a whole lot of fun for the children too. It starts around noon and the children play and swim in the lake and we have a huge picnic where everybody brings their favorite dish. We play games, from handball to soccer or touch football, and at night the kids are put to bed and the adults will have a party with drinks, dancing and the pods. Nobody under eighteen is allowed to participate in that part of the festivities."

"Well, it all sounds very intriguing...to say the least. I can't believe we moved to a valley with a secret. I have been all over the world and participated in many traditions, more than the average person...but I have to admit, I didn't see this one coming. I can't wait to tell Cotton about it."

"Remember, only Cotton, nobody else. Not your parents, not your brother or sister, only people in this valley."

"Well, I better get home. Cotton gets off at five today and I want to fix him a hot supper."

"I had a whole lot of fun today and I know Lucas and Logan loved it. Let's do this again soon," Robin told her.

"We would love to." They walked toward Logan's room where the boys were involved in crashing a train into a car left on the tracks they now played with. "Lucas, let's go home. Daddy will be home soon," Erica told him.

"Oh, already," he replied and stood up. "Can I come back, Mom?"

"I'm sure you can. Now tell Logan and Ms. Robin thank you for a wonderful afternoon."

After they said their goodbyes Erica walked home, insisting to Robin that it was too short of a distance not to walk back. Lucas was excitedly talking about the plans he had made with Logan for the next day, but Erica hardly listened, her mind still thinking about the valley's secret.

That night, after Lucas was asleep in bed, Erica and Cotton sat outside on the patio enjoying a glass of wine together. The mild evening breeze carried the scent of Honeysuckle up to them. Dino was lying at Erica's feet, totally content with the world.

"Did you see the shooting star just now?" Erica asked him, pointing toward the sky. Cotton looked up, but it was already too late.

"No, but isn't it amazing how many stars you can see? I could sit here all night and just stare at the sky."

"I was busting at the seams to tell you during supper, Cotton. Guess what? You won't guess in a million years," she told him animatedly.

"In that case I give up. What happened?"

"This valley has a secret. A secret nobody else knows about, except the people living here," Erica told him and waited for his reaction.

"What secret is that, Honey?" Cotton asked her, playing along since he saw how excited she was to tell him.

"Well, the valley is guarding a secret about a plant growing high up in the mountain. It is so beautiful it takes your breath away. Adam has seen it and painted a picture of it, which is hanging in their spare bedroom. Anyway, the plant produces pea pods and once a year they get collected by the Harvesters and each August the valley celebrates this plant by having an all day festival by the lake with picnics and paddleboat rides. It's called the Festival of the Pods and only residents of the valley are allowed to participate and receive one pod for their own use that night. The pods supposedly have three blood-red peas inside and if you chew them you basically get high and get such intense hallucinations and sexual fantasies that…"

Cotton started getting a laughing spasm looking at his wife, who he could tell was really into this story.

"You're not really falling for that, are you, Erica?" he asked her still smiling. "I think you watch too many movies."

"I should have known that you wouldn't believe me, but can we still go to the Festival of the Pods, even if it is just a gimmick?" Erica asked him.

"Sure, why not. It'll be a lot of fun for Lucas."

"Why do you always have to be such a cynic?" she asked him, upset that he didn't share her enthusiasm.

"Because I can't afford to believe everything somebody tells me. I can't afford to be gullible, not in my career," he answered her.

"All right, I can accept that, but I'm wondering what your explanation is going to be about the next thing I'm going to tell you."

"What is that? Another valley mystery?" he asked her, sipping his wine.

"Ha, ha. You're so funny. Well, it won't be so funny when you hear this. Robin told me that their house came on the market because the former owner committed suicide. How about that? Is that weird or what?" she told him, watching his face.

"That is strange. What happened?"

"It is horrible… he cut his leg off with a chainsaw and bled to death."

"That is horrible," Cotton remarked.

"But don't you think it's an eerie coincidence?"

"Yeah, it certainly is, but they do happen once in a while, Honey. Now stop thinking about it and come to bed with me."

Chapter Sixteen

August 8, 2009

Erica had been looking toward the Festival of the Pods with great anticipation, wondering if everything Robin had told her was really true. The day finally arrived. A huge rented canvas tent was erected by the lake to give shade to the tables filled with food and eating areas. Most of the people where familiar to Erica and Cotton, but they had never met some of the valley residents. The atmosphere was tingling, like everyone knew something big was going to happen, but didn't dare talk about it.

People were assigned jobs and responsibilities which had been organized by Robin weeks in advance. Erica and Rachel had volunteered to be in charge of the food and were standing behind one of the long fold-up tables deciding where every dish would go. The ladies were standing in line to hand them the homemade casseroles, potato salads, meats and desserts. Tea had been prepared earlier that morning and was now waiting in a huge tea cooler next to plastic cups. Fresh lemonade was waiting for the children next to the tea container. Erica was amazed at the incredible turn-out for the valley's festival. She had never seen this many valley folks in one place before.

The community had a festival meeting a month ago and had voted on renting a blow-up air castle with a large slide which was now floating fifteen feet from the water's edge. Lucas was in heaven, sliding over and over down the slide followed by Logan. Lee David was the designated lifeguard for the next two hours and would be replaced by Cotton who had also volunteered for the job. Robin was at the volleyball court signing up men and women to play in the tournament which would start at three-thirty.

The winners of the best team would each get a prize which Robin had purchased over a week ago. Adam was in charge of organizing the paddleboat contest and Jack Rutter would be driving the jet-ski pulling the kids around on a big inflated banana boat. His wife Ruth was in charge of making sure that each rider had their life-vest on correctly, before she would give her husband the okay to take the six passengers across the lake.

More and more valley residents arrived and spread their blankets onto the green grass. It all reminded Erica of an episode of Little House on the Prairie, one of her favorite television shows she used to watch when she was younger, where the residents of Walnut Grove would gather for a picnic. She felt the same carefree abandon now as when she sat watching the episodes. It was as if she lived in the same time period, like the modern civilization didn't exist, that outhouses and outdoor plumbing were the norm, that the microwave, refrigerator and electricity were decades away from being invented. Only that moment in time existed. You could depend on your neighbor and could call on the community to band together and face whatever lay ahead. If the valley could achieve this kind of atmosphere by creating a mysterious secret, than it was an awesome idea and all right with her.

Erica shook her head to get all the cobwebs out of her brain. When had she ever felt this way? When had she ever chosen the simple life over modern technology and conveniences? She couldn't quite understand what had come over her since she found out about the valley's secret; the elusive plant called the Trumpet Angel and its mysterious pods which supposedly held aphrodisiac powers. The painting had haunted her since the day she had laid eyes on it. She was obsessed with it. She tried to tell herself not to read too much into the whole fable Robin had told her. It was probably only a gimmick to keep the valley residents connected and to promote this festival. She figured that a mystery like this helped make the valley a more exciting place to live. Cotton had told her as much when she related the story of the Trumpet Angel to him, but on the other hand, Cotton hadn't seen the painting yet. Work had kept him awfully busy during the last few weeks leaving her and Lucas to their own devices.

When she brought up the topic of the pods last night, he once again told her not to believe everything she heard and then he smiled that all-knowing smile of his, which she hated so much because usually he was right.

"Let's just go and be part of the festival. Lucas will have a blast and I think the food will be outstanding. I always love home-cooked food," he told her.

"Didn't you listen to a word I said? I don't think this is just a gimmick. Robin was serious when she told me about the pods," Erica told him vehemently, angry at him now for giving her no credit. "I didn't just fall off the turnip truck."

"Yeah, and little green men will dance at midnight. Come on Erica, be realistic. Things like that don't really exist. If there was really a plant with mystical powers and the people in the valley know about it, don't you think that it would be impossible to keep it a secret? Not now with cell phones, texting, twitter, Facebook and instant news media. Think Erica. Don't be naïve."

"Maybe you're right, but… if I'm right and they really hand out pods tonight, I guess you won't object to me trying one, since you think that all this is a hoax anyway," Erica countered.

"I'll pretty much bet on it," he answered her.

"Okay, let's bet then. If I'm right I get a pod, if you're right I'll be your slave tonight after we get home from the festival."

"I think I can safely take that bet. You're on. But remember pot and mushrooms and the like don't count for your supposedly undiscovered pods."

"It's a deal."

They smiled at each other across the room, and he winked at her. Damn, she hated to lose to him, but there was a chance that she was right. She was counting on her instinct that she had read Robin correctly, but only time would tell.

She had signed up for a side dish and had prepared her famous oriental slaw for the picnic. At twelve thirty, Doug Manchester arrived at the lake and climbed on the three step podium. Erica was amazed at how quiet it became. Doug was an older man, she guessed to be in his early seventies, but in good physical shape. He had grey hair and very inquisitive eyes which strayed over the residents of the valley, now gathered in front of him. His eyes rested on each person, like they were his congregation. The thought occurred to Erica that he was looking for strangers among the crowd. Cotton stood next to her and gave her a mocking smile. She knew exactly what he was thinking. He's thinking that Doug Manchester is putting on a good show, that's exactly what he is thinking, she thought. She lifted up her arm and elbowed him in the rips. His grin only got wider. A silence came over the crowd and the only noise came from a couple of children, including Lucas, still playing in the lake. Doug cleared his throat and finally started to talk.

"Friends, I welcome each and every one of you to this year's Festival of the Pods. Two hundred fifty-five years ago a pioneer man named Bulk Horswell discovered this beautiful valley and made it his home. Other pioneer families followed over the years and Hunter's Valley developed into what it is today. But, it's not just an ordinary valley. Oh no. Far from it. It's a valley with a secret. A secret so well guarded that the rest of the world is still unaware of it. An exceptional accomplishment in these times we live in. A one of a kind plant is growing high up in these mountains and it is this plant which we are celebrating today. It is this plant which we are guarding. It is Hunter's Valley's plant."

Manchester continued, "The first Festival of the Pods was held in seventeen fifty-nine and if we are fortunate enough... we will... celebrate it next year. A lot of people have lived in this valley since then, honoring their promise to keep the secret of the valley safe. You must...do the same."

With even more conviction he continued, "But let us not haste toward the rewards of trustworthiness...the pleasures to come will wait for us. This day, let us enjoy the culinary miracles of our valley cooks. Let us enjoy our children's laughter at play, let us enjoy friendly competitiveness in the competitions to come, but most of all...let us enjoy this evening's pleasures which will start when darkness covers this valley. Enjoy the Festival of the Pods."

The people around Erica cheered and clapped. Not a bad speech for a mystical, non-existent plant, she thought and looked at Cotton who stood now safely a couple of feet away from her. He looked at her and lifted his shoulders like he was clueless of what just happened. She gave him her, I told you so smile, but she didn't think he got it.

"So, you think this is still just a big pretend?" She looked up at him with a teasing smile, challenging him.

"Listen, if you really think they are handing out pods which make you feel carefree and happy, by all means...have one, but leave me out of it."

Why did men always have to be so dim-witted when it came to the unexplained, Erica thought?

She started working in the food line until she was relieved by another lady then went through the food line herself with Cotton and Lucas. They moved to their picnic blanket and enjoyed the delicious food. Cotton had to be a lifeguard after the picnic and Erica splashed and played with Lucas in the water during the time of his commitment.

Robin caught up with her in the blow-up castle, sliding down the slide with Lucas.

"Are you going to do it tonight?" she asked her.   Erica knew what she meant, but hadn't made up her mind yet if she was going to try them or not, even though her bet said she could, if the pods really existed.

"You know, Cotton doesn't believe a word I told him about the pods. It serves him right if I just went ahead and did it."

The children had a blast in the water, going down the slide and riding the paddleboats. When Cotton was relieved from his lifeguard duty, they all three put on a life vest and went with Adam, Robin and Logan on the banana boat. They had a blast. Later they watched the volleyball competitions in which Adam and Cotton were on opposite teams which made it more exciting for the two women to encourage their husbands. It was Adam's team who won to the excited screams of half the valley's residents. The afternoon flew by and the evening arrived. They had hotdogs with chili and onions for supper and they ate them sitting on the picnic blanket watching the most spectacular sundown going down over the mountains. The hotdogs never tasted better and Lucas ate two of them.

"I had so much fun today, Dad. I never want to move away from here," he told Cotton as he stuffed the last bite into his mouth.

They walked home together and gave Lucas a bath and then tucked him into bed. He was asleep within minutes. Erica had asked a young girl of sixteen who lived in the valley to babysit for them so she and Cotton could go back and participate in the evening's festivities.

They left the house at nine to walk hand in hand to the lit up lake area. Loud party music was echoing up to them and even from a distance the place looked beautiful. Tiki torches on tall bamboo sticks were stuck in the ground next to the lake and the flickering flames mirrored themselves in the calm water, creating a festive atmosphere.

"Are you going to dance with me tonight?" Erica asked Cotton as they walked over the dam.

"I might," he simply answered and smiled at her.

"I'll believe it, when I see it," she answered, knowing it wasn't his favorite thing to do.

Robin and Adam were already drinking their first beer, sitting at one of the tables. Robin waved them over to sit by them.

"Hey, you made it. Logan fell asleep the moment his head hit the pillow. He was totally worn out."

"So was Lucas. Hasn't it been the most wonderful day?" Erica asked her friend.

"It sure was. I loved every minute of it. Especially when my husband's volleyball team beat your husband's team," she told her teasingly.

"The beer is in the cooler over there," Adam told Cotton and pointed to a large container by the wooden bar. Cotton walked over and grabbed two Coronas and handed one to Erica when he sat down at the table. More and more couples arrived and soon the wooden dance floor was getting crowded. Erica watched Robin and Adam dance together and made puppy eyes at Cotton until he finally got up and danced with her. Later she joined Robin and Rachel who had finally arrived at the festival. Adam had disappeared a while ago and Erica saw Cotton talking to Jack Rutter. He is probably asking him to do some gravel work on our driveway, Erica thought, then turned her attention toward the women.

"Have you made up your mind yet?" Robin asked her and she knew right away what she was talking about.

"Cotton thinks it's just a gimmick, a reason to celebrate," Erica answered.

"Well, he is wrong. Just wait. You'll see. Right, Rachel?"

"Hey, I'm just here to get my pod and then I'm off to my house to have my own private party. It's not much fun watching other couples having fun when you're by yourself, since my boyfriend isn't allowed to participate," Rachel told them. "But to answer your question. Cotton is so wrong." She looked at her watch then stood up. "Well, you two ladies have fun tonight, and so will I. I'll see you in a couple of days." She turned around and disappeared into the darkness.

"Where is she off too?"

"To get her pod, and it's time for us to do the same." She grabbed Erica's hand and pulled her with her.

"Wait, I'll have to tell Cotton were I'm going."

"Not a chance. He'll just talk you out of it." Erica looked at Cotton who was still standing with Jack Rutter, his back to her. She followed Robin to a camping tent set up to the side, where a constant stream of people had gone in and come out of. Two people were ahead of them standing in line.

"Is this where you get them?" Erica asked her, but didn't get an answer.

"Shh," was all her friend replied. Somehow a somber atmosphere had come over Robin and she was totally focused on the entrance of the tent. Rachel came out of the tent smiling at them. Finally it was Robin's turn. She motioned for Erica to wait right there and went inside the tent. Erica heard faint mumbling sounds and then Robin came back out grinning at her and told her it was her turn now and pushed her through the tent flaps. Adam and Doug were sitting at a card table. Adam had paperwork in front of him and Doug was guarding a wooden box.

"This is Erica Stancil, the newest member of Hunter's Valley. Erica, this is Doug Manchester, the Senior Harvester."

So this is it, she thought. The mystery is about to get unraveled.

"Nice to meet you, Doug," she answered, but he ignored her greeting.

"Erica Stancil, have you entered this tent with honest intentions?" Doug asked her.

Her first impulse was to laugh, but she didn't.

"Yes," was all she answered, taken aback by the seriousness in his voice.

"Will you guard the secret of the pods from strangers and not take them outside this valley? Will you swear to it?"

"Yes, I'll swear it," she answered.

"Then you shall receive your first pod tonight. Do not chew more than one, and chew it for fifteen seconds or so before you swallow it. Sign right here."

Erica bent down and signed the paper where Adam indicated. Hers was one name under many. She stood up straight. Adam indicated to her how to hold her hands out to receive her pod. Doug reached inside the box and retrieved a small Ziploc bag with a brown, four inch long single pod inside. He laid it into her open palms and closed her fingers over it. It reminded her of receiving the Lord's Supper in church.

Wow, Cotton would be impressed, Erica thought. They definitely are putting on a good show. She looked at the men who both nodded at her now, that she could leave the tent. She walked outside where Robin was waiting for her.

"I have to go and show this to Cotton. Maybe he'll believe me now."

"Oh, believe me, Honey. By the time this night is over you will have made a believer out of him." Robin smiled an all knowing smile at her then disappeared toward her picnic blanket still lying on the ground. Erica went back to the table and sat down. Cotton was still talking to Jack but saw her coming. He finished his conversation and then came back to the table.

"Look at this," she told him and opened her palm. "I received a pod. Doug and Adam are over there in the tent handing them out." She took the pod out of the Ziploc bag and opened the frail shell to find three of the most blood-red peas she had ever seen. The outer skins were wrinkled and looked shriveled, all three the size of little grapes.

"Let me take one, Cotton please. If you say it's just a big gimmick than nothing will happen. If you don't want me to, I won't, even though I won the bet," she told him.

Cotton picked one of the peas up and smelled it.

"It smells kind of sweet. It's probably just a raisin they treated with food color and soaked in alcohol and sugar for days on end to get the desired strength."

"In that case there is no problem with me taking one," she replied.

"All right," he answered finally. "Take one, but don't complain to me about a hangover tomorrow morning."

"They told me to only chew one pea," she told him and popped one into her mouth, then placed the rest of them into the bag. "Mm, sweet and gooey, almost sticky, but the flavor is totally intense.

"I can't believe you are falling for this hype. Don't you think that if they were really powerful and had healing strength, that they would be marketed by now?"

"I had to make a promise," she told him.

"A promise? You know how easily a promise can be broken when money enters the game, a whole lot of money?"

"Stop it Cotton. Just let me enjoy this. If nothing else, they taste really good," she silenced him, tired of his negative attitude. She swallowed the chewed up pea, taking extreme pleasure in the delicious flavor. All of a sudden her lips started to tingle and then her whole mouth. Little bursts of pleasure making every part of her mouth come alive. Her palate felt orgasmic.

"Wow, my mouth is tingly. It is bursting with tiny orgasms. I didn't know my mouth could feel this way." She giggled and looked at Cotton and he looked back at her and suddenly realized she was telling the truth. Her eyes were big and round, her pupils dilated.

"Shit," was all he said and jumped up. He saw Robin lying on her picnic blanket. He rushed over to her and leaned down to look into her face.

"Robin, what are the red peas you gave to Erica?"

"They are the magic peas," she answered with a smile on her face. He noticed her pupils were just as dilated as Erica's.

"You took one?"

"Of course I did? Why wouldn't I?"

"Robin, are they dangerous?"

"Would I take them if they were dangerous? Leave me alone, Cotton. I'm happy." She closed her eyes and started humming a song from the Beatles.

Love, love me do,
you know I love you,
I always be true,
so plea...se... love me....

Cotton turned around, realizing that Robin was out of it. He wouldn't get any questions answered by her so he walked back to Erica who was dancing by herself on the dance floor now, wearing a seductive grin on her face as she watched him come closer.

"Come dance with me, Cotton. Please." She placed her hands on his chest. "Please, Cotton," she purred at him.

"Do you feel all right?" he asked her.

"I feel fantastic. Come dance with me now."

Hell, he thought. She must be all right if she feels good enough to dance. Several couples were dancing to the Hollies,

All I Need is the Air that I Breathe, Yes to Love You.

They danced slowly, her warm body tightly formed against his. Her head rested against his chest. She looked up into his eyes and a warm feeling went through him.

"I love you," she purred up at him, beaming with happiness and his heart skipped a beat. Hell, this woman could still do it to him. She closed her eyes and rested against his chest again singing softly along with the song.

"All I need is the air that I breathe and to love you!
All I need is the air that I breathe…"

They moved to the rhythm of the song and he felt strangely exhilarated. He didn't even like dancing, had avoided it at all cost in the past, but now he enjoyed it. They danced to several more slow songs. This was the most mystical festival he ever went to, he thought. It had been a wonderful day and he knew that Erica and Lucas had enjoyed themselves, but this was strange, and the night wasn't over yet and promised to get better. They stopped dancing after a while and went back to the table. Adam had returned and sat next to them drinking a beer. Cotton was going to ask him something, but stopped short when he noticed that his eyes were also dilated. Adam had taken the peas too. Hell, was he the only one who hadn't? He stood up and walked to the dance floor where he stopped a couple from dancing.

"Can you tell me what time it is?" he asked them. They both looked at him surprised, their eyes dilated. He went to a second couple and repeated his question. Their eyes were also dilated. When he stopped the third couple only the man's eyes were dilated.

"You didn't take the peas?" he asked the woman.

"No. I'm pregnant, but I have in the past. Don't worry, they're harmless." She turned back to her husband who had waited patiently and continued to dance with him.

"Thanks," Cotton replied and walked back to Erica. "How do you feel now?" he asked his wife who looked dreamily at the stars.

"Like this is the most beautiful night in my whole life. Everything is so strikingly gorgeous. I see the stars the way I have never seen them before and the moon. The moon is breathtakingly beautiful. My senses are in overdrive and I'm so happy. I have never been this happy and carefree before."

Cotton kept a close eye on his wife for the rest of the night. At eleven o'clock she wanted to walk home. He held her hand and when they crossed the dam, she stopped and kissed him and it almost took his breath away. And then she started to describe the way she perceived the light of the sky reflecting itself onto the lake and he knew that he didn't see the same lake she saw. The lake she described was a thousand times more beautiful than the one he saw. He listened to her calm, soft voice describing the vivid colors and it was like her serenity was catching. He felt good himself, happy with the world, not worried anymore that the peas could cause her harm.

When they reached their house, he paid the babysitter and then they checked on Lucas. He was sleeping, holding his favorite superhero in his little hands.

They smiled at each other and walked to the master bedroom where Erica slowly undressed, then stepped into the shower tempting Cotton to join her. Her eyes locked with his and the promise he saw in them was too great to resist. A night of unbelievable fervor and bliss followed.

Annegret Werner Shaw

Chapter Seventeen

Three days after the festival, Erica passed Robin in her car on her way back from the grocery store. Robin was jogging around the lake and happened to be right on the dam when they met up. Erica stopped when she saw her friend waving at her. It was the first time they had seen each other since the festival.

"Come to my house later," Robin yelled at her, stepping in place. "Only one more lap around and I'm finished for today."

"All right, I have to put the groceries up first. I'll be there in an hour or so."

Fifty minutes later Erica knocked at her door. Robin came to the front entrance with a towel wrapped around her hair.

"Come on in. I just finished my shower. Get yourself something to drink, will you?" Robin walked back to her bedroom and finished dressing and blow drying her hair and then went to find Erica who sat outside in the wooden rocking chair sipping a Diet Coke.

She stepped out onto the patio and smiled a knowing smile at Erica.

"So, did you have fun last Saturday?"

"I sure did. It was incredible. Cotton is still teasing me about that night. And you were right; the feeling of pure happiness is still inside of me. In a way we both won our bet. I chewed the peas and he... well... you know."

"Well, maybe next year Cotton will join you and participate."

"I don't think so. He would never risk losing his job."

"Did you know that they handed out seventy-three pods this year? And there wasn't a single pod left over afterward," Robin told her.

"Is that unusual?"

"Well, it seems that there are always enough pods so that everyone who wants to participate will receive one. It is strange how the amount of pods grows with the amount of users living in this valley."

"How many people in this valley are non-users?" Erica asked her.

"Only three right now; Cotton, Betty Carr and Carl Scholl."

"Only three? That seems a low number."

"All I can tell you is that the Harvesters keep up with it. They keep really good records. Every single one of the pods is accounted for."

"It's a shame, no, maybe it's a blessing that there are no more," Erica replied. "I sure could get used to them." They both laughed.

"And nobody besides Adam and Doug know where the plant grows. It is probably a good thing."

"Yup, can you imagine what would happen if more people knew. There would be a race to where the plant grows every year. People would fight over the pods. It is a damn good thing that only two people know. Doug and Adam take their obligations as Harvesters very seriously. You can't even become a Harvester unless you've been a user for over five years and there has never been a woman who held the job."

"Really? So not even pillow talk can get it out of Adam?" Erica asked her, suddenly feeling ill inside for pushing her friend like that. What was wrong with her?

"That's right. I tried it several years ago when I was as fascinated with the plant as you are right now. All that Adam would tell me was that Doug kept an old journal which had been handed down through the centuries from one Harvester to the next, and that one day it would be Adams and he would be responsible for it. He saw it only once when

Doug showed it to him, so that he knows where to find it in case of Doug's unexpected death," Erica explained.

"An old journal… possibly hundreds of years old? Boy, that sounds so darn mysterious. Did he tell you what was in it?"

"Nope, he said he never looked inside it. He doesn't know, but he thinks it is important otherwise Doug wouldn't have told him."

Both women were quiet for a while. Erica was fascinated by the thought that there was an old journal in the valley which was as old as the plant itself and had served the Harvesters through the centuries. If she could just put her eyes on it, just once for a couple of minutes, read it…how thrilling would that be? She was consumed by the thought that the journal was right here in this valley, hidden inside a house on the other side of the lake.

"Are you hungry? I can make us a sandwich," Robin offered, but Erica just shook her head.

"I really have to run. Lucas gets off the bus soon." She jumped up out of her chair and ran down the wooden steps.

"Thanks for the Diet Coke. Don't be a stranger. Come and see me when you have time!" She climbed on the newly purchased four-wheeler and headed home. What wouldn't I give to put my eyes on that journal, she thought driving home?

The secrecy concerning the plant was becoming more interesting. Cotton still didn't believe that the plant existed. Man, would she love to prove him wrong, and to find the journal would do just that. Yeah, it was probably a made up story, just like Cotton told her over and over again, but what if it wasn't? What if it was more than Cotton suggested; raisins, food color and a whole lot of alcohol bought from one of those oriental food markets? Erica drove past Mrs. Wagner, Robin's neighbor, who was working in her yard waving at her, unaware of the old lady.

Annegret Werner Shaw

Chapter Eighteen

One year later

The day of Sarah David's baby shower arrived. Erica had ordered a beautiful cake from the bakery in the city over a week ago and she had to pick it up around four today. Who would have thought that Sarah would get pregnant so soon after the last baby? It was going to be a boy this time and she and her husband were thrilled. Erica and Robin were giving her a baby shower for the new arrival. Erica sent off the invitations three weeks ago and almost all of Sarah's friends and family were coming to the valley to celebrate that they were finally blessed with a little boy. Everything was ready; the only thing missing was to pick up the cake and take it to Robin's house where the baby shower would start at five. It was going to be a busy day.

On top of that, Doug Manchester had invited them to his birthday party. He celebrated it every year at the lake where he had refreshments and snacks for the children and beer for the adults. It was Saturday and the weather was beautiful. It would be another wonderful busy weekend.

As much as Erica loved the summer, their first winter in this valley had been a blast. It had been Lucas' first experience with snow and he had taken to it like a fish to water. They all learned how to snow ski and ice skate and had fun on the frozen lake. The valley had a four week competition going on where people from all around the area came to participate in the ice races where four-wheelers and dirt bikes competed on the frozen lake against each other. They even had a class for dirt bikes with training wheels and Lucas was so excited to see the young children compete in this sport that he talked Cotton into letting him participate the following year. People were sitting around the lake in their lawn chairs all snuggled up in blankets, drinking hot chocolate or coffee from the concession stands and eating hamburgers and sausages on sticks while watching the races. Winter in the mountains was just incredible.

Erica would never forget the first time Lucas woke up to a white winter wonderland outside his window. He had been so excited to get into the snow and build his first snowman that she had a hard time holding him back in his pajamas. The snow arrived on a Friday night, so Cotton was home the next morning to experience his son's enthusiasm. Half an hour later they were all outside, lying in the snow making snow angels, having their first snowball fight and building a huge snowman together with a large carrot nose Erica had purchased for just this purpose at the grocery store. They used two large charcoals for his eyes and used the colorful candy out of a Reese's Pieces bag for his mouth. Lucas named him Frosty after the song and Cotton donated his scarf and his black snookie to make Frosty come alive with character. The snowman stayed like this for almost the whole winter, except for the Reese's Pieces which seemed to disappear, and all three of them were sad when Frosty finally turned skinnier and skinnier until he vanished altogether with the warmer weather of spring arriving in the valley.

Erica walked downstairs and pushed the on button on the coffee maker. Saturdays were her favorite days. Cotton was home and they would usually ride the four-wheelers, explore the mountains, go swimming or have a relaxed day piddling around the house. Cotton loved to grill in the evenings and Erica would relax with a glass of wine and enjoy not having to cook. He would prep some vegetables and potatoes and put them on the grill next to the meat. The upstairs patio had become an integral part of their house. They ate most of their meals outside and relaxed in the lawn chairs, reading books or taking naps.

Lucas had taken to the valley faster than she had expected and hardly ever mentioned his former house or friends in Texas. He loved his school and teachers and was best buddies with Logan. Her parents had made the long drive and stayed for three weeks celebrating Christmas and the New Year with them. That first year living in the valley had just been perfect.

Erica stood by the railing looking over the valley waiting for the coffee to finish percolating. She was absorbed by the beauty of it all. This place had become their home so effortlessly and she couldn't imagine living anywhere else. Suddenly two arms snaked around her waist and she was pulled back against Cotton's chest.

"You were deep in thoughts," Cotton told her, "What were you thinking about?"

"How much I love this valley, and that I don't ever want to move away," she answered him as she turned around to face him. "I have made such good friends here."

Cotton smiled at her. "I'm happy that you're happy. Let's drink our coffee outside. It's going to be a beautiful day."

They walked inside the kitchen and fixed their coffees. Cotton liked his strong and black; she, on the other hand, liked it with milk and Sweet n' Low. Lucas came running downstairs already dressed in his jeans and t-shirt.

"Can I play with Logan later? We're going to build a clubhouse for boys only," he asked them, all excited about the day to come.

"Why don't you have breakfast first? How about some scrambled eggs and toast," Erica asked him.

"No, I would like cereal instead. It's faster. Can I leave after I eat it?"

"You can leave after you feed Dino," Erica answered him. "But you have to be back by twelve for lunch, and take Dino with you. Put your new watch on. Now that you can tell time, I don't want any excuse from you for being late, all right?"

"All right," Lucas grabbed his favorite bowl out of the dishwasher, which was clean, then filled it with cereal and milk and started eating it.

"Dad and I are drinking our coffee outside. Come and sit with us."

They all three walked outside and sat down at the table enjoying the early morning together, watching Dino who chased his first squirrel for the day up a tree.

"Dino is really good at that," Lucas remarked. "Do you think he is going to catch a squirrel one of these days?"

"I don't think so," Cotton replied. "I think it's more a game to both of them. Do you see how the squirrels come down the tree to tease him? Look, that one over there knows just the right amount of distance to come down the tree to keep safe."

"Yeah, I think they're just playing with each other," Lucas replied, satisfied with his father's answer. Fifteen minutes later he was off to Logan's house, Dino trotting along after him.

Cotton went to the shed and started to organize it. Even though they had lived here for almost a year, some of his tools had never been unpacked and he thought that the couple of hours he had this morning offered the opportunity to do just that. Erica used the time to plant some flowers in the front flowerbed. She had heard that they usually didn't get another frost in the valley after the beginning of May, so it was safe to plant them now.

When she finished transplanting the flowers, she walked upstairs and prepared tuna salad sandwiches for lunch. She added chips to the plates and carried everything to the patio, including a pitcher filled with lemonade.

She looked at her watch. It was twelve o'clock sharp. Lucas should return shortly. He knew that she didn't tolerate him being late.

She walked down the steps and went to find Cotton. She found him in the shed where he showed her proudly how he had organized his workspace. A mountain of empty boxes lay ready to be burned on the burning pile.

"Looks good in here, doesn't it?" he asked her.

"Sure does. Does this mean we are going to stay longer in this valley than the usual two years? In some of the other places you didn't even unpack all your tools," Erica replied.

"Maybe. In any case, it feels good to know where everything is in case I need it."

"It looks really nice. Are you hungry? I made some tuna salad sandwiches," she told him.

"Sounds good. I'll be up in a minute." He kissed her on the nose, a fond habit he just couldn't break. Her nose was just too darn cute. He smiled at her. It probably was good that she didn't know all his thoughts. She turned around and walked away wondering what was going through his head when he smiled like that. Lucas, Logan and Dino came running up the drive.

"Mom!" she heard Lucas yelling from a distance. "Mom, can Logan eat with us? His mom says it's okay if it's all right with you. Please can he, Mom?"

"Of course. In that case both of you wash up." Erica enjoyed moments like this. To see Lucas this happy and carefree was priceless. She went upstairs and fixed another sandwich just in time for all four of them to sit down and enjoy lunch together. Erica and Cotton didn't get a word in edgewise. They just took pleasure in listening to the boys talking about the clubhouse they were building and that they needed nails and a hammer to do it.

"Logan's father is letting him use his hammer and is giving him a lot of nails; can I borrow your hammer, Dad? I promise I will bring it back," he asked his father with his mouth full. Cotton looked at Erica, barely able to conceal his smile.

"All right, you can borrow my hammer if you promise to take good care of it."

"I promise," Lucas replied, grinning from ear to ear.

"Do you guys need any large card board boxes? I just emptied several of them. If you fold them together they could make good walls, strong enough to last the whole summer," Cotton suggested to them.

The two boys looked at each other, then shook their heads simultaneously.

"That's a great idea, Dad!"

After lunch the kids took off again, carrying the large boxes and the hammer into the woods behind Logan's house. Erica washed the dishes and then started to get ready for the birthday party. They were going to give Doug a bottle of wine and she still had to wrap it. Shortly after two o'clock they walked down to the lake, having told Lucas where to find them if he needed them. They were surprised at the huge turnout. Erica had never seen this many valley people in one place before, except at the Festival of the Pods. It seemed that Doug enjoyed a higher status by being the Senior Harvester; almost all of the users were present. I guess if you wanted something as bad as the peas you made sure you were at the Senior Harvester's birthday party, Erica thought, as she wished Doug a Happy Birthday.

Adam and Robin were also there and soon Erica and Robin were talking about the last preparations for the baby shower. Robin offered to drive with her into town and Erica happily accepted. One hour later they left the party, after they each told their husbands that they were officially in charge of the boys, then left to drive into town to pick up the cake.

Chapter Nineteen

August 2010

Rachel walked to the Festival of the Pods by herself, like she did every year since she moved to the valley seven years ago. It was here in this valley that she and her ex-husband Bruce bought their first house together after getting married. He never wanted anything to do with the festival and didn't go with her. But it wasn't just the festival he avoided; it was pretty much everything and everyone in this valley he kept away from. He was an introvert, a total bore, and to this day she couldn't explain how she didn't see it before she married him.

All he ever was interested in was to be home and on the computer checking the stock market. Granted, he was a broker and needed to stay on top of things, but with him it never ended. That's all he ever did and cared about. He was a damn good broker and made a lot of money, but she didn't care about the money. She wanted to feel alive, experience things with the man she married, but he wasn't interested. Living in this kind of paradise, how could he not go outside, sit on the patio, drink a beer and enjoy the sights? They could have lived in an apartment in the city and he wouldn't have noticed the difference. During the whole four years he lived in the valley, he never swam in the lake, went fishing, or even went for a walk with her and Tiger. He didn't like sports, didn't like to be active, except of course for sex. Maybe that's why she had stayed with him for four years. The sex had been good, but it wasn't enough for her. She finally had enough, couldn't take him any longer. And even though he told her that he still loved her, she insisted on a divorce, citing irreconcilable differences.

It had been three years now that she was alone, but the truth was that she didn't miss him at all. She would miss her dog a whole lot more, she thought as she crossed the dam. He at least stayed at her side from the moment she walked through the front door until she had to leave for work. They hiked together, swam in the lake together and even watched television together. At least she pretended he did, ignoring the fact that he lay next to her on the couch snoring contently. No, Bruce had been a loner, a big mistake she regretted. She on the other hand couldn't live without friends. She loved being around people, loved to be part of this valley and had insisted that she retained the house in the divorce.

Now Bruce lived in the city and she lived here in the valley with her dog. She met Mark Hiller, a fellow employee at the food company she worked for as a sales rep. and they had hit it off the second they met. It happened shortly after her divorce. He was handsome and outgoing, and she was attracted to him. In the beginning they had just eyed each other, until he found out that she was divorced and then he asked her out. He lived in town and had a six-year-old son. He saw his son every second weekend and on the weekends his ex had the boy, he came over and spent the night with her at her house. They had a routine and she loved the way he treated her. He made her feel like she was the most important thing in his life. He had asked her to marry him two times already, but she wasn't ready and said no. It was too soon for her. She hadn't even met his son yet, even though Mark had asked her several times to come over and spend time with them.

A child was a big responsibility and she didn't want to give either Mark or the boy false hope that she would become the new woman in their lives. She guessed she was gun-shy, not sure that it was the right thing to do yet. She still had time, there was no rush. She was thirty, gorgeous and supported herself and she liked it that way for now. There was plenty time to get married and be a mother later.

Going to the festival by herself was nothing new to her, but coming home and having to deal with a husband who didn't understand her needs on that particular night was frustrating. Good thing she didn't have to deal with that any longer. Now she went to the festival, enjoyed herself and when the time for handing out the pods arrived, she was one of the first ones in line. She never opened her pod at the festival as so many valley people did. She always took it home unopened, filled with high anticipation on her walk home.

When she arrived at her house, she unplugged her phone. She didn't want any unexpected interruptions. Then she got ready for an evening of pleasures and started with her taking a bath, adding expensive bath oils to the hot water and burning her favorite incense. She would listen to the music of her favorite musical, *The Phantom of the Opera,* and slipped into the hot, silky water. Oh, how she loved this night. Afterward she would dry herself off and add costly perfume to her soft skin, then dress in her favorite lingerie; delicate sleepwear from her favorite store in the city mall; Victoria's Secret. She would open a bottle of good champagne and light some perfumed candles in the living room, and only then would she open the pod and hope to find three peas inside. She would then sit on her comfortable couch and chew one of the shriveled up looking raisins, then relax back and wait for the wonderful erotic feelings to start. The peas would produce the strongest sexual feelings she ever experienced in her life. The hallucinations would take her out of the cedar cabin to a fantasy place she never wanted to leave. She would moan with pleasure and feel the ecstasy and rapture a woman could only dream of. No, the next couple of days belonged only to her, and only after experiencing three days of bliss would she enter the outside world again and wait another year for the next festival to arrive.

She had made it clear to Mark that she wanted to be alone this weekend, that she needed a couple days of rest and recuperation. She even took Monday off from work. Mark agreed with her and told her that he had plans of his own with his buddies. They were going on a cycling trip.

Rachel finished her warm luxurious bath and stepped out of the tub, her skin glistening from the bath oil. The last song was playing. She had seen the Phantom of the Opera in New York years ago and had loved it so much that she had bought the CD for this special night. She languorously rubbed her body dry as she listened to the lyrics;

> *"Pitiful creature of darkness, what kind of life have you known? God give me courage to show you, you are not alone..."*

Oh, how she loved those lyrics, those dramatic tunes and the beautiful voices. She just stood there in a trance as the song came to an end.

Realizing it was quiet in the house now, she moved to the CD player and shut it off. She turned her Sirius XM Radio to the contemporary Coffee House Channel then continued her routine by blow drying her blond hair, adding perfume to her neck and dressing in her favorite red lacy lingerie. Robin picked her glass up and refilled it again with the sparkling champagne. She took another sip, her nose tickling from the bursting little bubbles. It was almost time; everything was perfect.

The candles flickered from the ceiling fan as she sat down on the couch. The little saucer she had bought especially for the purpose of holding the peas was sitting on the end table. She had found the small antique saucer in an antique store five years ago and thought it perfect to hold the three peas. To her, the dish represented the peas in a way she could have only hoped for. The rest of the year it sat empty in a place of honor on her bookshelf. Everything was just right, the mood and atmosphere was set. One last look at Tiger who was sleeping on his pillow and she was ready.

She leaned back into the cushions and opened the pod, hoping to find three peas. Only once in all the years had she been disappointed to find merely two peas, but not this time. Three blood-red peas were inside and her heart leaped at seeing them. She placed them with the shell on the saucer, then took one of them and placed it into her mouth and started chewing it, the delicious indescribable flavor stimulating her palette so intensely that her eyes started to water. How could such a small pea expel such a strong flavor, she thought happily?

She closed her eyes and leisurely stretched out on the couch after placing the saucer on the end table next to her glass. Nothing mattered to her right now, except what was to come. She didn't have to wait long. Her senses started to tingle and then her lower body created urges and desires of an unbelievable strength. She started to moan, her mind leaving all of her problems behind and all she could do was to go with the feelings and enjoy them. She didn't think about Bruce or Mark, she didn't think about her mortgage or the car payment, her work or her life. All she knew was that she was experiencing pure ecstasy. All she could do was feel and experience... nothing else. Robin didn't hear the music in the background any longer, she didn't hear Tiger softly snoring on his pillow and she didn't hear Mark driving up in his brand-new black Tahoe coming to a screeching halt in her driveway.

The front door wasn't locked and Mark Hiller entered the house calling Rachel's name. Tiger jumped off his dog pillow and came running toward him, his tail waving excitedly. He petted him then moved through the foyer and entered the living room. The strong aroma of the scented candles hung heavy in the air. He was about to call Rachel again when he saw her lying on the couch dressed in the most sexy lingerie he ever had the pleasure of seeing her in. The music was playing softly and the whole atmosphere was surreal. When he saw her lying on the couch with her eyes closed, the first thought entering his mind was that Rachel had another man in the house. He looked anxiously toward the kitchen door, expecting a man dressed in who knows what to come out carrying two drinks. His anger flared up, he was jealous and it infuriated him that she could do such a thing to him. Maybe it's Bruce, he thought, but nothing happened. No man appeared and she didn't seem to notice that he was in the room.

"Rachel, what's going on?" he asked her as he walked closer, but she didn't reply. "Rachel, are you all right?" he asked her again and leaned down over her. He was just about to feel her pulse when she started to moan; sounds so sensual he had only heard from her when they had made love. Surprised he stood back and stared at her. What was going on? Her hips started to move up and down and her hands went between her thighs touching herself erotically.

Damn, what was going on here? Was she drunk? He had never seen her drunk before. He looked around for a drink, but all he could see was a bottle of champagne next to a half-full glass on the end table. He picked the bottle up. It was more than half-full.

"Rachel," he said her name again and bent down on one knee next to her. "Rachel, wake up." He touched her shoulder to shake her, but the minute he did her arms went around him and pulled him close. Her mouth opened and she kissed him with such favor that it took his breath away. She didn't taste drunk at all. Yet, he could detect a sweet tingling flavor inside her mouth he never tasted before. When he looked into her eyes they were half-open and she mouthed his name, her pupils dilated. She moaned and pulled him closer and kissed him again. "I want you," she moaned and tried to open his shirt. He had never seen her like this before, but hell, she sure was sexy and she wanted him. That was all the encouragement he needed. He was aroused. What was he supposed to do? Her arms held him tight and she moaned and kissed him over and over until he dropped his pants and slid into her. Hell, she didn't even wear panties.

When it was over she slept, still moaning once in a while. Mark put his pants back on and walked to the kitchen where he poured himself a strong drink. She kept the Ezra Brooks in the bottom cabinet. It was a good thing he knew where she kept the bourbon, because he sure needed a drink right now. If this hadn't been the weirdest thing? He walked back to the living room with his full glass in hand and stood in front of the couch looking down at her sleeping form. She sure was beautiful and she didn't taste or smell like alcohol. If she wasn't drunk, then what was she? He finished the glass of bourbon and was about to return to the kitchen to refill it when he looked at the champagne bottle and the half-empty glass, and that's when he saw the little saucer with the odd looking contents. What the hell was that? He picked the saucer up and sat down in the chair opposite the couch. What were these things? They didn't look like anything he had ever seen before and he was quiet familiar with drugs of all kinds. Was this what Rachel had taken to give her such a high? There was only one way to find out. He picked up one of the peas, smelled it and then licked it gently. The same flavor he tasted in her mouth was now on his tongue. This was what she had taken, he was sure of it.

Looking at the sleeping woman on the couch he figured that it would take a couple of hours until she would come around. He had time, since his cycling trip had been cancelled. He might as well see what these little peas were all about. He placed one of them into his mouth and chewed it, surprised at the incredible strong flavor. At least they tasted a whole lot better than the shrooms he once in a while chewed. He sat back and waited, anticipating something to happen and when it did he lost himself in hallucinations of such inconceivable magnitude, that it overwhelmed him with its intensity. He stood up and started dancing, his body swinging to the sweet singing of a nymph beckoning to him, luring him to come closer and he did and entered a zone he never entered before, saw things he never dreamed of and used his body as an instrument to receive unimaginable pleasure.

Mark came out of it three hours later, still numb, unable to comprehend what had happened to him. He couldn't make sense of it. It had been incredible. Never, ever had he experienced anything remotely comparable to this experience.

He wondered how come he never heard of these little peas before and how come Rachel knew about them and never told him, knowing that he enjoyed pot and the occasional shrooms? He looked at her and saw her stirring on the couch. Tiger went over to her and put his paw on her chest. She opened her eyes and looked at her dog with a smile then stretched her body with a satisfied grunt and then she saw him sitting in the chair watching her. She sat up with a start.

"What the hell are you doing here? How long have you been here?" she asked him, her voice loud and irritated.

"Long enough," he answered.

"What do you mean?"

"What I mean is that John broke his leg playing basketball. Our cycling trip was cancelled, so I thought I surprise you and obviously I did. You were high on those peas over there and seduced me," he told her without holding back.

"I did?" she asked him.

"Yes, you did and I enjoyed it very much, thank you. Why didn't you tell me about these peas?" he asked her.

"Because they are none of your business," she shouted angrily at him and jumped up. "I told you I wanted to be alone this weekend. You had no right busting in here. Rachel looked at the little saucer next to the chair he was sitting in and noticed that only one pea remained. "What happened to the other pea?" she screamed hysterically now.

"Well, it looked like you were having such a good time that I thought I try one," he answered her.

"You what? You idiot! You don't know what you did. They were my peas, for my use only!"

"What are you getting so upset about? I loved it. We can do this together from now on," he argued back. "It'll be awesome."

"No, we can't. Only residents of this valley can chew them and you're not one of them. Get out of my house and forget that you ever tasted one of these!" she screamed at him.

"What the hell is wrong with you? I don't see the big deal," he told her, totally perplexed by her strong reaction. "I don't get it? Why are you so mad at me?"

"Because this was my night! I have one weekend of the year reserved for just me and you busted in on my party...uninvited, that's why I'm so mad at you. Now go home and we'll talk later, all right?" She calmed down slightly. If he would just leave now she could still have a good day tomorrow. There was one pea left.

"The hell I will. I came all the way out here to spend some time with you and now you're kicking me out?" he yelled at her.

"Please Mark, leave," she asked him nicely now, thinking that it might make a difference.

"All right, I'll go, but I'll take the last pea with me. I'm sure you have more of them and if you don't, you know where to get them... I don't."

"No, I won't get any more for another year. Just leave and let's never talk about this again," she pleaded with him, hoping he would listen. "Please Mark."

He grabbed the little saucer and dropped the pea into his hand.

"The pea can't leave this valley. Give it back to me, right now," Rachel demanded. "You don't understand. Please Mark, listen to me. Give me back the pea."

"No, I won't. You can kick me out, but the pea is going to be my consolation prize," he told her, looking at the blood-red pea lying in his open palm.

"I said no," she screamed and moved closer to him, her hand slapping his open palm. She was faster than he had expected and the pea flew into the air. Tiger had been following the heated exchange between his owner and Mark, not knowing what was going on. He moved next to Rachel, his instinct to protect her on high alert.

The pea flew through the air and Tiger's natural reaction kicked in. Many times in the past had he caught a treat which Rachel threw to him and this time wasn't any different. Both Rachel and Mark watched the dog jump up. Time stood still for those few seconds. Unable to stop the animal they watched horrified how he caught the pea and swallowed it whole, never knowing that it wasn't a treat. After he swallowed the pea he looked from one to the other, totally ignorant of what he had just done, hoping for a second treat.

Neither one of them made a comment, the reality that the pea was now gone was too overwhelming. The thought that all three peas were gone festered inside of Rachel's mind and she turned furiously on Mark.

"This is entirely your fault!" she shouted at Mark and started pushing him with her hands against the wall.

"Hey, stop the abuse. What's wrong with you tonight?" he asked her, totally bewildered by her violent behavior. "Let's sit down and discuss this in a normal fashion."

"There's nothing to discuss," she shouted. Getting herself under control again she returned to the couch and sat down. "Please, just leave. I'm tired," she told him depleted.

"Not until you tell me where you got the peas."

"I will never tell you."

"Why not?"

"Because, I never will."

"In that case I will take the shell with me and take it to my friend William, the one you met three weeks ago at the bowling center. He will tell me exactly what kind of plant it came from." Mark took the shell off the saucer and stuck it into his pocket, just to make sure Tiger wouldn't get a hold of it. The dog had moved to his dog blanket and was sleeping now, making strange noises, like he was having a bad dream.

"Give me the shell back," Rachel insisted. "You have no right to take it."

"Tell me who gave you the peas, and what the name of the plant is."

"I don't know," she answered.

"Well, then I'll take it with me and find out for myself. I'm not walking away from the peas. I liked the effect it had on me and I want to get more." Mark stood up and looked for his shirt he had discarded a couple of hours ago. It was lying in a heap at the end of the couch.

"I beg you, Mark. Don't take the shell with you. The pods have never left the valley."

"I'm leaving. I have had enough of you. You're a strange bird tonight," he told her putting his shirt on. "See you at work."

"Mark, please don't," she pleaded, but he didn't listen. Mark turned around and walked out of the living room toward the front door without looking back at her.

What was she going to do now? Her peas were all gone and on top of that, the unimaginable had happened; an outsider was now in possession of a pod shell and would take it to the city to find out what plant it came from. She needed to do damage control; call Doug and tell him what happened. He would be pissed, but it wasn't her fault. How could she have known that Mark would come by tonight and chew a pea without her permission and then take the pod shell?

She picked up the phone and was just about to dial his number when she saw Tiger sit up with a start like something had startled him. He sat up unusually straight and she could see the hackles between his shoulder blades stand up. He looked at her and she opened her mouth to call him over to her, when he started to growl. The sounds came from deep down inside his chest and created goosebumps on her neck and arms. She had never heard him growl like that before. Mark heard it also and turned around. The dog looked first at her and then at Mark. Tiger started to snarl and his long canine teeth appeared beastly exposed. And then she saw his eyes. His usually soft, sad looking brown eyes turned black and then started to glow red. Deep fear entered her body. What was happening to her dog? Was she imagining all this because of the pea she had taken? She must be. This couldn't be happening for real. The thought barely crossed her mind, when Tiger leaped off his pillow and chased after Mark.

"What the hell!" Mark shouted and tried to close the door behind him before the dog reached him, but he was already too late. Tiger flew through the air and jumped on Mark throwing him to the ground outside. Rachel jumped off the couch and ran after the dog yelling for him to come back, all the while hearing Mark's inhuman screams. The picture which greeted her coming through the front door made her scream with horror. Tiger was on top of Mark who was lying in the green grass kicking his legs, his hands fighting the dog which had a hold on his throat.

"Tiger, off! Tiger!" she screamed as loud as she could as she ran over to them and started pulling and yanking at the dog's collar. Never, ever, had her dog shown this kind of behavior. He had never been aggressive and she couldn't grasp what was happening now. She felt the strength of his neck muscles, shaking his head back and forth, snarling and tearing at Mark's neck below him. Mark's terrified screams turned to gurgles... and then he was quiet... and Tiger let go of him.

The dog moved a couple steps away from the man and looked at his deed, then walked back to Mark and sniffed his lower body. He stopped sniffing by his right pants pocket and then, all of a sudden, ripped the pocket apart and ate the pod shell. Tiger looked up at her and then lay down in the grass. Totally stunned and numb with disbelief Rachel fixed her eyes on the bloody body below her. Mark's neck was ripped open. A deep gaping flesh wound exposed a torn artery, bones and grey looking shredded tubes. His blood was spraying out in the rhythm of his heartbeat as he tried in one last feeble attempt to lift his hand up to her. His mouth opened slightly and she saw his tongue move, but no sounds escaped his lips. She fell on her knees next to him and pressed her bare hand onto his open neck to stop the blood flow. The blood oozed out between her fingers and she watched as his hand fell limp onto the ground next to her…his eyes became lifeless.

Blood was everywhere; on the grass, on Mark's face, his arms, his clothes. She removed her hand and saw that the blood had stopped spurting and was now just trickling out of the wound. There was no doubt in her mind that he was dead. The blood puddle his head was lying in slowly grew larger. Refusing to accept the picture in front of her, Rachel looked at her own hands which were covered with blood as well as the rest of her body. Tiger was still lying in the grass looking at her. He looked like a lion which had just slaughtered a gazelle. His muzzle was covered with blood and so were his chest and paws. She thought she could see his pupils glimmering red. Like an extinguishing bed of coals the glow slowly went out. This just wasn't happening. This wasn't real.

And then Rachel started to scream and didn't stop; her system unable to take anything else in. She lost consciousness and collapsed to the ground next to Mark's mauled body. The dog stood up and walked over to her, his tail waving. He licked her face with his blood covered snout trying to wake her then lay next to her, resting his head on her chest.

That's how her neighbor Eddie Heinz found them, two bodies lying in a puddle of blood on the grass, with a blood covered dog watching over Rachel. He called 911 immediately and then he phoned Doug. It was three o'clock in the morning and it happened on the night of the Festival of the Pods. Being a user he thought Doug should know.

When Rachel came to she felt the uncomfortable tightness of a blood pressure cuff on her arm before she was fully awake.

"She's coming around," she heard someone say. Rachel was confused of where she was and what was happening to her. She opened her eyes slowly and recognized Martin Brake, one of the emergency crew members, who lived in the city. She looked around and discovered that she was lying on a stretcher in her own yard covered up with a blanket.

"What happened?" she asked Martin and then realization returned to her. Her face turned ashen and she felt like she was going to faint. Her eyes filled with horror and she started sobbing hysterically.

"Tiger... Tiger... killed Mark. Where is my dog?" she asked in between sobs.

"Eddie tied him up to a tree on the other side of the house," Martin told her as he removed the cuff then walked to a man talking on a cell phone.

Rachel looked toward the spot where even now Mark's body was lying and a wave of nausea hit her. She leaned over the stretcher and retched her guts out. She felt a presence next to her and looked up and recognized the man who Martin had talked to a second ago. He handed her a handkerchief and she took it.

"You won't believe how many of these I hand out in a month," he told her with a smile on his face. "I'm Mac Lockhorn with the Thorn County Sheriff's Department. Are you feeling well enough to talk to me?"

"No, damn it. What do you think?" she bitterly answered him as she snatched the offered handkerchief out of his hand and wiped her mouth, giving him an angry look.

Another wave of nausea hit her, but this time she jumped off the stretcher, discarding the blanket, and ran inside the house to the bathroom leaving him staring after her. Mac Lockhorn took a second look when he noticed that she was only wearing a sexy red lingerie outfit. This case is getting more mysterious by the minute, he thought.

After vomiting for what seemed an eternity, Rachel looked in the mirror and saw how her face was smeared with blood. She grabbed the washcloths and cleaned herself up then slipped on her white bathrobe which was hanging from a hook on the bathroom door, covering up her sparsely clad figure. When she returned to the front door a few minutes later she saw a multitude of people in the yard. A tall guy was snapping pictures from every angle of the corpse and she saw Mac Lockhorn kneeling over the body looking at the wound. Two uniformed cops were searching the yard with flashlights. And then she saw Doug walking through the gate. A police officer stopped him and she saw them talking and Doug looked around the yard until he saw her and pointed toward her.

Why was Doug here? Sure, she had wanted to call him to let him know about Mark chewing a pea and wanting to take the shell out of the valley, but she hadn't or...did she? Doug had never been at her house before and the only contact she had with him was when they acknowledged each other in passing or when they exchanged pleasantries at a party they were both invited to. Of course, he was the Senior Harvester and such was involved with anything that had to do with the pods and the peas, but what did Mark's death have to do with the pods and how did he know that Mark was dead, after all it was the middle of the night?

Whatever Doug told the person who stopped him, it worked and he was permitted to go to her.

"Rachel, are you all right?" he asked her and when she just stared at him uncomprehending; he stepped closer to her and whispered into her ear. "Listen...I don't know what happened here tonight, but I know it had something to do with the pods. Whatever you tell them, don't mention the peas to them." Disbelieving what she just heard, she looked into his eyes and the silent threat she saw there wasn't lost on her. "Rachel, do you understand what I'm saying to you?" he asked her, this time slightly louder. She shivered and nodded her head. "Good, then all is well," Doug responded and hugged her for show. "I'll come back and talk to you tomorrow and explain," he told her and then left the yard.

Rachel leaned back against the door frame and closed her eyes totally deflated. All is well...is that what Doug just told her...all is well? What just happened here? Doug had threatened her. Instead of sympathy and concern she was threatened and then told that all was well. In her weakened and shocked state she almost slipped to the floor, her legs giving out underneath her.

Mac Lockhorn noticed her crumbling frame and came running over to her, helping her to stand up straight again.

"Like I mentioned before, I'm Mac Lockhorn the lead detective. You look like you need to sit down somewhere."

All she could do was nod her head. Mac grabbed her by the arm and led her inside the house toward the kitchen. Had he been inside before to know where the kitchen was, she wondered. What the hell does it matter? Mark is dead and my dog killed him. He guided her to a chair and she sat down. The detective took the chair opposite her.

"Do you want some coffee?" he asked her, like he lived in the house. She shook her head. She didn't want anything. She didn't want to sit at this table, she didn't want to talk to him, and she especially didn't want to think. She wanted to take a sleeping pill and go to bed and when she would wake up in the morning she wanted all this to be a bad dream. But it wasn't going to happen and when she realized it she started to cry again. This time she reached for a napkin from the napkin holder on the table and blew her nose. He was quiet and waited, like he had all the time in the world. When she once again regained her composure, she looked at him.

"What happened here tonight?" he started off.

"We had a fight and... and my dog..." she swallowed hard to get the words out, "my dog... killed him," she answered totally unnerved from the night's events.

"With him I assume you mean Mark Hiller, the deceased. Am I correct?"

"Yes," she answered.

"And you are?"

"Rachel Young."

"May I call you Rachel?" he asked her.

"Sure," she answered, wishing he would go away. I want to sleep and wake up in…

"Were you and Mark Hiller dating?"

"Yes, he was my boyfriend." I can't believe I said the word was. He is dead. Tiger killed him, she thought.

"How long have you two been dating?"

"About eighteen months."

"Has your dog ever bitten anybody before?"

"No… never. I don't know what gotten into him to do such a thing."

"Did he ever show aggression?"

"No." Why can't you leave me alone?

"Did you tell the dog to attack him?"

"No…no, of course not!" she screamed vehemently at him. "Are you out of your mind?"

"What did you fight about?"

She thought about the peas and then remembered Doug's words. Don't mention the peas. Whatever you tell them, don't mention the peas.

"He came uninvited to my house. I wanted him to leave – he wanted to stay, so we fought." Let this nightmare be over, I can't take it anymore, she thought.

"That's it?"

"That's it." I'm not allowed to tell you anymore, now go away.

"Why did the dog attack him? Did Mark push or hit you?"

"No, I pushed him at one time, but only once, then I sat down on the couch and he left."

"Where was the dog at the time?"

"He was asleep on his pillow."

"What happened next?"

"Tiger, that's his name, he suddenly sat up…and started to growl and before I knew it, he went after Mark and by the time I came outside he already had him on the ground by his throat. I screamed and yelled and tried to pull him off by his collar, but he wouldn't let go until it was over."

"The vet is on his way to collect him. The dog is going to be put under observation and I'm sure they're going to run tests on him. Is he up to date on his shots, especially rabies?"

"Yes, he is." Stop asking me questions. I want to go to sleep.

"Which vet do you take him to? We will need the name and get all the dog's records."

"Doctor Eva Post. Her clinic is next to the Dairy Queen in Kingston."

I wish I could chew a pea right now and leave all this behind me. But I don't have any left…Mark chewed one and Tiger swallowed the last one… Oh, my God… Tiger swallowed the last pea… could that be the reason he killed Mark? Maybe the pea affected him differently then it affects humans. Her head started spinning, seeing the pea fly through the air and Tiger lunging for it and swallowing it whole. Oh…my God. That had to be it. The minute Rachel made the connection she jumped up and pushed the chair backwards that it fell with a loud crash to the kitchen floor.

"Are you all right?" Mac Lockhorn asked her concerned. You look as white as a sheet. Do you want something to drink?" he asked her, stood up and picked up the chair from the floor. "Here, come and sit down again." He guided her onto the chair. What a strange woman, he thought. I like to know what went on here tonight. She is definitely holding something back.

Rachel sat back down. The pea…the pea made him do it. If Tiger hadn't swallowed the damn pea Mark would still be alive. The thought was turning round and round in her head. Slowly through a fog Mac Lockhorn's voice penetrated her mind.

"Did Mark like the dog?"

"Yes, he did and Tiger liked him. I don't… understand… any of this. I'm getting such a headache. I'm feeling sick again," she said, stood up and walked to the bathroom, leaving the detective to stare after her. She was dizzy and the headache was becoming a throbbing pain in her temples. Rachel splashed cold water on her face then opened the medicine cabinet and looked for the Tylenol container. She found it pushed to the back of the cabinet, opened it and popped three pills into her mouth then flushed them down with water out of the faucet. When she returned to the kitchen the detective was still sitting there. Why couldn't everybody leave? She looked through the window and watched how three people lifted a black, heavy body bag onto a stretcher, then rolled it out of the yard and out of her sight.

"Was your dog ever trained for protection?"

Rachel sat back down realizing that he wasn't going to leave until she answered all his questions.

"No."

"Do you belong to a Schuetzen club?"

"No."

"Do you belong to any kind of dog training club?"

"No, he is just a pet."

"How old is Tiger?"

"Almost seven."

"Is he neutered?"

"No."

"Did you get him when he was a puppy?"

"Yes, he was eight weeks old?"

"Does he have a pedigree?"

"Yes."

"I would like a copy of it," he told her.

Rachel stood up and walked toward her little office. If she remembered right she placed the AKC papers in the bottom right drawer with all the other papers from the vet. Opening the drawer she saw the manila envelope and lifted it out. She handed the detective the envelope, barely functioning.

"It's all in here," she told him and once again looked out the window. A man was walking Tiger out of the gate. The dog was wearing a muzzle and didn't want to go, so the person was dragging him.

"Wait," she shouted, but she knew he couldn't hear her so she ran out of the door after him. "Wait!" she yelled again and this time she got the man's attention. "Where are you taking him?"

"I'm Doctor Smith. We have to take your dog in. It's protocol in a fatal mauling case."

He pulled out a business card and handed it to her. Tiger started whining, realizing something was wrong. Rachel bent down and hugged him. The blood had dried on his coat, but somehow she didn't care right then, realizing that she would never see her dog alive again, after all, he had killed Mark. She petted him, tears running down her cheeks and then she stood up, turned around and walked back to the house, putting her hands over her ears to drown out Tiger's pitiful howling.

Chapter Twenty

The following morning the news of Mark's death swept through the valley like a wildfire. It was Sunday, the day after the festival and Erica and Cotton woke up from the ringing of the phone. It was only seven-thirty when the phone rang and Erica reached for it, her eyes not quite open, her hands feeling for it on the night table.

"This can't be good," she mumbled drowsily. The phone clattered to the floor, but the insistent ringing continued. Finally she got a hold of it and answered.

"Hello," she breathed into the phone.

"Erica, wake up. This is Robin."

"Robin, do you know what time it is? Couldn't this wait until later?" she asked her friend, hoping for a yes answer so she could hang up and go back to sleep. She looked at Cotton who turned his back to her and pulled the blanket over his head to drown out the disturbing noise.

"Listen. Turn your television on to the local news station. Mark Hiller is dead. He was at Rachel's last night and Tiger killed him. It's on the news," Robin shouted into the phone, talking ninety miles an hour.

"Slow down. What did you say about Mark and Rachel?"

"Tiger, Rachel's dog, killed Mark last night. They are talking about it on the news right now. Switch it to channel forty-six and you'll see," Robin told her much slower this time.

"Oh, my gosh. How horrible." Erica sat up in bed now totally awake. Cotton heard his wife's words and knew something was wrong. He sat up next to her and looked at her concerned.

"Turn on the TV, channel forty-six," she told him and then told Robin that she was going to call her back.

"...death is still under investigation. Mark Hiller leaves his six-year-old son behind. Canine mauling's and fatal attacks have been on the rise. An estimated 4.7 million dog bites occur each year in America. The breeds most responsible for serious injury or death are Pit Bulls, Rottweiler and Wolf Hybrids. The dog in this case is a seven- year-old Golden Retriever who didn't show any aggressive behavior before and was familiar with the victim. He is currently held by the Thorn County Animal Facility awaiting results of the investigation; his own life now hanging in the balance."

Stunned, Erica shut the TV off and looked flabbergasted at Cotton who was just as taken aback by the news as she was. It was unbelievable. They knew Tiger as a nice, playful, gentle dog, who didn't have one single aggressive bone inside his body. Lucas and Dino had played with him many times. What happened last night at Rachel's house? When she ran into her at the party, she told Erica that she was going to get her pod and go straight home to enjoy it alone. Erica jumped out of bed, telephone in hand. Three seconds later she was talking to Robin again and they decided to go and see Rachel. Maybe they could help her in some way.

Rachel woke up to the loud banging on her front door. Who could that be, she thought, then the reality from last night set in and her stomach knotted up. She had taken two sleeping pills last night and slept hard, not wanting to deal with Mark's death. His poor son; he would be devastated finding out that he lost his father. And why did she feel so responsible? All she ever wanted was to have three days to herself, but everything had turned to shit. Mark was dead and her dog killed him. How could she ever come to terms with that?

The banging on the front door continued and Robin decided that whoever it was wasn't going to leave. She grabbed her robe and put it on, then walked to the door. Relieved, she found out that it was Erica and Robin, not the police. She opened the door and let them in. She didn't have to say anything; their concerned faces told her that they already knew what happened. They hugged her and they cried together and then Robin went to the kitchen to make coffee. Erica walked Rachel to the living room where they both used Kleenex to dry their tears.

"We had a fight last night, Mark and I... I had chewed one of the peas and... and when he came over he found me on the couch... high. He... he noticed the two other peas on my side table and... and decided to take one himself. When we both came out of it... I... was pretty upset with him... for chewing my pea and told him to go home. He said he was going to take the other pea with him since I could get more. When... when I tried to get it back from him... I slapped the pea out of his palm and... the pea... the pea... Tiger caught it and swallowed it whole. Mark then decided to take... the shell to a friend who works in the science department at the university to find out what kind of plant it came from. When he left, Tiger went after him and killed him.... It was... horrible... horrible," she told her, broken up, tears running down her face.

"And the worst part is... that I'm not allowed to talk about it to the police, them being outsiders. Doug came and threatened me not to mention the peas to them and he looked very angry when he told me. And now I'm going to lose Tiger on top of it. I... I just know it. All I can figure out is that the pea affected him differently and he went temporarily crazy. And I'm not allowed to tell the police. It's the only thing that could save him from being put to sleep. What am I going to do? Robin wouldn't understand; she doesn't own a dog, but you do. You understand, don't you Erica?" Erica nodded her head. "And she is married to the Junior Harvester, so don't tell her what I just told you."

Erica nodded her head again. She saw how frightened and miserable her friend was, but at the same time her own brain was going ninety miles an hour, digesting the information Rachel had revealed to her. Rachel started sniveling again.

"And you know... what Doug said to me before he left? You won't believe this. He said... all is well." She blew her nose and then continued. "Can you believe that? All... is well? What is wrong with that old man? I'm having such a horrible headache on top of everything else," she mumbled and rubbed her temples with both hands. "I need some Tylenol." She got up and went to her bathroom to take more pills.

Robin came out of the kitchen and walked to where Erica was sitting, carrying a tray with three filled coffee cups, cream and sugar.

"Where did Rachel go?"

"She is getting Tylenol for her headache," Erica told her.

Two minutes later Rachel came back and sat down again. "These pills just don't work."

"Have a cup of coffee, Rachel. It will give you some umph back." Rachel looked grateful at Robin and took a cup of coffee off the tray.

"It was on the news this morning," Robin told her, "but I already knew last night what happened. Doug called Adam and told him. He said that the yard was full of people, the sheriff department, emergency crew, the veterinarian and the coroner. I felt so horrible for you, but Adam told me to wait until this morning to come and see you. He told me you needed your rest."

"How did Doug find out?" Erica asked her. Both women looked expectantly at Rachel.

"Adam told me that Doug received a call from Eddie. He heard you screaming and walked over to your house and found you," Rachel explained.

"It was horrible. There was nothing I could do to save Mark," Rachel started crying again.

"I know, Honey. We're going to help you through this. If you don't want to be by yourself we can take turns staying with you or you can come to our house and stay as long as you need to. We can bring you lunch or supper or anything else you need. Just tell us what you need, all right."

Rachel nodded her head. She knew they meant well, but what could they really do to make her forget what happened? They couldn't erase the mental picture of Mark's mauled throat... the blood spraying out of the ripped artery... his hand reaching for her one last time... his dead eyes staring into nothingness. Robin shook her head.

"Thank you so much, but I just need to come to terms with what happened. Any time I close my eyes I see Tiger on top of Mark. There was nothing I could do to help him. It all happened so fast and it seems so unreal. I wish... I had..." The thought suddenly entered her mind and her face brightened for a second. Now that it was inside her head she wanted to ask it, but held back. Was it the right thing to do?

"What?" Erica asked her noticing the sudden change in her. You wish you had what? Tell us Rachel."

"Well, the truth is, I wish I had another pea so I could make the next couple of days disappear," she answered, her eyes large and wide, full with hope and expectation that one of her friends would come through for her.

"You already took all three peas?" Robin asked her, unaware of the conversation Robin and Erica had earlier.

"Yes, it was the only way I could get through last night," Rachel lied to her.

"Sure," Erica told her right away. "I have two left and you can have them both."

"You can have mine too," Robin added, never once doubting Rachel's words.

"You're good friends," she replied, her spirits slightly lifted.

Annegret Werner Shaw

Chapter Twenty-one

The next two days passed in record time for Rachel, partially because she chewed three of the peas her friends had given her to avoid dealing with reality. She experienced short times of wellbeing, but when the drug wore off she became extremely melancholy again. The mental picture of Mark being mauled by her dog wouldn't leave her mind. Now she only had one pea left and she guarded it fiercely. Maybe she would chew it after she returned home from the funeral.

Doug had come by after her friends left on Sunday morning. She had answered the door and saw Doug standing there. Her heart started hammering in her chest. There was only one reason he was there. They sat at the kitchen table wary of each other.

Doug asked her to tell him exactly what had happened the night before, and she did. She didn't leave anything out. When she finished she looked at him and waited for an answer. She expected some kind of advice of what to do next, but he was quiet. It took him quite a while to answer. He sat there with his elbows resting on the table tapping the tips of his fingers against each other, the distance between the fingertips becoming further and further apart. It drove her crazy sitting there, watching him think and waiting for an answer.

"Didn't you hear me? They are going to euthanize my dog unless I tell them that he ate a pea before his attack," Rachel told him, her voice raised, but Doug stayed silent, thinking.

Rachel was one of the few people in the valley he didn't know much about, in part because she was single and did her own thing. He knew she worked for a big company in Kingsville as a sales rep., but that was about it, except that she was good friends with Adam's wife. She is a single, independent woman, he thought. Would guilt work better on her or intimidation with violence? Man, he hated this job. It was the second time he had to deal with a woman concerning the peas. He decided to try it first with guilt.

"You can't let them find out about the peas. The secret of the valley has been kept for centuries. You just can't tell them," Doug started out, running his hands through his grey hair. "Listen to me, Rachel. This is serious. Very serious. A man is dead because of you."

"Because of me! What the hell are you talking about?" she shot back at him, getting extremely angry. How dare he say something like that to her.

"Listen, damn it!" he raised his voice. "If you had locked your front door this wouldn't have happened. Mark wouldn't have been able to come in, and if he wouldn't have come in, he wouldn't have been killed by your dog," Doug explained to her and continued with his plan.

"Tiger belongs to you and your boyfriend took the pea because he saw you and the way you reacted to it and he tried it. Who could blame him? Do you follow me, Rachel? Are you listening?" he asked her, putting all the responsibility on her shoulders. "Under no circumstances can you tell the sheriff's department about the pods."

"Oh, no, Doug. You can't put this on me. You make it sound like I killed Mark. You can't do this. I won't let you, and I won't let them kill Tiger either. It wasn't his fault. I didn't tell them last night, but I have to tell them today. It's the only way Tiger won't be put down," she answered, irritated that he was blaming her for what happened.

How dare he? He can't intimidate me this easily, Rachel thought. I won't let him. "My dog had a bad reaction to the pea he swallowed and that's all there is to it."

236

Doug just shook his head frustrated and irate now. All right, so guilt didn't work on her.

"No, Rachel. You can't tell them!"

"Yes, I can and I will!"

"No you won't," Doug shouted at her, this time his voice was angry and forceful.

"But my dog..."

"No, damn it!" Doug slapped her hard in the face. He was damn mad now, angry at her continued stubbornness. He jumped up and stood over her, taking her by the shoulders and shaking her violently.

"But, nothing! You don't mention the peas. For the sake of the valley and all its residents you don't mention them."

The fight was taken out of her by his aggressive behavior. Her cheek burned from his hard slap, tears entering her eyes. She looked into Doug's face. It was harsh and pitiless, his eyes malevolent. Rachel trembled with fear, unable to argue with him any further and felt like a rag doll, limp and lifeless in his hands.

"You promise right now that you will keep your mouth shut... or else... you hear me!" Doug shouted, as he shook her again. He waited a couple of seconds for an answer, but when she just stared at him with fear in her eyes, he yelled at her again. "You hear me, Rachel!"

"I... won't say a word," she stuttered, "I won't... I promise."

"I will hold you to your promise... don't doubt my words, Rachel. I will hold you to your promise."

Doug looked at her like he was trying to see if she was lying, his face hard and unsmiling, then he let go of her shoulders. He turned away from her and walked toward the kitchen door where he turned around one more time.

"It's for your own good, Rachel. Remember that," he uttered in a normal voice. "It's for your own good, damn it."

She heard the front entrance door slam shut then heard the motor of his Jeep start. She sat on the kitchen chair numb with what had just transpired. She touched her swollen cheek trying to digest it all. Never in her life did she think that Doug would hit her. Why was everything going wrong right now? She sat for quite a while in the kitchen trying to calm down. Slowly her heart rate returned to normal and her reasoning returned. How dare he hit her? Maybe she should report that to the police as well. He could go to jail for it. That would serve the bastard right. Her temples started to throb again. Damn Doug for hitting her so hard that it brought this horrible headache back, she thought, as she got up to find some more Tylenol. Her temples sure were throbbing.

She found the pills and popped three more into her mouth, then flushed them down with water out of the kitchen faucet. There was still some hope; hope that the veterinarian would find the presence of the pea in Tiger's system without her telling him. Surely, nowadays, with all the progress they were making in toxicology they would be able to detect the potent substance. Yes, Rachel thought, they will find the traces of the pea. It would be her way out of this dilemma and one day, when all this was over, she would give Doug a piece of her mind. She picked up the telephone and called Doctor Smith to get an update on the tests and Tiger's wellbeing, but it was too soon. He told her that the tests wouldn't come back for another couple of days.

On Wednesday morning, she went to Mark's funeral wearing her feelings on her sleeve. The morbid atmosphere added to her depression. The only bright moment for her was when she met Mark's son for the first time. He looked like a little version of his father and a smile came over her face. But it was short-lived, his ex-wife visibly guarding the boy from her. The woman stood behind him, her arms over his shoulders holding him against her and then she pulled him away after Rachel uttered a few sympathetic words of condolence to him. It started to rain heavily and she was soaking wet by the time she reached her car, not having had the forethought of bringing an umbrella on this overcast, gloomy day.

When she arrived home she thought about taking two sleeping pills and going straight to bed, but the telephone rang as soon as she unlocked the front door. Running to the kitchen phone she answered it, raindrops falling off her raincoat onto the floor.

"Hello," she answered out of breath.

"This is Doctor Smith," a man's voice told her.

"Doctor Smith, did you find something in the tests?" she asked him hopefully.

"I'm sorry, Ms. Young. The tests all came back negative. We're going to euthanize him tomorrow afternoon at four. I thought you should know, so you can come by and say goodbye to him."

"Oh, no. Isn't there anything I can do to prevent that from happening? What if he wears a muzzle and is always on a leash when I walk him?"

"I'm sorry, Ms. Young. I have been ordered by the court, he has to be euthanized. Are you coming tomorrow?"

"Yes," she simply answered, deep grief for her dog setting in. She didn't hear the veterinarian's reply or the click on the other end. She stood in the same spot for a while, numb with realization that she would lose her good friend, water still dropping onto the floor. Rachel finally took her wet shoes off and turned to walk to the entrance to hang up her jacket, but unexpectedly slipped on the wet tiles, her bottom hitting the floor so hard that she screamed out in pain. Totally deflated and miserable she continued to scream; her cries of wretchedness unheard in the empty house.

If Tiger had been home, he would have come running to her instantly, licking her face and making sure she was all right, but he wasn't home. He would never be home again. His soft, sad looking brown eyes would never stare at her again. He would never be the silent listener, never raise her spirits and never be the warm body next to her on the couch. And she couldn't do a damn thing to prevent his death.

She cried until she couldn't cry any longer. Why hadn't they found the substance in Tiger's body? It would have explained his behavior. It was a total accident that he ate the pea, an unforeseen, unplanned accident for heaven's sake. If Doctor Smith just knew he would recommend not to euthanize her dog. What if she asked him to keep it private? What if Doug never found out that she told him? All kinds of irrational solutions came to her mind, one better than another. Her thoughts were flying through her mind. There had to be a way, she just hadn't thought of it yet.

Then a different thought entered her frazzled mind and anchored itself deep inside her brain; she would take the last pea she had to Doctor Smith and convince him to test for it in Tiger. He would find out how potent and mind changing this drug could be, not only to people, but also to animals. The idea impaired her rational thinking and in her emotional state her foolish wish to save her dog rose to take priority over everything else.

She ignored the warning headache that warned her one final time to change her mind, but she was too emotionally damaged to heed the warning, just focused on the solution to save her dog's life. She reinforced her thoughts, getting more excited by the second. She would take the last pea to Doctor Smith right now. She ran upstairs and took it out of her night table. She would leave this instant and make him promise not to tell a soul. Maybe the confidentiality doctor-to-patient relationship applied to veterinarians as well. It was worth a try.

She ran back downstairs to grab her shoes, the headache now only a dull reminder in her front temples. Should she call Doctor Smith and tell him that she was on her way to see him? She turned toward the kitchen phone when something sapped through her brain and short-circuited her actions. She stood still, not moving a muscle then dropped her shoes onto the floor and walked toward the kitchen, not in a hurry any longer. Her legs felt lethargic, her arms heavy and stiff. Rachel slowly entered the kitchen and switched on the light above the kitchen table then walked toward the sink and threw the pea into the disposal and switched it on. Rachel's face showed no emotions as she watched the valuable pea disappear down the drain to the loud grinding sounds of the motor and the unheard protests in her mind.

Don't throw the pea away... I need the pea... I... need it. But her hand didn't listen and when the pea disappeared she turned the switch off. She spun on her heels toward the table... so fast, a move she had never done before and pulled a chair next to the table not knowing why. She lifted her foot and climbed on the chair and then on the table, totally amazed at her actions. Why was she doing this? She started to rebel. Get off the table - you're going crazy, but then her thoughts stopped all together and only her eyes and her heart reflected her terror of what was happening to her. She stood up straight and stared at the four lights attached to the ceiling fan, hanging over her head. Slowly she reached up and unscrewed first one light bulb and then a second one and smashed them together, breaking them into a thousand little pieces which fell on the table and onto the floor. Her fingers were bleeding, but she didn't care.

She stood still for half a minute, staring into the light of the other two bulbs, her pupils blood-red, and then she heard the front door open and Erica's voice.

"I'm glad you're back from the funeral. I brought you some potato soup. Where are you, Rachel?"

Rachel ignored her call, lifted both her hands and stuck two fingers into each empty socket. Her body shook back and forth until the dead weight of it pulled her fingers out of the sparking light sockets. Her body crashed unceremoniously off the table and landed in a heap on the kitchen floor.

Annegret Werner Shaw

Chapter Twenty-two

Erica was exceedingly concerned about Rachel and had checked on her friend every day since Mark's death. She could only imagine what she had been through. Rachel hadn't eaten right since the accident happened and was living on Red Bull, the energy drink, giving her the strength she needed to get through the day. In hind sight, it probably hadn't been a good idea to give Rachel the peas. They made it possible for her not to deal with reality. What would she do when the peas were all gone? She had to deal with the fact of what happened sooner or later.

Erica was taking her homemade potato soup and hoped that Rachel would eat at least a little bit of it. She had offered to go to the funeral with her, but Rachel had refused, telling her she wanted to be alone. She respected her decision and told her she would spend time with her later that day after the funeral. Erica had only met Mark once when he came to pick up Rachel at the lake where they had visited together, watching Lucas and the dogs swim in the lake. She hadn't exchanged more than ten words with him that day, since he was in a hurry. Rachel left with him to watch a movie in town and Erica had offered to bring Tiger home. That was over six months ago.

It was almost one-thirty and she was glad that Rachel had finally made it back from the funeral. Coming home from a funeral to an empty house had to be hard. She would try and cheer her up and talk her into going for a ride on the four wheelers in their rs. It would be a blast getting all muddied up, driving through the potholes filled with rainwater. Her car was in the front drive so she had to be home.

"I'm glad you're back from the funeral. I brought you some potato soup. Where are you, Rachel?" she shouted, when she entered the house.

She placed the bowl of soup on the entry table and hung up her raincoat. It was still pouring cats and dogs outside. She noticed Rachel's shoes discarded on the floor and several puddles of water next to them. Erica stepped carefully over the puddles on her way to the kitchen when she heard the loud crash. To her it sounded like something heavy hit the floor, a hard thump and then it was still.

"Rachel, are you in the kitchen?" she yelled at the same time that she observed the flickering of the kitchen lights and then the lights went out.

She entered the kitchen thinking that Rachel had beaten her home by barely a couple of minutes, since she didn't mop the water puddles up yct. The sight which greeted her was unimaginable. Rachel was lying on the kitchen floor, her crumbled body unmoving.

"Rachel!" she screamed and ran toward her, kneeling next to her still body, spilling some of the potato soup in her haste to put the bowl down on the floor.

She turned Rachel around to see her face. Her open eyes stared back at her, her pupils glimmered strangely then turned black. She picked up Rachel's hand and felt for a pulse, but found none.

"Rachel?" she screamed one more time, then jumped up and ran to the house phone.

She dialed as fast as she could and requested an ambulance, then ran back to Rachel and started CPR. She had taken several courses during her work at Sea World. The last time she took it was when Lucas was little, but never had to use her knowledge on anybody before. Now all of it changed and Rachel's life depended on it. Remembering the instructions she first straightened Rachel's head and checked her airway for obstructions, then took a breath and blew the air into her mouth. She then placed her hands over her sternum and pushed down hard; desperately trying to remember how many compressions she was supposed to give her, before she had to blow air into her lungs again. The number didn't come back to her, so she decided on seven, hoping that it was close enough.

Time dragged by while Erica repeated the steps over and over again. Finally, it seemed like forever, she heard the sirens of the ambulance in the distance getting louder, and a couple minutes later three EMS guys rushed inside the house.

"I'm here!" she shouted. "I'm in the kitchen. Hurry!"

They told her to step aside and started to work on the woman on the floor, taking vitals, hooking her up to a defibrillator and finally shouted the all clear before Rachel's body jumped from the shock of the electricity. They repeated the steps several times, all the while hoping they weren't too late. Erica stood to the side, numb from the shock, her legs shaking. She had to sit down or she would faint.

She leaned on the chair closest to her and pulled it toward her just in time to collapse on it. A dull pain coming from her right knee came to her awareness and she looked down; blood was running down her leg from a deep gash. A piece of glass stuck out of the wound and she pulled it out, wondering where it came from, then discarded it on the table and looked toward her friend lying lifeless on the floor. She watched the futile attempts of the EMS guys to revive her, but the longer it took the more hopeless it became. She heard another all clear, but again nothing happened. This just couldn't be happening. Rachel couldn't be dead. Tears started to run down her face as she watched one of the men close Rachel's eyes. He stood up, turned and looked straight at her, his eyes full of sympathy. He stepped toward her, his foot accidentally hitting the soup bowl, spilling the potato soup onto Rachel's kitchen floor. Mesmerized, both watched the spinning bowl until it finally came to rest next to Erica's feet. They both stared at it then he looked at her again and spoke.

"I'm sorry, Ma'am. She's gone."

Erica looked up into his face and realized the finality of his words. They hit her so hard that she jumped up and ran to the bathroom crying uncontrollably. She finally pressed her hand over her mouth knowing she had to get control of herself, then splashed cold water onto her face before exiting. She heard the EMS guy's voice calling someone on his cell phone. She wanted to ask him if she could go home, but somehow knew that she had to stay. She opened the front door and walked outside. The rain had stopped and the sun was out again. How fast the weather changes in this valley, Erica thought. We would have had a lot of fun on the four wheelers. The irony of it all mocked her. She had come to cheer Rachel up, but instead, she had to give her CPR. Her friend was dead. What in the hell happened to her? She didn't have time to think about it before, but what did Rachel do to get killed? Did she climb onto the kitchen table to change a light bulb in the ceiling fan light fixture and fell? The light bulb broke in the fall and that's how she cut her knee. That's where the glass splinter came from. It made sense.

"Ma'am!" The EMS guy came outside after her. "Ma'am, you know you can't leave yet. Someone from the sheriff's department is on his way. You're the one who found her. He will want to talk to you."

"I know," Erica answered and sat down deflated in one of Rachel's rocking chairs. She wanted to be anywhere but here, wanted her old life back, the one before she entered this house, but that would never happen.

I have to call Cotton and let him know what's going on, Erica thought. He has to be home when Lucas gets off the school bus. Who knows how long this is going to take. She walked back inside to the house phone and dialed Cotton's number. He answered on the third ring.

"Cotton, you need to come home. Rachel is dead. They told me to wait until someone from the sheriff's department gets here and I don't

246

know how long that will be. Lucas gets off the bus in one and a half hours."

"What? Rachel is dead?" he asked her.

"Yes... I went to Rachel's house to bring her soup. She is dead, Cotton. I can't leave. They told me to wait right here. You have to be home when Lucas gets off the school bus." She started crying and couldn't stop.

"Erica, Honey, I'll be home in forty-five minutes. Hang in there. Go and sit down somewhere. I'm on my way."

"Yes," she answered and hung up the phone. Cotton would handle it. He always did. She could always count on him.

Annegret Werner Shaw

Chapter Twenty-three

W hen Mac Lockhorn received the phone call to respond to a possible suicide, he was more than a little surprised to find out that it happened at the same address he'd been less than a week ago for the fatal dog mauling. Rachel Young, the woman who owned the dog supposedly killed herself. He received a call from Doctor Smith, the veterinarian, an hour ago informing him that the dog was being euthanized tomorrow. Is that why she did it, he mused, as he drove up the pass? Was she so distraught over losing her dog that she killed herself? Somehow he couldn't shake the feeling that there was a lot more to the story of her dog killing her boyfriend, but now he would probably never find out what happened that Saturday night.

A possible suicide, Mac thought. She electrocuted herself; definitely not the preferred way for a woman to end her life. Out of ten suicides by means of electrocution, only one of them was carried out by a woman. Supposedly she climbed on a table and put her fingers into the light sockets. Something was just not right.

He drove up the drive and saw a woman sitting on the patio looking distraught. That's the lady who found her, he surmised. He got out of his car and walked to the patio where he introduced himself to her.

"I'm, Detective Mac Lockhorn, with the Thorn County Sheriff's Department. Are you the person who found Rachel Young?"

"Yes. I'm Erica Stancil. I live in this valley. I was bringing her homemade soup and found her on the kitchen floor."

"I would appreciate if you stick around for a while longer while I go inside and look around. I have some questions for you later."

"Of course," Erica answered and watched him go inside.

Ten minutes later he came back outside. Erica was still sitting in the same chair.

"Now, I need your full name, address and telephone number," he started out and wrote everything she told him on a small note pad.

"Can you tell me what happened when you entered the house?"

"I came by to bring her some potato soup. I called her name when I came in, but she didn't answer me. I took off my raincoat and hung it up when I heard a crash coming from the kitchen and then I saw the lights flicker and go out. I didn't hear her scream or anything. When I entered the kitchen I saw her lying on the floor. I called 911 and then performed CPR.

"Is that how you hurt your knee?" he pointed to her leg. Erica looked down at her knee.

"Oh, that. I forgot about that. I got a glass splinter in it when I kneeled next to her to perform CPR."

"You might want to get that looked at," he told her.

"Believe me, it's no big deal. It doesn't hurt at all."

"Do you have any idea why your friend killed herself?" Mac asked her.

"She what… suicide? You think she killed herself? I figured she tried to change a light bulb and fell. That's probably the loud thump I heard. Why do you think it's a suicide, Detective? "

"Because in the normal scheme of things, you don't get electrocuted changing out a light bulb. There were two empty light sockets and two broken light bulbs on the table and floor, but no new light bulbs anywhere in the kitchen. Why would she climb onto the table without a new light bulb in her hand?" Mac Lockhorn asked her.

Erica was speechless. She had been sitting here thinking that Rachel broke her neck during the fall, but suicide never entered her mind.

"You're basing your theory of suicide on the fact that there were no new light bulbs in the kitchen? Maybe one was the old bulb and one a new bulb."

"Well, all right, here is my unofficial account of what happened, until I get the coroner's report. I found glass splinters from two light bulbs all over the table and on the floor. I found blood on her hands and on the empty light sockets and I'm sure once the Crime Scene Unit is finished they will have found blood on some of the shards of glass. She electrocuted herself by standing on the table and sticking two fingers of each hand into two empty light sockets at the same time. And she has burn marks on two fingers on each hand to prove it. Of course we will get the official version later. We have to wait for the coroner to get here. You heard her fall to the floor when you came in. There was nothing you could have done. It killed her instantly."

Erica couldn't believe what she heard. She was stunned. "If I would have gotten here just a couple minutes earlier, maybe I could have talked her out of it."

"It's hard to say, but you can't blame yourself. Do you have any idea why she would commit suicide?" he asked her.

"No, I don't. Sure, she was depressed about Mark's death and her dog, but I never expected her to kill herself," Erica told him. "No, there has to be more to this. She just wasn't the type to kill herself."

Chapter Twenty-four

Doug finally found the time to fix the broken rain gutter on his house which had irritated him for the last couple of months. The beautiful flower bed his wife had created in the last year of her life had taken a bad beating from the rain gushing out of the broken gutter, flushing the good garden dirt down the driveway. He stood on his tall ladder hammering nails into the wood, whistling the theme melody of *Doctor Zhivago*. He finally snapped back out of his depressing mood. Today was Mark's funeral and slowly things were getting back to normal. The secret of the pods was once more protected from outsiders, or so he thought.

His twenty-year anniversary of being the Senior Harvester was coming up next month. It wasn't like the valley celebrated this day; most people in the valley didn't even remember it, but for him it was important; important in the sense that his normal, carefree life had come to an end that day twenty years ago. It was certainly not a day to celebrate, but a day to curse until the end of his days. It was the day he became in charge of the old leather ledger and officially became the protector of the plant and the valley people, but only he and Satan's Angel knew it; nobody else. It was the day his life took a horrible turn and he would never forget it.

That day Chester Whitney's wife had called him to her husband's deathbed and what Chester told him that day behind closed doors made him regret that he had moved to this cursed valley.

"It's a... damn... hard... job," Chester had told him, the old man's labored breathing breaking the sentences up, his voice barely audible.

"I've... been the Senior Harvester... for thirty-five... years now... and I have seen it all... Don't ever... underestimate... the power of the plant... It's going to control you... now... that you're the... Senior Harvester. Take the ledger... with you today... it's in the top drawer... over there," his eyes looked to the right and indicated the chest of drawers. "Read it... and you will understand... what I'm talking about... It's all in there... all the suicides... all the horrible suicides... since the day the plant was discovered... and all that stands between the suicides... and the plant... is you."

A spasm went through Chester and he coughed; a cough so thick with congestion that he thought it would be the end of the old man right then and there. But eventually he caught his breath again and continued. "Prevent... them when you can... let them happen when you can't." He closed his eyes and Doug thought that Chester had fallen asleep.

"How, how do I do that?" he asked him, putting his hand on the old man's hand, hoping the contact would wake him up. Chester opened his eyes and looked at him with fatigue.

"I hated it... so much... and I'm glad it's... over for me... You will know... believe me, you will know... The feeling will come over you... after my death... the way it came over me... that awful feeling... when the Senior Harvester dies... It's a horrible... sickening feeling... and a headache you won't forget... you think you're dying... and the only way you can make it stop... is to take action... you may already be too late... or you may not... always look for the pod left behind... Any time the plant... senses danger... it will let you know... It's Satan's Angel come to earth... read Revelations 12:9 ... you will understand...

who knows… how many of THEM came to earth… all over this earth… but one is right here… living high up in the mountain cave… controlling our valley… read it… you will understand… He's tempting us… and he is collecting… and in the end, he will get what he came for… the souls… all the lost souls… and I helped him get them… I'm… afraid to die… I don't want… to walk… through the wrong… door… Help… me."

Doug had stared at him for a while, waiting for his next words, but there were none. Chester was dead. He stood up, still thinking about all the things he had told him. He walked to the chest of drawers and opened the top drawer. The ledger was right there. The last and only time he had seen it was over five years ago when Chester showed him the book and told him to find and take it after his death. That when the time came it would belong to him and he would be the new record keeper, the new Senior Harvester. He had asked him what he was supposed to take records of, but Chester only told him; "You will see… You will see. Don't show it to anyone else, keep it safe. Guard it with your life. It contains everything… everything."

He left the death room holding the ledger, passing Chester's wife in the hallway. He shook his head and told her that Chester was gone and hugged her. He couldn't give her any more without breaking down, his plate too full with his own emotions. He needed to get outside in a hurry, needed to breathe the clean mountain air and leave the gloomy atmosphere of the house behind. Chester's words weighed heavily on him. Were they the rambling words of a dying old man whose pain and fears clouded his mind, or where they words of wisdom and experience?

He walked up the mountain path behind Chester's house until he calmed down, then sat on a large boulder and opened the ledger, ready to find out what was inside. What he read changed his world forever. It was a day he would never forget for the rest of his life. That day he became a man without a choice; a man blackmailed by the brutal facts inside the ledger. Doing right and doing wrong merged together for him that day, the only other choice remaining was to choose death. Death…

the ultimate sacrifice... he wasn't ready or brave enough to die; ultimately he was already a victim of Satan's Angel, his soul forever lost to him.

For many months afterward he wondered what Chester had meant when he had told him about the awful feeling he would get, until he put it out of his mind. Three years later in 1993, he was mowing the lawn and the feeling Chester had talked about hit him for the first time. It was a feeling of utter doom coming over him out of nowhere. Like a dark heavy cloud settled over him, affecting his lungs with heaviness, making it hard for him to breathe. At first he thought he was having a heart attack, but there was no pain. He threw up, sweat running down his face. His head was throbbing with pain. Death was certainly around the corner. He battled it for two hours.

Strangely enough, he thought of Edward Hanks several times during this time of pain and agony and couldn't explain why his thoughts turned to him. And then the feeling of doom left him and he was back to normal. Fifteen minutes later he heard the sirens and found out that Edward Hanks had killed himself by setting himself on fire. And suddenly it all made sense to him, he figured out the connection between the feeling and the suicide. The words Chester had uttered to him entered his mind; always look for the peas left behind. He was too late to stop Edward from killing himself, but hadn't been too late to look for the pod. He found it in the glove compartment of Edward's car.

Since that horrible day, he experienced the feeling of doom several more times and he recognized it instantly. The next time Joseph Mass face came to his mind. He took action instantly, even though he was in a town thirty miles away from the valley, sitting in a dentist's chair. He jumped up, his mouth numb and swollen from the Novocain he had received, and left a stunned dentist behind holding his drill.

The symptoms disappeared the moment he took action. By the time he reached Joseph's house, he was already dead. He never found the pod, but Joseph's wife Muriel told him that her husband had had an

256

important meeting in town and hoped to get into some money. Doug knew that it involved the peas, but also knew that the plant was at peace again, not interrupting his thoughts any longer.

And then there was Old Man Cobb, Angela Barns and twenty-year-old Russell; they all became victims of Satan's Angel one way or the other.

And now all the problems he had with Rachel. He hated dealing with women.

It was the night of the Festival of the Pods four days ago, and he had just come out of his own trance, experiencing the most pleasurable dreams after chewing one of the peas as soon as he returned home. He had been in such a carefree state, when out of the blue a headache assaulted him so hard that his vision was temporarily blinded by the intensity of the pain. A woman's face entered his mind; Rachel Young's face. Doug sat down in his recliner and the phone rang. He could barely reach for it, his headache killing him. It was Eddie Heinz, and what he told him blew his mind. He jumped up; ready to drive over to Rachel's house and the headache diminished and then disappeared altogether. He never had much to do with Rachel, but he knew where she lived. By the time he reached her house it was already swarming with people. All he could do was to warn her not to talk about the peas.

And the next day he found out that her dog had swallowed one of the peas… if this wasn't the craziest situation ever. Rachel really loved that dog and he hated himself for coming down so hard on her, but what was he supposed to do? He didn't have any other choice. Nobody in this valley understood or realized that he would suffer the most severe consequences if he didn't handle the situation right, no matter if he liked it or not.

The only thing that mattered was that Satan's Angel was content with his actions, dealing with the problem. Rachel hadn't told anyone about the peas and she wouldn't, not after he got through with her. He hated hitting her; hated being him, but there was no other way to convince her to stay quiet. Oh, how he hated being the Senior Harvester and cursed the day he became one. It had become increasingly harder to keep the pods a secret, almost impossible with cell phones, texting, Facebook and instant messaging. It was a good thing that most cell phones didn't get reception this high up in these isolated mountains. The few people who owned Satellite phones in this valley were all users. Man was he glad that this business with Rachel was finally settled and over.

The horrible things he had to do to appease Satan's Angel. All the lives he had affected by his terrible deeds in helping to keep the secret of the valley safe. Doug didn't allow his thoughts to drift to those memories any longer, they were too horrible to revisit. But for some reason, he couldn't avoid thinking about them today. He had stooped down to the lowest level of humanity. He did things he never thought he was capable of, and if his wife would have known, she would have despised him for it.

The worst was when he was blackmailed by the plant into putting a crushed pea into sixteen-year-old Angela Barns' Diet Coke. She had talked about the pods on Facebook, telling her friends that her parents were taking them and that she wanted some. How the plant knew was only a guess on Doug's part, probably through the thoughts of her parents who were users. They scolded her and took her computer away from her for a month, but for Satan's Angel it wasn't enough. It wanted Angela under its control so it forced Doug to act.

He refused, had fought against it until he threw up from the horrible headaches it tortured him with, and eventually he gave up and did what it asked him to do. It wasn't that hard to accomplish. He placed the crushed pea into her Diet Coke when she went for a swim with her girlfriend. He pretended to take a stroll with Gabriel and rested by the picnic bench where he saw her drinking the coke. How was he supposed to know what consequences his actions would have?

One week later, Angela became the first runaway in Hunter's Valley history. He had written Angela's name into the ledger, not under the suicides, but under a new category; missing. Doug was the only one who knew that her absence was the direct result of the pods. Satan's Angel was smart. Smart enough to know that too many suicides in the valley would attract unwanted attention. A runaway teenager would never fall into that category. In all likelihood she was probably dead by now, but her parents were still full of hope that she would return home one of these days. He had to live each and every day knowing how much her parents suffered. At times it was unbearable. Beer was his answer so many nights; a whole lot of beer.

It felt good to have the plant at peace again. Four suicides during his reign as Senior Harvester were enough for him and he longed for peace and quiet. He was now seventy years old and knew he would hand over the torch to Adam soon. He felt it in his bones. His time on this earth was nearing its end. But it didn't bother him much that he would die, it bothered him much more to know that his soul belonged to Satan, the way it had bothered Chester before he died. He would walk through the wrong door, just like Chester and all his predecessors before him.

All these thoughts went through his mind on this beautiful morning. The birds were singing and the valley's heartbeat could be heard in the distance. One of his neighbors was mowing his lawn; another one was using a hammer somewhere down by the lake, the sounds echoing up the hill to him. He heard children playing in the distance and the occasional barking of a dog. Yes, it was a beautiful day in this God-forsaken damned valley.

He was just about finished with the rain gutter when he felt the first drop of rain hitting his hand. He looked up with surprise; the weather forecast had predicted no rain for the next three days. A dark cloud, heavy with unshed moisture, was approaching the valley from the north. Quickly he hammered the last two nails into the roof rafters and then climbed down the ladder, satisfied that he had finished the job before the downpour started

He collected his tools and took them to the shed, putting them exactly where they belonged, then returned to fetch the ladder. He was very organized, had been for all his life, a lesson he learned early on from his father. Everything had its place and if he needed something he would always know where to find it and not waste any unnecessary time looking for it.

Doug thought of his wife like he had every day since she passed three years ago. He missed her desperately. They moved to this valley forty-three years ago as newlyweds. It had been paradise for them. He became a user during the first Festival of the Pods, but not Betty. Oh, no. She had been so stubborn and refused to try them. Back then, he had thought that she was missing out, that she was narrow minded, not willing to try new things, but now he knew different. She had been the smart one, the strong one, never giving up her values. She watched him being a user for decades and stayed on her own path through all those years. When he became a Harvester, she had tolerated his obsession. He quit urging her to take the peas after he became the Senior Harvester, realizing she had been right all along.

And then she became sick. She was diagnosed with breast cancer and it devastated him. It was hard for him to see her suffer when she got sick, and even though he knew that the peas could ease her pain and maybe even extend her life for a couple more years, he resisted in giving them to her. He could have easily put the crushed peas in her drink, but he didn't. It was the one time in his life that he stayed strong, the one time he resisted. And now that he looked back, it was the best thing he had ever done in his life, his proudest moment. At least in that one instance he had been unselfish. She passed peacefully one night without falling into Satan's Angel's hands. Her soul was saved and it gave him great peace of mind to know that she was with God.

"Going to be a downpour in another minute," he told Gabriel, his Great Dane, who followed him as he carried the ladder to the back of the shed and hung it up on the hooks. "We better get inside before it hits."

Together they entered the house through the back door where Doug took off his shoes and slipped on his house shoes. It was only ten-thirty, but he already thought about what he could fix for lunch. Several options came to mind, but he didn't feel like spending a lot of time preparing it, so he decided on a simple ham and cheese sandwich with three bread and butter pickles on top of it and a cold glass of milk. He heard the raindrops hitting the tin roof over the patio. The noise was an instant invitation for him to take a short nap. He ate his sandwich and washed the dishes he had dirtied and then put everything back where it belonged. Doug walked to the living room and laid down on the couch, the Great Dane followed his example and plopped down on the opposite end. The rain was coming down hard by now, the noise lulling him to sleep. Within minutes both of them were dead to the world, unaware of the drama unfolding in the valley.

He dreamed of the plant; saw the plant getting larger coming toward him. The delicate flowers were closed. Satan's Angel was sleeping just like he was and he stared at it. How could something so beautiful be so evil? All of the sudden, the leaves and branches came alive and moved on their own accord. The blossoms opened up even though it was the middle of the day and then they started screeching angrily. He covered his ears to get away from the horrible piercing screams, but he couldn't.

It was two hours later that Doug woke up from the nauseating feeling he suddenly experienced. Dumbfounded, he sat up and a heavy, gloomy cloud settled over him, the feeling all too familiar. No, not again…what is happening now, he thought, still sleep befuddled. What is going on? Who? Where?

The face of Rachel Young entered his mind again and he jumped up, ready to drive to her house. What was the woman up to now? The feeling subsided instantly, his head now clear. He knew what he was supposed to do.

Chapter Twenty-five

Mac Lockhorn was questioning Erica outside Rachel's house when she saw Doug driving up in his jeep. What was he doing here and how did he know this time, she wondered? She certainly hadn't called him and neither did the EMS guy or Mac Lockhorn. Erica had an extreme aversion to Doug ever since Rachel told her what he said to her the night of Mark's death. That uncaring son of a bitch! He cared more about the pods than the residents of this valley. She watched him climb out of his jeep and walk over to them.

"What happened?" Doug asked immediately. "Did something happen to Rachel?"

"Why do you ask, Doug? How do you know that something happened?" Erica asked him agitated, not being able to resist.

"I... I came over to talk to Rachel and I'm just surprised to see the Detective here, that's all," he answered, slightly disturbed by her aggressiveness. How dare she? "What happened?" he asked again, ignoring Erica, looking straight at the detective, tolerating no more from her.

"Ms. Young is dead," Mac Lockhorn told him, sensing the tension between the two people in front of him. "She killed herself."

"What? Why?"

"We don't know," Erica answered, then remembered her manners. "Doug, this is Detective Mac Lockhorn with the Thorn County

Sheriff's Department," then she turned toward the detective and told him. "This is Doug Manchester. He lives in this valley."

The two men shook hands acknowledging each other.

"Didn't I see you the other night when Mark Hiller died?" Mac Lockhorn asked him.

"Yes, I was here to console Rachel. She is...was a good friend of mine," Doug told him, the answer sounding believable.

But Erica knew otherwise. She knew why Doug had come to see her that night and it wasn't because he wanted to console her; that much was for sure. A creepy feeling went through her. Something was horribly wrong in this valley and it all centered on Doug Manchester and the pods.

Voices were coming from the entryway and a couple seconds later Erica watched two men pushing the gurney with Rachel's body out of the house. A white sheet covered her body and was held in place by two straps. Erica barely kept her emotions under control. She didn't want to fall apart in front of the two men. All she wanted to do right now was to go home and be with Cotton and Lucas.

"What is going to happen now? Who is going to call her parents and her ex-husband Bruce? I've never met them." She felt so helpless. "Should I go inside and see if I can find some numbers?" Erica asked Mac Lockhorn.

"Let me go inside and talk to the coroner and the crime scene unit. I will know more after that. What is her ex's name?"

"Bruce Young," Erica and Doug answered simultaneously.

Dreading being alone with Doug, Erica tried to think of something she could do to avoid it, but nothing came to mind. The detective left and Erica turned to look at Doug. It seemed that he was evaluating her, like he was trying to figure out how she fit into this picture.

"Was Rachel a good friend of yours?" he asked her.

"Yes," Erica answered. For some reason she didn't trust this man.

"Were you here when Rachel killed herself?" he asked.

"No, I came right after it happened. I was bringing her some food."

"Did Rachel tell you anything about what happened to Mark Hiller?"

"She told me Tiger killed him. Why are you asking me all these questions?" she asked totally annoyed with him.

"Because... because I feel responsible. She was a user just like you are... and all users are my concern."

Wow, Erica thought. That was direct and unexpected. Was he trying to warn her like he had warned Rachel a couple of days ago? She didn't quite know what to say after that. She could ask him some direct questions like, how come there are so many suicides in this valley, but she didn't want to arouse his suspicions so she just stood there and waited.

"Do not talk to the detective about the pods. You know the rules," Doug told her. "It would be a horrible, bad mistake." They stared at each other.

"I have no such intentions," Erica answered him sarcastically.

"Good, then I can leave. My job here is done." Doug turned around and walked back to his vehicle. Erica watched him leave. Asshole, she thought, so much for being a good friend of Rachel's. The only reason he came was to protect the valley's secret. Mac Lockhorn came back outside carrying a piece of paper. He looked around for Doug.

"Did he leave?" he asked her. "I had some questions for him. It's the second time that he turned up shortly after someone dies. What did he want?" he asked Erica.

"I don't know. He didn't tell me."

"All right, I found a list of numbers next to the refrigerator. We will call the family and let them know. You can go home now if you like. If I have any more questions I'll give you a call."

"Thanks," Erica replied, relieved that she didn't have to call Rachel's parents. She left without looking back. How could life be so complicated and cruel?

Chapter Twenty-six

rica sat outside in her lawn chair staring at the street above the dam. The upstairs patio of her master bedroom offered the best view of the small road leading out of the valley. It was the only way through the pass and she knew Doug had to take it to get to his Doctor's appointment in the city. She overheard him last Saturday telling Adam that he had to go for his three month check-up this Wednesday morning, but she didn't catch the time of his appointment. She had been sitting on the patio ever since she put Lucas on the school bus, drinking her fourth cup of coffee.

It was almost nine-thirty and she was getting irritated with herself. Why did she feel so strongly about finding out what was going on? Couldn't she just leave it alone? But something told her that the valley's secret and the mysterious ledger had something to do with Mark Hiller's and Rachel's deaths, and probably all the other suicides which had happened in this valley over the last ten years. Was she the only one in the valley who thought it odd?

Everything pointed to Doug Manchester. Even Cotton didn't listen to her, but she just couldn't let it be, like some unknown force was driving her. Erica remembered Mac Lockhorn's words the last time she talked to him. He had told her that something just didn't seem right to him concerning Mark's and Rachel's deaths, but he couldn't put his finger on it. Well, she knew. She knew damn well what happened, but she didn't tell him. Rachel's death was officially declared a suicide.

The day after Rachel died, Erica went to the veterinarian clinic to be with Tiger when he was euthanized. She took him a pound of sliced roast beef and fed him each slice, talking and loving on him for the last time. She knew Rachel would have wanted her to do this. She cried when he was put to sleep and watched him fall asleep peacefully until it was over. The tears came running out of her and she knew that she was not just crying for Tiger, but also for Rachel. What a sad ending of their lives. Totally depleted of emotions she drove home, jumped on her four-wheeler and drove through the National Forest, gaining strength from the natural wilderness surrounding her. That was seven weeks ago.

If she could just have a look into that old ledger of his, she was sure that it held the answers. To her it was more than a coincidence that three people killed themselves in a small valley which only had one hundred twenty-five residents and only sixty of them adults. Three people, out of sixty, what did that equate to? One out of twenty? A week ago, out of curiosity, she went to the Internet and typed in Ratio of Suicides in the USA and according to the 2003 National Institute of Mental Health the statistics came up a whole lot lower than what it was here in the valley. The national average suicide rate for men was 0.01 percent which meant that out of a 100,000 men 10.6 would commit suicide. That was a staggering difference to the ratio in this valley. True, maybe she read more into this then she should, but she just had this gut instinct that something was wrong, that there was a reason and she had to follow up with the plan she concocted. The worst that could happen was that she would get arrested for trespassing. She could live with that, but she couldn't live with knowing that she stood by and waited until another person committed suicide.

Another car drove down the street and Erica picked up the binoculars to look at the driver, but even without them she could tell that it wasn't Doug's red jeep. Luckily there was such little traffic on the street that she could hear the vehicle's motor rumbling before it drove past the other side of the lake. In the time they had lived here she had come to recognize every resident's vehicle, but she wasn't going to take any chances. She wanted to see Doug's face behind the steering wheel to rule out any mistakes. She was going to do something illegal, but at least she was going about it in a smart way. She always applied her rule of eliminating as many risk factors as possible for anything she did, therefore lowering her chances of failure.

The last time she had done something this stupid was when she and Sandy, her best friend from high school, climbed the water tower in her home town, just because they wanted to. It was dark and they had climbed the fence, which was clearly there to keep people out, and ignored the no trespassing signs visible on all four sides of the tower. Nothing had deterred them.

They climbed the ladder seventy feet up and sat with their feet dangling off the top platform looking down at the lights of their hometown. They had sat up there for hours, talking about the future, thinking they owned the world, feeling like they were the only ones brave enough to do what everyone else secretly wanted to do. That was when she was sixteen-years-old, but she wasn't sixteen any more, yet, she was still an adrenaline junkie. She loved bungee jumping any chance she got and loved parachuting out of an airplane, but that only happened once in a while. She missed the daily excitement of training and performing with the killer whales, but at the same time she knew that she would never go back to it. If she was truthful with herself she would admit that this adventure, that's what she called it, that this adventure excited her. Her heart was beating just a little bit faster than normal.

She was just about to get up to refill her cup of coffee when she heard another car coming down the road. Even without the binoculars she saw that it was a red jeep. Looking through them, she saw Doug behind the wheel. Her heart started to beat faster now, the adrenaline kicking into high gear. It was time to act. She jumped out of the chair and ran down the stairs. The keys to the four-wheeler were lying ready on the kitchen table. Dino jumped up excitedly and waved his tail with anticipation, but she had to disappoint him.

"You have to be a good boy and stay right here," she told him then closed the door behind her.

Cotton purchased the four-wheelers half a year ago so they could take Lucas on the trails through the national forest surrounding the valley. One of them sat waiting for her in the driveway. Erica had driven Lucas to the bus stop on the four-wheeler this morning and left it outside to get to Doug's house in a hurry. She climbed on and started the motor. She figured that driving around the lake to the opposite side of the dam where Doug's house was would only take her eight minutes or so.

She drove over the dam and then turned left. In the back of her mind, she knew that Cotton would kill her if he found out what she was up to. B ut it was too late to turn around; her mind was made up. The opportunity had presented itself and she grabbed it, knowing that if she didn't she would regret it later. Too many horrible things had happened in this valley for her not to act and the mysterious ledger was tied to it all. To find it and to unravel the mystery of the plant, which supposedly held all the secrets, would be incredible. She would tell Cotton later… much later.

She simply had to find the ledger and put her eyes on it; find out once and for all if there was any truth to what Robin had told her. If all this turned out to be a big hoax she would be satisfied and relieved, but if it wasn't she would hopefully do something about it, even though she had no idea what it would be. She parked the four-wheeler higher up the road past Doug's house and then walked through the yard to his back patio. Slowly she climbed the wooden steps to the back door, realizing suddenly that there was one thing she had forgotten about and that was Gabriel, Doug's Great Dane.

She had heard Logan talk about Gabriel, the huge dog, to Lucas. How was she going to get past the dog? She had never met him and now realized that entering Doug's house would be more difficult than she had imagined. She took a deep breath and climbed the last two steps. She could handle this; after all, she wasn't afraid of killer whales, so why would she be afraid of a Great Dane? They weren't called the gentle giants for nothing. Suddenly a huge black and white dog came through the dog flap in the door and rushed at her, barking loudly. She stood her ground.

"Gabriel, come," she told him with a commanding voice, right away taking charge of the situation. The dog came to a stop and looked at her, confused. "Gabriel, come," she told him and he took a couple steps forward, close enough for her to touch him if she wanted to, but she held back, giving him time to adjust to her, getting used to her odor. She lowered her hand and let him sniff it. "Good boy, Gabriel," she praised him. "Good boy. Sit Gabriel," she told him, establishing dominance over him.

He sat down obediently, accepting her leadership. She patted his large head talking in a soft voice to him and after a couple of minutes of spending time with him she felt sure enough that the dog wouldn't give her any problems if she went inside the house. She moved closer to the big dog door and crawled on her hands and knees through the opening, the leather flap rubbing against the length of her back. Gabriel followed her inside and looked at her, his short stub of a tail waving back and forth, happy now for the unexpected company. She patted him affectionately then kept talking to him, just letting him hear her calm voice.

"Hey, Gabriel, why don't you show me where your master keeps the mysterious journal? It would save me a lot of time," she told him. Gabriel ignored her words and kept on staring at her, waving his tail. "Have it your way," she said and walked into what looked to be Doug's study. "Now, where would I keep something that important?" she mumbled to herself. "Not just anywhere in the open. No, it has to be in a special place; somewhere he thinks it's safe from anybody entering the house."

She had watched so many crime shows on television where people hid things and tried to recall their hiding spots. "Let's see, Dexter hid the blood samples of his victims in an air-conditioner. Well, there are no air conditioners in this house. How about some loose floor boards?"

She walked through the two bedroom house and checked for any loose floorboards, but couldn't detect any. She tried to find the attic access. Visitors wouldn't climb into an attic of somebody's house by accident, so it would be a safe place. Where in the devil was his attic access? She checked the hall way, the most likely place for it to be, but it wasn't there. He didn't have an attached garage so it couldn't be there either. She walked into each room and checked the closets. None had an attic access door. She checked the laundry room and after that walked into the kitchen and opened the pantry door, halfway not expecting it there. Surprised she looked at the small access panel over her head.

The pantry was about five feet by five feet, surprisingly large, with five rows of one foot wide shelves running along two walls. Cans of vegetables, cereal boxes and condiments were stacked in orderly fashion. Boxes of rice, pasta, Hamburger Helper, Betty Crocker scalloped potatoes and sweet potatoes were lined up on the bottom shelf. Anything you needed to make an unproblematic meal in a hurry. It was a well-stocked pantry with jars of alfredo sauces, pesto sauces and traditional red sauces. Who would have thought that Doug was such a stickler in his kitchen, she thought? This is the way my pantry should look. She looked around for a sturdy stool to climb inside the attic on, when she noticed the five rung step ladder folded and put up between the refrigerator and the wall.

Erica pulled the ladder out, careful not to leave a scratch on the wall and opened it up inside the pantry. She climbed up easily and lifted the white painted attic board to the inside of the opening then stepped on top of the fifth step, her head and chest passing through the opening. Gabriel came to the pantry, obviously curious as to what she was up to. He licked his jowls which looked humongous; clearly this pantry was the place where Doug kept the dog's treats, but she didn't have time to look for them now.

"Gabriel, be a good boy and lay down," she told him. "I'll be right back."

She hoisted her lower body through the opening inside the attic. It was a good thing that she was so athletic. She looked around the attic; the two sides of the slanted roof met in the middle about five feet above the attic floor, a small window and the attic access were the only sources which gave light to the attic. She looked for the pull string of the light fixture she knew was somewhere and found it to her right. The light turned on without any problem and now she could study the space without worrying that she would miss something. Erica couldn't stand up all the way, so she surveyed the small angled space bending down. Now where would Doug keep the darn journal, she mused, when she spotted the small military footlocker in the narrow part under the roof. Her heart started to hammer in her chest with excitement. Somehow, she knew that the journal was inside. She crawled to the far wall and pulled the footlocker toward her. Disappointed, she realized that it was locked with a typical five number lock, the same kind she had used for her school locker so many years ago. She was upset, realizing how close she had come to putting her eyes on the mysterious journal.

She sat there thinking of what to do next. Think, Erica, think, she told herself. Think this all the way through. Should she give up or should she try to open the lock by force. She looked at her wrist watch. Thirty minutes had passed since she had seen Doug drive past the mail boxes. She still had plenty of time to finish what she came to do. Doug was probably entering the city limits right now and would take another fifteen to get to the Medical Center to his doctor's office. She was safe for another two hours at the least.

She heard Gabriel whining down below and yelled at him to be quiet.

"Damn Gabriel, just a little longer. Be quiet and sit."

The whining stopped. Surprised that Gabriel listened to her she looked again at the footlocker, contemplating her options. If she did open it by force, Doug would know it the minute he came up here to get the ledger. But, he was seventy-years-old and she couldn't picture him climbing through the attic opening every day, so it would be a while before he found out that someone had looked at it. Would he report it to the police? She doubted it seriously; especially if nothing was missing. No, he wouldn't and he would never figure out who did it either. She surveyed the attic for something to use to open the lock and realized that she would make a poor burglar. She hadn't considered bringing a tool along for just this purpose.

Then a thought occurred to her. What were the numbers he had the lock set on? It read 32540. The last two numbers could be the year he was born. He turned seventy a couple of month ago. When had that been? She was horrible with dates, but she remembered the day so well. It was the day Lucas and Logan dragged the cardboard boxes into the woods to build their clubhouse. When did they celebrate Doug's birthday? She thought back, trying to recall anything to pinpoint the exact day. Something else was going on that day? What was it? It was a Saturday and Cotton was home. Lucas and Logan were building the clubhouse for boys only and she had been busy with what?

Think, Erica, think, she told herself. Something else happened that day, but what in the hell was it? And then it came to her. She remembered that she had to leave shortly after wishing Doug a Happy Birthday and left Cotton in charge of Lucas and Dino. In her mind's eye she saw herself shaking Doug's hand and then making her excuse to leave. Why did she have to leave? She left with Robin, and then she knew. It was the afternoon of Sarah's baby shower and she had been one of the hostesses in charge of the cake and the invitations. She had written the date twenty-six times on the invitation cards. The party had been on Saturday the sixth of May. Grinning from ear to ear, happy to recall the date, Erica moved the numbers of the lock to go with the month and date, hoping against all odds that she was right. Could she really be this lucky?

She turned and placed the numbers in the correct order 0 5 6 4 0 then pulled the lock, but it didn't budge. Disappointed she tried the second version of putting the numbers in order, 5 0 6 4 0. She tried the lock again and this time it opened.

Erica took a deep breath, happy that it worked. Wow, how lucky could she be? The lock was open. She had done it. She outfoxed the fox. Excited and proud of herself she unhooked the lock and lifted the top of the footlocker. She knew right away that she had found the old ledger. The wrinkled leather bound book was lying on top of hunting magazines and other papers looking extremely aged, frail and significant.

Hesitantly, she touched the brown weathered hide. Could this really be as old as Robin said it was? The outside binding was made out of thin leather protecting the pages inside. She lifted the book out of the footlocker and looked at it mesmerized. She realized that she was holding something out of the ordinary in her hands and was awestruck at her success in finding it. Slowly, she opened the ledger to its first page. A wave of uneasiness swept through her and she received a feeling of trespassing where no one had trespassed before. The feeling that this was a moment of importance, a discovery of a lifetime, struck her and she realized that she could never undo what she was about to do next; read what was inside the ledger.

She hesitated, realizing it was her last chance to back off, her last chance to keep her innocence and not be drawn into something way too big for her; something so unimaginable and malevolent that she would be horrified to understand its full meaning. But she shook the weird feeling off; something inside of her urging her on. She didn't come this far to turn her back on what she considered to be her duty and a great mystery. Maybe she would find out today what was going on in this valley and what caused all the suicides. After all, this was important to the wellbeing of all the valley's residents. One way or another she would find out if it was a big hoax. In that case, she would have a good laugh and feel stupid, but somehow she knew that that wasn't going to happen.

She felt something else inside of her, something foreign and unfamiliar and the feeling persisted. It irritated her, not because she was scared, but because she thought she knew herself and knew what she was all about, but in this instant she didn't understand herself. What was wrong with her? She felt strange, like she was not alone in her mind, but was being used and perhaps manipulated; but how could that be? Who would use her and for what reason? The feeling persisted. Weird thoughts not her own entered her mind.

Go ahead and read it. Find out the truth. You're just one of many players in my game. Read the words and be damned.

She shook her head. Shit, what was going on with her today? Where did these crazy thoughts come from? Maybe I should stop and go home, she thought, the weird sensations getting to her. I have no right being here, reading things which are not meant to be read by me. Erica hesitated, closed the ledger and was ready to put it back into the footlocker, but something took a hold of her; something stronger. She tried to reason with herself. It wasn't her fault that she was such a dare devil, it was her parents' fault. They had always told her to go after what she really wanted, and this was what she really wanted, wasn't it? Ever since Robin told her about the ledger, she had wanted to see it.

She finally opened the ledger to the first page and saw a hand drawn sketch of a plant. It looked familiar to her and she recognized the Trumpet Angel from Adam's oil painting. Small little penciled lines connected parts of the plant to the handwritten descriptions. She read them carefully:

Flower looks like a black Angel Trumpet - six blood-red, narrow fine lines feathering to the outer rim of each blossom - green oval shaped, hand-sized leaves have a narrow tip on the end - sturdy green trunk with little thorns - thin green tendrils curling around its branches.

Below the picture she read the next entry.

I found brown pods lying in abundance around the trunk of the plant. The flowers open up at sundown and only bloom from mid-June to the end of August. The pods are shed during the early days of August. Each pod holds three blood-red peas inside its shell, on rare occasions I only found two peas inside. They look wrinkled, the size of healthy grapes, but are extremely juicy and tasty. The plant doesn't require much sunlight or water. It is a mystery what sustains the plant. Efforts to grow more plants outside its habitat have proven futile.

Below the notes Erica read the signature and date.

Discovered 'The Black Trumpet Angel'
on August 3rd 1755
Bulk Horswell

Goosebumps covered Erica's arms and neck as she read the date, realizing how old it was. So, it was all real then, everything Doug had said in the opening speech was true and not made up. How amazing. She flipped to the second page and read on.

Loretta's recovery from the brink of death for the reason of childbirth was the result of her drinking a tea made from the crushed peas. To celebrate her recovery and the healing powers of the peas, we will celebrate the plant's existence by having an annual Festival of the Pods each August, commencing with church service to praise the Lord for his miracles.

Underneath the entry Erica found a set of rules.

Set of Rules

Only valley people can be users.
Users have to swear not to reveal the plant's
existence to outsiders.
Users have to swear never to take the pods
outside this valley.
Junior Harvester must be a user for five years
before being chosen by Senior Harvester.
Only the Junior and Senior Harvester
can know the location of the plant.
The position of Junior and Senior Harvester is for life.
The ledger has to be handed down to Junior Harvester shortly before
death of Senior Harvester.

September 29, 1758
Bulk Horswell

It was all right there in front of her; the rules the valley still followed today. It all happened so long ago. Totally spellbound, Erica read on.

She flipped through a couple more pages which held entries about the plant's growing cycle and sketches of the pods and the peas. She read everything, not wanting to skip any important information. The next pages were records of men who held down the job as Harvesters, starting with Bulk Horswell and Hank Horswell. The four vertical columns read; Junior Harvester, Senior Harvester, Date of Oath, and the last one; Date of Death. Looking at the years, Erica realized that some men were Harvesters for over forty years, some as short as two or three years. The Junior Harvester moved into the position of the Senior Harvester at the time of his death; the symbol of death neatly placed next to the date. It was a long list and she was amazed at all the different styles of handwriting and names. The last two names were all too familiar to her; Doug Manchester and Adam Fletcher.

To read the names of people she actually knew made it seem so much more valid. It was like the past was connected to the present and the empty pages following the last name pointed to the future. Nothing she read indicated any wrongdoing. She flipped through a couple more empty pages not expecting to find anything else, but to her surprise she came to a page holding only a few sentences. She quickly looked at her wristwatch, hoping enough time was left for her to read it. She had at least an hour before she had to get out of Doug's house. She concentrated back onto the page and was totally shocked at what she read next.

Two additional rules were written down. The script looked shaky, as if it was written with a trembling hand. It read;

Only the Senior Harvester will know about
the plant's mind controlling powers and suicides.
I urge every Senior Harvester who steps into my shoes to keep good
records of suicides in the valley.
I curse the plant's existence.
I curse the day I discovered it.
Beware, for it is Satan's Angel come to earth.

August 8th 1766
Bulk Horswell

Erica started shaking. She stared at the words in shock and slowly read the two sentences again. The words 'mind controlling powers and suicides' were underlined by the writer over two hundred years ago. She felt dizzy. What had she gotten herself into? She took several deep breaths to steady herself, then flipped back to the set of the first rules. Eight years had gone by since Bulk Horswell had written the first set of rules. Erica felt an incredible nervousness inside of her, yet, she couldn't keep from turning the page. She saw another list of names and years, starting in 1766, the same year the latest rules were added. Horrified she realized that it was a suicide list.

Edward Thompson – August 1766 – jumped off the cliff after discovering where the plant grows. Witnessed by Bulk and Hank Horswell.

Augustus Mueller – August 1771 – ran himself and horse off Hunter's Cliff.

Bulk Horswell – September 1771 – he was my brother and died a hero. He tied a rock to his leg and drowned himself in the valley's lake after trying to destroy the plant with his hatchet.

If anybody is brave enough in the future to follow in my brother's footsteps…destroy the tap….

Erica read the entry and was shocked. Bulk Horswell, the person who discovered the plant killed himself…and what did…destroy the tap… mean? She was shocked. She could suddenly sense evil around her and started to get nauseated, but forced herself to read on. This was too important. A fragile folded piece of paper fell out of the ledger when she turned the next page. She opened it and saw that it was a handwritten note and when she read it her head started spinning.

Hank, the plant is Satan's Angel come to earth to collect souls. I have been his helper for too long. I can't do it any longer. It needs to end today, before another person commits suicide. I have decided to destroy the plant and if I succeed you will never find this note or this ledger. God willing, I will survive. If I don't, please take care of Loretta and the children. Be reassured that I would never commit suicide on my own accord. God help me. God help us all! My faith will carry me through.

Don't follow in my footsteps. The responsibility lies with you now. Read this ledger and you will understand everything.

Bulk Horswell,

September 23,

in the year of our Lord 1771.

She read it a second time. Her thoughts were racing. She had stepped into something major, but she wanted to read on. She hadn't come this far to stop or get squeamish. Right now she just needed to find out as much as possible, and later, in the safety of her own home she would figure out what it all meant and what she could do about it. She steadied her nerves and then read on, her eyes getting larger with each name.

Hector von Steinbruch - August 1787 - hung himself inside his smoke shed.

William Dusk - September 1799 – shot himself with musket in horse corral.

Henry Koenig – September 1803 – hung himself in barn.

Milton Hall – August 1815 – cut his wrists in nearby woods with hunting knife.

Theo Johnson – August 1834 – ate poisonous mushrooms.

Brothers Victor and Scott McCormic – October 1867 – murder/suicide – shot Victor then set barn on fire, locked it from the inside and burned to death.

Harold Hammons – September 1871 – cut his throat in bed with hunting knife while lying next to his sleeping wife.

Erica read each entry, each more horrible than the one before. She couldn't believe it. She counted the names. Forty-nine suicides in this little valley, ending with the last five entries.

Edward Hanks – September 1993 – poured gasoline over himself and set himself on fire.
Joseph Mass – August 1999 – cut his leg off with a chainsaw and bled to death.
Old Man Cobb – 2003 - plant forced me to put a crushed pea into his beer – died in a car accident.
Angela Barns – September 2006 – runaway – plant forced me to put ground-up pea into her coke. (Presumed dead)
Russell Bradley - August 2007 – carbon-monoxide poisoning inside his car on top of Manitou Hill.
Mark Hiller – August 2010 – mauled to death by dog. (Dog swallowed one of the peas)
Rachel Young – August 2010 – electrocuted herself

Erica started shaking violently. Mark and Rachel, Rachel and Mark, Angela Barns and Old man Cobb. She had heard about the sixteen-year-old runaway a while back and now she found out that she unknowingly had become a user. And Old Man Cobb, the man who had rattled the secret to a doctor in town, was also dead because of the peas.

Erica felt dizzy, her thoughts catapulting in all directions. All the victims were users, and if they weren't, they were made to be users by Doug. How could he do such a horrible thing to an old man and a teenage girl? A moan escaped her lips as she remembered what she had read earlier. The plant had mind controlling powers and not just when you chewed a pea. It had control over its users mind… all the time.

"No… no, it can't be… nothing can be this evil," she whispered.

"I'm a user, Robin is a user, Adam is…. Oh, no…What is going to happen next?" Her head started hurting with the overwhelming knowledge that most of the people in the valley were users. An anxiety attack the likes she never experienced closed in on her and she snapped the book shut. She felt like she heard sinister laughing, like it was inside her head. Yet it was deathly quiet in the attic. She was losing it. She had to get out of this attic and get back home. Nothing seemed more important than that thought, but then her common sense kicked in. I'm strong, I can get through this, she told herself. I've done it many times swimming with the killer whales. I just have to.

Erica had been in dangerous situations before and staying calm was the only thing which got her through them. It would work again today. She took several deep breaths, regaining her control. Her anxiety disappeared to a certain degree. She looked at her watch. It was high time to get out of Doug's house. She chided herself for not bringing a small digital camera to take pictures of the records, but how could she have known what she would find? Wait until I tell Cotton, she thought. He won't believe it. If she just had more time, she could have cross-referenced the names. She was sure that she had seen several names twice; first as a Harvester and then on the suicide list. It had to wait; she had to get out of the house now, before Doug came home. She placed the book back into the footlocker, put the lock back the way she had found it and then pushed it back against the wall. She crawled to the attic opening and stepped on the ladder. One last look at the attic confirmed that she left everything the way she had found it. She shut off the light and placed the board back over the attic opening from the top step of the ladder and then climbed down.

Gabriel, in his excitement to see her, jumped up at her, placing his big paws against her chest unbalancing her. She screamed and fell from the last step hard against the pantry shelves. Recuperating from the unexpected pain of hitting her shoulder against the shelf, she heard a loud crash and realized that the bread and butter pickle jar had crashed to the floor.

"Shit," she shouted, then sprang into action.

She had to fix this mess before she left. She grabbed a couple of paper towels and wiped all the glass, pickles and juices into one pile. What was she going to do with the mess? She couldn't just put it into the trash. Doug would figure out that someone had been inside his house. She looked around and searched his kitchen drawers for a plastic bag and finally found one underneath the sink. Hurriedly she scooped up the mess and put it into the trash bag. She took two more paper towels and cleaned the floor with Windex she had noticed earlier under the sink. Hopefully the floor wouldn't stick when Doug walked inside his pantry the next time. Finally she grabbed the ladder, folded it up and placed it between the refrigerator and the wall. As far as she was concerned the place looked as good as when she came in. Maybe Doug would write the lost bread and butter pickles off to getting older and forgetful.

"Promise me you won't say a word," she told Gabriel as she patted him one last time before she once again crawled through the dog door, pulling the trash bag behind her.

Gabriel followed her, but she spoke sternly to him to return inside and he did so reluctantly. In a hurry now, she walked back to the four-wheeler and started the motor. Erica placed the trash bag on the back rack and drove down the hill. When she came to the mailboxes she stopped and checked to see if she had any mail. She saw the red jeep coming toward her and saw Doug driving past her honking and waving to her and she waved back at him, releasing a deep sigh of relief. This was way too close for comfort.

Erica reached her house and dropped the trash bag into her large can outside, still thinking how close she had come to running into Doug. Wouldn't that have been a mess? It wouldn't have been an easy situation to get out of, but she had been lucky. Someone was definitely looking out for her.

She entered the house and watched fascinated how Dino inspected her. He sniffed her pants and she almost felt like she had been cheating on him. She laughed out loud.

"Dino, cut it out. It's just Gabriel you smell."

She walked to the kitchen trying to ignore him smelling her pants, too deep into her own thoughts, and took an ice-cold Diet Coke out of the refrigerator. Popping the top she sat down at the kitchen table, musing over all the information she had found out. Man, if this wasn't the discovery of the century, no, make that centuries, she thought. This was so damn freaky; the perfect script for a horror movie. A plant who controlled minds and killed people; a plant who made people commit suicide, but why? Satan's Angel, was that what Bulk Horswell had called the plant? Satan's Angel? Wasn't there something in the Bible about Satan's Angel? Erica wanted to get the Bible out of the nightstand, but then she saw the pen and the grocery list she had written that morning lying on the table and thought it wiser to first write everything she remembered down before she would forget it. She ripped the front page off and put it to the side, then grabbed the pen and started writing the sentence down she had read earlier in the letter from Bulk to his brother Hank. She hadn't given it much thought, but somehow it seemed important to write it down now. For some reason the sentence was stuck in her head.

Hank, the plant is Satan's Angel come to earth to collect souls.

There it was again... the name... Satan's Angel. Shivers ran down her spine, but she tried to ignore them and instead focused on writing the names of the suicide victims down, before she would forget them.

Her temples started throbbing and she rubbed them, putting the pen down to do so. When had she ever suffered from such a horrible headache, she thought, annoyed at the interruption? She had written only three names down before the headache made it impossible for her to continue. It hurt so bad that she decided to get some pain pills out of the medicine cabinet upstairs in her bathroom. She drank one more sip of her Diet Coke, then walked upstairs to the master bathroom and opened the medicine cabinet. Her temples were throbbing and her mind was cloudy; strange thoughts like voices entering her mind.

I have tired of your participation in my game. Sadly - it must end now.

Damn there were those weird feelings again. Oh, she felt so eerie and the pounding in her head was killing her. Desperately, she picked up several pill containers and read the labels then flung them annoyed behind her. Why was she throwing the pill containers instead of placing them back on the shelf? She felt like she wasn't herself. She found the one she was looking for. Ambien, the sleeping pills she used once in a while. Why Ambien, she asked herself? Was I really looking for Ambien? She was astounded at herself. She couldn't think straight any longer.   She took the container back to the kitchen and sat down by her Diet Coke then opened the container and spilled the pills onto the table in front of her, some of them rolling off, but she didn't care. Slowly, as if in a trance, she picked up one pill after another and dropped them into her Diet Coke. She felt like she was screaming inside to rebel against her actions, but her body didn't listen. Horrified she watched how her hand swirled the Diet Coke then lifted it up to her ear and listened to the swishing sounds inside, her face a big grin she didn't feel or make, and then to her great horror she lifted the drink to her lips and drank the whole Diet Coke and its deadly contents in one setting, against her mental protest.

When she finished she put the Diet Coke down, wiped her mouth in an unladylike fashion, her face an emotionless mask... waiting... her pupils dilated and glowing blood-red... waiting... and then her head slowly dropped forward and hit the kitchen table with one single loud thump.

Chapter Twenty-seven

otton was driving his truck through the mountain pass toward home. He was in a good mood. It was a gorgeous day, he was off work and on top of all, one of his favorite Oldies was playing on the radio. His deep voice reverberated through the open car window as his fingers drummed the rhythm on the steering wheel.

"There is a house in New Orleans, they call the rising sun."

It didn't happen too often that he had an afternoon off, but an important meeting was cancelled and the rest of the afternoon belonged to him. Erica would be surprised to see him come home this early. Maybe they could talk Robin into watching Lucas for a couple of hours and he could take Erica to an early matinee and then to the new Sushi Bar in the city everybody was talking about. It wasn't exactly his cup of tea to eat sticky rice balls, raw fish and sea weed, but he hadn't spent much time with her lately so she deserved to be treated to something she liked; and she liked Sushi, so Sushi it was. A nice juicy steak and a baked potato would have been more to his liking, but he loved to surprise her and couldn't wait to see the child-like excitement on her face when he told her what he had planned.

He caught up to the school bus and waved at his son who was sitting in the back seat, smiling back at him with that one-of-a-kind smile children only have for such a short time, when their two front teeth are missing. We need to capture that smile in a picture, he thought before he watched the bus turn onto another street to let several other children off. Lucas would reach his bus stop in about fifteen minutes, belonging to the last group of children to be dropped off by the bus. If he hurried, he could tell Erica about his surprise and then they could sit together on the front porch and watch Lucas walking home across the dam with the other children, throwing rocks into the water.

Five minutes later he turned onto the small dirt road and noticed from a distance that Erica had taken the four-wheeler out for a ride. He wondered where she had gone. He honked the horn to let her know that he was home, but was surprised when she didn't come outside, happy to see that he had made it home so early.

He walked up the steps to the patio and opened the front door. Dino jumped up at him barking excitedly; something he hadn't done in a long time. He barked and yelped and wouldn't stop barking even after he yelled at him to do so. What was wrong with him? He looked up and saw Erica sitting on a chair, her head resting on the table. Was she asleep? She must be really tired, he thought. Maybe she was too tired to go to town later. Well, they could always have a nice romantic evening at home.

"Hey, Erica. I'm home, wake up," he told her as he took his uniform jacket off and hung it on the clothes rack next to the door.

She didn't stir. He walked up to her and put his hand on her shoulder to shake her awake when he saw the empty bottle of Ambien lying on the table. What the hell, he thought, then shook Erica harder, shouting her name. Erica's head rolled over to the side, her face deathly pale. A fist clamped around his heart.

"No!" he screamed. "No!"

Cotton grabbed the home phone from the wall and dialed 911. He screamed all the information into the phone then hung up and placed Erica on the kitchen floor and felt for a pulse. It was there, he could barely feel it, but it was there. His mind was racing, imagining all kinds of awful possibilities. Lucas, he thought, Lucas can't come home to this. I have to call Robin.

He dialed Robin's number as he sat next to Erica on the floor holding her hand. He told Robin to pick up Lucas from the bus stop and not to let him see the EMS vehicle coming to his house; that he had found Erica unconscious. He realized he was rambling on, but he couldn't help it and hung up without saying goodbye. He was shaking. It was a new feeling for him. He was usually the one in control, in charge of leading his men into dangerous missions in Iraq and Afghanistan, but never, ever, had he been afraid the way he was now.

This was personal, way too personal. He checked every other minute to see if Erica was still breathing and thanked God each time she was. The next fifteen minutes became the longest in his life and then, finally, he heard the sounds of the sirens. They were the best sounds he ever heard and he almost started sobbing, but he caught himself and stayed strong. Help was finally there, he just hoped it was in time.

He heard them drive into his yard and then heard the hurried footsteps on the stairs.

"I'm in here, in the kitchen!" he yelled and felt relieved when they took over.

He stepped to the side to give them room, but never took his eyes off his wife, his hands visibly shaking now. What was happening? How did his life change so fast? A thousand thoughts raced through his mind as he watched them work on Erica. Erica... Lucas... Sushi. How did his life turn so fast from happy to sad... how?

One of the men called in Life Flight, realizing that they didn't have much time. Erica was put on a gurney and carried to the ambulance, all the while being worked on by the crew. He climbed into the vehicle and sat next to her, watching them place an oxygen mask over her face and sticking several IVs into her elbow and wrist. The ambulance raced down the dirt road, over the dam and then toward the grassy area on the other side of the lake where they had spent so many happy moments.

Dino ran after the ambulance barking the whole time and followed them over the dam. A completely irrational thought entered Cotton's mind. If something happened to Dino, Lucas would lose two important beings in his life. Stop it, he scolded himself. You're losing it.

Life Flight landed five minutes later. Everything happened so fast after that. They told him the name of the hospital they were taking Erica to and then they were gone, up in the air again, the propeller pushing the air to the ground, the grass and bushes bending under the impact, creating ripples on the surface of the lake. A few seconds later Cotton watched the helicopter as it flew over the mountains and out of his sight, the distinctive whirling sound fading away on its way to the Medical Center with his unconscious wife inside, fighting for her life. Dino sat next to him whining.

He stared after the helicopter, numb with shock and pain. He couldn't believe what had happened in such a short time. One minute he was happy and had a healthy wife and child, and the next minute his world was in shambles. And the worst thing was that he didn't understand why. Why had Erica taken all of the Ambien? It was so unlike her to take a sleeping pill in the first place. For heaven's sake, what was happening? She only took one pill in the rarest of instances and usually a whole bottle would last her at least half a year.

The EMS offered to drive him back to the house and he took them up on it, wanting to get to the hospital as soon as possible. Dino ran the long way a second time and Cotton locked him inside the house when he got there.

The drive to the hospital seemed longer than the actual forty minutes it took him to get there. Thinking back to the last four weeks, he realized how little time he had spent with Erica; it drove him crazy with remorse. What if there were warning signs and he had been too busy to notice? What if he had paid more attention to her last night when she once again talked about Rachel and Mark? What if he hadn't worked so many hours lately, leaving her and Lucas alone? What if...? What if...?

Hell, what am I talking about here, he chided himself. I'm talking about Erica. Erica, who was used to fending for herself and Lucas. She did it for thirteen months when he was in Iraq three years ago and several times since then. He knew her well enough to know that she wouldn't try to commit suicide. No way, not Erica. She would never, ever do that to him or Lucas. She was full of life, but... now that he thought about it, so was Rachel. She had been one fun- loving woman, but Erica was his wife and he knew her better. Damn, what was going on here? Why hadn't he paid more attention to her last night when she tried to talk to him? He had been too absorbed with his own problems and worried about the up-coming meeting at work. He remembered her talking about the twenty-year-old medical student who lived in their house who killed himself, and also about the man, he forgot the name of, who used to live in Robin and Adam's house, and then of course of Rachel. She had talked about the valley's suicides and statistics she found on the internet, and now she tried to kill herself. And what did she say about Mac Lockhorn?

He couldn't remember. Damn his selfish ways. He should have listened to her, but he had been too busy thinking about his meeting which had been cancelled. Damn his priorities. Damn him.

His thoughts strayed into another direction. He remembered picking the Ambien up four weeks ago on his way home from work. Erica had probably taken three to four pills since then, so that left twenty-six pills in the container. Twenty-six pills for her to swallow. Could somebody survive that many pills in their system? The possibility that she wouldn't survive was just too horrible to contemplate.

Erica didn't seem depressed. Sure, the recent death of Rachel had affected her, but not to the point of committing suicide. He couldn't make any sense of it. Why? Why did Erica do something like this? Didn't she think about Lucas when she took the pills? That single thought alone brought Cotton back on track. Erica loved Lucas more than life itself and wouldn't do anything to put a cloud over his head. Something is just wrong with this whole picture…something is horribly wrong and I'm going to get to the bottom of it, he thought, turning into the hospital parking garage.

Chapter Twenty-eight

Doug drove home, glad that the visit with his doctor was behind him. He received a clean bill of health. Who would have thought so two years ago when he was diagnosed with stage four lung cancer? The doctor called it a miracle, but Doug knew better. It was the peas. He had chewed more than his share the same time he underwent radiation treatment and he knew that they had cured him.

Two large spots on his lungs disappeared into nothingness. The doctor had given him a year... at the most... but now look at him... healthy and fit as a fiddle. Sure, he had lost the tip of one lung and stopped smoking the cigars he liked so much, but he knew that it was ultimately the peas which had cured him. Now he was cancer free and could enjoy the rest of his life with only four yearly check-ups. But somehow he wasn't as thrilled as he thought he would be when he received the news today. In some way he had been ready to die. He wanted an end to his miserable existence, actually looked forward to it, but it wasn't to be.

He was cancer free. Words which would give a new lease on life to most people were disappointing to him. How could he keep on living and be happy, knowing what he had done to satisfy the plant? He was riddled with guilt and not one single day went by that he didn't suffer periods of severe remorse for his actions. He felt alone in this world. He had no one to confide in, not even Adam, who was clueless into what hellhole he had stepped the day he accepted the job as Junior Harvester. Poor Adam... poor, clueless Adam. His time would come soon enough. Yeah, he was alone with his knowledge; a wolf in sheep's clothing forced to do the devil's work. Maybe one day he would have enough courage to end it all, but it would never be enough to make everything he had done right again. Nothing could ever do that. Doug knew that in the end he would walk through the wrong door, like Chester did, and he was frightened of that moment.

He passed Erica Stancil who was picking up the mail on her four-wheeler and waved at her. She and her husband were a nice addition to the valley. Her husband Cotton is a non-user, Doug thought, one of the very few valley residents who didn't participate in chewing the peas.

There were three in the valley now; the first one being Betty Carr, a sixty-nine-year-old woman who never participated in anything the valley did. She had lived in her little cabin on the east side of the valley for over twenty-years now and in that time Doug had seen her maybe on ten occasions. She stayed to herself and had absolutely no interest in socializing. Secretly, he suspected that she was a closet alcoholic. In any case, she wasn't a problem. The second non-user was Carl Scholl, a forty-eight-year-old maintenance man who worked at the high school as a janitor. Doug always thought that he didn't have enough sense to hold down a job, but he'd been working for the school system for over twenty-five years so he must have been doing something right. Carl never married and lived in the valley with his four dogs he was totally devoted to. He didn't drink, didn't smoke and didn't date. He was a total loner. And now here was Cotton Stancil. He was different all together; a young man with strong morals. He had a back bone and determination, armored with a strong, likeable character which opened many doors for him. But so far the plant hadn't worried about him, didn't send him any ill feelings, and it was all right with Doug.

One thing was for sure, he never-ever wanted to put ground up peas into another person's drink again. He knew the fate of the person too well and didn't want another death on his conscience. No, he just wouldn't do it... no, not ever again.

The couple of times he talked to Cotton he found him quite interesting, being a former military man himself. Cotton would have made a better Harvester than Adam, Doug mused, but second guessing his choice wouldn't get him anywhere. At the time, Adam had been the best candidate for the job and so far he hadn't let him down.

He drove past the lake and up the dirt road toward his driveway. Gabriel heard the motor of his jeep and came running outside, glad to see him come home. The dog waved his tail and barked excitedly. Man, he loved that dog, his only companion since his wife died. He petted the huge Great Dane and walked to the back door and opened it, then went to the kitchen and grabbed a cold beer out of the refrigerator. He needed a beer, needed something cold to go down his throat. Why couldn't he be happier about his good report?

Damn, his life was one fucked-up mess. The only thing good was that the higher risk months for suicides were over. Just like certain states had a special season for hurricanes or tornados, in his mind there was a special season for valley suicides which started with the day of the Festival of the Pods until the end of September, when the peas lost their effectiveness.

Not a minute passed since he had this thought, that an eerie feeling went through him. It was not as strong as usual, but he recognized it none-the-less. Something was going on in the valley right now, but what? He sat down in his recliner letting the feeling grow stronger and waited for clues of what to do. Who would it be this time? It was mid-October and the peas were long dried up and had lost their potency. How could anybody else have gotten in trouble with them? What was going on and what was the plant trying to communicate to him? Was there another traitor amongst them? One thing was for sure; if there was one, the plant would take care of him like it always did, that much he knew. All he had to do was wait and the truth would reveal itself.

Strangely enough the feeling subsided and finally went away all together. Maybe the plant didn't need his help after all and all was well in the valley. He felt great relief flooding through him. All he wanted was peace, a couple more months of peace and quiet and maybe then he would get up enough courage to end it all on his own before the next Festival of the Pods arrived. He got up out of his recliner and ate a small lunch and then laid down on the couch and fell asleep, tired and worn out from his trip to the Medical Center. Doug took his hearing aids out and placed them on the coffee table next to him. He was snoring five minutes later. He didn't hear the siren of the ambulance on the other side of the valley, nor did he hear life flight landing by the lake.

Chapter Twenty-nine

C otton parked the truck in the hospital parking garage and rushed to the emergency room.

"Erica Stancil! I need an update on Erica Stancil. I'm her husband. She was brought here by Life Flight. Is she...?"

"The doctor is working on her right now, Mr. Stancil. Please have a seat in the waiting area. He will come and see you as soon as he can, Sir," a middle-aged nurse with thick rim glasses told him and pointed to an area down the hall.

Cotton let out a deep breath. The doctor is working on her. Thank God she is still alive, he thought as he walked toward the designated waiting area, where he became one of many people praying and wishing for good news. He sat down in one of the chairs even though he didn't feel like it. He was too nervous, too fidgety to sit still. How much misery, worry and hope is in this room, he thought as he looked around.

An elderly lady sat three chairs down from him holding a rosary in her hands, her lips moving to unheard prayers. A young man across from him tapped his feet nervously and looked at his wrist watch every few seconds. A young mother with a sleeping infant sat crying in a corner, her snivels subdued by a handkerchief. How much misery, he thought again, and so unnoticed by the rest of the world. Cotton felt insignificant sitting and waiting, the fate of his wife in the hands of others. He wasn't a religious man, never had been, but now sitting in the waiting room the thought of praying did enter his mind. He felt like a hypocrite, willing to do anything for Erica to get better. He didn't know how long he sat in the waiting area with morbid thoughts running through his mind. His elbows on his knees and his head in his hands, he snapped up as he heard his name.

"Cotton Stancil?"

"Here," he jumped up looking at the man calling his name. He was wearing a white coat and had stern eyes. His facial expression didn't reveal anything, not a smile, not an encouraging nod, nothing.

"Is she all right?" Cotton asked. He hated the man in front of him for making him ask.

"I think she'll be fine. She is a lucky woman. You found her just in time - another hour and she would have been dead. We pumped her stomach out and hooked her up to a dialysis machine to clean her blood."

Relief flooded through Cotton. Erica would be all right. The incredible pressure inside of him ebbed away. He thanked the doctor and asked permission to see her. He would talk to her and she would tell him what made her do it and together they would work through it and get her better. Whatever it took he would do it. He wanted her back and never ever wanted to go through something like this again. The doctor told him to wait another five minutes and a nurse would come and get him. Cotton sat down again; the tension slowly leaving his body. Erica would be all right. That was all that mattered to him. When he was finally allowed to see her she was still in intensive care waiting for a room. Her face looked pale, lying against the white pillow. Her eyes flickered open. They looked slightly swollen. She saw him and whispered his name, softly and worn out.

"Cotton?" The name he had heard her use a thousand times before now was a lifeline to a future with her. She had spoken his name when she was angry, happy, afraid, confused; she had screamed it in the throes of ecstasy, but never whispered it like she did now. Never like this, and it touched him deeply. The single word breathed ripped his heart out. To him, her whisper sounded like a desperate cry for help. Never had she spoken his name with such uncertainty, such confusion; her eyes mirroring her perplexity. Then she looked at the IVs in her arm.

"Cotton. What happened? Where am I?"

"You're in the hospital, Honey. They pumped your stomach out," he told her. "You took an overdose of sleeping pills."

"What? Sleeping pills?" she uttered, still incredibly drowsy. "I did what?" Her eyes were round with disbelief and he saw something else in them now... he saw fear. "Nooo...," she screamed the words. "How..."

He placed his hands on top of hers to calm her down. "Just rest for now," he told her. "The doctor said you're going to be fine. Don't worry. Lucas is at Robin's house. We will talk about all this later when you're stronger."

She wanted to ask him more questions, but her eyelids weighed a hundred pounds and sleep overtook her once more.

And then, as if to give her strength by saying it out loud, Cotton added; "I love you, Erica. I love you so very much."

But she didn't hear him, her mind lost in a dream of ambiguity; names and dates long forgotten floated through her unconscious mind, horrible deaths painted on oil paintings, blood gushing out of unimaginable wounds, death all around her. She moaned and moved around, her eyelids flickering rapidly as she slept through the nightmare; her mind tortured and guarded by an unseen presence inside her.

Cotton pulled up a chair and sat down next to her bed and watched her sleep. He noticed her unrest; she seemed so agitated, her fingers twitched and jerked once in a while and her almost unheard moans created a strong need in him to shake her awake, but he didn't. He watched her sleep and watched over her. As long as she didn't get any worse, he would let her get the rest she needed.

One hour later she was transferred to her own room, but didn't wake up during the move. He left the hospital around eleven o'clock that night, assured by the nurses that his wife wouldn't wake up until morning. Cotton had called Robin several hours earlier asking her if she could keep Lucas overnight and put him on the bus in the morning. Of course she had agreed right away and offered her help for anything else he should need. He told her that Erica had taken an overdose of sleeping pills, but was recovering.

Robin was shocked and didn't know what to say. An awkward silence hung between them and then she started to cry and he understood. There was nothing she could have said to make it better or make a difference and to him her crying said it all. She hung up the phone without uttering another word and the unspoken words meant more to him than anything she could have said. She was Erica's friend and words weren't relevant.

Cotton arrived back home around midnight and walked through the front door a different man. How many times had he come home from work, expecting his world to be perfect; a beautiful wife he adored and a young son who was so much like him that it took his breath away each time he put his eyes on him. And what had he done, besides bring his problems home from work every day and take his family for granted? Damn, if this wasn't one of life's hardest lesson.

Dino greeted him excitedly at the door, just like he did every day. The dog has no idea what's going on. He is clueless. He is so happy to see me even though my world has collapsed. How strange my thoughts are tonight, Cotton thought for the umpteenth time.

He petted Dino and then let him go outside to do his business, watching him run down the stairs into the darkness below. Cotton sat down on the patio chair, a broken man. All these years he had asked Erica to put up with his dangerous job of working in Iraq and Afghanistan, not thinking too much of what kind of daily sacrifice and anguish it required from her and Lucas. But now the shoe was on the other foot and he suffered the uncertainty of not knowing.

"Oh, my God," he uttered. "It's hard...so damn hard. Erica...I didn't know. I didn't know it was this hard. What would I give to hold you in my arms right now?"

He was miserable. A huge knot in his throat made it hard for him to swallow. Several minutes later, Cotton became aware of his surroundings again when he felt Dino's rough tongue licking his cheeks. Maybe he does know, he thought. Maybe he does.

He walked inside the house followed by Dino. Again in a rush now, he walked through the kitchen not able to look at the table where he had found Erica. He ran upstairs and was surprised when he saw the bathroom in such a mess; medication containers all over the floor. Did Erica do this when she looked for the pills? It was so unlike her to create a mess like this. Cotton put the disturbing thought out of his mind and took a quick shower, packed a bag with his clothes and then packed necessities he knew Erica would want when she woke up in the morning. He fed Dino, who followed him around like a shadow, staying close to him the whole time. He petted the dog before he left the house one hour later and drove through the black, moonless night back to the Medical Center, hoping that Erica had not woken up while he was gone.

As soon as he stepped out of the elevator onto the third floor, he knew something was terribly wrong. Two nurses were running down the hallway in the direction of Erica's room. Someone was saying some kind of code on the loudspeaker. His heart started beating faster as he ran after them, horrified to see them entering her room. As he turned the corner he was aghast by what he saw. Blood was covering the bed sheets and Erica's hospital gown. He looked at her face. She was unconscious, her mouth, chin and cheeks smeared with blood. A doctor came running in and pushed him to the side. One nurse was wrapping her left wrist while another man in a white coat worked on her right wrist, blood even now dripping out of the wound onto the floor. Another nurse tried to reinsert the IV back into her arm.

"What the hell happened?" Cotton shouted into the room. "She was fine when I left three hours ago."

"Sir, please wait outside the room," one of the nurses told him.

"The hell I will. This is my wife and I want to know right now what's going on!" Cotton shouted at her, scared to death to see Erica like this.

"Can't you see the doctor is working on your wife? Please, wait outside, Sir."

This time he listened, logical reasoning returning to him. He walked outside and paced the hallway, his look never wavering from the now closed door. Minutes, which seemed like hours passed painfully slow. His head was full with unanswered questions.

Finally the door opened and the doctor who he had seen working on Erica's wrist stepped out and walked toward him.

"What happened?" Cotton asked him.

"Well, the alarm went off to your wife's room and a nurse went to check on her and found her ripping the IV's out; but more disturbing than that was that she tried to…well…she tried to injure her wrists. All the blood you saw came from the wounds she inflicted on herself."

"What? What are you saying?" Cotton asked him confused. "She injured herself?"

"Yes, your wife was biting, no… ripping into her own flesh with her teeth. The nurse called for help and pulled your wife's wrist away from her teeth, but she then attacked her other wrist. I've never seen anything like it. I was the first doctor in the room and it took two nurses and myself to keep her from hurting herself. She is all right for now, but she did damage the main artery in her right wrist. Most of the blood came from that wound. We called in a hand specialist and he will perform surgery on her as soon as he gets here. She is stable right now.

We had to give her a sedative. She fought us with everything she had, like a wild animal bent on self-destruction."

Cotton noticed that the doctor was really distressed by what he had witnessed, and for a seasoned doctor it probably took a whole lot to accomplish that. That fact scared Cotton more than anything else. He had seen this kind of shock on many occasions in Iraq.

"What... what is going on with her? I don't understand...?" Cotton shook his head, a huge knot in his throat then wiped a tear away with his hand. "What are we going to do? What is the next step?"

"Right now she's going into surgery and after that your wife will be put on suicide watch. I'm going to bring in Doctor Carson for a mental evaluation. He is the best in his field and will help us shed some light on what is going on with her. He will want to talk to you as well. I suggest you get some sleep in her room while she's in surgery. There is nothing you can do right now, but rest up for when she wakes up in about three hours."

"Thank you, Doctor..." Cotton told him, his emotions barely under control.

"Doctor Gardner," the doctor filled in.

"Thank you, Doctor Gardner," Cotton finished his sentence.

Doctor Gardner put his hands on Cotton's shoulder. It wasn't his custom to touch family members, especially not men, but in this case he felt compelled. "Hang in there," he told him and walked off shaking his head with disbelief. He thought he had seen it all, but what he saw today...he still couldn't wrap his head around it.

The door to Erica's room finally opened and Cotton watched her being wheeled outside and down the hall in her hospital bed. Her face had been cleaned up and her gown and bed sheets were changed. Right now she looked like she was sleeping peacefully. Both her wrists were bandaged and lay motionless next to her body. What is happening to her, Cotton thought? What is happening to us? Why is she doing this? We were so happy.

He watched her as they wheeled her into the elevator, then he turned around and walked to the men's room. For a second time a huge knot filled his throat making it hard for him to swallow. Overwhelmed physically and emotionally, he leaned against the restroom wall and felt like hitting it, feeling totally helpless with what was happening. A couple minutes later he got himself under control and splashed cold water on his face, then walked disillusioned to Erica's hospital room. He picked up the two small bags he had dropped when he had entered the room earlier, now pushed against the wall. He closed the door behind him and was at a loss for what to do next.

For a man of action, ineffectiveness was an intolerable situation. There was a pull-out couch, but he knew he couldn't sleep so he walked to the recliner and sat down, placing the bags on the couch next to him. He stared at the empty place where the hospital bed had stood such a short time ago. Erica, he thought, his Erica. They were married for ten years and there wasn't anything he didn't know about her, or so he thought. They were each other's best friends for heaven's sake. He couldn't figure out what led her to do such a horrible thing.

Self-destruction... that just wasn't Erica. She couldn't stand watching a horror movie and would always look away when anything bloody happened. She abhorred violence of any kind and he had to be the disciplinarian with Lucas if he ever needed a spanking. Cotton's hands went through his black, unruly hair, frustrated with his inability to find the reason why his wife tried to kill herself. Exhausted, he leaned back against the recliner and stared out of the dark hospital window, his mind in turmoil, pictures of Erica with blood dripping down her cheeks and mouth flashing through his mind. What was he going to tell Lucas? What was he going to tell his son about his mother? What?

Chapter Thirty

C otton woke up startled. He had dozed off, but was suddenly wide awake. It felt like he had slept for only a few minutes, but in reality he had been out for two hours. He saw the door to Erica's room open and jumped up out of the recliner he had fallen asleep in. Two nurses pushed the hospital bed, with a still unconscious Erica, back inside the room.

"Everything went very well," one of the nurses told him as the other nurse plugged the cables of the automatic hospital bed into the outlets. "The doctor will come and talk to you in a few minutes. Your wife should wake up pretty soon."

"Thank you," he told the nurses as he walked closer to Erica's bed and picked up the hand closest to him, staring at the white bandages around her wrist. One nurse left the room while the second one finished attaching all the little sensors to Erica's skin and turned the monitors back on.

"I'll be right back," he heard her say when she finished. "I forgot the straps to tie her down."

Oh my God, Cotton thought, has it come to that? Erica has to be tied down. He sat down next to the bed and looked at her. She looked so innocent, so incapable of doing what she tried to do. He placed his palm over her hand, careful not to hurt her, feeling the warmth of her. Her fingers twitched slightly. He looked at her face and saw that she was trying to open her eyes. With a smile on his face he waited for her to open them all the way. He wanted her to see him and be reassured that he was right there with her and everything would be all right.

Her eyes slowly opened. She looked disoriented and then she smiled at him, a sweet, soft smile, but it only lasted a second. Panic and fright entered her eyes making them look larger than he had ever seen them, like they filled with awareness and insight of what had happened to her. He also saw a desperate need to communicate with him. She opened her mouth and tried to say something, but the sounds came out raspy. Cotton leaned closer to be able to hear her.

"What is it, Honey?" he asked her.

"The plant... the plant is trying to kill me," she whispered.

He thought he didn't understand her right and leaned closer, but she didn't say anything else. It took all her energy to say those few words. He leaned back and looked at her, thinking about what he thought he heard her say. Her eyes were still open and he saw terror in them. Cotton started to say something to her when he saw her face change.

Her eyes became wider and rounder and the fright and panic he had just seen in them, now filled with...with...? He couldn't quite make it out. But then it came to him, her eyes filled with loathing and disgust. But why...how? Erica looked at her bandages and lifted her upper lip exposing her teeth, something he never saw her do. What in the hell was wrong with her?

She didn't leave him much time to think. Her upper body suddenly rose up and she started to scream an inhuman scream as she ripped her hand away from underneath his and started tearing at her bandages. It all happened so fast, so unexpectedly, that it took Cotton totally off-guard.

He jumped up and yelled for help, his voice desperate. He grabbed her arms to hold them down, but she was so strong, like a wild animal fighting him every step of the way, all the while screaming this inhuman shrill sound. Fear so deep, he never felt anything like it, filled him with horror. He pinned her arms down on the bed. It took all his strength to do so. She got loose and scratched his face with her free hand drawing deep bloody gashes on his cheek, then lifted her free wrist to her mouth and began attacking the bandages with her teeth, like a rabid dog, ripping and snarling; her eyes wild with hate, her pupils unusually large, glimmering blood-red. Cotton screamed with whatever strength he had left in him and finally staff came running into the room helping him get her under control and her wrists out of harm's way.

Cotton's eyes never left hers. He was drawn to them, like seeing them would make it more real, that it wasn't a trick of his imagination. He watched her pupils turn black again and then her eyes closed as the drug they administered into her vein finally took effect. He let go of her arm, mentally and physically exhausted. He stood up and moved to a corner in the room and watched like an outsider, not comprehending, not functioning, not capable of anything right then. The nurse repaired the damage done to her bandages and then tied her to the bed by her arms and legs. He couldn't take it any longer, couldn't see her like this; he had to get out.

He turned around, away from the nurses working on his wife and walked outside the room, down the hall and out of the hospital like a desperate man trying to put distance between what he had just witnessed and what he was able to comprehend and deal with without going crazy. He drove away in his truck, not caring in what direction he drove, just away from what he witnessed, away from what didn't make sense to him anymore, away from what was destroying his whole world.

During all his military time he had always known, without a doubt, who the enemy was and what he had to do to fight them, but tonight he had witnessed something so horrible, so unbelievable, that it shook the foundation of his sanity. What he witnessed surpassed everything imaginable and he felt totally helpless. He didn't know how to fight it, how to save his wife, his son and his own existence. His innocent son, who was asleep in Robin's house, not aware of what was going on. How could he save his family?

Half an hour later he stopped the vehicle beside the road and stepped out of the truck. It was still dark, but he didn't care. He felt like he was ready to explode with frustration if he stayed another second inside the truck. He had to do something, had to get back to normal. He slammed the door shut, let out a loud scream and slammed his fist into the car window, glass splinters flying everywhere. The sharp pain in his hand brought him back to reality. Three of his knuckles were bleeding and a long gash in the fleshy part between his thumb and index finger was dripping blood on the ground. Damn it hurt, but it felt good at the same time. Cotton shook his hand to flip the loose glass splinters and blood off then took off his t-shirt and wrapped it around his hand.

"That was about the dumbest thing I've ever done," he mumbled to himself. He didn't regret it; he had needed the pain to get focused again. Nothing could bring a person back to reality the way pain could. He got back into the truck and looked into the rear view mirror. Three ugly, bloody scratches covered his left cheek. Damn, I look a fucking mess, he thought, turned the car around and headed home.

Chapter Thirty-one

C otton arrived home at the crack of dawn. The sun was not yet out, but the birds were already busy greeting the new day with the chirping he usually loved to listen to. Today he barely noticed it as he climbed up the stairs and entered his house. He picked up the phone and called Robin and told her to tell Lucas to come straight home after school. Robin asked him about Erica, but he couldn't answer and just uttered that he couldn't talk right then and hung up the phone. He didn't realize that it had been way too early to call her; his usual thoughts of consideration now replaced by his worries. The second call he made was to his work to request a week off from work due to a family emergency.

Next, he walked upstairs to the bathroom to take care of his hand and face. Again he saw the mess in the room. The medication cabinet stood wide open; pill bottles and tubes were flung everywhere, in the sink, in the bathtub and on the floor. No, this just wasn't Erica. She would never have done this. He found the peroxide and rinsed his whole hand and then poured the liquid down the three gashes on his cheek. He added Neosporin to the wounds and then wrapped his right hand the best he could. It had to do. He didn't have time to see a doctor.

Cotton walked back downstairs and poured himself a strong drink, then sat down in the chair Erica had been in, when he had found her yesterday afternoon. Had it really been just yesterday afternoon? It seemed like a lifetime ago that his life had changed so drastically. It seemed almost impossible that so much could have happened in such a short time. He still couldn't believe what he had witnessed. It was like it wasn't Erica he had seen... but someone else. Her mannerism, her facial expressions, and the incredible strength she displayed... where did it all come from? He outweighed her by a hundred pounds. Sure, she exercised regularly, but it was nothing compared to him. He was in excellent condition; he did weight training five days a week.

What he had witnessed and felt when he tried to restrain her was downright impossible... and what about the glow in her eyes? It was inhuman. If he didn't know better he would say that he saw evil in his wife's eyes, like she was possessed by something horribly malicious, and he had no idea how to fight that.

He was used to dealing with men's horrible cruelty and the aftermath of slaughter and massacre. He had pulled corpses out of the Tigris in Baghdad so badly decomposed that the bodies fell apart. He had collected body parts and put them in plastic bags for identification after a suicide bomber blew himself up next to two of his men. He knew how to handle tragedies of war. He would shut off his emotions and deal with it the best he could, even though it was extremely hard. He didn't like it, but he understood men's cruelty to each other. What he witnessed today he didn't understand and it scared the crap out of him.

Cotton chided himself for his inability to deal with it. Erica needed him and he had to snap out of it...he didn't have a choice. Something was going on and he had to find out what it was, natural or unnatural. It didn't make a damn difference, he had to fix it. Erica and Lucas needed him to be strong and make the right decisions. If he could just understand it; if he knew what he was dealing with? How could he fight it, if he didn't know what he was fighting?

Those eyes... what could make them glow red like that? Like two glimmering coals in a fire. He shook his head trying to get the horrible picture out of his mind, then placed his left elbow onto the table and rested his tired head in his palm. He felt exhausted, totally bushed, mentally drained. He closed his eyes wondering if he should sleep and revitalize himself with a short nap.

He opened his eyes again and that's when he noticed the papers lying on the table. Tired, he pulled one of them closer and recognized the grocery list Erica had written yesterday morning, asking him several times what else he wanted from the store. He put the list down, shattered by the memory of a normal weekday morning with Erica. The ink pen she had used was lying on the second piece of paper. He pulled it closer to see what she had written on it and read the strange sentence.

Hank, the plant is Satan's Angel come to earth to collect souls.

Who the hell is Hank, Cotton thought? He read on; two words written in capital letters and underlined.

SUICIDE LIST

The words instantly grabbed Cotton's attention. Intrigued he read on, his instinct now on high alert. *Forty-nine suicides in Hunter's Valley since 1766*

Erica had written names underneath the heading he never heard before, except for the first one. If he remembered right, he was the guy who discovered the supposedly mysterious plant several hundred years ago.

Bulk Horswell,
William Dusk
Henry Koenig
Augustus Jordan,
Rachel Yo...

311

Erica had stopped writing in the middle of Rachel Young's last name. Stunned at what he read, he read it a second time and then a third. All he knew was that these were the last words Erica had written before she took an overdose of sleeping pills. Why had she stopped in the middle of Rachel's last name... and what did the sentence, "Hank, the plant is Satan's Angel come to earth to collect souls," mean? What was she trying to tell him?

The words Erica had whispered to him before she became so fierce and violent in the hospital came back to him. "The plant is trying to kill me." She had looked afraid when she said it... and she had been herself when she said it. It happened just a couple seconds before she turned into something else, something evil. Whatever it was, it stopped her before she could tell him more. Was that also the reason she stopped writing in the middle of Rachel's last name? He thought about her words. What did they mean? Did she mean it literally, that the plant was trying to kill her? The plant he never believed in.

Those eyes... blood-red... glowing? Suddenly Cotton knew what they reminded him of. They looked like the peas Erica had chewed at the Festival of the Pods. The peas he thought were rum soaked raisins.

The hair on his neck stood up and a chill went down his spine as he put it all together, realizing the truth and the enormity of it blew his mind. He stood up... too driven to sit down... and paced the floor, thinking the facts through over and over; his thoughts jumping all over the place. Could it really be true? Could a drug like the peas control a person's mind and make them want to kill themselves? Why were there so many suicides in this valley? He remembered the twenty-year-old young man who had killed himself on top of Manitou Hill, and then there was Rachel. Why were all these people killing themselves? Erica had mentioned to him that the dog ate one of the peas. Cotton hadn't thought anything of it at the time, but now he began to understand. Could it be the reason that Tiger acted so out of character and killed Mark Hiller? And now Erica. She was trying really hard to kill herself.

But why...why? Erica must have found out something. She must have found out that the suicides were connected to the plant and that's why the plant was trying to kill her. The plant had stopped her each time. By killing Erica the secret of the valley would stay safe.

Wow, this was huge - unbelievable - but huge. Did strange things like this really happen? He believed in facts. He believed there were bad people in this world doing bad things every day, but could there be other sources which influenced people to do or commit acts they normally wouldn't do, like drugs? How many times had he heard or seen something on television about drugs which caused the user to become abusive, violent or act out of character. How many times did people overdose? Wasn't it the dulling effects of the drug itself which caused the miscalculation of the dose which led to the death of a person? Was it so far-fetched then that these peas had the same power over its users, except that the powers never wore off, that they stayed with the user forever?

The question was, what was he going to do about it?

Annegret Werner Shaw

Chapter Thirty-two

B ad news traveled fast in Hunter's Valley. Everybody knew everybody and when something bad happened it went through the valley like a wild fire.

Doug's telephone rang at eight o'clock the next morning. He had just finished shaving and walked to the living room to pick up the phone, mumbling something about calling too damn early.

"Morning Doug. Thought you were up by now and wanted to know what's going on in Hunter's Valley," Charles, his closest neighbor and friend, about the same age as he was, told him.

"What in the hell can be going on this early in the morning?" he asked him, grouchy at the early morning interruption. "Can't a man have his first cup of coffee before his nosy neighbor interrupts his routine?" he goaded, but knew that his blunt statements wouldn't upset Charles.

They always treated each other like this, antagonizing the other person on purpose to get a rise out of each other. Two decades of humorous bickering and witty sarcasm had strengthened their friendship through the years and they counted on each other to add extra zest to their daily lives. Both knew it, and wouldn't stop if their lives depended on it, until one of them was dead.

"Well, then drink your damn cup of coffee and call me later," Charles replied, knowing full well that Doug wouldn't let him off the hook.

"Damn fool you are. It's too damn late for that. You might as well tell me now. What the hell is going on?" he replied.

"Erica Stancil was picked up by life flight yesterday afternoon. It landed next to the lake. I'm surprised you didn't hear it."

"I took my hearing aids out after I got home from the doctor, not that that is any of your damn business. What the hell happened to her? I saw her at the mailbox picking up her mail on my way home, must have been around one or so."

"Robin told me she took an overdose of sleeping pills, tried to kill herself, that's what she told me," Charles answered.

"Shit, is she all right?" Doug inquired.

"I don't know, but I saw Cotton driving up to the house real early this morning and Robin told me he would take care of Lucas after school. I called the hospital, but they didn't want to tell me anything either, not being a relative you know."

"Well, maybe I'll give Cotton a call later on. Now get off my phone and mind your own business," he told Charles and hung up the phone before he could answer anything back.

Wasn't that the darndest thing? Erica Stancil? He didn't see that one coming. Why the hell was she a danger to the plant? Had she told the detective about the pods? If she did, why did the plant wait this long to deal with her? No, he didn't think that was the case. It had been the second time that she received a pod and she had told him that she had given two of her peas to Rachel after Mark was killed. She didn't have any peas left to take out of the valley and she didn't seem the type to want to make a profit from the peas, otherwise she wouldn't have given Rachel the two she had left. He had to find out. He dialed Cotton's number and heard him picking up after only three rings.

"Hello," he heard Cotton's voice, sounding almost normal.

"Hello, Cotton. This is Doug. I just heard that Erica is in the hospital. How is she doing?" Doug asked him.

Cotton was caught off guard. He hardly ever spoke to Doug and here he was calling and checking on Erica. A warning bell went off in his head. What had Erica tried to tell him about the Senior Harvester about a week ago? Why hadn't he paid closer attention to her? Damn, what kind of a husband had he been lately that he didn't know what was on his wife's mind? Was it a coincidence that the person calling about Erica's wellbeing happened to be the same person who is in charge of the plant?

In any case, he wasn't in the mood to talk to anyone, especially not to him. Why was he calling him anyway? Was he trying to figure out what Erica knew?

The way Cotton saw it, Doug was to the plant what the Pope was to the Catholic Church. What a horrible example, Cotton thought and then tried to sound grateful for Doug's interest in his wife's welfare. The best defense is a good offense, he thought.

"She is fine. She is recuperating nicely. I'm taking Lucas to see her this afternoon."

"That's good to hear," Doug replied, wondering what else he could say to gain more information without sounding too obvious. "What in the hell happened? I saw her yesterday around one by the mailboxes and she seemed fine." Even to him it sounded nosy and way too blunt. He waited for a reply, but when Cotton didn't answer he added; "Listen, Cotton, I know you got your plate full right now, but if there's anything I can do to help give me a call, all right?"

"Will do, Doug. Thanks for offering." Cotton hung up the phone deep in thought.

Boy, hadn't that been obvious. He had a feeling that Doug knew why Erica tried to commit suicide and was fishing for more information. One thing was for sure, if the plant was responsible for Erica's suicide attempts, then he had to destroy it, before it succeeded in killing her. There was only one problem; he didn't know where it grew.

317

He had been all over these mountains riding his four-wheeler, but never came across a plant looking like the plant in Adam's oil painting. Erica had shown it to him one night when they were playing poker at Adam's house. He had liked the picture, but never thought anything else about it, thinking that it was just a made-up fantasy picture of a mystical plant. Back then, he never imagined that there was any validity to the secret of the valley.

Only Adam and Doug knew where the plant grew, and they wouldn't go back up the mountain for another nine months. He couldn't wait that long. Erica would die if he didn't destroy the plant or she would spend the rest of her life in a straitjacket somewhere in an institution, so she couldn't harm herself. He wouldn't let that happen. That was no life for her or for Lucas and him. Lucas needed his mother and he needed her. No, he had to find another way. What about Adam, he thought. Would Adam tell him where the plant grew? He had to get Adam to talk. After all, he was a good friend. He just had to understand the dilemma he was in. Doug on the other hand would never give him the information he needed. He was the Senior Harvester, set in his ways, and he carried the weight of his knowledge and the responsibility too long to give it up. Who knows what hold the plant had on him?

No, he was going to talk to Adam tonight and see if he could persuade him to reveal the plant's hiding place. He went over all the arguments Adam could bring up. He had to be prepared. How much did Adam know about the plant? How much would he reveal to him? Would he put Adam's life in danger by asking him to reveal the location of the plant? After all, the people who committed suicides were all users and so was Adam. He hadn't thought of that before. He had to tread very carefully. After all, if the plant had the power to make users commit suicide it could also have the power to make users commit murder. It was a good thing that he never chewed the peas. Thank God for that. But Adam had chewed the peas and that made him just as vulnerable as all the other users. How could he protect Adam? He had to come up with a good answer; otherwise he didn't stand a chance to destroy the plant. Damn, this was a horrible situation to be in.

Apply your training, he told himself. Think... cover everything; who, what, when, where and why... start with where... where... the valley.

As far as he knew the suicides occurred in the valley. Could it be that the plant's powers didn't reach past the mountains? How could he test this theory? There just wasn't a way or was there? But then he remembered Erica's reaction when she woke up in the hospital. Erica was thirty-five miles away and the first thing she did was to rip the bandages off her arms, abhorred at the realization that she was still alive. He would never forget the look of loathing in her eyes, the way she had fought him and the nurses until she was drugged again and fell back into unconsciousness. Maybe if he took her back to Texas. Maybe Texas was far enough away from the plant were it couldn't reach her. It was worth a try. Distance made everything less; heat, cold, sound, even light, so why couldn't it work with the plant?

He would wait for Lucas to come home from school and then he would take them to Texas. The talk with Adam had to wait; Erica's welfare was more important right now. Having made up his mind, he called Lucas' school and told them he wouldn't be back for a while due to a family emergency. It was eleven o'clock in the morning now and he would have a couple more hours before school let out and Lucas would come home on the bus.

He decided to call the hospital and check on Erica. They told him that she was resting comfortably now, but that they had to give her more medicine two hours ago when she woke up and fought the restraints trying to get loose. It was a horrible picture to think of Erica that way; never the less, he had a plan now and would see it through and he needed all his strength for that.

Cotton walked to the couch to lay down. Dino followed his example and plopped down on his dog pillow. Trained to fall asleep in the strangest places Cotton was dead to the world five minutes later, getting the rest he needed.

Three hours afterward, he walked outside and sat in the wooden rocking chair on the patio waiting for the school bus to drop off Lucas. It would be any minute now that he would see the yellow bus coming around the corner on the other side of the lake. He heard the bus before he saw it. It was somehow strange how everything sounded louder in the valley, echoing off the mountain walls. The bus stopped at the mailboxes and five children exited. Lucas was wearing his bright yellow shirt and he could spot him easily among the children who were running down the incline of the road toward the dam. It had become a contest between them to see who could throw rocks the farthest into the lake. He smiled to himself, enjoying watching such innocent childhood games and hoped and longed for more such moments in the future.

His thoughts returned to his problem. He was taking Erica to Texas where her family could take care of her. He would send Lucas along to be out of harm's way and after a couple of days only he would return to the valley, find the plant and destroy it.

Ten more minutes passed as the children slowly walked home, laughing and shouting. They split up at the bottom of the dirt road and Lucas walked up the incline toward their house. Dino ran down the road to greet him and Cotton could hear his son's excited shouts of seeing his dog. Another minute passed before he heard him stomping up the wooden steps. When Lucas appeared around the corner he noticed his father sitting there and his face brightened with that toothless smile he loved so much. Cotton's heart lurched and he had to swallow.

"I didn't know you were home, Dad. Where's Mom?" he asked innocently then his eyes became big and round. "Dad, what happened to you?"

"Happen to me?" Cotton asked him confused.

"Your face... and your hand, Dad." Lucas stepped closer to inspect his face. "You look like you fought a bear."

"Oh, that," Cotton replied suddenly understanding. He had totally forgotten about his hand and the scratches on his face. "Umh... it wasn't a bear, but I did have a little accident. I slipped and fell and got all scratched up, that's all."

"Does it hurt a lot?"

"No, son. I had already forgotten about it," Cotton told him.

"Where is Mom?" Lucas asked him again, dismissing his father's injuries.

"Didn't Ms. Robin tell you that mom is in the hospital?" Cotton asked him surprised.

"No, she only said that I was supposed to spend the night at her house and you would explain later. Why is Mom in the hospital? Is she sick?"

"Well, she kind of had an accident with some medication. We will go and visit her after you have a snack."

"Will she come home with us?"

"No, but if the Doctor says it's all right I would like for her to go to Nima and Papa's house in Texas so they can take real good care of her until she gets better. Would you like that?" he asked his son.

"Wow, I would like that a lot. I haven't seen Nima and Papa in such a long time," Lucas replied excitedly then his face turned serious. "You would come too, right Dad?"

"For a couple of days, Lucas, then I have to come back here and finish some important work."

"You're not getting a divorce, are you Dad? Kevin's parents told him they were moving and then he found out they were getting a divorce," he told him serious as could be, his face looking worried.

Cotton had to smile at his son. "No, your Mom and I love each other very much and we love being married to each other. We're a family, Mom, you and me, and we're going to stay together as long as we live."

"All right, Dad," he answered, satisfied with his father's answer.

"Well, eat your snack now and then we'll put some clothes for you and Mom in a suitcase to take to Nima and Papa's house." He pulled one of the snack packs out of the refrigerator which Erica always kept in abundance for Lucas and placed it on top of the kitchen table, then filled a small glass with milk to go with it. "Go and wash your hands," he told Lucas.

"They're not really dirty," his son answered and held his hands up for his inspection.

"I watched you throw rocks into the lake. Go and wash your hands," Cotton told him sternly.

"All right, if I have to," Lucas answered, defeated by his father's stern reply.

He left the room and thirty seconds later Cotton heard the water coming out of the bathroom faucet. When Lucas finally ate his snack he walked into the master bedroom and made two phone calls, the first one to his in-laws in Texas, explaining to them that Erica needed help recovering from an accidental overdose, telling them he would explain everything in detail when they arrived. The second call was to Robin, asking her if she could take care of Dino for a couple of days.

Chapter Thirty-three

Five hours later, Cotton sat with Erica, Lucas and a nurse he had hired, on a plane leaving for Houston, Texas. It was a good thing that they had some money saved up. The last minute tickets in first class had cost him an arm and a leg, but money didn't seem important compared to his wife's health. He gladly would have given anything he owned to get her back to normal. The doctor had reluctantly given his permission, along with drugs to keep Erica calm. His only other condition was that Cotton take a nurse along to administer the shots and check her vital signs on a regular basis, until she was taken care of by a doctor in Texas.

Cotton cooperated and with the Doctor's recommendation found Linda Beige, a thirty-seven-year-old nurse who agreed to accompany them on the flight to Houston. She was friendly and Cotton felt good to know he had medical assistance if he needed it. The last thing he wanted was for Lucas to witness one of Erica's mad panic-stricken attacks to get out of the restraints and hurt herself. Erica was sleeping when Lucas first saw his mom in the hospital room.

"Mom is sleeping. Should we wake her up and tell her that I'm here?" he asked his father, his eyes big and round.

"No, we'll let her sleep. We have a long trip ahead of us." Cotton was glad she was asleep. Lucas sat on his father's lap and together they watched her for a while until the nurses and aides entered the room to get her ready for transfer. Cotton thought it wiser to step out of the room with Lucas and walked to the waiting area by the elevator. Twenty minutes later a nurse came around the hallway corner pushing a now semi-awake Erica with her wrists tied to the armrests of the wheelchair. Lucas jumped out of his chair and ran toward her.

"Mom, we're going to Nima's and Papa's house!" he shouted excitedly, then stopped short when he saw her face. Cotton caught up to him and saw his shocked little face staring at her. Erica's eyes were half open. It pained Cotton beyond description to see his wife so pale and lifeless, being wheeled out of the hospital room by the nurse, but it pained him even more to see the shock on his young son's face when he saw his mother. Erica was full of drugs. It was like she didn't take anything in, staring through objects and people, like she couldn't see them. She didn't react to Lucas saying her name over and over again and not to her husband's kiss on her cheek and his reassuring voice that everything would be all right.

Lucas was holding on to his father's hand. Cotton could tell how upset he was and squeezed his little hand reassuringly.

"What's wrong with Mom?" Lucas asked him, tears starting to run down his face. "She isn't talking to me."

"The doctor gave your mom some medication. She is very sleepy right now, son."

"Will she get better? She didn't hug me back either."

"She will get better once we're in Texas. I promise," Cotton answered him, not wanting to consider the alternative.

This just had to work. The only other thing which could work was to wait until the effects of the peas wore off. But how long would that take? There was just no way of knowing. It could take months, it could take years, it could take forever. Cotton couldn't wait that long.

Erica didn't register that she was first transported in a handicap bus to the airport and then transferred from the wheelchair to the comfortable first class seat in the airplane. When Linda Beige tied her arms to the armrests her eyes finally closed, she was once again asleep.

They sat in silence. Cotton sat next to Lucas and across the aisle Linda Beige kept a close eye on Erica. If all went well they would be in Houston within four hours. Erica had received her last shot right before they boarded the plane and hopefully would sleep the whole flight. She looked so fragile, her face pale with dark circles underneath her eyes, her hands bandaged and tied. Every once in a while she moaned and moved her head from one side to the other and Lucas would look worriedly at his mother, the center of his universe, not understanding what was going on.

"Why did the lady tie mom's arms to the seat?" he asked Cotton after they took off.

"Remember, I told you earlier that mom has a lot of medication inside her body. Well, the medication makes her do strange things. We just want her to be safe, that's all," his father explained to him. He looked at his son, so innocent, so untouched, so saddened. Cotton wanted to see Lucas smile again, see the gap his lost two front teeth created and know that he was happy. He would do anything to make that happen.

Lucas turned toward the window and looked out. The plane was climbing in altitude, but the joy his son usually exhibited watching the world get smaller and smaller wasn't there. Lucas didn't say another word and thirty minutes later he fell asleep, his little body leaning against his father's side. Cotton laid him down on his lap and covered him with the blue courtesy blanket. The rest of the flight Cotton spent in silence, feeling the warm sleeping body of his son on his lap and keeping an eye on Erica who was also sleeping. His heart filled with tenderness toward his wife. Her curly long hair framed her pale face, but even like this, she was the most beautiful woman in the world to him.

They had to wait for all passengers to exit the airplane before they could transfer Erica back into her wheelchair. Cotton carried his sleeping son off the airplane as Linda pushed Erica toward the gate.

Erica's parents were waiting when they came out and waved excitedly to them, but when Erica's mother, Edith, saw her daughter in such an unresponsive state she started crying. Cotton's father-in-law, Dan, shook his hand then took the sleeping boy from his arms wile Cotton hugged Edith and then introduced Linda Beige as Erica's nurse.

"Mom, Erica is still out of it," Cotton told Edith.

"But Cotton, what's wrong with her? Why are her wrists bandaged and tied to the armrests, as if..." she couldn't finish the sentence.

"I promise I'll explain everything when we get home," Cotton answered and pushed the wheelchair toward the exit. Lucas woke up before they reached the car and was overjoyed to find out that his Papa was carrying him.

He squeezed him hard around the neck and then shouted excitedly at his Nima.

"Mom and I are going to stay with you for a while, Nima. Aren't you excited?" he asked his grandmother who looked sad to him.

"Yes, Honey. I'm very excited," she answered.

They all laughed at his enthusiasm and kept up the positive attitude all the way home for Lucas sake. It was exactly what everybody needed. Lucas told his grandparents about his school and all his new friends. He told them about the clubhouse he and Logan built, the picnics they had by the lake and that he was a very good swimmer now. He talked excitedly the whole drive home.   One hour later he was sound asleep in the guest bedroom. Linda Beige was assigned the second guest bedroom and Erica was put in her old room she occupied when she was a young girl. Linda was sitting at Erica's bedside watching her while Cotton talked to her parents downstairs and filled them in on the whole situation. He didn't keep anything from them and, even though they seemed extremely skeptical, he asked them to be patient and give him the time he needed to find out if his theory of distance worked.

It was way after midnight by the time Cotton relieved Linda and told her to rest. He sat in a recliner next to his wife's bed and watched her. She was still sleeping and even though she looked peaceful, her hands were tied to the bed. He didn't want to take any chances with her. It had been almost seven hours since she had received the last shot. The moment of truth was getting closer and Cotton started to get nervous. What if all this was for nothing? What if it didn't work? What else could he do to save her?

Erica slept through the night, longer than he had anticipated. It was getting daylight outside and she still slept. At seven o'clock, his mother-in-law knocked on the door and brought him coffee. He was grateful for the interruption. He was so tired that the coffee was a welcome sight. This was the longest Erica had gone without medication since she had been brought to the hospital. She looked so serene, her beautiful face relaxed, her eyeballs moving just a little bit behind her closed lids. What was she dreaming of, he wondered? Was she still being tortured by the plant's powers over her mind?

It was after Cotton finished his coffee that she started to wake up. Her eyes flickered and she moved her head from one side to the other, then she tried to lift her arm but couldn't and her eyes opened. She looked at him, then looked around the room and then at her tied wrists.

"Cotton, we're at my parent's house. How did that happen? What are we doing here?" Her eyes were clear and she looked normal, but it could be a trick. How would he know for sure? Maybe it was the plant talking through her, trying to trick him into loosening her ties.

"What do you remember, Erica?" Cotton asked her, his heart hammering in his chest waiting for an answer.

She looked at him, trying to figure it out, her forehead crinkled up, her eyebrows furrowed.

"I don't remember how I got here," she answered. "How long have I been here?"

"We arrived last night."

"Is Lucas here too?"

"Yes, he is. What do you remember, Erica?" Cotton asked her again. "Tell me the last thing you remember."

"I… I was sitting at the kitchen table at home…writing you a note about…about what I found out about the plant. It has the power…to make people… to make people commit suicide… if they try to harm it or reveal the secret to outsiders," Erica stumbled over the words as the memories rushed back to her consciousness. "Oh, my gosh, Cotton! What did I do?" she looked at her bandaged wrists and then looked at Cotton, instant panic written all over her face. "Did I try to kill myself? Did I cut my wrists?"

She knew the answer the moment she asked the question and started sobbing, overwhelmed with the knowledge of what she had done to herself. "Oh, no. How could I do such a thing? Cotton help me." Her body shook from the realization. "I'm… so… afraid." She couldn't catch her breath. Cotton jumped up from the chair and put his arms around her.

"Calm down, Erica. Take a deep breath. You're hyperventilating." She heard his reassuring voice through the fog she was in. "Everything is all right now. You're safe. The plant can't harm you here. That's why I brought you here. You hear me, you're safe now."

Cotton's comforting voice finally penetrated her mind. She did as he said and took several deep breaths of air and then released them slowly through her mouth. Cotton grabbed a tissue from the night table and dabbed her tears away. She laid back down on the pillow, her arms still tied to the bed frame.

"Did Lucas find me after…? I…?" she left the words hanging, unable to say them out lout. "Oh, my God. Please tell me that he didn't…"

"Honey, stop. I found you. I came home early to surprise you and found you unconscious at the kitchen table. Lucas doesn't know. Robin picked him up from the school bus and took care of him. He thinks you got sick from taking medication. That's all. He's fine. I promise."

"Thank God for that. What are we going to do now, Cotton?" Erica asked him.

"First you have to tell me more about the plant. It stopped you from doing so when you tried to write the list of the people who had committed suicide and later in the hospital when you came to, and it will do so again if it still holds power over you. It's the only way to find out if your mind is free from it."

Erica started talking and explained to him how she had found out from Robin that Doug Manchester was in the possession of an old ledger which was handed down from one Harvester to the next since the discovery of the plant hundreds of years ago.

"I just had to find out if all the suicides were connected to the plant, so I waited for Doug to leave for his doctor's appointment in town. When I saw him leave, I climbed onto the four-wheeler and went to his house. I entered through the dog flap in the back door," Erica rattled on, eager to tell him everything.

"You did what?" Cotton raised his voice at her. "You trespassed!"

"I knew you wouldn't like it - so I didn't tell you. I had to. I somehow knew that the pods had something to do with the suicides. Remember, I told you about it a while back, but you just wrote it off to coincidences. I couldn't. I had to find out, so I did."

"All right, go on. What did you find out?"

"Well, I found it in his footlocker in the attic. And what I read in the ledger blew my mind. It is a record book about all the suicides in the valley; forty-nine of them since… I think… 1766 and all because of the plant. Whenever the plant felt threatened by a person, that was planning to take it out of the valley or reveal its secret, it killed that person by controlling their mind and forcing them to commit suicide. And when I tried to write the list, it tried to kill me. I got the worst headache of my life and…I don't remember anything past that."

She was quiet for a while, suddenly realizing that she would probably never be able to go back to the beautiful valley she had come to love so much. "What are you planning on doing?" Erica asked him.

"Well, how do you feel?"

"Fine."

"In that case, I'm going to take those ties off your wrists. You're fine… no headache… nothing?"

"No, nothing."

He reached over and untied her right wrist and then the other and then on impulse leaned down and kissed her. And the kiss which was meant to be short and comforting turned passionate with all his pent-up emotions coming to the surface. Erica's arms reached around his neck and pulled him closer turning their passionate kiss into a heated encounter.

And that's how Lucas found them. He entered the room without knocking and looked at his parents kissing, standing but a mere two feet from the bed.

"Is Mom feeling better?" he asked innocently, wiping his sleep-filled eyes, bringing the ardent kiss to a sudden stop. They both looked up, taken aback, and when they saw their son standing there in his pajamas, looking from one parent to the other, they started laughing and Lucas smiled his toothless smile brightening the room.

"Come and give me a good morning kiss," Erica told him and a second later Lucas was on the bed with them, hugging his mom.

There was a knock on the door and Cotton stood up, calling for whoever it was to enter. Linda Beige came inside the room and was positively shocked to see Erica talking energetically to her son, looking rested and in good spirits.

"What happened?" she asked and looked at Cotton, who just grinned at her. She turned toward Erica. "How are you feeling, Mrs. Stancil?" Erica looked up at her and wondered who she was.

"I'm fine. Thank you, but who…"

"I forgot to tell you, Honey," Cotton interrupted her. "This is Linda Beige, the nurse I hired. She accompanied us on the flight in case you needed medical assistance."

"Oh," Erica answered. "Nice to meet you, Mrs. Beige."

"You too," Linda replied. "Especially now that you feel better. If it's all right, I would like to take your vitals and change your bandages. It looks like you made a miraculous recovery from yesterday."

Cotton picked Lucas up off the bed and told him to go back to his room and get dressed when Erica's parents walked into the room.

"Erica!" her mother shouted. "You're awake!"

"Mom is all better now," Lucas told them proudly then marched past them to his room.

"I can't believe it. We were so worried about you." Her mother rushed toward the bed and hugged her daughter and her father waited patiently to get his turn.

"Does this mean it worked? Are we in the all clear?" her father asked Cotton after he kissed his daughter.

"It sure does. All she has to do now is rest up and heal the wounds on her wrists."

Erica threw the bed sheets back and started to climb out. Cotton immediately came to her side and helped her.

"Shouldn't you stay in bed," he asked her, "at least for today?"

He looked toward the nurse, who had just finished taken her vitals, for support. "Don't you think so, Mrs. Beige?"

"Blood pressure, pulse and temperature all look good. Let's play it by ear. I saw a comfortable couch downstairs for her to lie down on."

Erica gave her a brilliant smile and grabbed her robe from the end of the bed, which Cotton so thoughtfully had brought along for her. Lucas came running back into the room dressed in his Superman shirt.

"Nima, I'm really hungry. Can we go downstairs and eat breakfast?" he asked his grandmother and pulled her hand in the direction of the door.

Cotton smiled, grateful that his son was resilient enough to bounce back quickly from the shock he received of seeing his mother so incoherent. They all walked downstairs to the breakfast area where Edith had hot coffee, biscuits and scrambled eggs waiting for them.

Erica rested for two hours after breakfast on the living room couch. Edith and Dan took Lucas for a walk to the neighborhood playground and would be gone for at least an hour. Cotton finally had a chance to ask her more questions. He fixed two glasses of ice tea and brought one to Erica and sat next to her.

"Will we ever be able to go back home, Cotton?" she asked him.

"I don't know. It all depends on if I can find out where the plant grows. I'm going to destroy that son of a bitch. Tell me more, what else do you remember?"

"I read an old letter from the man who first located the plant, Bulk Horswell. He wrote a note to his brother that he was going to destroy the plant, but he killed himself. He didn't succeed, Cotton. He died a horrible death by tying a rock to his leg and drowning himself in the lake. It is so horrible to think that the lake we swim in and enjoy so much became his grave."

"Doug called me the morning after you were admitted to the hospital and inquired after you. He was really trying to fish for information," Cotton told her.

"Stay away from him. He is so deep into this. He always knows when something is going on in the valley concerning the plant. He appeared after Mark was killed and Rachel committed suicide. He was there before anybody else. You know what I read in the journal that would blow your mind?"

"What?"

"Well, do you remember when Robin told us about Angela Barns, the teenager who ran away? Doug has her name written under the suicide list. He put a crushed pea in her drink and she disappeared. Old Man Barns, who spilled the beans about the pods to a doctor in the city, he is also on the list. Do you know what happened to him? Doug put a crushed pea in his beer and he had a fatal car accident. It was a suicide. And both times Doug wrote that he was forced by the plant to do it. He will try and do the same thing to you, Cotton."

"My gosh, I never imagined he would be capable of something like that."

"Maybe he didn't have a choice? He is, at any rate, under the influence of the plant and he will find out what you're up to. After all, you have to either ask him or Adam where the plant grows. The plant can't control you, but it will and can control Doug."

"That reminds me." Cotton pulled the piece of paper which Erica had written the suicide list on out of his pocket. He never could make any sense out of the one sentence she had written above the suicide list.

Hank, the plant is Satan's Angel come to earth to collect souls.

He handed the paper to Erica.

"What does this mean? Do you know? He couldn't possibly mean it literally, could he? That the plant is one of Satan's Angels?"

"Why not? Think about it. Evil takes many forms. How do we know why so many bad things happen here on earth? If the devil was thrown out of heaven and his angels with him, how do we know what form they took? We will probably never know what influence the devil or his angels had over Hitler, Saddam Hussein, Stalin, Gaddafi, Idi Amin, Pol Pot or other evil men throughout history. Look at World War

I and World War II, the Korean and Vietnam wars. Maybe the real reason for all this evil has always been invisible to the human eye."

"Yeah, I guess you're right. Even now as we speak we have dictators who are ruling countries where people are dying of famine, are killed out of hatred or tortured. Come to think of it… you know what is really strange, Erica?" Cotton asked her, suddenly connecting the dots.

"What?"

"Is it just a coincidence that so many mass murderers and school shooters commit suicide? Even Adolf Hitler, one of the worst mass murderers of all time, committed suicide by taking cyanide and then he shot himself. Even as far back as 30 BC, Mark Anthony, the Roman politician and general killed himself with his own sword and Cleopatra, the Queen of Egypt…she killed herself by letting a poisonous snake bite her. I guess we will never know how many suicides were the work of Satan's Angels. Oh, man… I really have to give this a lot of thought."

"Cotton?" Erica asked him disillusioned, "Did you ever think something like this could happen?"

"No, not in my wildest dreams."

Erica continued to get stronger and three days after they arrived, Linda Beige announced that she was flying back home, reassuring Cotton that Erica's wrists were healing nicely and that in another week she should get the stitches pulled by a medical practitioner. Cotton stayed at his in-laws house a couple more days until the following Friday, then flew back home to Hunter's Valley.

Chapter Thirty-four

C otton arrived home around five o'clock on Friday afternoon and didn't see any reason why he shouldn't go and talk to Adam right away. He had called them once to give them an update and to check on Dino. They were probably wondering how Erica was doing. He would grab the bull by the horns and talk to Adam. He had to do it without Robin around. Cotton took two of his finest cigars, that Erica had given him for his last birthday, out of his humidor and grabbed a bottle of red wine, a small token of his appreciation to Robin and Adam for watching Dino. The cigars would be the perfect reason to get Adam outside on the patio, away from Robin's ears, since she abhorred the smell of them. Adam definitely appreciated a good cigar, something they had in common.

He closed the door behind him and walked the short distance down the incline of his road, then turned and walked along the lake to their house. Robin and Adam's house was the third one on the left and it only took him five minutes to reach it. He knocked on the front door, hoping they would be home. Then he heard Adam laughing inside the house and relaxed. Adam came to the door and was genuinely happy to see him. They shook hands and Adam inquired after Erica's wellbeing. Robin came to the door and invited him in and he handed her the bottle of wine.

They sat in the living room and Cotton told them how much Erica had improved and how much she enjoyed being pampered by her parents. He also told them how happy Lucas was that he was with his grandparents again. They invited him to stay for supper, but he declined claiming he grabbed a Subway sandwich less than an hour ago on his way from the airport. Dino came running in from the patio and greeted him excitedly, waving his tail and licking his hand over and over again.

"Did Dino give you any trouble?" Cotton asked them, knowing that they wouldn't tell him if he had.

"He was the perfect dog. He can be our houseguest anytime," Robin answered him. "When are Erica and Lucas coming home? Logan is really missing his friend, and so am I."

"We are playing it by ear. Hopefully pretty soon," Cotton answered her, knowing full well that he wasn't telling the truth.

It depended all on if he would be successful in destroying the plant.

"I brought you a cigar," Cotton told Adam. "Is it all right if we smoke it on the patio?" he asked Robin.

"Of course, go ahead. I have to check on supper anyhow. Do either one of you want a beer to go with it?"

"No," both men answered simultaneously and all three of them laughed.

Seated outside on the patio, they snipped the narrow end of the cigar then rolled the end evenly over the flame of the lighter to achieve the perfect draw. Both men appreciatively inhaled a deep lungful of the cigar.

"I'm so glad everything is going to be all right with Erica," Adam remarked and then added. "We were really worried about her."

"Is that because there are so many successful suicides in this valley?" Cotton asked him. Adam looked at him perplexed.

"What the hell are you talking about?"

Cotton didn't say anything else and let the silence sit between them. Why would Adam act like he didn't know anything about all the suicides? Cotton had become an expert in reading the body language of people he was interrogating in his line of work. The lives of his troops depended on his astuteness, but Adam didn't show any signs of lying to him... yet. Cotton had to follow through in the chance that he was wrong.

"Adam, you're my friend and Robin is Erica's friend. You have to help us. I know that the plant kills people by controlling their minds and making them commit suicide. It killed Mark and Rachel and tried to kill Erica... for heaven's sake. It has no power over me since I never chewed the peas, so it can't hurt me. You have to help me. You can leave the valley for the time that it takes me to do so. I will pay for airplane tickets for you and your whole family. I'll fly you all to Texas and only when you are safely there will you tell me where it grows. That's the reason I took Erica there. The plant doesn't have any power over her mind that far away."

Adam looked at his friend totally speechless. What the hell was Cotton rambling on about?

"Cotton, what are you talking about? That's crazy. The plant doesn't control users' minds. You get a big high when you chew the peas and you feel good for weeks on end, but that's it. I swear to you, I have never heard anything about mind controlling powers. That's ridiculous, downright... absurd. I have been a user for ten years. Don't you think I would know if my mind was controlled by anything else besides me?"

"Adam, you're the Junior Harvester. Are you telling me that Doug never told you the connection between all the suicides and the plant?"

"No, he didn't, but I'm certainly going to ask him. Who told you such nonsense?"

"It doesn't matter. All that matters is that you have to tell me where the plant grows."

"You know I can't do that. I swore an oath and I'm abiding by it," Adam told him getting more and more upset at Cotton.

"Adam, you have to help me. I beg you, for the welfare of every person living in this valley. The suicides need to stop."

"I think you better leave now." Adam stood up, irritated by Cotton's persistence. "I can't help you. And if you're smart, you won't say another word about this to anyone. People in this valley want to believe in something and this custom brings them together and makes them happy. Nobody forces you to participate and nothing bad has ever happened because of the pods. The valley is a good place to live and raise a family, but if you have a problem with it, you should consider moving and leave us be. We like our custom!" Adam shouted. "Now leave!"

Adam threw the barely smoked cigar over the railing. He turned around and stormed inside the house slamming the screen door behind him with such force that it crashed loudly into the latch.

Cotton stayed behind, dumbfounded with what just happened. This was not the way he had anticipated the conversation would go. He was at a loss of what to do next. Should he talk to Adam some more or go home? He chose the latter, realizing that Adam was just too angry and had to digest what he had told him first. Cotton walked inside the house, grabbed Dino's leash from the entrance hook and shouted a goodnight to Robin who was still cooking in the kitchen. He didn't hear her reply, as he had already closed the front door behind him.

Cotton walked home. What was he going to do next? He thought about his dilemma all the way home, wondering if his life would ever be simple again. He missed Erica and Lucas. Somehow he had to get through to Adam how dangerous this plant was, but how was he going to convince him? He walked inside his kitchen.

Food didn't appeal to him right now, even though he hadn't eaten anything since this morning before he took the flight back. He hadn't had a sandwich like he told Robin. He was going to put the house on the market tomorrow. No way would he ever bring Erica and Lucas back to this valley. He opened the pantry and retrieved a can of Pedigree dog food for Dino and mixed it with the dry dog food. Why would Adam deny knowing about the suicides? There was only one reason; he really didn't know. He reached for the phone and called Erica.

"Listen Erica, I talked to Adam and he told me that he knows nothing about the suicides," Cotton told her. "I didn't get anywhere with him."

It was quiet on the other end of the line. "Did you hear me, Erica?"

"Yes, yes... I just remembered something. Adam told you the truth. I don't know why I didn't remember this earlier? There was a set of rules in the ledger. Only the Senior Harvester knows about the mind controlling powers of the plant and the suicides. The ledger only comes into the Junior Harvester's possession shortly before the Senior Harvester's death."

"Damn it, Erica. It would have been nice if I had known that fact before I talked to him."

"I'm sorry. I just now remembered when you said something about it."

"I guess I'm going to have to change my whole damn plan. How are you feeling?"

"Really good. I really miss you a lot and so does Lucas."

"I miss you both too. Give Lucas a goodnight kiss from me."

"I will... and Cotton?"

"Yes?"

"There is something else I remember now. I don't know why it comes to me in bits and pieces. It's like I remember more and more of what I read in the ledger. When Bulk Horswell committed suicide after trying to destroy the plant, his brother documented his death into the journal. And he wrote a sentence underneath. If I remember correctly it read; if anybody is brave enough in the future to follow in my brother's footsteps, destroy the… and then the letters "t" and "ap"… and then he stopped writing just like I did when I tried to tell you about the suicides."

"T" and then an "ap"?" Cotton asked her.

"Yes. What does it mean?"

"I don't know yet, but I'll figure it out."

"Oh, I hope you will. I love you, you know and… Cotton… promise me that you will be careful."

"I will, I promise and I love you too," Cotton replied and hung up the phone. Dino looked up at him with his big soft eyes. He petted the dog and rubbed him behind the ears. "You miss them too, don't you old boy?" he asked him then walked to the liquor cabinet and fixed himself a drink. He sat down in his recliner and relaxed. He had all night to come up with a new plan and to figure out what "tap" stood for. He took a couple of sips of the drink, but sitting in his recliner all alone in the big living room made him miss Erica and Lucas even more. He stood up and took his drink with him upstairs to the master bedroom.

Cotton jumped into the shower hoping to let the hot water revitalize him. What could tap stand for? Tap… tap… tap… what was the man trying to write down so many centuries ago? It had to do with the plant. Think… man… plant… leaves, flowers, fruits… damn it, he never was a plant person. He had taken survival training in Special Forces, knew what kind of plants you could eat and which to stay away from because they were poisonous. He had learned to cook roots and live off them, but he didn't know much about… and then he suddenly knew.

Roots… as in taproot, that's what it was. He didn't destroy the taproot of the plant, that's why he failed. Well, that was good to know. He wouldn't make the same mistake. He stepped out of the shower, grabbed a towel and wrapped it around his waist then walked to his computer and researched the word taproot just to cover all his basis. It was the main root of a plant usually stouter than the lateral roots and growing straight downward from the stem. He didn't want to make the same mistake. The plant grew somewhere on the mountain and it meant that the roots had to be strong, resilient, tough and able to grow under the harshest of conditions where rocks, stones and boulders were its foothold. Cotton took another sip of his drink. That poor man all those hundreds of years ago. He didn't know what he was dealing with. He didn't know that the root grew deep into the mountain rocks. Petroleum products weren't available to him back then. He had no idea that the root would survive and kill him.

Cotton went to bed early, but couldn't find sleep. He tossed and turned for several hours, throwing ideas around in his mind of how to handle Adam and how to destroy the plant. He finally fell asleep around three in the morning. He knew finally what he had to do.

Annegret Werner Shaw

Chapter Thirty-five

obin stood by the oven sautéing onions and bell peppers when she heard Adam slam the patio door. Surprised at the unexpected noise, she looked up and saw her husband walking past the kitchen to his study and heard him slamming the study door as well. His face was red. Wow, she thought. What the hell happened out there in such a short time? The two men were good friends and got along well. A few seconds later Cotton entered and shouted a goodnight to her. She paused again and stared befuddled out of the kitchen window after him. He was walking in hurried steps away from the house, Dino running around him, excited to get home. She noticed the moon rising on the other side of the lake, reflecting bright streams of light across the water. It will be a full moon in a couple of days, she thought, then went back to stirring the onions.

Five minutes later she finished cooking and shouted for Logan and Adam to come and eat, but neither one of them listened or answered her. She turned the burner off and went looking first for her son, whom she found deeply engrossed building a space ship out of his Legos. She told him to wash up and come for dinner. When she looked in the study, she found Adam pacing the room like a caged animal. When she told him that supper was ready he ignored her, too mad to even notice her.

"What happened between you two?" she asked him concerned. Adam rarely ever got this angry.

"It doesn't concern you," he remarked, extremely short with her. "Leave me alone for a while. I have to think."

"Why can't you tell me what it is about?" she asked him, feeling rebuffed. "Maybe I can help."

"I doubt that very seriously. Please, Honey, just leave me alone for a while and close the door behind you."

Disappointed, she left the room and closed the door. She was dying to find out what happened, but in the current state Adam was in, she knew she wouldn't get any information out of him. As much as she hated to, she just had to wait.

Adam kept pacing the room. Eventually he calmed down enough to sit behind his desk. How in the hell had things taken such a bad turn tonight? What did the damn plant have to do with the suicides in the valley? Sure, he had to admit that it was strange that Rachel killed herself and Erica followed in her footsteps, but to blame the plant for it was absolutely ridiculous. Damn this whole situation and damn the position it put him in.

He wished he'd never taken the position as Junior Harvester. It wasn't right for Cotton to ask him to reveal the location of the plant. Cotton was stepping over the boundaries of their friendship and it made him furious. Another thought crossed Adam's mind. Was he obligated to tell Doug about what happened? He remembered the talk he had with Doug when he chose him for the Junior Harvester position. "Always report anything you hear concerning the plant to me immediately," he had told him, and he remembered another thing which had been strange at the time, but now made sense. Doug had told him; "only the Senior Harvester will carry the burden of knowledge," and then, "and one day it will be your burden to carry, when you become Senior Harvester." He hadn't given those statements much thought back then, but now… could they have anything to do with what Cotton was talking about?

Adam thought about it for another minute then reached for the phone. He held it to his ear, but then decided against it. It would be better to talk to Doug in person. He wanted to see his eyes. He wanted to see his eyes to see if Cotton was right. It would be too hard to tell if Doug was lying to him over the phone. Resolutely he stood up and walked out of the room, passing the kitchen as he grabbed the jeep keys off the front foyer table.

"I'll be right back!" he yelled at Robin half-way out the door.

"But supper is ready!" she shouted after him. "Where are you going?" She didn't receive an answer. Men, she thought, must be the most complex beings in the universe.

Annegret Werner Shaw

Chapter Thirty-six

D oug was watching his favorite T.V. sitcom *"Two and a Half Men,"* when he heard loud banging on his front door.

"Who the hell can that be?" Doug cussed, annoyed at being interrupted. "Doesn't anyone in this valley know what time it is?" He slowly raised himself up out of his recliner and walked to the front door where Gabriel already waited excitedly waving his tail. "If you're that excited to get company, why don't you entertain whoever it is waiting on the other side and I get back to my show," he mumbled disgruntled. He opened the door and was astounded to see Adam standing on his porch.

"What brings you to my house this late?" he asked in surprise.

"Something happened that I need to discuss with you," Adam replied and walked passed him inside the house.

Doug closed the door frowning. He hated unexpected visitors, especially this late at night when he watched his sitcoms. It was the only time of day that he truly felt carefree and happy, laughing at the funny jokes the thirty minute show brought to his life. Annoyed, he followed Adam to the living room and shut off the television. Damn, he hated to miss the rest of the show.

"Do you want a beer?" he asked Adam, walking past him to the refrigerator.

"No."

"Well, have a seat then. I'll be right back."

Adam heard the refrigerator door open and close and then Doug reappeared and sat across from him. Gabriel walked toward his master and laid down by his feet.

"Now," Doug said, twisting the top off his bottle. "What's on your mind that can't wait until tomorrow?"

"It has to do with the plant. I think trouble is coming our way."

Doug sat up straight in his recliner. "What are you talking about? What happened and be specific, man. I'm in no mood to ask you a thousand questions. Start from the beginning."

"All right, all right," Adam replied. "Cotton is back in town. He came over to my house and I knew right away that he had something on his mind. He told me about this far-fetched theory of his, that the plant is responsible for Erica's suicide attempt, and not just that, he thinks that the plant is responsible for all the suicides in this valley. Can you believe that?" He stopped talking and looked at Doug to see his reaction.

He expected him to laugh it off or tell him that Cotton must have been drunk, but he did no such thing. He just sat there and didn't even try to deny it. A couple seconds passed and the horrible truth that it was really true penetrated Adam's mind.

"Say something, Doug. Is it true? Is Cotton right?"

But Doug didn't talk; his thoughts were in turmoil. How in the hell did Cotton figure it out? Where had he gone wrong and what was he going to do about it?

Adam waited for an answer, but Doug sat in his chair, looking like he was in another world.

"Cotton took her to Texas, you know," Adam continued, not being able to stand the silence. "We all thought it was because her parents could take care of her, but that wasn't the reason." He stopped talking again not sure if Doug was listening.

"Go on, man. Tell me," Doug surprised him by asking. "Why did he take Erica to Texas?"

"He took her to Texas to get her away from the plant's power over her mind and according to him it worked. Erica is doing really well. And listen, Doug, now comes the crucial part. He wants me to tell him where the plant grows so he can destroy it."

"He what?" Doug shouted and jumped out of his recliner, upsetting Gabriel. The dog jumped up as well and started growling at the unknown danger, sensing his owner's agitation. "Shut up, Gabriel," Doug shouted at him, irritated at the dog. Gabriel whined and laid back down. He wasn't used to his master talking to him in that tone.

"He wants me to show him where the plant is located so that…"

"I heard you the first time. What the hell did you tell him?"

"I was angry with him and told him never to ask me again. I told him to forget about the plant and move away from the valley, if he didn't like it here."

"Hmmm…" Doug expelled the sound. "Hmmm…do you think he is going to listen to you?"

"I really don't know. He seemed so determined."

Doug sat back down and for the next two minutes neither man spoke, each brewing his own thoughts.

"How did he find out?" Doug asked him.

"How the hell do I know?" Adam answered him honestly. "I have no idea… is it true then that the plant is responsible for the suicides, that it can control user's minds?"

"Yes, damn it. Do you think they made up all those rules just for fun? They were written hundreds of years ago to protect the residents of this valley. You would have eventually found out when you became the next Senior Harvester, but hell, it doesn't make any difference to me if you find out now. You can't do a damn thing about it one way or another, or you will end up like the other suicide victims, dead as a door nail. The plant won't tolerate traitors."

Adam's throat tightened up as he listened to Doug's words. What had he gotten himself into? Why in the world had he ever thought that being a Junior Harvester was an honor; to be selected from so many other men who wanted to get the job? He had been proud and tried to do a good job, never realizing it would become the job from hell.

"How can a plant have powers over people's mind? How can that be possible?" Adam asked him.

"Because this isn't just any plant we're talking about, Adam. This plant is one of Satan's Angels who was thrown out of the heavens. The plant is leading us astray and tempting us, by getting us addicted to its peas. Just like Adam and Eve, we've become Satan's victims. Any person who has chewed the peas is under his control. We are his pawns to do with as he pleases."

Adam's face turned white as a sheet as he listened to Doug's explanation.

Doug started laughing, tears running down his eyes. "I guess that's how I looked when I found out what it was all about, the day I became Senior Harvester. The thing is, you and I never stood a chance, never had a choice. The day we became users was the day that our choices were taken away from us. If you try to get out of your obligation to become Senior Harvester, you will most certainly die before you leave this valley and Satan will claim your soul. Many have tried to leave this valley, but all have died except Erica. Maybe it is because Cotton isn't a user. He is a very determined young man. I kept my eye on him from the moment I found out that he wasn't going to participate in chewing the peas."

This was just too much for Adam to hear. "How can I…"

"How can you what? Get out? I told you… you can't. Try and leave this valley. Your thoughts are known to Satan's Angel. You don't stand a chance. You don't stand a chance in hell. Read the journal. You will understand it all if you read the journal. Everything is documented in it and it will take your breath away the way it did mine when I first read it," Doug told him and then he suddenly saw a connection.

"Ahhh… the journal, that's it. I told you about the journal years ago. Did you tell anyone about the journal, because I know for a fact that I haven't told anyone about its existence?" He let the suggestion hang heavy in the air. Adam looked at him stunned.

"You don't think that I told Erica, do you? You must be out of your mind if you think that," Adam shouted, suddenly angry as hell, the blood vessels on his forehead protruding out dangerously.

"What about Robin? She's your wife. Did you tell her anything? Anything at all?" Adam looked at him, but now swallowed the words he was going to say, as a hot wave flushed over his face.

"No, no, of course I didn't tell Robin anything," he finally shouted, but it was already too late. Doug noticed his hesitation and the red hue on his face and neck. Small glistening sweat pearls started to cover Adam's face.

"You son of a bitch! You did tell her!" Doug shouted at him. "What did you tell her? Answer me, you worthless piece of shit!"

"Nothing, really! It was nothing. All I told her a while back was that you were in the possession of the record journal, that's all. I swear, Doug. I never mentioned anything else to her. She doesn't know where the plant grows. Hell, do you think I'm crazy? I took the job as Junior Harvester serious. Think this through, if it is true that the plant controls user's minds and kills those who mean it harm, I would be dead already, wouldn't I?... Think, Doug… If I had told her something important the plant would already have taken care of me and her, and I wouldn't be standing here in front of you right now. Don't you see that? The plant didn't feel threatened by me or Robin!"

"Maybe you're right… Let me think about all this. Why don't you go home and I'll let you know tomorrow what we're going to do about Cotton," Doug told him, stood up and walked him to the front door, Gabriel by his side.

"I swear to you, Doug. All I told Robin was that you had the old journal, nothing more."

"It's all right, Adam. Go home now." He patted him on the shoulder and watched him walk away with the thought that he had been wrong in choosing Adam to be the Junior Harvester.

Tired to his bones, Doug walked back to his recliner and sat down. He felt worn out, totally spent. Deflated from the evening's events, he leaned back in his chair. He noticed the full beer bottle forgotten in the heated discussion. He didn't feel like drinking it anymore.

Damn, he hated to protect the plant, but like he mentioned to Adam earlier, he didn't have a choice. Think… think really hard, he told himself. How did it all connect together? Maybe if he knew how Erica found out about the suicides he would know what to do to fix it. Did Robin tell Erica about the journal or maybe Rachel told her something? That was probably it. Rachel watched her dog kill Mark. She probably figured it out and told Erica. That's probably why the plant tried to kill her as well. It all made sense to him now.

She couldn't have read the journal; after all, it was safely tucked away in his footlocker in the attic and Gabriel wouldn't have let her in, never having met her before. But how could he be sure? Damn you… Satan's Angel… if you're in my head then help me figure this out. Do something! Do something for heaven's sake.

He relaxed back into the soft cushions of his chair and closed his eyes, giving himself totally up to thinking clearly, without any other stimulus. His arms rested on the arm rests. His thoughts became clear.

In his mind's eye, he saw Erica the way she had looked that day by the mailboxes. He saw her waving back at him, sitting on her four-wheeler, getting the mail out of her mailbox. It was the same day she tried to commit suicide, the same day he had been gone for hours to see his doctor. Where had Erica come from when he saw her? Think, think. It's right there in front of your eyes. She was on her four-wheeler. Which direction did the four-wheeler face? There it was; the answer he was searching for. The four-wheeler was turned in the wrong direction.

If she had been coming from her house, it would have been facing the opposite direction. Why turn the four-wheeler around, when there was no need to do so? No, she had just come from the opposite direction.

His house was in the opposite direction. Damn, he had been wrong, she had been inside his house; and there was only one reason why she would have been in his house while he wasn't home. He jumped up and rushed to the kitchen and tore the pantry door open. He switched the light on and looked up. The attic board looked like it hadn't been moved. He surveyed his stock on the shelves. Everything looked the way it should. Nothing was out of order, except, except... he couldn't put his finger on it and yet he knew something wasn't right. He studied each shelf at a time. He was a stickler for keeping his pantry organized ever since Martha died. If nothing else, it gave him something to do.

Suddenly it hit him; the Bread and Butter Pickle jar was missing. He loved those pickles and knew for a fact that he had purchased a jar last time he was in town. It should be sitting right there, he thought, and placed his hand on the empty spot. He bent down on his knees and swiped his palms over the pantry floor.

"Damn," he shouted as a sharp glass splinter entered the soft flesh of his palm. He leaned back and looked at the spot where the blood trickled out. A sharp quarter inch long splinter protruded out of his skin. He pulled it out with one quick jerk. It was thick and probably came from the pickle jar, he thought as he got up. He threw the splinter into the trash can then walked to the refrigerator and pulled the step ladder out. Three minutes later he was inside the attic. He pulled the cord for the light and crawled to the footlocker. Everything looked fine to him so far. He pulled the footlocker out of the narrow space and looked at the combination lock. It was still locked; the numbers were the same as he left them. There was no way that Erica could have figured out the date of his birthday and put the numbers in, could she? But he had underestimated her; she was a lot smarter and braver than he gave her credit for.

He unlocked the lock and opened the lid. Sure enough, the ledger was facing the wrong direction. He always had the top front facing left, no exceptions. Now it was facing right. Damn that woman, she had read the damn journal. Nobody but the Senior Harvesters had ever held this journal in their hands. It was his job to keep records and in a couple of years it would be Adam's job; but now she, Erica, an outsider, had seen and read it. The thought created goosebumps on his arms and neck. Why did the plant fail in killing her, he asked himself? She was a user and the plant would have known her thoughts. Why did it let her find the ledger? Why didn't it kill her right there in the attic or on her way home when she was riding the four-wheeler? It would have been so damn easy. Weird thoughts not his own entered Doug's mind.

"It's the game, you idiot, the challenge. I played her."

"A fucking game!" Doug shouted into the empty attic. "A fucking game! That's what you think this is? Well, it looks to me like you're losing this one!"

He started laughing hysterically not able to stop. "She is in Texas now…out of your reach. Why did you fail, you son of a bitch?"

"Because all I do is listen… every hour… every day… every year… every century… if anybody plots against me. It gets boring. I like to play with them. In the end they will all become mine, including you."

Doug realized that it was the truth. He already belonged to Satan and somehow, even though he didn't know how, so would all the others and there was nothing he or anybody else could do about it. Suddenly the attic became too small for him… he had to get out. He couldn't tolerate the foreign thoughts any longer. He grabbed the journal and didn't bother locking the footlocker. What the hell for? Climbing downstairs his head cleared up, but he still needed something to calm his nerves. He walked over to the beer bottle and finished it in one setting then went and got another one out of the refrigerator.

There was never a recorded failed suicide in the journal's history. Did he need to write it down? He sat down at the kitchen table and picked up his pen.

Erica Stancil – October 2010 – unsuccessful suicide by sleeping pills, moved to Texas, out of range of plant's power.

Depressed he put down the pen. What was he going to do next? Should he talk to Cotton and tell him to leave it alone, that he had no business messing with something so powerful? Would he listen to him? Could he take that chance? He was so tired of protecting the damn plant; tired of fixing problems.

"Why don't you just kill me!" he shouted into the quiet room. "I'm tired of protecting you! Come and get into my head so I can kill myself, because I don't have the guts to do it on my own."

He waited, but nothing happened. Doug closed the journal, too tired and worn out to climb once more into the attic. I'll take it back into the attic tomorrow, he thought, as he hid it underneath the towels in the kitchen drawer. Heck, if Erica knew how to find the journal so did Cotton now. It probably was a lot safer right here underneath the towels than in the footlocker.

He saw Gabriel sleeping peacefully on his dog blanket. I can't even depend on my own dog, he thought, then got up and walked to his bedroom where he laid down on his bed fully dressed. He didn't care if he ever got up again, closed his eyes and waited for sleep to overtake him, but he couldn't sleep.

His thoughts drifted to Old Man Cobb, the old uptight geezer who rattled the valley's secret to his doctor in town. When that happened, Satan's Angel had been furious and entered his head constantly, whispering an awful act of revenge into his head. The plant needed him to do it since it had no power over Old Man Cobb, him being a non-user. Doug had resisted, pushed the thoughts out of his mind for over three weeks, but the headaches became unbearable and finally he had yielded to the plant's instructions and put a crushed pea into his beer. It made him feel like shit, but he didn't have a choice. It was either him or the old man, and at that time Martha was still alive and he didn't want to die.

The next day Old Man Cobb had a fatal accident. Only Doug knew that it was a suicide and he had been an instrument to make it happen. He was guilty of murder. It had been the perfect murder. Tears of regret ran down his cheeks. He should have had the guts to kill himself back then, but he didn't. If he could just change what he had done, maybe life could be worth living again. One thing was for sure; his soul belonged to Satan and there was nothing he could do about it, but he wasn't going to do it again. No, he wouldn't take a father away from his son.

His thoughts finally drifted off, and he fell into a deep, dreamless sleep unaware that Gabriel jumped next to him onto the bed and laid his heavy head on his chest.

Chapter Thirty-seven

The sun was shining bright through the bedroom window when Cotton woke up. He jumped out of the bed, remembering the plan he had formed the night before. After showering he put on his oldest pair of jeans and T-shirt, then took his brown metallic 1911 .45 pistol out of the night table and shoved the magazine he kept in a separate space inside the pistol grip. He looped the Kydex holster through his belt and placed the pistol inside, then went downstairs to get his coffee.

He grabbed a cereal bowl, filled it with his favorite cereal and ate it within five minutes. He learned how to eat fast in the military. Cotton was out of the house ten minutes later, letting Dino do his business while he walked to the tool shed behind the house. He grabbed his machete from the bench and then looked for his three gallon gas container. He found it in the back underneath a shelf and checked to find that it was still three quarters full. Satisfied with the amount of gasoline inside, he took both items to his truck and put them into the bed.

His military ruck hung from a hook and he took it down and opened it. He grabbed a handful of large, half an inch wide by one foot long, black zip ties, duct tape, knife, lighter and ant spray and put the items inside the ruck and carried it to his truck. Dino came running toward him and jumped inside, excited to go on an outing with Cotton, but he told him to get out and put him back inside the house. His mind made up he went to the truck and drove it down the incline toward Adam's house.

Adam and Robin were sitting down for breakfast when they first heard the noise of the truck and then loud banging on their front door. They looked at each other wondering who it could be. Adam got up and walked to the front door which was still locked. Shocked, he realized that it was Cotton. Why in the hell did he come back? He had had a horrible, restless night behind him trying to figure out how he was going to deal with what Doug had told him.

"Open the door, Adam! I need to talk to you!" Cotton shouted at him through the door.

"I don't have anything to say to you!" Adam shouted back. "Go home, Cotton. You're wasting your time with me."

"Open the damn door, Adam, or I will shout what I have to say to you and the whole valley will know your business."

Sighing deeply, Adam unlocked the door and Cotton stepped inside.

"It's not going to make any difference to me what you have to say, I will not tell you where you can find the plant," Adam told him.

"Oh, yes you will," Cotton told him as he pulled the gun out and put it underneath his chin. "Listen to me. I don't want to shoot you, but I will if I have to. I'm a desperate man and therefore very dangerous. Tell Robin that you are going off-roading with me."

"I will not go anywhere with you," Adam told him.

"In that case I will take both of you. It's your decision, man. Make the right one," Cotton hissed through his teeth.

Adam looked into Cotton's eyes and what he saw scared him. He wasn't kidding. He heard Robin coming up behind him. Cotton put the gun behind his back, his eyes daring Adam not to mess up.

"Morning, Cotton. What's going on?" Robin asked him, entering the foyer.

"Morning, Robin. I invited Adam to go off-roading with me. I hope you don't mind if I steal him for a couple of hours?"

"Robin, I know I promised to stain the patio today, but… can I put it off until tomorrow? I'll be back this afternoon, all right?" Adam told her.

"You men are all alike," she joked. "You make promises you don't keep," she smiled up at him. "Go on and have fun, but be back soon. I love you."

Adam bent down and kissed her on the mouth. "I love you too," he whispered, then turned around and walked outside with Cotton.

"Get in the truck," Cotton told him. "And do exactly what I tell you unless you want to die, and I don't mean by my hands. Put your hands behind your back." Adam did as he was told. Cotton looped one of the zip ties then took a second one, looped it through the first one and told Adam to put his hands through each loop then tightened them where Adam couldn't get loose.

"It will be uncomfortable, but it can't be helped."

"Where are we going?" Adam asked him.

"Up to Manitou Hill." Cotton started the truck then pushed the play button of the CD player. "Sing along with it. Your life depends on it. Don't think about anything, but the lyrics of these children songs. Only stop to tell me if you're getting a headache."

The CD started playing. It was Lucas' CD, filled with his favorite children songs, which his grandparents had given him for Christmas.

"He's got the whole world, in his hands."

When Adam heard the song he looked at Cotton like he had lost his mind.

"Are you serious?"

"Do it, man. I didn't lie to you yesterday. The plant will kill you if you don't channel your thoughts away from what is happening right now."

"I know you were…" Adam started to tell him, but Cotton furiously interrupted him.

"Chill the fuck out, Adam! Sing! Damn it! Not another thought about it! Don't you understand! Don't you get it!" he shouted at him. Adam all of a sudden understood and started singing along with the lyrics.

"He's got the whole world, in his hands.
He's got an itty biddy baby, in his hands…"

Cotton joined him and soon both men were driving down the road singing the children's song together. The truck window was still broken and their voices echoed up the hills. If it hadn't been so serious they would have cracked up. They drove about ten minutes until they reached the path up to Manitou Hill. Cotton turned the truck onto the barely traveled path and slowly drove up the steep trail. They were still singing children songs, Adam a willing occupant since he now fully understood the consequences.

Cotton had twice before been up to the plateau and he remembered the lonely pine tree sitting on top. It was perfect for his plan. The panoramic view was spectacular from up there, but since the Russell kid killed himself, hardly anybody came to see it anymore. It was sad that something so heartbreaking and tragic kept people from avoiding Manitou Hill.

Once on top, he told Adam to get out of the truck and they climbed up between two rocks until they reached the top of a huge bolder, Cotton carrying his ruck and tools. The solitary pine tree, growing out of a gap in the boulder, stood proud and erect as ever. It was the perfect spot for Adam to wait while he destroyed the plant. He could even see the valley below from here.

"I want you to sit right here and lean back against the tree. I'm going to cut the tie wraps." Adam did as he was told. "Now put your hands around the tree." Adam did again as he was told and Cotton tied him up again, applying the same techniques as he would to insurgents in Iraq or Afghanistan. Once finished with the hands, he moved to Adam's feet and did the same. "I'm going to hurry as fast as I can. You're sitting in the shade until way after three so you're going to be all right, unless I fail. Can you move?" he asked him. "Are you comfortable?"

Adam tried hard to get loose, but he couldn't, no matter how hard he tried.

"Yes, I think they will hold me. I can't get them loose. What happens if you don't come back? I'll be dead before somebody finds me up here."

"Don't worry. I thought about that. I wrote a note and left it in your mailbox this morning. The latest Robin will find it is on Monday. You won't die in that short time."

"Thanks man, my arms will probably be worthless by then."

"It beats killing yourself," Cotton told him. He took the ant spray out of his ruck and sprayed a liberal amount around the tree and where Adam sat. "Just so the ants won't take a liking to you," Cotton joked. "I sense that you do understand why I'm doing this now? Am I right?"

Adam nodded his head in agreement.

"I went to see Doug after you left last night and he told me that it was true. He told me that he never had a choice and that I didn't either."

"That's right, and what happened to Erica can happen to Robin. I didn't tell you this yesterday, but it was Robin who told Erica about the journal. She is a user and she spilled the beans about the journal. She could commit suicide any time the plant decides to do away with her. Tell me if you are getting a headache. It is the first sign of the plant entering your mind."

"I really didn't know, Cotton," Adam told him.

"Well, I didn't know that yesterday, but I do know it now, that's why I came back this morning. When I called Erica last night, she told me that she read it in the journal; that only the Senior Harvester knows about the mind controlling capabilities of the plant. Do you really want that job one day?"

"Hell no!"

"All right, then listen. It will probably take me four hours or so to find and destroy the plant, right?"

"Right," Adam agreed.

"Okay, tell me where the plant grows and let this show get on the road."

"Have you ever been on Pitch Fork Mountain?" Adam asked him.

"Only once. We drove the length of the ridge. It's pretty steep up there."

"Well, do you know where the three cliffs stick out like a fork and to the right is a small plateau."

"Yeah, I know where that is."

"Well, there is a boulder next to the cliff. Go home and get your climbing rope. You have to tie it around the boulder and let yourself down over the rock face, about sixty feet or so until you come to an opening in the rock. Follow the tunnel to a huge alcove and you will find the plant inside. Be careful man and get the job done. I don't want to stay tied to this tree forever," Adam told him encouragingly.

"There is one more thing I have to…"

"Shit!" Adam shouted suddenly.

"What's the matter?"

"I'm getting a fucking headache, that's what. It's starting."

Cotton grabbed the duct tape out of his ruck and started wrapping Adam's forehead to the tree. Adam fought him every step of the way, swinging his head right and left to avoid being taped to the tree, screaming an inhuman sound. When he finished with his head, Cotton wrapped the duct tape several times around his feet and hands for extra measure, just in case. He never dealt with this inhuman strength before.

"Sorry, man. Just want to make a hundred percent sure that you don't get loose and I don't want you to smash your head in against the tree either."

He looked at Adam who now looked like a stranger. His face was contorted by hate and anger; his eyes were large like they would pop out of their sockets at any moment, his pupils glimmering red and blood curdling sounds were coming out of his mouth sounding more like a wild beast than a human being.

"I'll be back as soon as I can. Hang in there, Adam, and thank you for doing this. It has to be hell for you right now," he shouted, knowing there was nothing he could do to help him. He ran back to his truck and jumped in, then drove back to his house where his four-wheeler was waiting in the garage. He didn't waste any time, ran inside his shed and grabbed the climbing rope and a flashlight. He attached the machete to his ruck and put it on, then tied the gasoline container to the four-wheeler and took off in the direction of Pitch Fork Mountain.

What an appropriate name for a mountain which offered shelter to the plant, Cotton thought, as he drove toward the outer edge of the valley. Pitch Fork Mountain was the tallest mountain and the most dangerous one to explore. The one time he and Erica had been up there, they had made sure not to veer off the designated path. It definitely had been an adventure. He reached the small narrow trail which would take him through boulders and trees up to the ridgeline. The trail was steep and washed out in several places and two small creeks crossed its path. Twenty minutes later he reached the three cliffs which stuck out like the fork Adam had talked about. The Devil's fork protecting the devil's plant, Cotton thought. How ironic.

Cotton parked the four-wheeler next to the tree, then grabbed his rope and looped it around the boulder and made a double knot, then looped two smaller ropes through the handle of the gas container and attached it to his ruck. He needed both hands free so he could safely climb down the rock face. One last time he went over his mental list of things he needed to successfully destroy the plant then walked to the end of the cliff and threw the length of the rope down.

He had learned to mountain climb in Ranger school and again when he was taking the Mountain Course in Tenth Group when he was stationed in Colorado, so he shouldn't have any problems descending the rock face. Carefully he put the rope around him and started to lower himself down the cliff. Not in a million years would someone ever check for the plant down there, he thought, as he lowered himself step by step downward, the heavy gas container making it hard for him to keep his balance.

Chapter Thirty-eight

Doug was preparing himself a mid-morning snack, when a slight headache started to bother him. It's the damn plant again, letting me know that all is not well in the valley, like I don't know that already, he thought. The impulse to do the same thing to Cotton as he had done to Old Man Cobb entered his brain.

"No, I won't do it," Doug shouted out loud, knowing that it hadn't been his thought, but the plants. "No, never again! Not this time. Just kill me right now, right here. I won't do it! I won't lift my hand against another human being ever again!" Then he suddenly laughed, a thought entering his mind. "There are no peas left anyhow, so that idea won't work." He snickered to himself and realized what he was doing. I'm going crazy, he thought. I'm going fucking crazy and really don't give a shit.

Several other solutions entered his mind. Maybe he would go and talk to Cotton this afternoon. He didn't stand a chance to find the plant if Adam and he wouldn't talk. Maybe Cotton would give up and leave it be. On the other hand, maybe he could tell him that he would show him where the plant grew next harvest. And then you give him the juices of the peas in a drink.

"No, I said I won't do it. I said no and I mean it! Never again! Do you hear me! I said no! Not now and not next year! I will never do it again!" Doug shouted into the empty kitchen. His headache grew worse. "Bring it on, then! Make me kill myself!" he shouted. "I'm ready!"

Damn that horrible headache, Doug thought and walked to his bathroom where he kept the Tylenol. He popped three pills into his mouth and flushed them down with a handful of water from the sink, knowing full well that the pills wouldn't help. He laughed again out loud. That would be something; creating a drug which would prevent the devil from entering your mind... evil would be eradicated from the world... no murders, no wars, no cruelty, no... just peace and quiet and love. That's what heaven must be... full of peace and no worries... just calmness. A heaven I will never experience, he thought sadly.

He walked back to where his sandwich lay halfway made on the cutting board, picked up the knife and sliced the tomato just the way he liked it, not too thick and not too thin, then put it on top of the sandwich. All that was missing now was the Bread and Butter Pickles. His last jar, he thought, since the other one was broken. Damn that headache. His temples were throbbing with pain. He turned around and opened the refrigerator to grab the half full jar. Ignore the pain, he thought. Ignore the pain. You can do it.

Suddenly he found himself holding the refrigerator door open and reaching for something, but what? His headache was receding. Maybe the Tylenol was working after all. But he felt so strange... something changed inside of him... making it... hard for him to think clearly... pushing his thoughts aside and... Doug's face changed to a death mask, not a muscle moved, he didn't blink. His pupils changed from black to blood-red and his body moved without him giving it a command. He let go of the door and turned away, leaving it open, not worrying about the escaping cold air. Gabriel, who had been sleeping on his dog pillow stood up and growled at him as he walked past.

He stopped and stared at the dog and watched how the usually unafraid canine tucked in his tail and disappeared with a strange whining sound into another room. Doug walked to the front door, not knowing where he was going to go or able to stop himself. Adam's face appeared in front of him, but he didn't know why. He felt like he was a little man, inside his own body, watching his transformation from the inside out. All he could do was to observe his own actions, horrified and scared to death what was happening to him, unable to change anything, at the same time not really wanting to. He was ready to die. Finally… all this… would be behind him… soon. Was hell… worse than this… ungodly existence? He would… finally pay the price… for all his sins and… weaknesses. He just hoped… death… would… come… fast.

He opened the front door and walked outside, climbed on his four-wheeler and started it. He started screaming inside of his mind, but no sounds came out of his mouth. He turned the four-wheeler around and drove down the dirt road way faster than he had ever driven. Suddenly his hands hit the brakes so hard that his body almost slammed over the four-wheeler. Dust settled around the vehicle as Doug's stiff neck turned awkwardly to the right.

He had come to a stop right next to the valley's mailboxes. Doug was aware how his eyes moved from one mail box to the next, reading the names, until they came to rest on the name Fletcher. His hands opened the mailbox and pulled out a handwritten note. He was able to still comprehend what it said; "You will find Adam on Manitou Hill."

He tucked the note inside his pants and continued his drive toward Manitou Hill. What was going to happen? His mind was a helpless hostage. When he reached the small trail leading up to the top of the mountain, his hands turned the throttle to full speed, not heeding the danger lurking on both sides, racing up the hill faster than common sense would allow. Doug expected to die at any minute by veering off the paths into the deep gorges next to the road, but it didn't happen. When he reached the top of the hill, he killed the motor and climbed off to survey his surroundings.

He could see what the beast inside of him let him see and watched his body move toward the pine tree by the large boulder. He saw Adam sitting tied to a tree, his forehead taped to the trunk, his eyes closed. Inside his head he screamed a warning, but not a word came out of his mouth, like all his emotions and commands to warn Adam ricocheted off the glass bubble which surrounded his mind. He had an inkling of what was coming and he screamed in protest. I don't want... to hurt... another person. I don't... want...to kill... Adam. Kill me... now!

Adam thought he heard steps. His fight to free himself had stopped several minutes ago and he was ecstatic when the powerful urge to kill himself, which had overcome his mind so forcefully, had left him. Never in his life could he have imagined such a force to enter and replace his mind, such a numbness which had overtaken him, leaving him totally helpless to fight it. His mind and thoughts were replaced by such a feeling of self-destruction and hate toward himself, that he now lay worn-out against the trunk. Cotton would come back soon, he hoped, glad his mind had returned to normal.

Again, he heard twigs snapping and roused himself, mentally exhausted from his ordeal. He opened his sore eyes and saw Doug at a distance walking toward him.

"Doug, what are you doing up here?" he shouted, surprised to see him, but Doug didn't reply.

Adam watched him coming closer and noticed that his body movements were different, awkward. He walked kind of hunched down, tiptoeing, his feet touching the ground way too narrow to each other like he was walking a tight rope. It was almost funny to watch him. What was wrong with him? And then he knew. Alarmed to the core, he stared into Doug's face which looked like a contorted mask and when he saw his blood-red pupils he knew that he didn't stand a chance. He watched helplessly as the old man stuck his hand slowly into his own pocket and pulled out a white piece of paper. He held it in front of Adam's face so that he could read it; "You will find Adam on Manitou Mountain" then ripped it to shreds with such spine-chilling laughter that Adam wanted to cover his ears.

Doug bent down awkwardly in front of him and reached for his throat as his mind cried out; "I'm sorry, Adam! I'm so sorry!" It was at that moment that Adam knew he was going to die.

"No, Doug! No! Don't do this!" Adam screamed as Doug's hands closed around his throat. He felt incredible pressure on his windpipe as his air supply was cut off. He couldn't breathe any longer and he couldn't do anything about it. He felt pain inside his throat, heard the crushing of his windpipe and then eerie victory laughter filled his brain as he slowly lost consciousness. The last thing which entered his fading mind was the picture he always carried in his wallet; a picture of a smiling Robin holding a one-year-old Logan in her arms, then all went black.

Chapter Thirty-nine

C otton lowered himself down the rock face until he reached the cave. He safely stepped onto the lip of the opening and let out a deep breath. He had made it this far, now all he had to do was destroy the plant. He had been in dangerous situations before, had stared terrorists in the eyes and killed enemies, but this felt totally different to him. He was going to fight something which had superhuman powers. He was going to fight Satan's Angel. He never thought anything like this was possible.

All he had ever known was evil created by men, but this was evil in its purest form created by Satan himself, and it frightened him. He took off his ruck, retrieved the flashlight out of it and then carried everything through the tunnel guided only by the bright beam of the flashlight until he reached the large alcove Adam had told him about. Once there, he placed everything on the ground and grabbed the machete. Cotton looked around. Any other time he would have been impressed.

He was in a large cave with four vertical openings in the outer rock wall which let in enough light to see everything clearly. Cotton saw the plant. It didn't look like the one he had seen in the picture Adam had painted. There were no black flowers, just green stems and branches which were tangled up with tiny vines. The green leaves looked almost wilted and many of them lay scattered around the trunk of the plant. It's getting ready for winter, Cotton thought.

The wind stirred and moved the plant slightly, or was it the wind? Cotton moved closer and watched fascinated how the plant sensed his closeness or perhaps the danger it was in. It came to life; the vines twisting away from the branches, reaching for him, making him come closer, trying to ensnare him. He could smell faint perfume so sweet and tantalizing that Cotton found it hard not to bend down and inhale it deep into his lungs, but he knew he would be drugged by the potency if he was exposed to it for a longer time.

Incredible, he thought, the plant is capable of expelling this scent without the flowers. He took off his t-shirt and wrapped it around his nose and mouth, preventing the sweet nectar from entering him. Stepping closer now, he was within arm's reach. He pulled the machete back. The plant started to wriggle with incredible speed. It twisted and turned as he lowered the machete to its trunk and started chopping at it. Shrill, ear-piercing sounds escaped the plant, but he didn't stop, swinging the machete with all the strength he had and severed the trunk from its roots. The noise stopped, but the cut off vines kept on wriggling in a futile attempt to entangle him then slowly quit moving. The green leaves started to shrivel up and finally after thirty seconds they lay withered on the rocks.

Cotton retrieved the container of gasoline and poured its content over the plant and its roots. He let it run deep into the crevice where the taproot grew and let it soak until it ran out of the hole. He wouldn't make the same mistake Bulk Horswell had made. Satisfied that the crevice was full with gasoline he poured a trail of gasoline through the tunnel back to the opening. That task completed, he went back to retrieve his backpack then walked back outside. Ready to burn the damn plant to Kingdom Come, he lit a match and threw it on the gasoline trail then jumped behind a boulder by the cave opening. The gasoline trail burst into a huge, soaring blaze and rushed through the tunnel at an incredible speed. A loud explosion shook the cliff as Cotton hung on to the boulder. A firewall soared past him, as rocks and smoke escaped through the tunnel and the four vertical openings in the cave. Satisfied he watched the smoke rise into the blue, cloudless sky above. There was nothing left of the plant, he was sure.

Satan's Angel, which had ruled Hunter's Valley for centuries was destroyed and couldn't cause any more harm.

Chapter Forty

Satan's Angel's use of Doug's body was complete and merciless. He raced up the path to Pitch Fork Mountain in a frantic battle against time, without any regard to his prisoner's old, frail body. He took chances the real Doug would've never taken, speeding over rocks and holes, so close to the edge of the gorge that it was insanity. Eerie screams coming out of Doug's mouth didn't belong to him, but to the fanatical evil spirit of Satan's Angel.

Dust rose up behind the four-wheeler as it raced higher to the top of the mountain, Doug's body being bounced around without pity, his hands so tight around the handle grips of the four-wheeler that his knuckles stuck out white. His muscles hurt all the way up his arms into his shoulder blades. If he could just jerk the four-wheeler to the side and go over the edge to end this torturous masquerade, was the only thought Doug was allowed to have, like it added extra pleasure to Satan's Angel to tease him with a merciful death he knew he wouldn't get from the malevolent occupier of his painful body. Finally he reached the ridge, still screeching this inhuman shrill scream and raced to the three cliffs and the plateau. A loud explosion shook the ground beneath the four-wheeler and five dark columns of grayish-black smoke rose from the cliff and climbed up into the sky.

Doug felt deep horrible pain inside his body. He was burning from the inside out and it was unbearable. His possessor snarled with anger and hate, spit running out of his mouth, dripping over his clothes and then a howling so inhuman came out of him and echoed down the mountains and over the valley that Doug knew Satan was losing his Angel. The smoke was the symbol of his defeat. With the little strength Satan's Angel had left over the old man's body, he tried to conquer his last soul. He had to act fast, his strength was fading. In just a few more minutes he would lose control over Doug's mind and Doug would be in control again. He couldn't let that happen and he couldn't let his destroyer go unpunished. He jumped off the four-wheeler and ran to the rope tied around the boulder. His fingers clumsily fumbled with the knot and finally loosened it. With a loud scream of hate and defeat he threw it over the cliff to the depth below. Nobody would ever find the slayer of the plant and he would rot in hell for all eternity like the other two humans who had dared so many centuries ago to destroy him. Satan's Angel's time was almost up. He didn't want to leave anyone alive who knew the plants resting place. He had to act fast.

His movements were awkward and slow as he climbed back on the four-wheeler, damning this seventy-year-old body. He circled the plateau in a frenzy and then drove head-on into Cotton's four-wheeler pushing it over the cliff. The last trace of his presence on the ridge now vanished into the canyon below. Satisfied and howling into the quietness of the mountain, he made one last final effort, circled around the plateau and then gave gas and sped in a straight line over the cliff's edge, yelling an eerie victorious howl and then vanished into the depth of the canyon, exploding on impact.

Chapter Forty-one

otton stood at the opening of the cave and listened to the soaring sounds of the fire as it was slowly getting weaker. Suddenly an eerie howling sound echoed through the valley and he realized that it originated from the plateau above him. What could have happened? Cotton grabbed the rope and was about to climb up when he saw it falling past him. Instinct made him hold on to it and he pulled it inside the opening. What the hell was going on up there? The rope couldn't have untied itself, that much was for sure.

Had Adam gotten loose and come after him? How would he get back up? He was stranded. Cotton looked up to see if an ascent to the top was possible without a rope, when he saw his four-wheeler being pushed over the cliff. Eerie laughter echoed down the canyon as he watched his ATV plummeting into the canyon below where it smashed to pieces. It all happened so fast. In the next instant he saw another four-wheeler, carrying a person, flying over the cliff into the air until it lost momentum and crashed to the canyon floor, the eerie laughter echoing from the canyon walls. Only after the four-wheeler exploded did the canyon become quiet again.

Dumbfounded, Cotton scratched his cheek. Had he seen correctly? Had that been Doug on the four-wheeler? And then he understood. Something he hadn't considered before now became crystal clear to him. When the plant hadn't been able to control Adam, it changed tactics and controlled Doug's mind instead. Damn the plant, why hadn't he thought about that possibility earlier? Did Doug get to Adam? If he killed Adam then his chances of ever being found were close to nil. Adam was the only one who knew where he was. Cotton never anticipated this turn of events.

He sat down on the rock totally deflated, totally at a loss of what to do next. The rope wasn't long enough to lower him to the canyon floor. The cliffs were way too steep and flat for him to climb up or down and the only two people who knew about this cave were now dead. He wouldn't be found for a long time, if ever. His only option was to wait and see if someone in the valley had noticed the smoke and would come and investigate. One thought gave him hope; maybe a helicopter would fly by in the search for all three missing men. At least they would find Adam's body, since he left the note in his mailbox.

Cotton laid down on the warm ground, resigned to wait. He had a lot of time left before he would try something desperate, like climbing down the rope to see if the rock face turned rougher way down below. All that mattered to him right now was that Satan's Angel was destroyed.

Chapter Forty-two

The day waned into the afternoon and Adam didn't come home as promised. Robin was glad that the two men had overcome their differences and were friends again. No matter how hard she tried last night, Adam wouldn't tell her what the fight had been about. It was now six o'clock at night and Adam still hadn't returned. Maybe he had decided to hang out at Cotton's place and drink a couple of beers with him. She ate with Logan around seven then let him watch a Disney movie on the big screen while she cleaned the dishes and put a plate of food for Adam inside the refrigerator. He probably would be starving when he returned home. It had become their custom to have family movie night on Saturdays with popcorn and root beer. Tonight Logan was watching the old Swiss Family Robinson movie and she could hear him laughing out loud from the kitchen.

When Adam didn't return by eight o'clock, she started to get concerned and dialed Cotton's home phone number, but nobody picked up. Where could they be? They had left in Cotton's truck. It suddenly came to her that Adam didn't use his dirt bike or his four-wheeler. Why didn't that occur to her earlier? So what did he use to go off-roading with? The jeep was still sitting in the driveway.

"Logan, Honey, I'll be right back," she yelled at her son, grabbed the jeep keys and drove to Cotton's house which sat in total darkness, not a single light was on. The headlights of her jeep revealed Cotton's truck parked next to the open garage and she could see Erica's four-wheeler parked inside. Cotton's four-wheeler was gone. There is no way that both guys rode on one four-wheeler, she thought. Something just wasn't right here. She drove back home and looked in on Logan. He hadn't moved a muscle since she left, probably never even noticed that she was gone. She picked up the kitchen phone and started calling some neighbors, but nobody had seen the men. She finally called Doug's number hoping to enlist his help, but he didn't answer his phone either. She didn't know what to do. Adam would be mad with her if she called the police unnecessarily, but what the hell, he should have told her where he was going. No, she thought, I'll wait a little longer.

Robin went to bed at eleven. Surely Adam would come home during the night. The guys had never stayed out this long before, but Erica wasn't home and it was a weekend night. She laid down wondering what could have happened to them and fell into a light sleep, every so often waking up to look at the digital clock.

The telephone rang and startled her awake. It was one-thirty. A horrible feeling came over her. A telephone call at this time of night couldn't be good. She picked up the phone and answered.

"Hello?"

"Hello, Robin. This is Erica. Something is not right. I tried all day and night to get in touch with Cotton. He doesn't answer the phone. Is Adam home?"

"No, he isn't. I'm worried too," Robin told her.

"Call the police. Something is terribly wrong."

They started the first search party at dawn. Word traveled fast and by the time it was ten o'clock, over a hundred volunteers had gathered to search for the missing men. Nobody had seen them during the last twenty-four hours.

Erica stayed in Texas. As much as she hated not being able to help in the search efforts, she had sworn to Cotton that she would stay

380

where she was. He had explained to her that if something happened to him, Lucas would have lost one parent, but for her to come back to the valley and fall again under the spell of the plant would mean he would lose both parents. As badly as she wanted to, she had to keep that scenario in mind and stay right there in Texas for her son's sake, sitting next to the phone, waiting and hoping for good news. But it didn't come and the longer she waited the harder it became for her not to get on the next plane.

Robin's parents and in-laws rushed to her side to be with her during those awful hours. They took care of Logan and tried to keep Robin's spirits up.

Chapter Forty-three

T he day waned into late afternoon and Cotton prepared to spend his first night in the cave. Nobody would come looking for him until the next day. Robin and Erica were probably frantic by now, not knowing where their husbands were. It had gotten fairly chilly outside so he grabbed his ruck and moved inside the cave. The fire had extinguished hours ago and the smoke and dust had finally settled. The moonlight shone through the vertical openings as he sat down against the cave wall.

His stomach growled loudly and he realized how hungry he was. What wouldn't he give for a juicy burger right now? He searched all the pockets of the ruck. Maybe he would find gum inside, but to his great joy he discovered a forgotten MRE in one of the side pockets. He opened it carefully, realizing he could use the slick airtight bag to catch the drops of water he heard dripping somewhere in the cave. He opened the ration and found a pound cake inside, one of his favorites. Slowly he started eating the snack savoring each bite. A good thing the rations lasted forever. The next thing he would do, would be to find the water he heard dripping somewhere. He had to find it in case he was stuck in this cave for a longer time. Looking around, Cotton marveled at how peaceful and serene the cave appeared now. It almost had a romantic touch to it the way the moonlight illuminated the walls and the deep crater in the middle of the cave, where Satan's Angel had its foothold such a short time ago.

Cotton had been brought up as a Methodist. When he first heard as a child attending Bible school that the devil was cast out of heaven, he never became frightened, never once did he consider that it would affect his life, thinking that hell was deep down in the earth, far away from anything that kept him safe. All through his growing-up years he considered himself out of harm's way and later, after he joined the military, he assumed that all the evil he dealt with in Afghanistan and Iraq were man-made. Sitting alone in the cold, dark cave now, he could only marvel at how wrong he had been. What he had witnessed in the last week was beyond his comprehension.

The next three days became the longest in Cotton's life. Sunday passed without him being found and on Monday he finally decided to climb down the length of the rope to see if the surface of the cliff changed below, but there were no crevices he could use for a foothold and the rope was way too short to reach the canyon floor. Disappointed he climbed back up and waited and kept himself hydrated thanks to the small amount of water he drank. He saw a helicopter in the distance and fired shots into the air, but they went unnoticed. For two nights he had used his flashlight to try and attract attention to his location, but nobody saw it. The batteries died around ten the night before and Cotton threw the flashlight disappointedly against the cave wall.

Adam's body was spotted on Monday afternoon by a helicopter pilot flying low over Manitou Hill. When the rescue team finally reached him half an hour later, he was barely alive. If it hadn't been for the tape around his head holding his neck up so he could still breath, he would have been dead hours ago. He was transported to the Medical Center by Life Flight where Robin stayed with him. The doctors weren't sure if he was going to make it. Erica called Robin every day to inquire about his health and stayed in touch with the continued search efforts to find Cotton and Doug, who was also missing. It was only because of her father, who talked some sense into her, that Erica stayed put in Texas, hanging onto some hope that Cotton was still alive.

Adam stayed in a coma for the next three days and when he finally woke up he still couldn't speak, his throat too damaged to do so. He requested a notepad and inquired after Cotton. When Robin told him that he was still missing, he wrote down where they would probably find him. When Erica received the news that Adam had come out of the coma and written down where they would find Cotton, she was elated and stayed next to the phone for the rest of the day.

Cotton resigned himself to dying in the cave after he spent six long days and nights without being rescued. On Thursday afternoon, he was resting in the opening of the cave dosing and dreaming about Erica and Lucas. If he could just speak with them one more time, put his eyes on their beautiful faces, he would die a happy man. He suddenly heard his name being called from above him and jumped up with renewed strength, hope surging through him. Did he imagine it? He heard his name again and relief flooded through him.

"I'm down here! Can you hear me? I need a rope to climb up!" he screamed from the top of his lungs.

"You got it," someone yelled back at him. "Do you need help? We can lower a harness down?"

"I can do it! Just get me a rope!" he yelled back.

A couple minutes later a rope was lowered down to the cave and Cotton was able to climb up on his own accord, his machete attached to his ruck was on his back. The rescue team gave him a bottle of water and a sandwich and Cotton devoured both. He showed them where the two four-wheelers and Doug's body were located. A recovery group was sent into the canyon and Doug's burned up body was retrieved.

The full story of exactly what had happened was never revealed to the public. Cotton found the journal in Doug's house and took it with him, burying it deep inside his own military locker. The following day he visited Adam in the hospital and together they agreed to keep the true secret of the valley, so insane and unbelievable, to themselves. To know what had really happened would scare mankind since it could happen anywhere else on earth. They left the story the way the police perceived it; that Doug had lost his mind and attacked Adam, whom he tied to a tree and then strangled, then he untied Cotton's rope and threw it down the cliff, hoping Cotton would die an agonizing slow death of starvation. Doug then killed himself.

No one ever entered the cave again.

Erica and Lucas came back to the valley after the investigations into the case were over. It was a happy day in Cotton's life when he picked them up from the airport and took them to their home in the valley they loved so much.

Life was good again.

Epilogue

Three years later...

A beautiful sunset went down over Hunter's Valley. It was a peaceful evening with homeowners happy and content; some of them watching the sunset from their patios, others sitting in front of their televisions, unaware of the beauty outside.

On Pitch Fork Mountain one single, beautiful, black flower in the shape of an angel trumpet opened up to the warm summer's night, basking in the knowledge that it would never die. It would take time to grow back to its former glory, but it had time. It had all the time in the world.

It would always be Satan's helper, mercilessly teasing and taunting its victims and putting temptation in their paths. There would always be a few who couldn't withstand the enticement and fall to its' prey. This was the way it had been for thousands of years and it would be this way again. This is how it was written.

"Watch and pray, that you enter not into temptation: the spirit indeed is willing, but the flesh is weak."

Matthew 26:41